For Tom Kelleher

Acknowledgments

Much thanks go to the following people for their assistance in making this book a reality: Jude Pittman and everyone at BWL Publishing, Michelle Lee for her always amazing cover art, Eileen Charbonneau for her superior editing, the members of my writing group who have listened to and commented on every Chapter (Lee Baldarelli, Janice Hitzhusen, James Pease, Barbara Lamacchia, Cindy Shenette, Rebecca Southwick, and Jane Willan), Victoria Belisle, costumed interpreter at Old Sturbridge Village, who spent time explaining to me the dairying and foodways of the 1830s, professional folklorists, Dr. Sara Cleto and Dr. Brittany Warman, who guided me to some great resources for learning about the field of folklore, and, most importantly, my dear friend, historian Tom Kelleher, to whom this book is dedicated and who knows more about the history of this time period than anyone I know. Tom, you are a goldmine of information and a beloved friend.

The Folklorist

Eileen O'Finlan

Print ISBNs
Amazon print 9780228627951
Ingram Spark 9780228627968
Barnes & Noble 9780228627975

BWL Publishing Inc.

*Books we love to write …
Authors around the world.*

http://bwlpublishing.ca

Author's Note

Many readers may be surprised to learn that the historical event around which this novel revolves really happened. There was not one instance, but several, throughout the 19th century. It would eventually come to be known as the New England Vampire Panic. Every state in New England experienced at least one case.

The account which Seth reads from the newspaper incorporates a real account in Woodstock, Vermont in 1817 with a fictional one in 1831. Charlotte reads about the real case of Mercy Lena Brown from an actual article in a 1970 issue of Yankee magazine. The account of the Kendall family is entirely fictional as is the family itself. For those readers interested in learning more about the New England Vampire Panic, I highly recommend folklorist, Michael E. Bell's book, Food for the Dead: On the Trail of New England's Vampires.

Other than the two "vampire" cases mentioned above, every character in this story is fictional. However, the folklorists Charlotte mentions by name were real people.

Table of Contents

Chapter 1

July 1973
Middlebury, Vermont

"Guess how he greeted me. 'How's our little folklorist this morning?'" Charlotte jammed her key into the lock of her apartment door.

Heidi followed her into the apartment. "What did you say?"

"I said, 'Good morning.' What else could I say? He had the president of the museum with him."

Charlotte had stopped at the market on the way home from work. Heidi, who lived across the hall with her aunt, helped her carry up the bags.

"What's his sign?" Heidi asked.

"No idea."

"I'll bet he's an Aries. Find out his birthday."

Her back to Heidi, Charlotte rolled her eyes as she stacked salad fixings on the counter. She ran a colander filled with lettuce under cold water. "I've only been working there for three months and already I hate my boss. I hate that I hate my boss."

"But you like the job, right?"

Charlotte pulled out a cutting board to slice the cucumbers. "I'd love it if I could do what I'm supposed to be doing. I mean, everyone said, 'What job are you going to find with a degree in folklore?' Then this opening for an assistant director of programs at the New England Folklife Museum comes up." Charlotte stopped slicing, looked off in the distance as if reliving the moment. "A museum dedicated to my field. And it's in Vermont, where I've always wanted to live. I'm fairly

close to my grandmother who I adore. I love
Middlebury. What's more perfect?" She resumed
hacking at the cucumber. "And then I get Brad Louden
for a boss. Male chauvinist pig!"

"Let me do that before you chop off your fingers."

"Thanks. I'll go check my bean sprouts."

The salad was made, a large slice of homemade
bread smeared with butter and liberally sprinkled with
garlic placed in the oven, and a smattering of herbed
tofu, snow peas, broccoli, mushrooms, and water
chestnuts sizzling in the wok when a knock sounded at
the door. Charlotte opened it to find Heidi's aunt, Iris
Pleasant.

"I thought I heard you girls come up the stairs."

"Heidi's in the kitchen."

"I wanted to make sure you both had enough to
eat," Iris said as she followed Charlotte.

"We've got plenty," said Charlotte, forcing a smile.
She pulled the garlic bread from the oven. She'd been
living across the hall from Heidi and her widowed aunt
for three months. In that time, she and Heidi had
become good friends, but Iris Pleasant drove her up the
wall.

"What are you having besides bread and salad?"
Iris asked, glancing around the kitchen. "What on earth
is this?" She peered into the wok as if aliens had landed
in it.

"Tofu and vegetables," said Heidi. "It's very
healthy."

Iris looked sideways at her niece. "These rabbit
food side dishes are all well and good, but they're not
enough. You should come home for supper. Charlotte,
you come, too. I have a meatloaf and baked potatoes in
the oven."

"Mrs. Pleasant, I'm a vegetarian, remember? Said
Charlotte.

"Oh, I keep forgetting. I'll bring over a few baked potatoes for you when they're done. I don't want you to go hungry."

"You don't need to do that."

"It's no problem, dear." Then turning to Heidi, she said, "If you're going to stay, don't be too late coming home. You'll still be hungry. I'll keep the meatloaf warm. You both need some fattening up."

Fattening up was the last thing Charlotte wanted. She worked hard to keep a trim figure while she was pretty sure that Heidi could eat all she wanted without gaining an ounce.

"Thank you, Auntie," said Heidi, kissing her on the cheek while ushering her out the door.

"Sorry about that," she said when she returned to the kitchen.

"Don't be. She means well." *I think.*

"So, back to your situation," said Heidi as they sat down to eat. "Thinking of quitting your job?"

"I'm not letting Brad Louden drive me away. I just can't figure out why he hired me if he doesn't like me."

"What makes you think he doesn't like you?"

"Our *little* folklorist?' In meetings, he never asks for my opinion. When I do say something he either cuts me off, talks over me, or ignores whatever I've said. I'm just supposed to get the coffee and take the minutes. My title is Assistant Director of Programs, but he thinks I'm his secretary."

"Probably an Aries. Have you talked to him about it?"

"No. We've been busy getting ready for the Fourth of July." Charlotte took a sip of lemonade. "And that's another thing. Calendar customs are one of my specialties, but will he listen to any of my ideas? No. Everything has to be exactly as he dictates. I'm only there to carry out his plans."

"He's the Director of Programs, right?"

"We're supposed to work as a team. The two of us and the curators. He listens to them. He takes their advice. When I tried to make suggestions for Bennington Battle Day he wouldn't even listen."

"I'm a nurse, but I can't tell the Director of Nursing what to do."

"I don't want to tell him what to do, Heidi. I want to be included as a valuable member of the team. I want to be heard."

"You're new. Give it some time. When he realizes how good you are at your job, he'll come around."

"Why are you sticking up for him?"

"I'm not. I'm trying to figure him out. I can see my dad saying that and not meaning anything by it. Talk to Brad."

"Your father is of a different generation. Brad's closer to ours. In his thirties, I think. He should be a little more liberated. I've never heard him call Paul or Jonathan our little curators. It's not because I'm new. It's because I'm a woman. And since that's not going to change, neither will he."

* * *

As she drove to the museum the next morning, Charlotte thought over her dinner conversation with Heidi. Maybe Heidi was right. Maybe she should speak to Brad. She couldn't very well continue to complain if she didn't at least take steps to rectify the situation.

After leaving her purse in her desk drawer, she went to Brad's office to ask if he could make time to meet with her.

"No time like the present," he said, motioning towards the chair across from his desk.

"It's about my job," she began.

"Everything okay? How's the Fourth of July exhibit coming?"

"Fine. That's not what I wanted to talk about, though."

"Okay. Shoot."

Charlotte sat straight, the hem of her paisley maxi skirt making a cool arc around her sandals. The light breeze wafting from the open window billowed the sleeves of her poet's blouse. She leaned forward slightly.

"I'm don't feel that my strengths are being well utilized."

She watched as he smoothed his mustache. Something in the gesture repelled her. "I do have a master's degree. And since calendar customs are one of my specialties, I–"

"I've read your resumé," he interrupted.

"Yes. Well, in the three months I've been here, I have made several suggestions, but I don't feel as though any have been taken–"

"We work as a team, Charlotte." He cut her off again. "No one person gets to dictate. I hope you weren't expecting to run everything. That's not how we do things here."

"I love the idea of working as a team. It's what I want, but–"

"Then we have no problem." He shot up from his chair. "Listen, I've got a meeting with the president this morning."

"I thought you had time to talk with me."

"We talked." He came out from behind his desk. Standing over her, he put a hand on her shoulder, rubbed her upper arm. "You just keep being a good team player and everything will be fine." He made a fist and bumped the thumb side against her shoulder. "Okay? Gotta go. And you get over to the exhibit site. Paul brought out a box of stuff after you left yesterday. I'm sure they need dusting before they go into the exhibit."

He winked at her before walking away.

Returning to her office, Charlotte dropped into her chair. The box could damn well wait. What had just happened? Hadn't she gone to Brad to talk professional to professional? Within minutes she was dismissed like a child from the principal's office. What the hell? She glanced at the clock. With a heavy sigh, Charlotte started to get up when the phone rang.

"Assistant Director of Programs, Charlotte Lajoie speaking," she answered.

"Charlotte, good, I've caught you."

"Grandma!" Her grandmother's voice snapped her out of her despondency. Realizing this was a long-distance call, she suddenly panicked. "What's wrong?"

"Nothing's wrong." Her grandmother's voice, smooth and comforting as her homemade butterscotch pudding, set Charlotte's mind at ease. "I'm sorry to bother you at work, but I find I forget too easily these days so I have to do a thing when I think of it, or I might not do it at all."

"It's no bother, Grandma. You can call me anytime."

"You're so sweet. I'll only keep you a moment. I wanted to know if you can come down this weekend. I was rummaging in the garret, and I came across something I'd forgotten all about that I think you would find interesting."

"I'd love to. What is it?"

"Oh, that's wonderful. I'd love to see you. It's been a while."

"It has. I'll come on Friday, but can you tell me what you want to show me?"

"It's something that goes way back in the family. Back to your great, great, great grandmother, Jerusha Halsey. I won't say anything more. I want it to be a surprise. Let's just say there's no one better in the family to give it to than you."

Charlotte hung up the phone feeling elated, her meeting with Brad almost forgotten. Intrigued at her grandmother's hints and delighted about spending the weekend with her, she got through the rest of the work week riding on that high.

Chapter 2

Late July 1830
Birch Falls, Vermont

An ear-splitting crack of thunder woke Jerusha Kendall with a start. Heart pounding, she had no time to collect herself as her sisters clambered out of their bed. Seeing the shadowy cluster of their forms at the garret window, she rushed to join them. A great fork cut through the air, lighting up the barn and pasture. Jerusha clapped her hands over her ears as the thunder boomed the next instant.

"Will we be washed away?" asked Josie, the timid one of Jerusha's sisters.

"Of course not," Lizzy answered. "Though I do worry for the chickens."

Jerusha wasn't so sure. It had been raining, often in torrents, for five days without stop. Fields were flooded, crops destroyed. Mr. Haskell had been on his way home when the rain began on Saturday. He'd stopped in at the Kendall farm to wait out the storm. That was five days ago. He had yet to leave. Last night, when Jerusha's father and brother, Seth, had come in for supper dripping wet, they'd said that the barn was ankle deep in water.

Jerusha, at eight, the youngest of the Kendall brood, squeezed in close to Lizzy, her favorite sister. As another streak of lightning lit the sky, Jerusha glanced up at Lizzy's face. The eerie light gave her grinning mouth and wide eyes a maniacal appearance. The next crash of thunder propelled Jerusha's arms around Lizzy's waist, her head buried in her sister's shift. She could feel Lizzy's heart pounding but knew it was caused by excitement, not fear.

"We are safe," Lizzy told her, holding one arm tightly around Jerusha while she stroked her dark curls.

Jerusha thought Lizzy, at thirteen, quite grown up and felt safe in her fearless sister's embrace. She'd become especially sensitive, frightening easily, since their sister, Rebecca, had died one year ago from consumption. It was the first real loss in Jerusha's young life. The specter of more loss raised by Josie's fearful question unnerved her.

The pounding rain and crashing thunder muffled other sounds, so the sisters never heard the footsteps on the garret stairs. They startled and turned quickly when a voice behind them said, "Girls, come away from the window."

It was Susannah, the oldest of the Kendall children. At twenty and recently married, she no longer slept in the garret; she and her husband taking the spare room on the second floor.

"Is the house flooding?" asked Josie.

"Just the cellar. But it's not safe to stand near the window in a storm such as this."

"How did you know we were up?" asked Jerusha.

Susannah laughed. "The thunder woke us all. Mother asked me to look in on you. I suspect Lizzy was the first out of bed to view the excitement?"

In the dim light of Susannah's candle, Jerusha could just make out her eldest sister's form. Tall and willowy with long, dark hair hanging to her waist, even in near-darkness she cut an imposing figure of authority. Jerusha thought she could just make out a wry smile cast in Lizzy's direction.

"Come, girls. Back to bed."

"Must you always be so bossy?" said Lizzy, who always chaffed at Susannah's authoritarian demeanor.

"Shall I have Mother come up, then?" asked Susannah.

"No," said Lizzy, dropping onto the bed.

In the morning, Josie nudged Jerusha awake. The thunder and lightning had stopped, but the rain still pelted the roof and streamed down the windowpanes. In the kitchen, Jerusha's mother stirred a pot hanging above the fire. She turned as the girls entered the room, smiling at them. They approached the table with mincing steps, unlike most mornings when they would bound into the kitchen eager for breakfast. Nothing seemed normal since the storm began. Only Lizzy went about her morning chores with her usual alacrity.

"Pots, Jerusha," said her mother.

As though in a trance, Jerusha went about her morning task, emptying all the chamber pots and returning them to their rooms. She finished just as Mr. Haskell entered the room and breakfast was being set on the table.

The kitchen door opened admitting Jerusha's father, her brother, Seth, and brother-in-law, Zachary Wall. Rain, pushed through the door by the wind, splattered onto Jerusha's skirt.

"The barn floor is drenched, but the hay seems dry enough," said her father. "Seth's not getting wet at night."

Seth, the only son in the family, slept in the hayloft.

"He should come in the house at night, Eli," said their mother. "I do not like him out there in this weather."

"They hayloft is as dry as the house, Mother," said Seth, kissing her cheek. At sixteen, he was taller than she and had to bend.

"But in this weather?"

"He is capable, Mary, and we need someone to keep an eye on the water level. It is bad enough we have lost so much of the crop to this never-ending storm. If we lose the hay, we will lose the livestock as well.

"I wish I could sleep in the hayloft," said Lizzy. "Mother, could I not just once?" she begged.

"We have discussed this before Eliza Louise Kendall. The answer is no."

As if to punctuate her mother's words, Josie tried to stifle a cough, producing a choked, gagging sound. "Excuse me, please," she mumbled and hurried from the room. When her coughing did not abate, their mother followed.

"Are any of the crops to be salvaged?" Susannah asked her father.

"Some, but much has been lost. I have never seen such a torrent. Have you Chauncey?" he asked, looking towards their house guest.

"Never. And I have seen a good many things in my time. It puts me in mind of a story I heard when I was a boy, though."

"Tell, please," Lizzy begged, always eager for a story from the elderly widower known throughout Birch Falls for his endless storehouse of tales.

Jerusha glanced at Mr. Haskell. His eyes gleamed as they always did when he launched into a story.

"Seems there was a young lady, oh, about your age." He nodded towards Susannah. "Lovely young miss, she was. Lived up to Winooski, just the other side of the Onion River. Well, I heard tell that one night she was standing at her bedchamber window waiting for her beau. Her parents did not like the fellow, so they planned on running off together, don'tcha know."

Unable to tear her gaze from his face, Jerusha put down her spoon. As she listened, she pictured a girl, much like Susannah, standing before their garret window.

"A light rain began to fall, and she hoped he would hurry before it got worse."

"Did he make it?" Lizzy asked.

Mr. Haskell's mouth screwed up. He scrunched his eyes tight and slowly shook his head.

"What happened?" asked Jerusha, feeling a touch of irritation when Seth snickered.

"As I heard it," Mr. Haskell continued, "the rain picked up, the wind began to howl, and before you knew it, the thunder was chasing the lightning across the sky."

"Like last night!" said Lizzy.

"Just like last night. She'd a been smart to move away from that window, but she was afraid she would miss her lover and since her parents were sending her to her aunt's house all the way down to Wallingford the very next day, she dared not take the chance. So she stayed right at that window."

Jerusha hadn't any idea why Susannah had told them it wasn't safe to stand near the window in a storm, but she felt she was about to find out.

"The rain was coming down hard now, you understand, and she could not see well at all," he continued. "So she opened the window and leaned out."

"And she fell out of the window?" asked Lizzy.

"No. No." He laughed. "She didn't fall out." His tone grew serious again. "What happened was far worse."

Jerusha held her breath, unable to think what would be worse than falling out of the garret window.

"It was then that a giant fork of lightning split the sky in two." He leaned in, looking intently at his captive audience.

"We saw one like that last night. Remember, Jerusha?" said Lizzy.

"Lizzy, if you do not stop interrupting, Mr. Haskell will never get to finish his story," said Seth.

Lizzy heaved an exaggerated sigh in Seth's direction before turning back to Mr. Haskell. "Sorry. What happened?"

"What happened is, the end of the lightning fork struck that young lady."

"Struck her?" Lizzy's eyes widened. "Did she die?"

"Oh, yes, I am afraid she did. Threw her clear across the room. Her poor parents rushed in to find her in a heap on the floor. Had to bury the poor darling the next day."

Jerusha felt heat rise from the pit of her stomach to her head. She wasn't sure she could finish eating.

"I told you not to stand near the window in a thunderstorm," said Susannah, trying unsuccessfully to suppress a smile.

"What happened to her beau?" asked Lizzy. "Did he get there?"

"Strangest thing," said Mr. Haskell. "At just the moment when the lightning struck her, the rain washed out the bridge he was riding over, and he was drowned in the river below."

"How sad," said Lizzy, looking downcast.

"Thought you heard Mr. Haskell say he was a no-good rascal," said her father.

"He never said that."

"He said the girl's parents did not like him."

The sparkle in Mr. Haskell's eyes grew brighter. "They say," he continued, "That on stormy nights when the lightning flashes you can still see that girl standing at the window looking for her lover who will never come."

Jerusha glanced around the table. Lizzy looked stricken, Seth rolled his eyes, Susannah almost giggled, her father and Zachary went on with their breakfasts, and Mr. Haskell looked well-satisfied. Jerusha was still trying to decide what to make of it when her mother's voice called from the parlor, "Eli! Come quickly! Josie cannot breathe."

Chapter 3

October 1830
Birch Falls, Vermont

Jerusha and Josie sat at the kitchen table peeling apples. The fruit's sweet tang filled the kitchen. Josie's cough had grown worse in the three months since the morning she had excused herself from the breakfast table. That first coughing fit a few months ago that was so relentless she'd been unable to catch her breath had frightened her mother. Jerusha was afraid now, too. Josie complained of a sore throat and pain in her chest and shoulders. She had been set to doing only quiet chores as too much effort made it difficult to breathe. Though her parents did not speak of it in front of her, Jerusha knew from their worried faces and overheard bits of conversation that they feared Josie was consumptive.

She glanced at Josie concentrating on her apple and wondered if she knew. Always thin and pale, Josie's cheeks were becoming hollow, just as Rebecca's had done shortly before she died.

"Father says we're fortunate the orchard wasn't destroyed by that awful storm in July," said Jerusha.

Josie nodded.

"Hannah's family lost all their apples, but Betsy's kept most of theirs. They said they would share." Hannah Small and Betsy Runyan were Jerusha's best friends. She worried about them almost as much as about her own family's situation since that storm had washed out a good many farms and even taken a few houses along the river.

"Good," said Josie.

"I hope someone will have a frolic," Jerusha continued. "They are fun and the work goes faster."

"Perhaps the Wickers will have—" Josie began, but a coughing fit overtook her.

Jerusha waited, hoping it would subside quickly.

"Perhaps the Wickers will have one," Josie tried again, her voice strained. "Their orchard had the least damage so—" again the coughing stopped her. This time it did not cease. She put down her apple and knife. Bent over, her body shook with spasms.

"Josie? What should I do?"

When her sister could not answer, Jerusha fled from the kitchen for help. She found Susannah and Lizzy in the dooryard doing laundry.

"Come quickly," she said, racing to them. "Josie is coughing hard. She cannot stop."

"Go for Mother," Susannah ordered Lizzy who hastened up the hill towards the Wicker farm.

Once back in the kitchen, Jerusha watched from a corner as Susannah bent over Josie's crumpled form on the floor.

"She's in fever," said Susannah. She gathered the girl in her arms and carried her to a room near the kitchen.

Jerusha followed but stayed beyond the doorway. This was the room where Rebecca had died. Jerusha did not like it.

"Fetch me a pitcher of cold water," Susannah ordered.

Jerusha was glad of something to do. She ran to the well, filled a bucket, and after pouring it into a pitcher, carried it to Susannah. Once delivered, she backed out of the room to resume her spot beyond the threshold.

Susannah dipped a cloth into the water to mop Josie's head and neck.

"A cup, please."

Jerusha fetched it. She watched as Susannah lifted Josie to a sitting position, trying to get her to swallow a sip of water. Josie only groaned as a small stream trickled down her chin.

Jerusha turned at the sound of hurried footsteps. Her mother brushed past her into the room. A moment later, Lizzy arrived with her father bringing the scent of hay and cows.

"I will go for Doctor Eacker," he said, hurrying from the room.

"Bring Caroline, too," her mother called.

"Send Lizzy," he answered, halfway out the door.

Lizzy did not wait but bolted from the house. Jerusha ran after her.

"Let me come with you," she yelled, trying to catch up with Lizzy.

Jerusha was out of breath by the time she reached the home of Caroline Cutting. Lizzy had outdistanced her easily, reaching the house enough ahead that Mrs. Cutting was already gathering up her basket by the time Jerusha got there. Lizzy looked at her quizzically, only just realizing that she'd been followed.

"We will take the wagon," said Mrs. Cutting, while her eldest son hitched it to the horse.

When it was ready, Mrs. Cutting gave Jerusha a boost up while Lizzy scrambled into the seat beside her.

"Will Josie die?" Lizzy asked.

Jerusha's stomach flipped.

"That is in the Lord's hands," answered Mrs. Cutting.

"But she has the same signs as Rebecca. She must have consumption, too."

"I have yet to lay eyes on the girl," said Mrs. Cutting. "I cannot say."

"She coughs so much and gets fevers. She has grown thinner than ever. Her throat–"

"Those are all signs of things other than consumption."

"So, she could have something else?" asked Jerusha, hope billowing in her chest.

"She could." Mrs. Cutting glanced down at Jerusha. The shadow that crossed her time-worn face tossed Jerusha's nascent hope to the wind.

"Can you help her, Mrs. Cutting?" Jerusha pleaded.

"I will do my best."

Caroline Cutting was the midwife who had delivered her and all her siblings. She was the one her mother turned to when illness in the family was beyond her own nursing skills. Her remedies always worked. Except for Rebecca.

Jerusha's father preferred Doctor Eacker. Unlike most doctors, he'd been to college then studied with a practicing physician. He knew the latest treatments. But he could not save Rebecca either.

"Will we all get sick and die?" asked Lizzy.

"I pray not."

"I wonder how it feels to die. You have seen many die. Do you know how it feels?"

"Not having done it myself, no. And there is need for you to dwell on it, Miss Eliza," said Caroline as she pulled the wagon up to the Kendall home.

"Thank the Lord you are here, Caroline," said Jerusha's mother as they entered the sickroom. "Her fever has not come down."

"Let me," said Mrs. Cutting, taking the cold cloth from Susannah. She sniffed it, then said, "You need to add vinegar to the water. It helps." She removed some herbs from her basket. "Sweet balm and catnip," she said. "We will make a tea with these for the fever." Pulling out more, she added, "And coltsfoot and flaxseed for the cough."

Jerusha watched, transfixed, as Mrs. Cutting's hands, beginning to gnarl with age, moved deftly amongst the assortment of herbs she pulled from her bag.

"Girls," said their mother. "Go back to your chores."

Susannah rose but her mother stopped her. "Stay with us, Susannah. You must learn."

Jerusha remained in the doorway when Doctor Eacker arrived. A mild row ensued between him and Mrs. Cutting when he insisted that she leave the room. He did not want her "potions" interfering with his scientific remedies. Caroline stood rooted to the spot, hands on hips. "My *potions* have been saving lives in Birch Falls since before you were born."

They glared at each other. In the end he allowed her to stay, but kept his back to her, purposely walking in front of her, blocking her view. After the doctor left, Jerusha's mother apologized to Mrs. Cutting.

"No matter," said Mrs. Cutting. "I am growing accustomed to his rudeness. It seems more of Birch Falls engage his services all the time."

Mrs. Cutting's lips tightened to a thin line as she resumed preparing tea for Josie.

Jerusha's mother caught sight of her in the doorway. "Did I not tell you to go back to your chores? Go then."

Jerusha felt unnerved the rest of the day. It was not until evening that her disquiet began to abate. The family, except for Josie, gathered in the parlor. Her mother sewed by the firelight. Susannah snuggled up to Zachary while she knitted and he whittled. Lizzy mended, her father wrote in his account books, and Seth read aloud from the Burlington Free Press. Jerusha worked her sampler. She'd finished the alphabet and moved onto a little house with trees on either side. The slow rhythm of communal evening work calmed her.

Much of what Seth read from the paper meant little to Jerusha, but she liked the timbre of his deepening voice. She looked up when she realized he'd been silent for a while. Deeply engrossed, he held the paper close to the firelight.

"Is something amiss?" asked their mother, who along with the others, looked towards Seth.

"Strange doings in Woodstock," he mumbled.

"What sort?" asked Susannah.

"The gruesome sort."

"Read it aloud," said Lizzy.

Seth cleared his throat then began.

"On Saturday last, the residents of Woodstock undertook an odd sort of ritual by which the family of the late Isaac Pearson hoped to rid itself of the specter of death haunting his family. Isaac Pearson, by all accounts a youth of good Christian morals, went to an early grave on April the tenth when consumption carried him off at the age of seventeen. Within two months he was followed to the afterlife by a sister, Ellen. Shortly thereafter, his brother, Benjamin became consumptive and showed signs of becoming the third in a sad trio. Upon consulting with Doctors James Blake and Lester Merriman, the family resorted to an unconventional method of treatment.

"Said treatment was not in the form of one of modern day's more bizarre remedies. Instead, they looked to the past for inspiration, invoking a ritual known to have been used in Woodstock in 1817 and likely used in many other locales before that.

"Believing the illness to be caused by one of the deceased family members having returned to feed off the living, their solution was to exhume the bodies of Isaac and Ellen to see if either showed signs of having returned from the grave in search of sustenance.

"Upon opening Ellen's coffin, she was determined to be in a normal state of decomposition, and nothing appeared out of place in her grave. Thus, she was vindicated of any post-mortem wrongdoing.

"Isaac's corpse, however, did not fare as well. Upon prying open the coffin lid, it was discovered to be in a different position than that which it had been

in when buried. It seems that Isaac had turned onto his side sometime during his eternal rest. Given that suspicious maneuver, it was clear further examination was warranted.

"Doctor Merriman was called upon to ply his trade and he soon discovered that Isaac's heart contained fresh blood. The culprit had been unearthed!

"Now what to do? The good citizens of Woodstock reached back in their memory for what was done to the corpse of Frederick Ransom in 1817. His heart had been removed and taken to the blacksmith's forge where it was burned. The ashes had been buried, the corpse reinterred, and the ritual concluded, though it must be said that Frederick's mother, sister, and two brothers died of consumption thereafter. The remedy did not appear to have worked.

"Nonetheless, and perhaps knowing of that outcome, last Saturday's Woodstock contingent did their earlier counterparts one better. They brought Isaac's ailing brother to the blacksmith's shop and insisted he breathe in the ashes as his brother's heart burned. This, they believed, was the missing piece in the earlier ritual.

"As of this writing, Benjamin Pearson still resides among the living, though by all accounts has not improved. Whether inhaling the ashes is truly the key to recovering his health remains to be seen."

There was silence when Seth finished reading. Jerusha looked about. Susannah was intent on her knitting and Zachary on his half-whittled stick. Mother stared at a spot on the wall. Seth peered into the fire. Father's elbow rested on the parlor table, his head in his hand. Even Lizzy appeared uncomfortable. As unnerved by her family's responses as by the images conjured by the article, Jerusha fought back tears.

"Is there nothing in the paper about the troubles in France?" her father asked, his voice barely above a whisper.

Jerusha listened to the rustling as Seth turned the pages hoping he would find something, anything to take her mind off people dying of consumption and being dug up to have their hearts burned.

As Seth resumed reading, Jerusha's needle poked through the canvas of the sampler. She would have to rip out the house later. Her hands shook too much to keep the line straight. But for now, she kept the needle moving.

When Seth finished reading the paper aloud, Mother proposed the others go to bed while she stayed with Josie.

"I will spell you in a few hours, Mother," Susannah told her.

Seth moved to tamp down the fire.

"Leave it," said their mother. "I will work a bit longer and take care of it before I go to Josie."

As she climbed the stairs, Jerusha glanced over the banister to see her mother standing alone before the hearth, newspaper in hand. An odd expression passed over her mother's face as she flung the paper into the fire.

Chapter 4

June 1973
Bennington, Vermont

The sun was setting when Charlotte pulled her Volkswagen Beetle into her grandmother's driveway. Her sandals crunched on pebbles as she stepped out. She'd played the radio on the way down to keep at bay her curiosity about whatever her grandmother wanted to show her. Jim Croce's "Bad, Bad Leroy Brown" continued to play in her head as she wrested her suitcase over the spare tire in her trunk.

Before she reached the door, Grandma Tessier came out onto the porch.

"Grandma!" Charlotte broke into a run, ignoring the awkwardness of the suitcase and shoulder bag.

"Hello, ma pet," her grandmother called, flinging wide her arms.

Dropping her bags, Charlotte threw herself into her grandmother's embrace, breathing deeply of the rose-scented dusting powder her grandmother always wore.

"Have you had supper?" she asked, ushering Charlotte into the house.

"I grabbed a quick bite before I left."

"Room for a piece of pie?"

"Yours? Always."

"Bring your things up to Beatrice's room while I warm a piece for you."

The bedroom her grandmother referred to had belonged to Charlotte's Aunt Beatrice as a girl. When her parents brought Charlotte and her siblings to visit as kids, it was the room she and her sister, Tracy, shared while her parents stayed in her mother's old room and her brother, Russ, took Uncle Will's old room. Aunt Beatrice died in a car accident three years ago. Yet there was still so much of her here. Her bird books resided on the headboard shelf. The caricature of her drawn at a country fair hung on the inside of the closet door. The top left-hand drawer of the vanity held old, beaded necklaces and antique broaches, while in the top right was an empty bottle of Tabu. The remnants left behind when Aunt Beatrice moved to Connecticut years ago.

Charlotte dropped her shoulder bag and suitcase next to the bed. As was her custom, she opened the bureau drawer, withdrew the empty perfume bottle and breathed in the spicy, citrus scent. An image of Aunt Beatrice formed behind her closed eyelids. Tall, slender, dark haired, and well-dressed. The woman who never married because she'd rather have a career. The woman who loved to travel, trained to be a stewardess but could not find a job because she wore glasses and couldn't get used to contact lenses, so she became a secretary at an insurance company instead. All the while, she continued to write letters and op-ed pieces about the unfairness of the airlines' hiring policies regarding women. The woman who always told Charlotte that she could be anything she wanted and to never let anyone stand in her way. The woman taken suddenly and far too soon. The woman Charlotte wanted to emulate.

"That smells good," said Charlotte, returning to the kitchen to find two wedges of peach pie with a scoop of vanilla ice cream next to each, and two tall glasses of milk on the table. Charlotte felt engulfed by a sense of comfort. Eloise Tessier was, in Charlotte's estimation, the perfect grandmother. A sweet face, gentle blue eyes, and soft white hair piled atop her head, she was, as always, dressed in a neat house dress and apron. She appeared the epitome of the kindly little old grandmother.

"Tell me all about your new job," she said as they sat together indulging in the sweetness of the pie and ice cream. "What do you do at the museum?"

"So far I mostly help set up the exhibits, but I was hired to create public programs centered on New England folkways," she said.

"That sounds fascinating. What's to be your first program?"

"I'm not sure yet. We're still tossing around ideas." Charlotte did not want to ruin the profound sense of peace that always overcame her the moment she arrived at her grandmother's house by talking about work problems. "I'm dying to know what you wanted to show me."

Grandma Tessier's blue eyes lit with a hint of mischief. She smiled, but said nothing as she crossed the kitchen, pulled open a drawer of the Hoosier cabinet, and reached inside.

Charlotte forgot the pie and ice cream when her grandmother set a small, aged book on the table.

"What is this?"

"A very old diary. I found it in the attic. I've had it for years, but I'd forgotten all about it."

"On the phone you said it belonged to an ancestor."

"Yes. Your great, great, great grandmother, Jerusha Halsey. My grandmother gave it to me. I would have given it to your mother or Beatrice or Will, but none of them ever seemed interested. Instead I packed it away and forgot about it. Fortunately, I had a burst of nostalgia recently and decided to go through some of the old trunks in the attic. I tried to read it again, but my eyesight's not what it used to be."

Charlotte wiped her hands before gently opening the cover. The small, brown book was frayed, the pages cracked and, in places, beginning to turn to dust.

"I should be wearing gloves," she said. "It's too delicate." She closed the book.

"I'll get you a pair," said her grandmother.

"Not winter gloves, Grandma. Cotton gloves. It's what we use for handling artifacts. I wish I'd known to bring some."

"I understand. Like the white ones I wear at night after I put on my hand cream. I'll get them. Don't worry about getting them dirty. I have several pairs."

She left the kitchen and returned moments later with the gloves. Charlotte donned them, moved to the other end of the table away from the food, and opened the diary. The browning pages looked as though they'd been soaked in tea. For a moment, the looping cursive words appeared foreign, but soon Charlotte's training set in allowing her to decipher the script. The first entry was dated January 1, 1839.

"Did you read it when your grandmother gave it to you?" Charlotte asked.

"Yes, but that was a very long time ago. All I remember is that Jerusha was seventeen when she wrote it and that she was trying to understand a family matter."

Charlotte looked up. "Really?"

Something had happened when she was younger. Something she didn't understand. If I remember right, she used this diary to sort out her thoughts."

Charlotte laughed. "Keeping diaries was popular in the nineteenth century and not just among kids. Everyone did it, even men and women. Usually, they were filled with comments about the weather and listings of their daily activities. They're helpful to historians for understanding daily life, but they don't always make the most scintillating reading."

"There's probably a good bit of that in there, as well. But I thought you'd like to have something from one of your ancestors. A piece of family history."

"I do, Grandma. Thank you so much for thinking of me." She reached out to cover her grandmother's hand with her own. "I can't wait to read it."

That night Charlotte sat by the window in Aunt Beatrice's room, the waxing gibbous moon shining down on the decaying diary pages. Despite the lamp and the magnifying glass her grandmother had loaned her, she struggled to read.

The first entry established that Jerusha had received the diary as a New Year's gift – a more common time for gift-giving in Yankee New England than was Christmas Charlotte knew – and that she was living in Birch Falls, Vermont, a hamlet tucked into the Champlain Valley. Charlotte also learned that January 1, 1839 was a Tuesday, cold but clear, and that Jerusha had celebrated the new year by going sleighing with her father and someone named Nathan. A brother, perhaps?

The following diary entries were much the same, though sleighing was not mentioned again until mid-month. Her ancestor wrote of the endless sweeping of wood chips, pine needles, and dirt that fell from the wood brought in for the fireplaces, mending and knitting accomplished, and complaints of snow drifting in through the window at night to dust their blankets.

Jerusha wrote of her parents, a sister named Susannah who had moved to Ohio along with her husband Zachary, and Nathan who, apparently was not her brother after all. An entry towards the end of January stated, *Nathan speaks little of his family in Connecticut.* Likely, a hired hand, then. Very common for New Englanders at the time.

Charlotte's eyes were close to giving out as she neared the end of January's entries. It was nearing midnight when she came to the final one for that month.

January 31 Wednesday
Cold today. Father and Nathan brought in more wood. Isaiah and Frederick Wicker helped. I spent the day with Mrs. Wicker as payment for work done by

Frederick. I so wish she could teach me to weave. Instead I have been spinning. For years I have watched as she works on the loom longing to try my own hand at it so when she asked if I still wished to learn, I nearly burst into tears. Oh, how I do wish Mother and Mrs. Wicker were friendly again so that I would be allowed.

"Interesting," Charlotte whispered. "I wonder what that was all about."

Though intrigued, the ancient script was proving too much for her tired eyes, and the handwriting began to blur. It would have to wait until morning.

Chapter 5

December 1830
Birch Falls, Vermont

"Some tea, Mary," whispered Lavinia Wicker, setting the cup on the little table. Mary sat in a chair next to Josie's bed, rubbing her tired eyes.

There were others in the room as well. Caroline Cutting was there along with Susannah and a handful of neighbors. They'd been gathering for three days, taking turns holding vigil, getting meals, helping with housework, and anything else that needed doing. Many came, stayed awhile, then returned home to come back later. Only Mary had barely left Josie's side from the moment Caroline had told her that she thought the end was near.

A light snow had fallen during the night giving the landscape the appearance of having been dusted with flour. Mary stared out the window. The sky was bright blue. Even from inside she could tell that the morning air was crisp. It was the type of day Mary loved. Brisk enough to be invigorating, but not freezing. Ordinarily, she would like to be outside on a day like this. She loved the cleanness of a new-fallen snow, a bright sky, bracing air. Today it seemed wrong. She felt almost offended that creation should offer up such a favored vignette while she sat inside waiting for another daughter to die.

"Mary, drink. You need it," urged Lavinia.

She sighed. "Alright." The heat of the tea was soothing, which also seemed wrong.

"Mother." The voice, at once quiet and raspy, pulled her attention immediately to the emaciated child next to her.

Mary moved instantly from the chair to sit on the edge of the bed. She took Josie's hand in her own.

"What is it, my darling?"

"I love you, Mother."

"I love you, too."

Mary brushed the sweat-soaked hair from Josie's eyes, leaned forward and kissed her forehead. She felt a tear drop from her eye, landing on Josie's face. She moved to brush it away. As her hand neared her daughter's eye, the lid did not blink, the eyes stared up, vacant.

"No," Mary whispered. "No," she repeated louder.

Caroline Cutting moved in from the other side of the bed. As Mary stared at Josie's face, Caroline's hands came into view, her fingers feeling for a pulse at the neck. Then they became a blur as tears flooded Mary's eyes.

"She is gone," she heard Caroline say.

Mary felt strong arms wrap around her, pulling her up from the bed, turning her around. Eli. They stood together by the bed holding each other tightly, not saying a word, both staring down at the still form under the covers. Others bustled around them. Caroline's quiet but assured voice gave orders. Preparing the body would now begin.

Mary took a deep breath, stepped away from Eli and moved towards the bed to help. She felt as though she barely breathed throughout. It had been the same when Rebecca died, as though she was simply repeating the same motions, which, in a sense, she was.

"I will take care of the looking glass," said Lavinia once they had finished, though Mary barely registered the words.

She heard the kitchen door open and close, smelled woodsmoke and cold air as Eli returned. He had gone to the cabinetmaker to order a coffin as soon as the women began preparing the body.

"It will be ready on the morrow," he whispered to her.

"Go now, Mary," said one of the neighbors, she took no notice who. "Get something to eat. We will stay."

"No. I must stay with her."

"No, Mary," said Eli. "You need to keep up your strength. Come. Susannah has prepared something."

With his arm wrapped around her shoulder, Eli ushered her from the sick room. The scent of roasted meat set her mouth to watering. It was true, she was hungry though she felt a twinge of guilt for it.

"Take the dishes to my house when you are done and I will wash them, Susannah," said Lavinia.

Mary looked up, saw Eli shrug in Susannah's direction.

"I will do that. Thank you, Mrs. Wicker," said Susannah.

Mary again had the feeling of reliving Rebecca's death. She knew if she looked, she'd see that Lavinia had covered the small looking glass with a cloth. It was common enough to do so upon the time of a death, it not being fitting for one to preen at such a time. Mary, however, did not subscribe to the old belief that one's soul might become trapped in the looking glass should one peek while the body was still in the house. Lavinia, of course, did. Her superstitious nature was so powerful that she feared any reflection, even the distorted glimpse one might catch in a tub of dishwater. Mary had no more strength to argue the point today than she had a year ago, so the dishes would go to Lavinia's house for washing until Josie was buried. It was easier that way.

For the next two days, the house was full of people. Josie's body, now lying in the coffin would not be unattended from the moment she died until she was buried. Day and night family and neighbors kept vigil.

Though crowded, the house was nearly silent. People spoke little and when they did it was in subdued tones. Mary was grateful for the many neighbors. Their presence held her up when she felt she could not even stand any longer. It also allowed her to sleep at times knowing Josie was never alone.

"Thank you, Lord, for my good neighbors," she prayed upon laying down. She meant to pray more, to ask blessings upon each family member and neighbor who filled her house, helped her with meals and cleaning, and, most of importantly, stayed by Josie's body for hours on end, but exhaustion overtook her, and she fell asleep.

Two days later Mary sat on the parlor sofa, her head on Eli's shoulder. They had buried Josie that morning. The temperature the past few days had been just high enough that a grave could be dug. Mary was numb throughout the service in their parlor, the procession to the graveyard, and the burial. Upon returning home, there were guests to feed, condolences to accept, the kitchen to be put to rights after everyone had left. She'd felt herself constantly moving, heard her own voice, though she'd no idea what she'd said or to whom. It felt eerily like a repetition of the day they had buried Rebecca.

Now with company gone, their surviving children in bed, and the house quiet, Mary had nothing to prevent the image she'd been fighting all day from rising in her mind.

Josie.

The little girl who hated the cold asleep in a box buried in the almost frozen ground. Asleep, not dead – Mary's mind could not accept that yet. Outside her home. In a dark, cramped box. In the cold.

"Mary." Eli's voice was barely above a whisper.

She realized she was squeezing his hand hard enough to hurt them both.

"I am sorry," she said. "I was thinking about—"

"Shh. I know."

But he didn't. Not really. He likely thought she was remembering Josie's soft eyes, her smile, her sweet demeanor. He could not imagine that she pictured their child's corpse, shivering beneath the ground. She would not tell him. Could not. What would he think of her? Yet, she could not force the image from her mind, so badly did she ache to wrap her child in blankets and hold her close until she was warm again.

"Can you spare one of the girls for a day with Lavinia?" Eli asked, getting up to pace the room. "My accounts show that we owe the Wickers a half day's labor. Phineas says Lavinia could use some help."

"Send Lizzy." Mary heard herself reply, but the words seemed to come from someone else. She could not do something as ordinary as speak of chores at this time. Four children gone from her now. First her two infant boys and now two of her daughters. Life was no longer ordinary, and she could not at this moment believe it would ever be so again.

"Very well, then."

Mary's heart rebelled momentarily at Eli's casual talk. She stole a glance at his face in the dying firelight. The dusting of white in his chestnut hair looked more profuse, but perhaps it was a trick of the firelight. Lines deepened around his mouth as he clenched his jaw. The light was not enough for her to see his eyes clearly, but she did not need to. His heart ached as much as her own. She knew he was fighting the truth, too. The sight of him trying to hold it in broke something in her. Tears streamed down her face as a moaning sob escaped before she could clamp her hands over her mouth.

Eli was kneeling before her in an instant, his arms around her, pulling her into his embrace. She slid from the sofa. They sat in a heap, Mary half in his lap, arms tight around each other. They made little noise, their faces pressed into each other's shoulders, but their bodies heaved with their almost silent weeping.

All that had been pent up in Mary since Josie took her last breath was bursting forth. Eli gently but firmly gripped her shoulders pushing her back enough to look into her face. The only light was from the dying embers and the moon. She could see only the barest outline of his face, but she felt his breath as he spoke.

"She is with the Lord. At peace. We must remember that."

Mary nodded. She tried to speak, but as she opened her mouth, she felt her face crumple. Eli held her close again until she stopped.

"Let us go to bed," he whispered.

Later she would have no memory of getting up, climbing the stairs, and slipping into bed beside her husband. The only thing she would remember was the sound of a cough drifting down from the garret.

Chapter 6

June 1973
Bennington, Vermont

"Who's that?" Charlotte asked, glancing out the window at a young man mowing her grandmother's lawn.

"His name is Keith Perry. He lives up to Poultney, but he's spending the summer with his grandparents across the way. I've hired him to do my yardwork for the summer. I did it for a few years after your grandfather died, but it's too much for me now."

"I'm glad you have him, then." Charlotte felt a hint of worry. How old was her grandmother? It was a question that children were never allowed to ask adults. She wasn't sure she could ask now. A quick calculation put her grandmother in her seventies. What would she do in the winter when the driveway needed shoveling?

"Did you get a chance to read any of the diary yet?" asked her grandmother.

"I read all of January's entries last night. The last one said something about Jerusha wishing her neighbor would teach her to weave, but for some reason, couldn't. It seems Mrs. Wicker and Jerusha's mother must have had a falling out."

Eloise Tessier pulled up a chair at the kitchen table. "I was trying to remember what in that diary made me think Jerusha was trying to figure out some big family secret. It was too long ago. My memory isn't what it used to be. But now that you say it, I do think it had something to do with her mother and a neighbor. And something to do with one of her sisters, as well."

"Sisters? She's only mentioned one so far. Susannah. But apparently, she had moved to Ohio with her husband by the time Jerusha started keeping the diary."

"There had been others. They'd died by the time she wrote that journal. It was rare in those days for all the children of a family to live to adulthood."

"I know, Grandma. How hard it must have been for them."

"Losing a child is the worst thing that could ever happen. It doesn't matter how old they are, either." She lifted her gaze, staring past Charlotte, and she knew her grandmother was thinking of Aunt Beatrice.

"I'm so sorry, Grandma," Charlotte whispered, reaching across the table for her grandmother's hand.

A knock sounded on the door of the screened porch. Charlotte opened it to find a young man of seventeen or eighteen with shoulder-length brown hair, soft brown eyes, and bell bottom jeans covered in grass stains.

"You must be Keith," she said.

"That's me. You must be Charlotte. Your grandmother mentioned you were coming."

"Come in," she said, ushering him into the sunporch.

He stepped inside, but only a pace beyond the door. "I'm a mess," he said. "I don't want to get dirt and grass clippings all over the place."

Charlotte's grandmother joined them.

"Good morning, Mrs. Tessier," said Keith. "I finished the lawn. Would you like me to weed the gardens for you?"

"That's very thoughtful, but I can manage, and I like to do it. Charlotte, would you help me?"

"I'd love to, Grandma."

"Okay, Mrs. Tessier," said Keith. "But if you need anything else besides mowing let me know. I can fix stuff around the house, do heavy lifting, whatever you need."

"Thank you, Keith. I'll keep that in mind."

"I'm gonna go, then. Nice to meet you, Charlotte," he said backing out the door.

"He seems like a nice kid," said Charlotte.

"Oh, he is," agreed her grandmother. "His grandparents are awfully fond of him, and I can see why. They do wish he'd cut his hair, though."

"Oh, Grandma!" Charlotte laughed, shaking her head.

"I know. I know. You young people like it," she said, holding up her hands to ward off any criticism from Charlotte. "It's just that to us older folks, it looks a might peculiar to see a boy with long hair. Now, how about we get after those weeds?"

Charlotte was relieved to see her grandmother's vigor. Eloise Tessier had always loved her gardens – flower and vegetable. Her home and yard were like a scene from Currier and Ives. Two tall maple trees stood on either side of the front walkway. Roses climbed a trellis against the side of the house. Luxurious wisteria dangled from the awning over the back door. The draping sallows of a weeping willow on the side lawn had formed a childhood playhouse for Charlotte whenever her family visited in summer. Flower beds edged the house all around while a vegetable garden provided nourishment all summer and fall.

As Charlotte pulled weeds from around a cluster of petunias, she glimpsed her grandmother's hands working in the section next to her. They were not as swift as they once were, but they moved with the assurance of a woman who knew what she was doing. Charlotte felt a pang of melancholy at the thought that one day, maybe in the not-so-distant future, those hands would no longer coax flowers and vegetables from the earth.

"How old is Keith?" Charlotte asked.

"Just turned eighteen. He's going away to college in the fall. He's too young for you."

Charlotte nearly choked. "Grandma! That's not why I asked. I'm worried about you here all alone. I wish you had someone like him nearby all year if you need anything."

"I'm not that old, yet. I just need a little help with the heavier work."

This was spoken in the tone Charlotte knew meant the discussion was at an end. She would let it go for now.

As they straightened up from pulling the last of the weeds, they noticed the mail truck pass by.

"I'll grab your mail," said Charlotte, heading towards the front.

Back in the kitchen, Charlotte gathered bread, bologna and cheese for her grandmother and a heap of salad vegetables for herself to go with the potato salad her grandmother had made the day before.

"Here's a letter from your mother." Her grandmother held up a cream-colored envelope, a cluster of tulips in the corner. "Thank goodness she uses normal stationery. The last time I got a letter from Tracy the paper was round. She wrote in a circle from the inside out. I got dizzy reading it."

Charlotte made a mental note to tell her sister to forgo the fancy stationery when corresponding with their grandmother.

"What does Mom say?" asked Charlotte as her grandmother sliced open the envelope.

"Oh, good news! They are coming up to stay for a week and leave Tracy here for the rest of the summer. Charlotte, can you take a week off and come, too?"

"I just started my job. I won't have any vacation time for a year."

"Too bad. Come for the weekend they're here, at least."

"I'll try. Does she say anything else?"

"Russ is home for the summer. He'll be a senior next year, won't he?"

"Yes."

"It seems like you were all tiny tots just yesterday."

Charlotte smiled. Her childhood visits to Grandma and Grandpa Tessier were among her best memories. She felt free here. Never judged. Just loved.

"I'm thankful that Russ went to college," said her grandmother. "It kept him from being drafted. Keith has an older brother. He's there. In Vietnam."

"Thank God the draft is ending. Now if the war would just end," said Charlotte. "I can't imagine what it would be like to constantly worry about Russ if he was there." She set the plate with the sandwich before her grandmother then poured them each a glass of milk.

"I don't think I slept a wink the entire time your Uncle Will was in Europe." She shook her head. "Let's see what else your mother has to say. Tracy is planning to have a group of girls sleep over for her sixteenth birthday in September. Ha! That should be a noisy night for your parents. Is Tracy still doing all those acrobatics?"

"Gymnastics. Yes. Ever since she saw Cathy Rigby in the 1968 Olympics she's been hooked. Watching Olga Korbut last summer put her over the edge. She's been taking gymnastics lessons three days a week for the past five years."

"Last summer I watched her do those flips across the back lawn. It nearly gave me a heart attack."

"Then it's a good thing you haven't seen her on the balance beam." Charlotte laughed. "She's very good."

"I know. I just pray she doesn't get hurt."

"Tracy has no fear. One day I saw her doing back handsprings down the stairs."

"Don't even tell me about it. Your poor mother!"

"Well, when she goes to one of Tracy's competitions, she glows with pride. When are they coming up here?"

"They'll arrive on Saturday, July fourteenth."

When they'd finished lunch and cleaned the kitchen, Charlotte's grandmother announced that she was going to lie down. "I take a nap every day at this time. I never used to nap, but now I need it."

Deciding it was a good time to read some more of Jerusha's diary, Charlotte retrieved it along with the cotton gloves from Aunt Beatrice's bedroom. She thought she would go outside to read, but upon seeing that the sky had grown overcast decided to sit on the sun porch instead.

She sank into the cushioned seat of her favorite chair; the one Grandpa had made long ago. When she was little and her family came up from Massachusetts for a summer visit, Charlotte would spend hours on the porch curled up in the chair, a stack of books on one of the rounded wooden arms. A tray lamp, also made by Grandpa, held her lemonade and a plate of cookies then as it did now.

The air had taken on a slight chill with the darkening of the clouds. Charlotte could smell rain. She breathed deeply of the invigorating scent. Opening the diary, she began with the first entry for February. She was impressed that Jerusha had rarely missed a day, though often it was merely a mention of the weather and a rundown of the day's tasks.

On the twenty-first of February 1839, Jerusha had written, *Today begins my seventeenth year.*

Ah, Jerusha was sixteen. Charlotte understood her grandmother's confusion. But she was well-versed enough in the parlance of the nineteenth century to know that Jerusha would have considered the day she was born the beginning of her first year, making the first day of her seventeenth year her sixteenth birthday.

"Sweet sixteen," Charlotte whispered, remembering her own sixteenth birthday. Her mother had gone all out reserving the banquet room at Devon Brawn House, the fanciest restaurant in Charlotte's hometown of Westcott, Massachusetts. All her friends had been invited. They'd gone through all the rituals of the Sweet Sixteen party – the candle ceremony, the father-daughter dance, the passing on of the heirlooms, and the shoe ceremony – her first time in high heels. Charlotte ate it up, even then showing signs of the folklorist she would become.

Jerusha's sixteenth was nothing like Charlotte's. Besides the mention of it being her birthday, the only other indicator of it having been a special day was that her mother had given her a new pair of gloves – a simple necessity that was perhaps a gift to mark the day.

Yet, Charlotte knew that turning sixteen was as important for Jerusha as it had been for her. It was a time of coming of age. In folklorist terms, Jerusha had moved into a liminal time. She was at one of the great thresholds of life, times always marked by some sort of ritual whether planned in advance or not. Charlotte had studied the ways in which such rituals were acted out. She hoped the diary would tell her how Jerusha had done it.

She finished reading the entries for February. There was nothing more about weaving with Mrs. Wicker. Would weaving have been done in the winter? She didn't think so.

A light tap at the screen door pulled her from her thoughts. It was Keith. The rain had let up, but it was still sprinkling. She ushered him into the sun porch.

"I'm going to the market for my grandmother. She asked me to see if Mrs. Tessier needs anything," he said.

"That's nice of you," said Charlotte. It comforted her to know that her grandmother was well looked after by the neighbors. "She's napping right now. She's low on bread. Come into the kitchen. I'll look around to see if there's anything else."

Keith followed her, waiting just inside the kitchen door as she perused the refrigerator, cupboards, and pantry.

"I can't see anything else she needs." Opening the Hoosier cabinet drawer, Charlotte found the spare change her grandmother kept in it and gave him what he'd need for the bread.

"I won't be long," he said, turning to leave.

Suddenly, the sky opened, the rain quickly turning into a pelting torrent.

"Why don't you wait until it lets up," said Charlotte. She handed him a bottle of Coke, grabbed one for herself, and fished the bottle opener from the drawer. "Have a seat," she said, dropping into a chair at the table.

"Grandma says you'll be leaving for college in the fall. Where are you going?"

"UVM."

"Great school." Charlotte was a little envious. She would have loved to have gone to the University of Vermont, but they didn't have her major. "What will you be studying?"

"Education and history."

"Double major. That's ambitious. You want to teach history?"

He nodded. "High school, I think. Maybe junior high. But I want to make it more interesting than most of my history teachers did. I love going to museums and reading about history, but just memorizing all those dates and battles is a real drag. I want to help kids fall in love with it."

Charlotte watched his eyes light up as he spoke. It was the most he'd said at one time since she'd met him.

"We've got some great history around here," he continued. "Vermont has Ethan Allen, the Battle of Bennington. Just down to Massachusetts there's

Lexington and Concord, all the stuff in Boston, Plymouth, you know?"

"I do. I'm from Massachusetts. I majored in folklore with a minor in anthropology at the University of Pennsylvania. I took a lot of history courses. Even worked at Old Sturbridge Village one summer."

Keith's eyes widened. "Did you wear a costume?"

"Yes."

"I'm hoping to go this summer. I want to take my brother with me."

"I thought he was in Vietnam."

"That's Roy, my older brother. My younger brother's Alan. He's almost sixteen. He's not interested in much besides goofing off. I had to promise to drive him and his friends over to Fair Haven one night next month to get him to agree to come with me."

"What's in Fair Haven?"

Keith glanced away and Charlotte detected a faint blush on his cheeks. "An old barn that's looked like it's about to fall in on itself for as long as I can remember. I can't believe it's still standing."

"What do they want to go there for?" Charlotte asked.

"It's supposed to be haunted. They say some guy hanged himself from the rafters and now he haunts the place."

Chalotte couldn't help grinning. "So, they want to go legend tripping.

"Go what?"

"Legend tripping. That's what Gary Hall calls it. He's a folklorist who just wrote an article about it. Kids have been doing it forever – going to a site of tragedy that supposedly is now haunted. It's a rite of passage. They do it to show their bravery, then have a story to tell. But mostly it's a psychological release, though the kids don't realize it. Sixteen is about the right age. They're on the verge of adulthood but not quite there yet. By going at night to a place far enough away to have to drive, they are pushing the boundaries of parental control. Because they are placing themselves into a scary situation, one that forces them to face death and the supernatural, they have to prove their courage to go through with it. In reality, they're perfectly safe, but in their minds, they're taking a huge risk. Hall gave it the title Legend Tripping."

"Huh. I never knew that crazy stuff we all did had been studied."

"You did it, too, then?" Charlotte wished she had her tape recorder.

"Yeah. We all did. It's a tradition."

"Exactly! I'll bet you went to the same barn with a bunch of your friends. Got some older kid to drive?"

"My friend Frankie's older brother. He'd gone with his friends a few years before."

Charlotte nodded. "Yup. That's how it works. Kenneth Thigpen did a study on it a couple of years ago. He said there are three parts to the legend trip. I'll bet you followed the pattern. On the way there, you told stories about the place, the hanging, the ghost. Anyone who'd done it before related their experiences. And you went over the rituals that would have to be performed once you arrived in order to make the ghost appear. Am I right?"

"Wow! It's like you were in the car with us."

She laughed. "What were your rituals?"

"We had to park in a specific patch of grass so we were facing the side of the barn. Then flash the lights twice, beep the horn three times, and everybody in the car yells, 'John Green, John Green, let yourself be seen.' John Green was the guy who hanged himself."

"And then what happens?"

"You're supposed to be able to see a shadow of John Green hanging from a noose tied to one of the rafters. It shows up on the outside of the barn. Swings back and forth a little, too. It's weird, now that I think about it. Why would it be a shadow on the outside of the barn? He hanged himself inside it."

"Doesn't have to be logical," said Charlotte. "Did you see it?"

Keith scrunched his face. "Kind of."

"What do you mean?"

"I saw something. Some kind of shadow on the barn, I think. To tell the truth, I was pretty scared. We'd worked ourselves up good on the way there. It was probably the shadow of a tree limb or something."

"That's the point of phase one. Getting yourselves into a state where you can talk yourselves into seeing or hearing whatever is supposed to happen. The power of suggestion."

"Is the light flashing, horn beeping, and chanting phase two?"

"Yes. That and whatever is supposed to happen because of it."

"What's phase three?"

"Talking about it afterwards. Recounting everything that happened. Did anyone claim to see the shadow?"

"Oh yeah. Roddy Wilkins. He was talking for days about how he saw the perfect outline of John Green swinging away on the side of the barn. I heard he told some kids who weren't there that he got out of the car and went right up to it, touched it, and it disappeared. That's crap, though. He never left the car."

Charlotte threw back her head and laughed. "Classic! Well, Keith, you now know that you have taken part in an age-old rite of passage, and you are poised to assist your brother and his friends in doing the same. It's harmless as long as no one gets hurt and no damage is done. Unfortunately, a lot of kids like to drink and get high on the way. Not that great an idea combined with driving, though I'm sure it almost guarantees they'll see whatever they're expecting to, and maybe a few other things as well. Vandalism sometimes occurs, too. Also, not advisable."

"We didn't do any of that when I went. Well, okay, there were a few beers involved. Nobody vandalized anything, though. I'll make sure my brother and his friends behave."

The rain let up and the sun poked out from between the clouds.

"I'd better go. My grandmother will think I drowned in the rain. I'll be back with the bread soon. It was cool rapping with you."

After Keith left, Charlotte returned to the sun porch, slipped the cotton gloves back on, and took up Jerusha's diary. She read through March and April. Most entries were about weather and spring cleaning. Charlotte thought of helping her mother with their own spring cleaning, a ritual she'd always hated. It had nothing on what Jerusha and her mother had had to do. Nor did Charlotte have to make her own soap from lye and animal fat or starch from mushy potatoes. Reading Jerusha's entries made her grateful for the relatively easy workload she had when it came to keeping house, especially when she read the entry about scalding mattresses to rid them of bedbugs.

One April entry mentioned that the Wicker family had taken a large amount of wool to the carding mill. Later in the month, Jerusha wrote:

Hoped to go to Mrs. Wicker today. Mother insisted I churn butter for her instead.

Charlotte swore she could feel Jerusha's disappointment pulse from the page.

The rain picked up again making the porch air a little too damp for comfort. Charlotte decided to continue her reading in the living room. Upon entering she found her grandmother standing with her back to her, looking down at something in her hands.

"Grandma?"

She turned. "Oh, Charlotte. I didn't hear you come in." She was holding a framed picture she had picked up from the end table.

Charlotte moved closer to her. It was a picture of Aunt Beatrice.

"Did you have a good nap?"

"Fine, I guess. I dreamed of Beatrice." Her voice sounded far away.

Charlotte glanced down at the picture. It was Aunt Beatrice's high school graduation picture.

"You make me think of her."

"I do?" Charlotte glanced again at her aunt's picture. Aunt Beatrice had light brown hair cut short and full of curls. Her face was long and narrow, her smile wide. Though the photo was black and white, she remembered her aunt's blue eyes. Charlotte's own hair was a rich, chestnut brown, thick and reaching to her waist. Her eyes were green and her face full, with what she thought of as 'chipmunk cheeks.'

"I don't think we look very much alike."

"Not your looks," said her grandmother. "Your spirit. Beatrice was full of life. She had so many things she wanted to do, so many places she wanted to see. It was a shame the airlines wouldn't take her just because she wore glasses. So foolish! Still, she loved having a job and an apartment, making her own way in the world. She wanted to get married and raise a family one day, too, but she was in no hurry. Independent. That's the best word to describe her." She continued to gaze at the photograph.

"I miss her," Charlotte whispered.

She looked up at Charlotte. "She was proud of you. But she'd be even more proud if she could see what you've made of yourself."

"I haven't done anything yet."

"But you have. "You've graduated from college and earned a master's degree. Now you've got an important position at that museum. You're going places, ma pet."

Charlotte felt her stomach tighten. She was going nowhere if Brad Louden had anything to say about it. And she had no idea what to do. She wished she could ask Aunt Beatrice.

Her grandmother returned the photograph to the table and held Charlotte's hands. "You are going to do all the things Beatrice wanted to do and more. You will rise above anything or anyone who tries to hold you back. You're smart, courageous, and strong. Just like Beatrice."

She reached up, caressing Charlotte's cheek. "I am so proud of you."

Tears stung Charlotte's eyes. She felt like a fraud. I'll do my best, Grandma."

Chapter 7

Late April 1831
Birch Falls, Vermont

Jerusha and Lizzy were tasked with all the housekeeping while their mother and Susannah spent the day making enough soap for the year. The girls escaped outdoors as often as they could to feed the chickens, gather eggs, milk the cows, and carry water from the well. It was damp and chilly, but Lizzy loved to be outdoors and ever since Josie had died, Jerusha stuck close to Lizzy.

"I wish I could have gone with Father and Seth," said Lizzy. "I could do the same work as them."

Jerusha took the full pail of water Lizzy handed to her before Lizzy turned back to the well to fill a second pail. Even at thirteen she was strong as a bull. Certainly, she could have helped Father and Seth with some of the maple sugaring, but Jerusha was glad Lizzy was home with her just the same.

They brought the water buckets into the house, set them in the kitchen, then rushed upstairs to make the beds.

"Mrs. Wicker is going to teach me to weave," said Lizzy, reaching into the mattress to fluff up the ticking. "We will start as soon as it is warm enough to work without a fire."

"I wish Mother would let me go, too," said Jerusha.

"I wish you could go instead of me. I hate all that flax and wool. After it rains, that house smells like wet sheep." Lizzy pulled a face that made Jerusha laugh.

Jerusha had always been fascinated by Mrs. Wicker's big wooden loom. She'd seen her neighbor work the treadles with her feet making the heddles move up and down while passing a shuttle through the heavy threads, pulling, and pushing the breast beam. In the end she would have a finished piece – a coverlet, a blanket, a counterpane – some with intricate designs. Most of Jerusha's winter clothing had been made on Mrs. Wicker's loom as were her father's and Seth's work pantaloons and her mother's and sister's petticoats. Mrs. Wicker was one of the few women in Birch Falls who still wove on a loom. Her work supplied many in the community. To Jerusha the process of making the many items from simple wool and flax was a great mystery. The loom, that hulking piece of machinery was the key to unlocking it. She longed to understand its complexities.

"Hannah says her mother has asked Mrs. Wicker to make a new counterpane for her and Betsy's brothers all need new pantaloons. You will have lots of practice."

"I don't care a fig about learning to weave," said Lizzy. "I think it dull. I would rather work outdoors."

"You help Mother in the garden."

"I mean like what Father and Seth do – chop wood, mend fences, plow the fields."

"You've never done any of those things," said Jerusha.

"Only because I am not allowed. If they would let me, I know I could."

Jerusha shook her head at Lizzy's bravado. She could not fathom her sister's desire for men's work, but she did know that Lizzy had an abundance of vigor and that if she set her mind to something she would do it.

As Jerusha threw the counterpane over the bed a fine dust arose tickling her nose so that she sneezed. Lizzy sneezed, too, then began to cough.

"Lizzy?" asked Jerusha when her sister's coughing did not abate. "Lizzy, are you alright?"

Lizzy nodded but kept coughing. She doubled over onto the bed. "Should I get Mother?"

"I am here." Before Jerusha could turn around her mother was brushing past her towards Lizzy.

"It's the dust." Lizzy choked out the words. Her face had turned red, and tears glistened in her eyes.

"Jerusha, fetch water, please," her mother ordered.

She ran from the room, heart pounding.

"Where are you going in such a hurry?" asked Susannah, straightening up from stirring the kettle of animal fat and lye, a hand rubbing her lower back.

"Dust made Lizzy cough. Mother said to fetch water."

"It is only the dust, then, Jerusha," said Susannah, her voice soft and comforting.

Ever since Josie's death the slightest cough had unnerved their mother. Her fear was contagious. The others were better able to disregard it, but Jerusha seemed to absorb her mother's fear through her skin.

"She will be fine after a swallow or two," said Susannah as Jerusha left the room, cup in hand.

Susannah was right. Lizzy gulped the entire cup of water, wiped her eyes, and, after clearing her throat a few times, spoke hoarsely. "I feel fine now."

Jerusha heaved a sigh of relief. Her mother squeezed Lizzy tightly before leaving the room.

Jerusha's father and Seth returned in time for supper, having taken their noon meal at the sugaring camp. Jerusha and Lizzy ran to them as they came through the door, burying their noses in their father's coat.

"Father, you smell good." Jerusha breathed deeply of the scent of wood smoke and maple sugar.

Eli laughed, throwing an arm around each girl.

"May I go with you and Seth tomorrow?" Lizzy begged.

"Now, Lizzy, you are needed here."

"Mother has Susannah and Jerusha. You need me."

"The camp is full of men," said Seth, hanging his coat on a wall peg and grinning at Lizzy. "You would only be in the way."

"I will not be in the way, Seth," Lizzy growled at him.

"True, Little Ox, because you will not be there."

Seth had called Lizzy Little Ox ever since the time at age nine when she tried to help the oxen pull the hay wagon. "Lizzy, get away from there. You are not one of the oxen," her father had called which sent Seth into gales of laughter. He had never forgotten it. Though Lizzy appeared to bristle whenever Seth called her Little Ox, Jerusha was sure she secretly liked the nickname. It did, after all, support her belief in her own physical strength.

"Father, would I be in the way?"

"You? Never!"

"Ha!" she threw at Seth. "Then I can go, Father?"

"I fear you are needed more at home."

"But—"

She was interrupted by her mother. "You are to go to Mrs. Wicker tomorrow, Lizzy. Now come to the table."

"Jerusha can go in my place. She wants to learn weaving."

Jerusha's heart skipped a beat. The thought that she might replace Lizzy and learn to weave was worth missing her sister for the day.

"Jerusha is not old enough for that yet," said her mother, dashing Jerusha's hopes. "You will go."

"But, Mother I—"

"Eilza!"ended the conversation.

Just then Susannah's husband, Zachary, returned from his position as store clerk.

"Busy day at the store?" Eli asked.

"Fairly. Mr. Hapgood will give me leave whenever you are in need of me, though. Will you start plowing soon?"

"Not much longer."

"Will you begin working with Seth and the girls, Zachary?" asked Mary.

"Whenever you like."

Zachary had been a schoolmaster prior to marrying Susannah. As the winter school term had just come to an end, he had agreed to continue their lessons in the evening.

"Seth may not have as much time now," said Eli. "He will be busy on the farm this year. But if you can make certain he understands how to keep accounts, I would be obliged."

Zachary nodded. Preparing to inherit the farm?"

A wide grin spread over Seth's face. "Someday."

"I wish I could learn the same as Seth," said Lizzy.

"Seth learns for the future, as do you," said her father.

"Mother does not weave."

"Mrs. Wicker needs help," her mother told her. "She has no daughters. It is our Christian duty to help one another. So, you will go to Mrs. Wicker, and you will do whatever she asks, and we will hear no more about this. Is that understood?"

"Yes, Mother." Lizzy dropped her gaze to her plate.

"If fresh air and exercise is what you are after, daughter, there will be plenty of it before long," said her father. "The garden will need to be in by this time next month."

"Churning butter, too," added Susannah. "That will require your strong limbs."

"Mother, may I go with Lizzy to Mrs. Wicker's tomorrow?" asked Jerusha.

Jerusha waited while her mother thought it over for a moment, then said, "I believe we can spare you."

Jerusha nearly leaped from her chair with joy. "Thank you, Mother!"

"But you will be needed at home before long. Spring cleaning is just around the corner."

After supper, the women and girls cleared the table while the men headed to the barns. A knock sounded at the door. It was Caroline Cutting.

"I am on my way home from seeing Amy Clement," she said. "I have just delivered her of a baby boy. He seems of good health and Amy rests comfortably at present."

"Praise be to God," said Jerusha's mother, seating Mrs. Cutting at the table. "Tea?"

"No, thank you. I'll not tarry. I stopped to ask that you look in on Amy. Her mother and sister may need help."

"I will go, of course, but if she and the babe are well..."

"You know how she was before, Mary."

"Yes, but she has shown no signs for months."

Jerusha glanced at her mother whose voice had gone to a whisper. Amy Clement was frail. She'd been wracked with cough on and off for years. Hers was the lingering type of consumption. Amy's two aunts had shown signs for nearly twenty years before succumbing to the illness. It had been but seven years for Amy. It was assumed she would be like her aunts, still having a decade or more ahead of her.

"She is well enough at present. But I have seen it happen before. In the time leading up to the birth, the woman loses all signs of the illness but soon after she has delivered, she is taken with an awful relapse. Many times it carries her off."

Jerusha watched the color drain from her mother's face.

"Susannah and I will go tomorrow."

"Thank you. They will be grateful for your presence."

That night Jerusha snuggled close to Lizzy. She tried to think about learning to weave, but her mind kept returning to Amy Clement, wondering if within the next few days, the new baby would be bereft of his mother.

Chapter 8

June 1973
Middlebury, Vermont

Charlotte and Heidi sat at the table in Charlotte's kitchen. Heidi had talked Charlotte into learning her latest craft – soap-making.

"None of that legend tripping stuff in my wild years," said Heidi. "There was a haunted cemetery a lot of kids hung around in after dark, though," she said, removing the contents of the kit. "Mm…smell this," she said, handing a small vial to Charlotte. "Roses. And this one is lavender."

"Ever go there?" asked Charlotte, sniffing the vial.

"Sure. I went with friends and one time alone."

"Were you spooked?"

"No. I wanted to communicate with the spirits. We'll have to wear these," she said, handing a pair of gloves to Charlotte. "We aren't supposed to touch the lye with our hands."

"Communicate with the spirits?"

"Yes. That wasn't the first time. I've always been sensitive, but it was the most powerful experience I'd had up to that time."

"What happened?" Charlotte asked.

"I walked around the cemetery for a while. I got really strong vibes near this one gravestone. The name on it was Hannah Morton. She was eighteen when she died. Anyway, I put my hands on the stone, trying to get the vibrations to come through. It took a while, but finally I heard a girl's voice."

Heidi put down the vial of pure olive oil and absentmindedly tucked a lock of her blond hair behind her ear.

"What did she say?" asked Charlotte.

"I am not finished." Heidi said this in a higher register than her own voice but didn't appear to realize it. A shiver ran down Charlotte's spine.

Shaking her head, Heidi resumed taking the other oils from the box. "That was all. Just that one sentence. It was amazing, though."

"How old were you?"

"Almost sixteen."

Charlotte had only known Heidi for a few months. Was it possible her friend was unstable? She was a nurse. She'd need to have her wits about her for that, wouldn't she?

"You don't believe me?" Heidi's voice was tinged with hurt.

"I'm trying to take it in."

Heidi shrugged. "Don't folklorists run into that sort of thing?"

"The supernatural is often part of folklore, isn't it? Have you ever had an experience you couldn't explain? Ever encountered a spirit?"

Charlotte's mind flew to an experience she'd had as a child.

"Once," she said. "When I was about five or six. I remember I went with my dad to the home of some man. I guess he was going to do some work for this guy. Anyway, I got bored standing around while they talked and decided to go exploring. I wandered off into another room. There were no lights on, and it was really dark. I felt like there was someone else in the room watching me. Then I heard a man's voice from behind me say, 'What do you want?' He sounded angry. When I turned around, I could just make out the outline of a chair. I could almost see a man sitting there. He was smoking a pipe. I saw and smelled the pipe smoke. It frightened me that someone would be sitting alone in the dark like that. I let out a scream and ran.

"My dad and the man he'd come to talk with came to see what was wrong. I threw myself into my dad's arms and told him the man in the other room scared me. The one sitting in the chair smoking a pipe.

"As Dad was carrying me out of the house, I heard the other man tell him that the only person who had ever smoked a pipe in the house was his father, but he'd died a few months previous. At that age, I don't think I understood death very well, but something about what he said scared me even then."

As she finished the story, Charlotte realized her heart was beating fast.

"Far out," said Heidi. "After that experience, why don't you believe mine?"

"I honestly don't know what to believe. I know I was scared out of my wits that day, but I was just a little kid. Kids have wild imaginations, right? That's what my mom said when my dad told her what happened."

"The man said his father smoked a pipe. How would you have known to imagine that?"

"Maybe because I'd seen men smoking pipes. My dad smokes one."

"You had a true paranormal experience." There was conviction in Heidi's voice. "Maybe you have a gift."

"I doubt it. I never saw anything like that again."

Heidi was quiet. She scooped the solidified palm and coconut oils into an old saucepan she'd brought from her apartment. "Have you ever felt like you're not alone when you know you are?"

Charlotte thought a moment. "Well, yes, but I think most people have that experience once in a while."

"I think most people have the ability to reach beyond, but don't develop it. Aren't you curious about what you experienced when you were little?"

Charlotte sighed. "Yes and no."

Heidi threw her a questioning look.

"Part of me is fascinated with the whole idea of ghosts. I don't know if I believe in them or not. On one hand, it seems ridiculous, the stuff of tall tales and–"

"Folklore?" Heidi's eyes glimmered, making Charlotte laugh.

"Yes. But on the other hand, I don't think there is a known civilization in human history that hasn't had some form of belief in ghosts or a spirit world or something of that nature. That has to mean something."

"Is that why you went into folklore?"

Charlotte nodded. "I'm enthralled by hearing what people have experienced. I love their stories. I love collecting them to see how they fit together, what they have in common. But I'm not sure I want to encounter any of it myself."

"Why not?"

"What I remember most vividly about that one experience was how terrified I felt. I don't think I've ever been that frightened before or since. I don't ever want to feel that scared again."

"Haven't you put yourself in a job where you might?"

Charlotte laughed. "At the moment I think I've put myself in a job where I'm more likely to be bored to death than scared to death. At least I will be if Brad doesn't let me do more than dust the stuff he wants to put in an exhibit."

A knock at the door interrupted their conversation. Charlotte answered to find Heidi's aunt standing there in her bathrobe and slippers, her hair wrapped in a mass of pink curlers.

"Come in, Mrs. Pleasant."

"I'll only stay a moment." She stepped into the kitchen to address her niece. "What's all this?" she asked, pointing at the assorted bags, molds, pans, and vials on the table.

"We're making soap," said Heidi.

"Soap? Why would you make soap? You can get all you want at the store."

"It's a craft, Aunt Iris," Heidi explained. "We're doing it for enjoyment."

"How is that enjoyable?"

"It's relaxing. Here, smell this," she said, handing a vial of lavender fragrance to her aunt.

"Mm…that does smell good, but can't you get scented soaps at the store?"

Heidi sighed. "Yes, but we want to make our own. It's good to get in touch with how things were done in the past. It's more natural."

"Uh-huh. Well, dear, I just came to let you know that I'm going to bed now. You should come home soon. It's getting late. You have to get up early for work in the morning."

"I know Auntie. I'll be home in a little while."

Charlotte had to fight to keep from rolling her eyes. When she'd first met Heidi and Mrs. Pleasant, she thought how fortunate it was for Heidi to live with her aunt who was struggling after her husband died. They had been living together for just over a year. It gave Heidi, who had taken a nursing position at Porter Hospital, a place to live close to work and Mrs. Pleasant company and help with the rent and expenses. At first, Charlotte had been a bit envious of their arrangement. Her own apartment consisted of three tiny rooms – kitchen, living room, and bedroom – along with a small bath. Sometimes she felt as though she could barely turn around in it. Heidi and her aunt had a larger apartment with two bedrooms. While Charlotte scraped by, Heidi usually had a bit to spare. When they went to the movies or out to lunch, Heidi often paid for them both. It hurt Charlotte's pride. She thought about picking up a second job but decided that would have to wait until she felt more established at the museum. After she got to know Iris Pleasant better her envy dissipated.

"All right, but keep an eye on the time," Iris said.

She turned to leave but stopped in front of Charlotte. "Don't you have to work in the morning?"

"Yes."

"You should go to bed soon, too." She turned back, taking them both in. "When we don't get enough sleep, we don't look our best. You're both such pretty girls. You don't want to lose your looks. How will either of you find a nice young man that way?"

This woman was too much for Charlotte. Did she ever think of anything else? "That's not why I'm working, Mrs. Pleasant."

Iris turned her attention back to Charlotte. "After all those years at college and never finding a husband, I'd think you'd try at work. All the men you work with aren't already married, are they?"

Charlotte folded her arms across her chest. "Not all, but it doesn't matter. I didn't go to college to find a husband and that's not what I'm looking for at work, either."

Iris Pleasant gave her a sideways glance – a look Charlotte had come to know and dislike. It was a look that said she knew better than Charlotte, knew she wasn't being truthful. It set Charlotte's teeth on edge.

"Heidi is hoping to marry a doctor. That's why she became a nurse. I don't understand why you chose to study fairytales–"

"Folklore," Charlotte corrected.

"Isn't that the same thing? Anyway, if you were going to go to college you probably should have chosen something where you could meet a nice man who would make enough money to take care of you properly. But…" she shrugged and let out a *what's done is done* sigh.

It was moments like this when Charlotte understood where the term making one's blood boil came from. She swore her own blood was bubbling in her veins throwing off steam that would escape through her ears any second. Before she could speak,

Heidi scooped up the soap-making supplies and tossed them into their box.

"You're right, Aunt Iris. It's getting late. Let's go. Charlotte, I'll talk to you later." She ushered her aunt out of the apartment before Charlotte could blow.

Once they were gone, Charlotte flopped on the couch. The uneasy feeling brought on by recounting her childhood memory was now compounded by her irritation at Iris Pleasant. Needing something to calm her agitation, she got up, put Van Morrison's *Moondance* album on the turntable making sure the volume wasn't up too high so as not to disturb her neighbors. The last thing she needed was Iris Pleasant coming back. She lay back down on the couch and closed her eyes.

The first song on the album was "And It Stoned Me". Though the song had nothing to do with drugs, Charlotte couldn't help but associate it with getting stoned. She knew a few people from college who, if they felt as she did now, wouldn't hesitate to roll a joint. Charlotte had tried it a few times, but rather than relax her as it did most people, it made her more agitated. Pot obviously wasn't for her. A glass of wine would not have been out of the question if she'd had any, but liquor of any kind was too expensive except for the cheap malt liquor masquerading as wine. She'd had enough of that in college, too.

Instead, she immersed herself in the music. Laying on the couch with her eyes closed, she let the bluesy strains and Morrison's rich voice seep into her brain. By the time "Into the Mystic" played, she was mentally floating on undulating waves letting the music rock her own gypsy soul.

Chapter 9

May 1831
Birch Falls, Vermont

"Mother, might I speak to you about a delicate matter?" asked Susannah.

Mary Kendall glanced at the anxious face of her eldest daughter as they walked the muddy road towards the home of Amy Clement. There had been a look of apprehension about Susannah of late.

"What is it?"

"A fortnight ago I thought I was with child. I was mistaken."

Mary gazed on the bowed head of her daughter. Susannah had seemed so withdrawn lately she had feared something far worse. "Do not be discouraged. It will happen in God's time."

Mary took a deep breath of the clean air. All around her grass was becoming green and lush. Trees were sending forth buds. Today Eli would hitch up the oxen to plow the kitchen garden for her. Tomorrow she and her girls would begin planting.

Mary and Susannah had been visiting Amy regularly since Caroline Cutting had requested it just a few weeks ago. The baby was well. Amy, though she had relapsed after the birth, was not any worse than she had been before. The freshness of the spring morning lifted Mary's spirits.

"I fear it."

The words were spoken so softly, Mary almost didn't catch them.

"Fear what, Susannah?"

"Being with child." Susannah kept her head bowed as they walked.

Mary placed a hand on her daughter's shoulder. "It is not unusual. It will be a new experience," she said, her voice calm and soothing. "But it is a natural one. I will be with you throughout, God willing. And Caroline will be there at the birth. There is no one better to have at such a time than Caroline Cutting."

Mary watched Susannah's bonnet bob as she nodded her agreement, but still she kept her gaze lowered.

"What if..."

The catch in Susannah's voice made Mary stop walking. Turning Susannah towards her, she took the young woman's face in her hands. "If what, Susannah?"

"If it dies. I could never bear it."

Mary drew in a sharp breath. Susannah, the oldest, could remember the two baby boys they had buried, one stillborn the other gone at two months. Susannah did not know of the miscarriages Mary had suffered as they happened while she was too young to have understood. Mary gazed at Susannah unsure what words would bring her reassurance when truly there was none.

"It was the Lord's will that he should take your brothers to him so quickly. We cannot fathom the mind of God but must trust in his mercy."

"How did you survive it?"

"It is too common to expect otherwise. When I married, my own mother counseled me not to allow myself an attachment to a child before its first year. Even then to be wary of too much tenderness towards the child until it seemed it would live. I confess I found myself incapable of conforming to such advice. Had I been able to I might have saved myself much heartache."

"I fear I will prove just as unable," said Susannah as they resumed walking. "When I thought I might be...you know, I felt love right away. When I discovered I'd been mistaken, I cried for the loss of something that never was. How could I survive a real loss?"

"With the help of the Lord and those who love you," said Mary. "At the time it seems impossible that your heart will ever mend, but it does. Patched, at least, though not like new."

They arrived at the Clement house to find Caroline Cutting hovering over Amy's bed. Amy's sister, Julia, took them aside to relate that Amy had grown much worse during the night. "She coughed all night, blood coming out in clots. She said her chest felt as though a boulder had been placed upon it."

It had been but a few days since they had last visited, but Amy's appearance had changed rapidly. She'd lost a great deal of weight in a short time. Her sunken cheeks were bright red, her eyes fever bright. She lay in bed moaning as Caroline wiped her forehead with a wet cloth and her mother gripped her hand and prayed. Mary pulled up a chair next to Amy's mother, placed an arm over the woman's shoulder.

"Caroline?" Mary asked.

"As I feared. Like so many consumptives who seem to improve until their time has come but once they've borne the babe, the malady returns more ferociously than ever."

"Is there no hope, then?"

Caroline dropped her gaze to her patient's face and shook her head. A whimper escaped Amy's mother. Mary pulled her close.

For the next three days and nights Mary and Susannah gathered around Amy's bed with Amy's husband, mother, sister, Caroline, and Lavinia Wicker. Other neighbor women also came and went. Many brought food. Some did chores. Together they all prayed, spoke gently with Amy, tried to make her comfortable, listened for her last words, and, finally, saw her off to eternity.

Throughout those days and nights, Mary's thoughts returned often to the talk she'd had with Susannah as they'd walked to Amy's house on the morning when they'd found her so stricken. How she wished there was a way she could spare her daughter knowing the pain of the loss of a child. Mary's own mother had lost three children before Mary was born. She did not know a single married woman who had not lost any either by miscarriage or from having died as babies. Mary had not been quite truthful when she'd told Susannah that her heart would be patched in time. Each of Mary's losses had broken off a piece of her heart. It might go on beating, but those pieces would always be missing, buried in the ground with her children.

* * *

Once they had plowed the land for the kitchen garden, Eli and Seth moved on to finishing repairs to the fences, plowing the fields, and planting the English grasses of Timothy, clover, and red top which would eventually become hay. Because of the time spent watching at Amy's bedside, Mary and Susannah had not been able to help put in the garden. Lizzy and Jerusha had been left to do it on their own.

"The girls have done well with the garden, Mary," said Lavinia Wicker as they walked home from the gathering that followed Amy's burial.

"Indeed. I am much pleased that they have learned so well."

"Your Lizzy works like a demon."

Despite the solemnity of the day, Mary could not help a smile. "When she puts her mind to something she goes at it hammer and tongs not to be stopped until the task is done and done well."

"To be sure. I wish I had a girl like her. My niece was a good, obedient girl. She did her best while she was with me, but she lacked Lizzy's vitality."

"Ten men together lack Lizzy's vitality," said Mary. Both women laughed then glanced sheepishly at one another.

"Still," Lavinia continued, "I am sorry my niece had to return home. She was of great help to me. You are fortunate in your girls, Mary. I know you would have liked more boys, but at least you have Seth. As the saying goes, 'pity the man who has no sons and pity the woman who has no daughters.' Phineas has as much help as he needs, but my work falls to me alone."

"Does not Lizzy help you when I send her over?"

"She does, of course, though I suspect she does not care much for weaving. Jerusha is the one who takes an interest. I would like to train her to weave when she is older, if you consent."

"Jerusha is taken with the loom, I believe."

"She will do well, then."

The sun was playing peekaboo with the clouds. Every time it hid, Mary shivered a bit. Though it was not late enough in the day for the shadows to be long, she felt cold as though Lavinia's larger form were casting shade over her. She told herself it was due to the funeral. It brought back too many memories, the most recent still being too fresh.

Mary took comfort in the presence of her friend. She had been Lavinia Wicker's neighbor all her married life and had known her since they were girls. Lavinia was older than Mary by a few years, so they had not become close until they were grown, and age no longer mattered. Still, she sometimes thought of Lavinia as "the older girl." Perhaps it was a remnant from youth or because Lavinia was much bigger than Mary. Lavinia was only a bit taller, Mary being a tall woman herself with a stately bearing one could call statuesque. Lavinia was heavier than Mary, not fat, but sturdy, with a square face, strong jaw, and shoulders made for a milkmaid's yoke. Her hands and forearms made Mary think of kneading dough. Lavinia had a motherly air about her. With the raising of five boys, she was by turns tender and stern as circumstances necessitated and always there when needed.

Mary gazed up at the clear, blue sky. "It is good weather for planting. I will gather my girls and we will come 'round now to put in your garden. We shall have it done before the sun sets."

"You are a good neighbor and a good friend, Mary," said Lavinia, absently tucking in a strand of wheat brown hair that had escaped her bonnet.

"It is you who are good to me," said Mary, thinking of all that Lavinia had done for her in the days following the deaths of her two baby boys and, more recently, the deaths of Rebecca and Josie. Despite all she had to care for in her own home, Lavinia had come by day after day bringing meals, helping with mending and cleaning, sitting with Mary and letting her cry then, eventually, insisting she return to her own cooking and housework and rejoin the world of the living. Mary wondered often how she would have made it through those terrible days without Lavinia.

Chapter 10

Late June 1973
Middlebury, Vermont

"So, Halloween," said Brad. "Any ideas?"

Brad, Charlotte, and the two curators, Paul Bentley, and Jonathan Du Prés, sat at the round table in the meeting room.

"I've been thinking we could do something on the progression of Halloween from its ancient Celtic origins to today and show the connections between the old and the current. For example, showing Jack-O'-lanterns using both turnips and pumpkins and–"

"I think we want something more substantial than Jack-O'-lanterns," said Brad. "Paul? Jonathan? Anything?"

Cut off mid-sentence, Charlotte was left with her mouth open as Brad turned his attention to the curators. She had spent weeks thinking about a Halloween exhibit that would be both informative and entertaining. She waited for a break in the conversation and tried again.

"Maybe I shouldn't have started with Jack-O'-lanterns," she said, a nervous laugh escaping. "What I was trying to get at was creating an exhibit where visitors can learn about Halloween customs as they were brought from Europe to New England and how they have evolved over time. I'd like to bring in Cabbage Night, as well."

"Pumpkins, cabbages. Leave it to a vegetarian," said Brad. The three men laughed. Charlotte forced a laugh, too.

"Yes, well, I wasn't really intending to bring that into it," she said. "But seriously, Halloween is a really fascinating holiday from a folklore point of view."

"The Cabbage Night aspect sounds interesting," said Jonathan. "How were you thinking of presenting it?"

Charlotte turned eagerly toward Jonathan. Perhaps if one of the curators showed interest in her ideas Brad would be forced to at least hear her out.

"Most people today don't even know about Cabbage Night. I first heard of it from my dad. He told me about how he and his brothers and cousins observed it. All the pranks they pulled. Now older kids do things sort of like that on Halloween. I think we should show how that happened."

"It is something no one will be apt to see anywhere else," said Paul. "I'd almost forgotten about it until you brought it up."

Paul and Jonathan were older, around Charlotte's father's age. They could have engaged in some Cabbage Night pranks themselves.

Charlotte hazarded a glance at Brad. He was leaning back in his chair, arms folded across his chest. He appeared to be clenching his jaw.

"It sounds good for showing how Halloween folk traditions have built on each other and transformed over time," said Jonathan. He jotted notes on the pad of paper in front of him.

Charlotte's heart soared. Both curators though her idea was good and were willing to go with it. The three of them continued to brainstorm for several minutes while Brad remained silent.

"What do you say we all go over to Collections and look at what we've got? We can start setting aside what we want to use."

Brad held up a hand. "We need to cut this meeting short. I have an appointment. Whatever you're thinking Charlotte, put it in writing. I'll look at it when I've got time."

"I will," she said. She thought that request sounded promising, but when Brad shoved back his chair and stalked out of the room, she wasn't sure what to think, especially when she caught the look that passed between the two curators.

"You've pushed his buttons," Jonathan told her.

"What did I do?"

"Came up with a good idea," said Paul.

"Isn't that what he hired me for?"

Paul gave a snort and shook his head. "That's what he was supposed to have hired you for, but Brad doesn't really want an assistant. Shepherd didn't like the department being a one-man show."

"He's not going to make it easy on you," said Jonathan. "I think he hired a woman because he thought it would be easier to keep her in line. You know, not show him up."

"Because a woman couldn't be as good at this job as a man?" asked Charlotte, knowing the answer.

"In his mind," said Jonathan. "You're proving him wrong, though."

"You might want to be careful," said Paul. "If you're too good, it could cost you your job."

"Being too good at my job could get me fired? That's completely unfair!"

Paul shrugged. "Brad's very insecure. Tread lightly."

"There's nothing stopping the three of us from going over to Collections now, is there?" asked Jonathan.

As they walked to the adjacent building, Charlotte couldn't stop thinking about the conversation they'd just had. She'd gone from elation at being taken seriously and having her ideas validated, to excitement about sinking her teeth into this project, to frustration and indignation at what Paul and Jonathan had revealed about Brad's motivation for hiring her. What was she supposed to do? Give a half-hearted effort, fail just enough to assuage Brad's ego but not so much that she lost her job? She was trying to build a career. She'd thought this position would be a perfect opportunity to prove herself. Instead, she now felt as though she was walking a tightrope.

* * *

At home after supper, Charlotte collapsed into a beanbag chair, Jerusha's diary in hand. She'd spent most of the morning in Collections with Paul and Jonathan. They'd compiled a list of possible items to use and some they might try to borrow from other museums or private collectors. After that, she'd returned to her office to type, in painstaking detail, her idea for the exhibit. Near the end of the day, she'd brought it to Brad.

"What's this?" he'd asked.

"My idea for the exhibit. You asked me to write it up."

He gave her a blank look before taking it from her. "Oh, yeah. I forgot." He'd tossed it onto the table in his office that was littered with papers, files, and books. "Thanks. I'll get to it when I can."

Now, cleaned up from supper and exhausted, she wanted only to relax in Jerusha's simpler world for a while.

The entries were the ordinary listing of tasks until Charlotte reached the one for June twenty-seventh 1839. It read:

Mrs. Wicker came to the dairy room today while Mother and I were skimming the milk. She told Mother she needed help and couldn't I please go to her. Mother barely spoke, saying only that she was in need of me. Mother said nothing after that but went about her work with her lips pressed tightly together as though Mrs. Wicker were of no more account than a fly after which Mrs. Wicker bid us good day.

I have often longed to know why Mother cannot be civil to Mrs. Wicker when they used to be such dear friends. Something happened between them when I was but eight or nine, that turned them from friends to foes. I asked once what had happened, but Mother said it was none of my concern and that I was not to inquire about it again. Father will not speak of it, either. I wonder if I asked Mrs. Wicker would she tell me. If only I knew, perhaps I could find a way to mend the breach.

The next few entries made no more mention of this situation. Jerusha had obviously been too busy to write of it if the long lists of tasks were any indication. Her interest piqued, Charlotte read on hoping Jerusha had found out the reason for the rift and confided it to her journal. The next entry of interest was that of July fourth.

Sunny and warm today. Spent the day in town with Mother, Father, and Nathan. Listened to Mr. Henley's oration on our revolutionary past and had a picnic on the Common. After the Declaration was read, there was a parade. Father went to the tavern to toast the nation with the gentlemen. Mother found Mrs. Cutting and sat with her on the Common. Nathan and I walked together. He has been with us two years now, but he did not walk with me last year. I asked after his relations in Griswold, but he said he knew little of them, there only being a few cousins left. His family had been taken off by consumption, so he had left Connecticut for the home of an uncle in Vermont. When he arrived, he found the uncle had gone west. Old Mr. Haskell had sent him to us knowing that Father needed the help as our last hired man had recently left and Mother did not approve of Frederick Wicker taking his place.

Nathan said Mr. Haskell mentioned that he had something in common with us but never said what. I supposed it was the consumption as it took all of Nathan's family and much of ours and said so, but Nathan got the feeling there was more to it than that but could not think what it might be. I reminded him that Mr. Haskell is a great teller of tales and likes to keep an air of mystery. After the fireworks we went home.

So, they had a resident storyteller in their village, thought Charlotte, wishing she could have heard old Mr. Haskell tell his tales. Her folklorist mind wondered if they were stories he'd made up or if he had been the history keeper for the community. She couldn't help but think it a loss, not having storytellers of that sort anymore. Not that it would be practical. People did not live in such interdependent communities anymore. That thought returned her mind to the earlier entry about Jerusha's mother and Mrs. Wicker. Charlotte knew that in a society where community members relied heavily on one another, a falling-out of the magnitude Jerusha's diary indicated could have had serious consequences. Only something truly terrible could have caused it, especially since, as Jerusha wrote, they had previously been "dear friends."

Chapter 11

June 1831
Birch Falls, Vermont

The loom took up a good portion of the back room in the Wicker home. Between that and the walking wheel there was little room for much else. There was a chest of drawers upon which Mrs. Wicker kept much of her sewing and weaving implements, the bench on which she sat when working the loom, several bags of wool, two ladderback chairs, and a small table piled with finished items. Though Jerusha was now coming regularly to help Mrs. Wicker, the sight of the loom never failed to enchant her. On rainy days when the house smelled of wet sheep, the odor that so repelled Lizzy, Jerusha breathed deeply, drawing in its scent.

She had yet to begin weaving, though Mrs. Wicker had begun showing her how to dress the loom, putting the fiber through slots and heddles, readying it for its work. Soon she hoped to learn a plain weave. She watched carefully as Mrs. Wicker set up the sixteen treadles and eight harnesses, committing everything she saw, and all Mrs. Wicker told her, to memory. Though she was set to spinning, she hardly took her eyes off the woman who passed the shuttle through the warp while pressing a different treadle depending upon the design she wanted. It seemed a sort of magic to Jerusha that out of these great skeins of yarn should emerge a pattern of colors that when finished would make sense to the eye in just the way Mrs. Wicker had planned before she even began. She longed to know the secrets of the loom that worked such a wonder. She would have to wait longer than she wanted to before she could actually try her hand at it. At only eight years of age, her feet didn't reach the treadles yet. But she could learn from watching and listening so that she'd be ready when the day came that she was tall enough to work the loom herself.

On this day, Jerusha was spinning, having just finished helping Mrs. Wicker to dress the loom for making a coverlet. Lizzy was outside, weeding the kitchen garden. As it was a warm day, the door had been left open.

"Your sister is much happier with this arrangement," observed Mrs. Wicker, settling herself on the bench before the loom.

"We both are," said Jerusha.

"I am glad to hear it," she said. "Have you been sleeping well, Jerusha?"

"Yes, Ma'am," she answered, thinking this an odd question.

"No strange dreams? No dreams of water, or falling, or picking blueberries."

Jerusha stifled a giggle. "No, but I look forward to picking blueberries with Hannah and Betsy. Mother said when they are ripe, we can pick to our hearts' content then bring them home for pies." Jerusha realized why she was being asked these questions and hoped to change the subject. Mrs. Wicker had a strong propensity towards superstition. She believed an endless store of them. Jerusha knew it was the one thing about Mrs. Wicker that exasperated her mother. She and her siblings had been counseled to be polite, but not to take any of Mrs. Wicker's superstitions to heart.

"But no dreaming of it?"

"No, Ma'am."

"Good, as these are signs of a coming illness. Now, your mother wants a new coverlet for your bed. Yours has worn thin, she told me. She wants to be sure you are warm this winter."

"Winter is a long way off," said Jerusha.

"It is, but I will make it now so your mother's mind will be at rest."

Jerusha thought she understood. When they'd done the spring cleaning her mother had lamented over the state of the coverlet on the bed Jerusha and Lizzy shared. Her mother had developed a great fear of illness since Josie's death and anything that might bring on illness. It seemed to Jerusha that her mother saw death lurking in every corner now and meant to be prepared to fight it off at all costs.

"Will you make it today?"

"I will begin it today, yes."

Both turned toward the open door from which direction came the sound of laughter.

"I cannot imagine what Lizzy is finding so humorous in the vegetable garden," said Mrs. Wicker.

Jerusha dashed to the door to see.

A goat had strayed away from the flocks grazing in a nearby meadow and was nibbling Lizzy's bonnet strings.

"Stop! Stop it now!" Lizzy tried to command the goat, but she was laughing too hard for her words to have any effect. Having a fondness for all animals, Lizzy was delighted rather than annoyed by their antics. "A kindred soul," Mother always called any of their mischievous farm animals who seemed to get into scrapes mainly in Lizzy's presence.

"Come now. You must get out of the garden," Lizzy instructed the goat, backing away so that the animal, who had let go of her bonnet only to grab a mouthful of her apron front, could be led away.

Jerusha ran out to help her sister. Together they got the goat back with the others before hurrying away. By the time they returned to the garden, Lizzy was laughing so hard she collapsed on the ground.

"Are you alright?" called Mrs. Wicker from the doorway.

"Yes," said Jerusha. "A goat got loose and was trying to make dinner of Lizzy's apron. We took it back."

"Why is she on the ground?"

Jerusha looked down at her sister still crumpled in a heap at her feet. She was about to say that Lizzy was laughing too hard to stay upright when she realized that the sound emanating from her contorted form had changed. Lizzy's laughter had become a racking cough.

Mrs. Wicker must have discerned it, too, as she was beside them in an instant, lifting Lizzy to her feet. The amusement Jerusha had felt moments ago was replaced by dread when she saw Lizzy's face red from strain, tears shining on her cheeks.

"Come inside," said Mrs. Wicker with an arm around Lizzy's waist, coaxing her towards the door. "Jerusha, go for your mother."

"No." The word was expelled from Lizzy's mouth in the midst of a cough. She reached for Jerusha's arm. "I am fine," she said, her voice hoarse.

"Shall I get water?" asked Jerusha.

"Yes. Quickly, please," said Mrs. Wicker.

Jerusha ran to the well. When she returned, Lizzy was inside seated near the loom. She was gulping for air but had ceased coughing. Mrs. Wicker had a cup ready.

After finishing the water, Lizzy was able to speak more clearly. "I feel fine," she said. "I just laughed too hard. I can go back to the garden now. Please do not trouble Mother about it. She will only worry, and it was truly nothing."

"Very well," said Mrs. Wicker. "But tell me first, what did you dream of last night?"

Looking puzzled, Lizzy threw a quick glance at Jerusha. "I do not remember," she said before heading out the door.

Jerusha returned to her spinning. Lost in thought, she spoke little the rest of the day. Lulled by the rhythmic clack of the loom and the chirp of the spinning wheel, her thoughts kept returning to Lizzy. Several nights during the past few weeks, Lizzy had awakened Jerusha with her coughing. She would not allow Jerusha to go to their mother nor even tell her of it. Lizzy kept assuring Jerusha it was nothing. She felt fine. The cough was a dry one. She brought nothing up. There was no reason to fret.

It was true Lizzy had no less vigor than usual. Her apple cheeks glowed red; her eyes shone brightly. She seemed to go at her work with even more zeal than usual. But thoughts continued to spin in Jerusha's mind as persistently as the fiber spun on her wheel. Red cheeks and shining eyes were signs of robust health, but also of consumption. Yet Lizzy, was sturdy as ever. She had not lost weight, was not wasting away.

But consumption was a disease that often took its time. Even at her young age, Jerusha had become familiar with its machinations. She had watched its progress in both Rebecca and Josie. She'd known villagers who had been plagued by it since before she was born. Some of them were gone now, but some continued on, laboring under its tyrannical rule. Some were taken quickly, others lingered. But always, at the end it was the same. The victim seemed to melt away before their loved ones' eyes. The fever that had previously come and gone finally came to stay. Blood, at first just drops then, at the end, great clots, was expelled with the rattling cough. Unable to rise from the bed, feeling as though a heavy weight lay upon their chest, the victim took on a cadaverous appearance, racked with pain until claimed at last by death's cold grip.

Images of Rebecca and Josie in their final days haunted Jerusha. Thankfully, she was unable to conjure an image of Lizzy in the same condition. Strong, sturdy Lizzy could never dwindle away as had their sisters. Josie was always small, lean, and prone to illness. Rebecca had not been as delicate as Josie, but neither was she as robust as Lizzy. Jerusha knew consumption could come for anyone, man, woman, or child. It could turn the heartiest to a frail shadow. But not her Lizzy. Please, God, not her Lizzy.

Late in the afternoon as the two girls wended their way down the hill towards home, Jerusha plucked up the courage to ask Lizzy for the truth.

"Are you well, Lizzy? You cough so much lately."

"I am fine."

Jerusha stopped walking, caught her sister's hand. "I do not think so."

Lizzy looked Jerusha in the eye. "Why not?" Her voice sounded wary as if she were asking what had given her away.

"Your cheeks turn bright red and your eyes shine."

"So?" she said, dropping Jerusha's hand.

"All the coughing at night."

Lizzy shrugged as she resumed walking. "It is dusty in the garret."

"The heat."

Lizzy stopped, turned towards Jerusha. "Heat?"

"At night you become so warm it awakens me. Is it fever?"

Lizzy turned away. "The nights are growing warmer."

"Not that warm. And it has been happening for months, though more so recently. You should tell Mother."

"If I was truly ill, wouldn't Mother know? She knew when the others were sick. They did not have to tell her."

"They were not trying to hide it. You are."

They were nearly home now. Lizzy rounded on Jerusha so forcefully it almost bowled her over.

"You are not to speak a word about it to Mother. I am quite fine. It will only upset her."

"But Lizzy—"

"If I become ill, I will tell Mother myself. Or I will be so sick she will know it. I will not have Mother distressed over a little coughing."

"Do you promise, Lizzy? Promise you will tell her if it gets worse." Jerusha reached for both of Lizzy's hands, tugging them, not wanting her to get away until she'd pledged her word.

"I will promise only if you vow not to say anything. If Mother thinks I am ill, she'll have me in bed for a fortnight and I cannot bear it."

"If I have your word that you will, then I shall promise."

"I, too."

With that Lizzy pulled her hands away. She swept ahead of Jerusha into the house.

Jerusha stared after her, wishing she had not made such a rash oath. Lizzy was so stubborn. It could be too late before she made any mention of it to their mother. But Jerusha had given her word.

Chapter 12

June 1973
Middlebury, Vermont

"I wonder how long this will go on for," Heidi said, glancing at the television. She had invited Charlotte over to share her latest craft project while Heidi's aunt Iris was out grocery shopping.

"Aren't you interested?" asked Charlotte. "It's important." Black and white images of a large group of men shuffling papers, gathering in clusters to talk, and walking importantly around a large room appeared on the screen. The televised Watergate hearings had been going on since mid-May.

"I know and I am interested, but it just seems so relentless. Should I leave it on or shut it off?"

"Leave it on. We can listen while we work. Unless you really want to shut it off."

"It can stay," Heidi said, handing Charlotte a wide, glass candle holder.

They were sitting on the living room floor by a low, round coffee table on which was spread a variety of magazines along with all the materials for decoupage, Heidi's latest craft.

"I got as many old magazines as I could find. Aunt Iris never throws anything out."

"Does she know we're going to cut them up?"

"Oh, yeah. She's fine with it. She said she always knew there was something she was keeping them for."

Charlotte chuckled, rifling through them. "So, what do we do with these?"

"Decide on a theme. Cut out the pictures you like. Use lots of different shapes and sizes. Then glue them to your candle holder collage style. I like to burn candles while I'm studying astrology so I'm looking for something that would fit. What's your theme?"

"Don't know yet." This was not Charlotte's idea of the best way to spend a Saturday afternoon, but she had nothing else to do and she did enjoy Heidi's company, if not always her crafts. "What's this?" asked Charlotte, holding up a copy of *Ms.* she'd uncovered from beneath the strewn issues of *Life, Look, Yankee,* and *Lady's Home Journal.* "Your aunt reads *Ms.* magazine?"

"Are you kidding? That's mine. She doesn't know. And if she comes back before we're done, stick it and any others under the pile."

Charlotte snickered. "What will she do if she sees it? Send you to your room? It's not like it's a copy of *Playgirl.*"

Heidi laughed. "No, but she will lecture me. I'd just as soon not listen to it."

"Honestly, Heidi, I don't get her. I mean it's bad enough that we have to put up with chauvinistic attitudes from men. Do we have to get it from women, too?"

"It's the generation gap, you know. She truly thinks a woman's place is in the home. It's how she was raised. Anything else is just wrong in her eyes."

"What about you? You went to nursing school. You work. Tell me you're not really doing it to find a doctor for a husband."

"Of course not. Though it if happens, I won't complain. But no, that's not why I became a nurse. I'm very interested in medicine, and I love helping people. As far as Aunt Iris is concerned, nursing is one of the few professions suitable to a woman. That along with teacher, librarian, and secretary. I think that's it," Heidi said, counting them off on her fingers. "At least until she's married. Then she's supposed to stop working and just be a wife and mother."

"I'm surprised she lets me in her apartment," said Charlotte.

"To tell you the truth, I don't think she knows what to make of you. But I think she's fascinated by you."

Charlotte snorted.

"No, really. She's always asking me questions about you. About what you think and how you see things."

Charlotte pulled a few copies of *Yankee* from the pile. She had no idea what theme she wanted but felt they might have the best shot at inspiring something for her.

"She really does hang on to these. This is three years old," Charlotte said, picking up a copy from 1970. "So, what kind of things does she ask about me?"

Charlotte barely heard Heidi's answer. She had come across an article in the 1970 copy of *Yankee* about the account of Mercy Lena Brown, a young woman who had died of tuberculosis in 1892 and whose body had been disinterred by her family and neighbors looking for signs that she had not been resting easy in her grave. Indeed, they had found such signs and, deciding Mercy was responsible for the illnesses continuing in her family, they removed her heart and burned it.

"Charlotte?"

"Huh, what?" she looked up.

"You must have found something awfully interesting," said Heidi, grinning. "You haven't heard a word I've said."

"Oh. Sorry. It's this article. Listen to this." She read the entire article aloud.

"That happened here? In New England?" asked Heidi.

"In Rhode Island. I've read about it. This wasn't the only one. There were several others."

"People really thought they were vampires?"

"Sort of. They didn't use that word, though. But they did think someone who had died was returning to feast on their surviving family members. They didn't understand tuberculosis or how it was transmitted. They called it consumption because the person who had it wasted away. It looked sort of like they were being consumed."

"I know. I've studied tuberculosis, but I didn't know the vampire part. Too bad that wasn't part of my lessons."

"The author of this article doesn't quite understand it, though," said Charlotte, thoroughly intrigued by the story.

"What do you mean?"

"He's writing about Mercy's brother, Edwin. He was the one who got sick with TB after Mercy died from it. He seems to think...well, here, listen. 'The family and friends of Edwin Brown unanimously agreed that it must be a vampire that was sucking his blood and causing his loss of strength.'"

"Well, isn't that was a vampire does?"

"In our post-*Dracula* understanding, yes. But at the time this happened that book hadn't been written. In fact, a newspaper clipping about this very case was found among Bram Stoker's belongings after his death. But the writer of this article is projecting a modern-day view of vampirism based on Stoker's *Dracula* onto the Brown family that they would not have comprehended. Can I keep this magazine? I've always though some angle on this whole vampire thing would make a great dissertation."

"Sure. Does that mean you're planning to go back for your doctorate?"

"I don't know. Maybe," said Charlotte. "I think about it sometimes. I'd love to do it. But I have to make a living so..."

"You should. Charlotte, you're so smart. You'd go further in your career with a Ph.D., wouldn't you?"

"I suppose. I'm in awe of Linda Dégh. I would love to be half as good a folklorist as she is."

Heidi was looking at her as though assessing something.

"What?" Charlotte asked.

"Your whole face lit up when you were talking about it."

"It did?"

"Uh-huh. Charlotte, I'm getting a really strong vibe that this is something you need to do." Heidi's soft blue eyes took on a dreamy look. Her lips parted in a half-smile. The end of a strand of her bone-straight blond hair hung dangerously close to a puddle of glue. Charlotte wondered if she was going into some sort of trance. But then she jerked as if suddenly awakening. "Oh! I know what your theme should be."

"For my dissertation?"

"No, for your candleholder."

"Oh, that," said Charlotte, having forgotten the craft they were supposed to be doing.

"Your theme should have something to do with this vampire thing. Are there pictures with the article? After it's finished, you should burn a candle in it whenever you work on it. This woman is buried in Rhode Island?"

"Exeter," said Charlotte, bemused at Heidi's sudden animation.

"Hmm…I wonder if we can go there. Do you know what cemetery?"

"You want to visit her grave?"

"Of course. I think she's led you to this. That's why you found that article. Don't you see? She's helping you. I bet if we went to her grave, I could contact her. She could tell you what to do."

Charlotte was certain Mercy Brown was long past telling anyone what to do, but her interest was certainly piqued.

"I'm sure her grave is a legend-tripping site. The story is likely well-known by the locals. But unless I'm doing actual research for a dissertation, I don't think I can swing going to Rhode Island."

Heidi let out an exasperated breath. "Okay, but if you decide to do it, please let me go with you."

"You'll be the first to know."

Charlotte managed to find enough pictures from the October issues of magazines suitably spooky enough to appease Heidi. Heidi gave up on the assorted issues, broke down, and sacrificed some of the pages of her beloved horoscope magazines. They worked quietly together, listening to the Watergate proceedings.

After a short time, Heidi broke the relative quiet by asking, "Were the vampires all in Rhode Island?"

"No. They were throughout New England."

Heidi looked at Charlotte, eyes wide. "Any in Vermont?"

"Yeah. A few, I think. Woodstock had one or two."

"How do you know about them? I've never even heard of any of this."

"I came across them when I was studying folk remedies." Charlotte grinned at the puzzled look on Heidi's face. "Not a remedy you studied, huh?"

"I don't even get the connection."

"They weren't looking at it as something to do with the supernatural or the occult. At least, not exactly."

"Since when aren't vampires supernatural?"

"Since before Bram Stoker wrote *Dracula*. You've got to get away from your modern-day notions of vampires to get it. They didn't understand how tuberculosis, or consumption as they called it, passed from person to person. They just knew that one family member after another took ill with the same disease that wasted them away making them look like corpses while they were still alive. Their forebears had brought from Europe the folk belief that a dead family member could come back and feed off the living. Not bite their neck and suck their blood but drain the life from them."

"So how did they think the dead person turned into a vampire?" How did they get out of their graves?"

"It wasn't so much that the person turned into a vampire, but that something, I guess like an evil spirit, they didn't really have a name for it, used the body as a host. It left the grave, I suppose, as a vapor or something."

Heidi tilted her head to one side, her brows knit in concentration. "So, they didn't bite their victims but drained the life from them. By what? Osmosis?"

Charlotte shrugged. "How exactly it was done is kind of a gray area."

"Weird."

"Yes, but to them, perfectly reasonable."

"But can you imagine digging up a dead body? Especially a family member. One of your kids? It's ghoulish."

"Again, by our standards, yes. I'm sure it wasn't pleasant for them, but they were trying to save their remaining family members. It was meant to be a cure. That's why I bumped into the practice while studying folk remedies."

"So this stuff was in one of your text books?"

"Actually, I found old newspaper articles that reported on it at the time."

Heidi's brows shot up. "You're kidding? I would have thought they did this stuff in secret. At night."

"You're still thinking like a modern-day person. Sometimes they had town meetings to decide on whether or not to do it. I think that happened in Vermont. The whole town turned out for it. It was winter and the article mentioned that the sleighing was good that day."

"Was that in Woodstock?"

"Yup."

"I can't believe I've never heard about any of this. Is it just me? Is it common knowledge that I somehow missed?"

Charlotte laughed. "Not at all. It was sporadic and spread out. Not like the witch hysteria in Salem that happened all at one time in one place. It was just as scary, but in a different way. Death was a regular visitor then. Very few families saw all of their kids reach adulthood. It was more or less taken for granted that some of them would die young. And consumption was rampant, especially in New England. So, for them, it was probably more sad than frightening.”

“Still. Digging up the bodies. Ugh. I’m sorry, but I can’t get my head around it.”

“It would be an outrageous thing to do today so that’s not surprising.”

“So, once they’d dug them up, what told them whether or not the person was a vampire or whatever they called it?”

“They were looking for bodies that didn’t appear the way they thought they were supposed to. They were particularly looking for fresh blood in the heart or blood on the mouth. They were also looking to see if the body was in a different position from the way they were buried.”

“If they didn’t think the person drank their victim’s blood, why were they looking for that?”

“Blood is a lifeforce. They didn’t think a dead body should have fresh blood in it. If it did, something was very wrong. Very unnatural.”

“But didn’t a lot of that depend on how long the person had been dead and how cold the ground was?”

“Sure, but they didn’t know much about decomposition. At least not to the extent that say a coroner today would. They knew the body decomposed and about rigor mortis. Prior to the Civil War they didn’t do any embalming. They got the person into the ground quickly before the body could start stinking up the place, so they had little idea about the process of decomposition and all the variables that go with it.”

“Wow. This is blowing my mind.” Heidi shook her head. “But you said the grave sites of the people they dug up are legend trip sites now. So, some people must have known about them.”

"Well, yeah. I suppose people who live near any of the sites have heard about them. Undoubtedly, the stories are jumbled now. That's what usually happens. But, still, there's a story about them. Maybe that the person was a vampire, or by now the story might be that they're a ghost or that the graveyard is haunted, or something. Sometimes families carry the story of what happened through generations, so descendants might know about it. They might have a more accurate account, but it would still probably be changed a bit. It's like the game Telephone. Passing it on by word of mouth, especially over decades or centuries, almost guarantees changes in the details."

"You're right, Charlotte. This would make a good dissertation topic. You already know a lot about it, and you're obviously very interested. I really think you should do it."

Charlotte had toyed off and on with the idea of getting a doctorate. She doubted she'd be able to make a mark in the study of folklore without it. Yet when she'd once broached the subject with her parents, her mother had insisted she'd spent enough time in college and needed to find a job and start paying off her loans. But, oh, to see her name attached to research that would be respected by the likes of Linda Dégh or Alan Dundes. To be in their company, teach at a major university. It was her dream. Sure, she loved the idea of the museum and knew it was great practical experience, but she wasn't sure she wanted to do it forever. If she would have to put up with attitudes like Brad's, she could do without it. She wondered if Linda Dégh ever had to deal with anything like that. She couldn't imagine her taking the kind of crap Brad was dishing out.

"Maybe," she said. "I'm still new at the museum. I can't take on more schooling right now. Maybe someday I'll be able to take a sabbatical and then I can do it."

"How is it going at the museum? Brad still being a jerk?"

"And how!" Charlotte caught her up on all that had happened since the meeting about the Halloween exhibit.

"What did he say about the idea you wrote up for him?"

"I don't think he's even read it. The last time I brought it up, he gave me a dirty look and walked away. He's probably sick of me asking about it."

The door opened and Iris Pleasant entered carrying a bag of groceries. "Would you girls help me with these, please?" she asked.

"Of course," said Heidi.

After bringing up all the bags, Charlotte and Heidi unloaded them and helped put everything away. Charlotte noticed Iris eying her as she worked. She wondered about Heidi's claim that her aunt was intrigued by her. She was amused by the thought the Iris Pleasant found her such an oddity.

"So, what were you girls talking about while I was gone?" Iris asked.

Charlotte couldn't help herself. "Vampires, digging up dead people, the decomposition of corpses, you know, the usual stuff."

Iris stared at her, mouth agape.

"Charlotte," Heidi hissed under her breath, but Charlotte noticed she was fighting a smile. "We were talking about folk remedies, Auntie. Did you know that a long time ago people thought their dead relatives were coming back as vampires and killing the rest of the family members?"

Iris gave Heidi and Charlotte a bemused look that quickly changed to the expression Charlotte so disliked, the one that said she knew they were making things up and was on to them.

"How is your job going, Charlotte?" Iris asked.

"Fine, thanks."

"Have you met a nice man, yet?"

Charlotte sighed heavily. "There are lots of nice people at the museum."

"Anyone special?" The smug expression returned.

"Nope."

Iris tsked. "What are you going to do if you can't find a husband?"

"Take care of myself? I am capable, you know."

"I'm sure you are dear, but why would you want to be alone?" A dismayed look crossed Iris's face as she glanced from Charlotte to Heidi and back again. "You're not...I mean, you do like men, don't you?"

Charlotte closed her eyes and drew a deep breath. When she thought she could control her voice she said, "Yes. I like men. I'm just not looking for one at the moment. I'm focused on building my career."

The look that Charlotte was beginning to think of as a cross between a sneer and an expression of self-satisfaction reappeared on Iris's face for the third time since she'd returned from the store. "If you could just find yourself a husband, you wouldn't have to worry about that, dear."

"I want to worry about that. I want a career. Why can't you understand that?"

Iris laughed. It was a soft sound, but not a pleasant one. It was more an auditory compliment to the look Charlotte was growing to despise.

When Iris took a bag of toiletry supplies to put away in the bathroom, Charlotte turned to Heidi. "Sorry, but she was really getting to me. Why does she even care what I do?"

Heidi shrugged. "That's my aunt. She thinks she should tell everyone how to live their lives."

"What about you? I know you date now and then, but you're not serious with anyone. Does she do this to you?"

"A little, but I work in an environment where I'm guaranteed to meet a lot of eligible bachelors. She's convinced I'll wind up marrying a doctor so she's okay with me. At least for now. She knows what doctors and nurses do for a living and can understand why someone would want to do it. She has no idea what a folklorist does. Or anyone else at the museum, for that matter. Besides, all you're really supposed to want is a husband, a bunch of kids, a nice house, and a really good washer and dryer."

Charlotte laughed. "Well, I am sick of the laundromat."

Chapter 13

July 1831
Birch Falls, Vermont

"I am frightened." Mary took the cup of tea Caroline offered. Her hands were shaking.

"I should wonder if you were not," said Caroline, taking the seat across from Mary at the kitchen table.

Lavinia Wicker had told Mary about Lizzy's coughing fit. There was no dust that time, only exertion. It wasn't as though Lizzy was a stranger to that. Mary had paid closer attention to Lizzy ever since. She noticed the periodic reddening of her cheeks coupled with a luminosity of her eyes, neither of which could always be attributed to fresh air and exercise. She saw, too, how Lizzy sometimes kept herself quieter than usual or stopped some activity abruptly as if it had suddenly become too taxing, especially if she thought no one was looking. Unable to sleep some nights, she'd heard the faint sound of coughing coming from the garret and knew it was Lizzy.

"Am I going to lose another?" Mary asked, unable to keep the pleading from her voice.

"She has some signs of it, but they might be of other things as well."

"Things that can be cured?"

"Perhaps."

Mary looked into the older woman's soft gray eyes. They were filled with compassion, but she was not sure she saw hope.

"I never thought it would be Lizzy," said Mary, barely above a whisper. "So full of life. How could death claim her so soon?"

Caroline reached across the table to lay her strong, calloused hand over Mary's. "It has not, yet. Do not bury the girl while she still lives." There was a slight, gentle smile on Caroline's face.

Abashed, Mary glanced away. "I hope never to bury another child."

Returning her gaze to Caroline's face, she asked, "How can I help but suspect it when she follows the same pattern as Rebecca and Josie?"

"Lizzy is unlike them in her constitution," Caroline said in the practical, reasoning tone she used with patients. "Rebecca was slight of stature. She was prone to sore throat, fevers, and coughs long before she became consumptive. Josie was even smaller. She had a narrow chest. Her skin was always pale, though her cheeks were rosy. These are all signs of an invalid constitution. Lizzy's composition is quite different. Her form gives no suggestions of an invalid nature. That is in her favor."

"Except the cough. And the fevers."

"As I said, those are signs of other ailments, as well."

Mary's spirits lifted a bit, until another thought crashed in on her. "There is Zachary, too. And now I will lose Susannah."

"It may indeed save them."

Mary nodded, though tears stung her eyes as much from shame at her own selfishness as at the thought of Susannah moving far away. Zachary had recently suffered a consumptive attack. He'd been plagued with them years ago, but they had stopped. He'd not had one until recently. Doctor Eacker had strongly suggested a trip. A long one. On horseback, not enclosed in a carriage. Zachary, it seems, had been considering a move west. The doctor's advice persuaded him it was the right decision. He would go to Ohio he'd recently told them all over dinner. He planned to open a store. He would get settled then return for Susannah. They would make a life there as part of the push westward that was beginning to lure so many Americans. Mary knew it was sensible in regards to his health and the likelihood of a more profitable future, but it only felt like another loss. So many who went west were never again seen by the families they left behind.

"Haying will be upon us soon," said Caroline. "Lizzy is bound to be in the thick of it. Watch how she fares."

* * *

Haying that summer was a mad flurry. Rain had prevented the start, pushing it to the very end of July. Eli hired three young men from town to help. Spread out in a staggered line, they along with Eli, Seth, and Zachary swung their scythes in rhythmic unison cutting a swath across the field. Mary sent Lizzy and Jerusha to them at dinnertime. Knowing they could not take time to come in, the girls brought dinner to them which they ate right there in the field. Along with food, Mary sent extra switchel knowing how thirsty they would be. What they'd taken with them in the morning would likely be gone.

"Is Zachary well?" asked Susannah when the girls returned.

"In fine fettle," said Lizzy.

"I thought he looked a bit tired," said Jerusha.

"Of course, he is tired," Lizzy shot back. "He is working hard and has been all day."

Mary turned in surprise at Lizzy's harsh tone. It was unlike her to snap at Jerusha. But Lizzy, Mary noticed, had become short-tempered whenever illness was mentioned or even alluded to.

"I meant more so than the others," Jerusha said in a quiet tone.

102

"Come girls," said Mary. "We have lots to do. They will need our help soon so we must get our work here done quickly. There's no time to bicker."

Lizzy bustled about the kitchen far more quickly than was necessary as if determined to prove herself full of vigor. Mary watched, knowing Lizzy would deny it if she asked was something wrong. Susannah and Jerusha seemed to notice, too, as they stared at Lizzy with puzzled expressions.

Once Lizzy had everything on the table, she looked up, glanced at each face, and asked, "Why are you all staring at me?"

"Because you have turned into an even greater whirlwind than usual," said Susannah. "What has gotten into you?"

"Nothing," she said, her cheeks reddening. "Mother said we needed to hurry."

Mary thought Lizzy looked as though she'd just been caught in some mischief. She cleared her throat. "Well done, Lizzy," she said. "Girls, let us eat."

The men returned when it became too dark to see. Mary set out food for the hungry lot including the three from town. They'd be staying with them, sleeping in the barn with Seth until the haying was completed.

The next day they were all in the field. The men continued the cutting while the women and girls spread the newly cut hay out to dry and raked the previous day's cuttings into windrows. As they were finishing the midday meal on the third day, Eli told Jerusha to weed the cornfield when she was through eating.

"I will do it, Father," Lizzy said

"No. We need your help here," he told her. "Jerusha can do whatever she can on her own."

Lizzy looked crestfallen. Mary was puzzled at first. Lizzy loved to be in the midst of haying, zealous about pitching in with the men and had always been resentful about being sent to do another job before haying was completed. While helpful, in the past she'd been too young to contribute as much as she did this year. Now her father admitted that he needed her help, the thing Lizzy longed most to hear. Instead of beaming with pride, she'd asked to be sent off and was disappointed when denied. Mary couldn't help but think she was feeling poorly enough to want to be alone, unseen by the others.

"What's this, Little Ox?" asked Seth. "You want to quit on us? Is men's work too much for you?"

Momentary relief flooded Mary as she watched Lizzy's eyes narrow.

"Race me back to the field and find out," she challenged her brother and was off and running before he could rise from the ground. The hired men followed them.

"It is me you should have sent to the cornfield," said Zachary after Jerusha left.

"Are you not well?" asked Susannah, her voice quivering slightly.

"Not especially," he said.

Eli rose to his feet with a groan. "You need to stop?"

"No, no. I can manage. I am just not as strong this year as in the past."

"You will need to be on your way to Ohio, soon. Best to go before it turns cold. Doctor Eacker says a long ride in the open air is just what you need."

"I expect he is right," said Zachary. "Once we finish getting the hay in, I will make arrangements to go."

Mary's heart plummeted. She knew it was necessary, but it was still difficult. She would have Susannah a while longer, though as it would take some time for Zachary to settle in Ohio and either return or send for her. It would mean a delay in Susannah's conceiving a child, but it could not be helped. Susannah had confided in her that though she longed to be a mother, she was still terribly afraid.

On the fourth day of haying, an incident occurred that shook Mary's world beyond anything she could have expected. While helping to load the hay onto the wagon, Mary glanced up towards the men cutting in the field. Seth who worked harder than anyone during haying, always hoping to be declared the best by the end, an honor sought after by all the young men, suddenly collapsed. Mary's breath caught. She'd seen his last swing. Even from a distance she was sure he hadn't cut himself and could not understand what caused him to fall.

A shout went up. The other men rushed towards Seth. Mary's stillness caught the attention of the others loading the wagon.

"What is it?" asked Susannah.

"Seth. He fell."

They were all watching now. The figures of the other men bent over Seth who had still not risen.

"Stay here," Mary said to the others and raced into the field.

When she reached the group of men, Seth was sitting in the tall grass. His face looked strained as he tried to catch his breath. The telltale wet streaks lining his face made Mary's heart plummet.

"The way he coughs all night," said one of the hired men, "I am surprised it has not happened sooner."

"Coughs all night?" asked Mary. "How long has this been happening?" she asked, dropping to her knees next to Seth.

"Not long," he choked out.

"How long, exactly?"

Seth shrugged. "A while. From the hay, I expect."

"You will sleep in the house from now on," she said.

Seth did not argue, perhaps because he hadn't enough breath. Instead, he reached for the scythe. "Let's get back to work," he said.

"You need to rest," said Mary.

"I am fine, Mother. It took me by surprise, is all."

"Seth, you cannot–" she began.

"Mary," said Eli, leading her away by the elbow. "Leave him be."

"But, Eli—"

"I will keep watch over him. Go on back to the hay wagon. We must get this finished."

Frustration rose in Mary. They could not stop the work of haying. It was one of the most important tasks on the farm as it would feed all their livestock throughout the winter. They had to work while the weather held. The faster they got it done while the sun was shining, the better. Wet hay would mold making it useless or worse, causing it to spontaneously combust and set the barn on fire.

"Stop him if it seems too much."

"I will, Mary. Now go on back."

A terrible sense of helplessness came over Mary as she walked back to the hay wagon. That and a dread that the future held only the decimation of her family.

Chapter 14

July 1973
Middlebury, Vermont

"Charlotte, you will never guess what happened today!"

"Come in and tell me."

Charlotte handed Heidi an Orange Crush once they'd entered her apartment then, grabbing one for herself, plopped down next to her on the sofa.

"I was talking with some other nurse at lunch. I told about your vampire article. I thought no one would have known anything about it, but it turns out one of them did."

"Oh?"

"Yeah. Angela Preston. She grew up in Vergennes. Actually, it's in Birch Falls, but that's near Vergennes. Anyway, she said all the kids have known about it for ages. They do that legending thing at a grave because it's supposed to contain a vampire."

"Legend tripping."

"Yeah. So she said she's been to the grave. There's some weird inscription on it."

"What's the legend associated with it?"

Heidi looked blank. "I don't know. She just said kids go to the grave at night. They say sometimes you can hear Eliza say something, but that's all I know."

"Eliza?"

"The vampire. Eliza Kenner or Kendall or something."

"Kendall?" Charlotte felt a flash of recognition. Jerusha's maiden name had been Kendall and she'd lived in Birch Falls. Charlotte didn't remember the mention of an Eliza, but her grandmother did say that Jerusha had sisters who died early.

"I guess. Anyway, she said that the kids leave fake vampire teeth like the ones for Halloween costumes. It's really weird, too, because no grass grows on her grave.

"That's part of vampire lore. Grass isn't supposed to be able to grow on their graves. Most likely it's because it gets a lot of visits from people who keep trampling it down."

"Maybe. Anyway, Angela said that a guy her friend used to date dug up the grave one night."

"Oh?" asked Charlotte, unable to keep the skepticism from her voice. "What did he find?"

"She wasn't very clear on that. It's amazing she knew about it, huh?"

"I'm not surprised. People who live in an area where it happened know the local legends about them. Do you know what year Eliza died?"

"I could ask."

"I'd like to know. Jerusha lived in Birch Falls. I'm wondering if it was before or after her time."

"You think she might have known about it?"

"Maybe."

"Did she mention anything in her diary about it?"

"Not so far, but I haven't finished reading it."

The conversation with Heidi sparked Charlotte's imagination, so after supper she immediately resumed reading the diary. She didn't honestly expect to find a reference to any vampire activity, though she did wonder if Eliza Kendall was related to Jerusha.

The evening was warm, so Charlotte sat close to the open window, bare feet propped up on the coffee table. The entries after the fourth of July were routine again for a while until she reached the one for July tenth.

Hot and humid today. Was sent to Mrs. Wicker by Father as he said we owe them a day's work for help Frederick gave us last week. Mother said nothing but looked like a thunder cloud. Spent the day dying cloth.

Endeavoring to learn the source of Mother's ill feelings towards her, I spoke about the corn husking frolics we had and how much we all loved the pies she and Mother baked together. I thought she looked wistful at that so I plucked up my courage to say that I wished they would do so again. She only said those days are at an end.

I told her it makes me sad to see her and Mother no longer friendly and she allowed that it makes her sad, as well. When I asked what brought about the rift between them, she only said, 'You must hear it from your mother.' When I said Mother will not tell me she said to tell or not is for Mother to decide. She then went to tend the garden and I saw little of her the rest of the day.

Jerusha continued her musings in the entry for the following day.

Rain today. Worked at home. I was tired as I slept poorly last night. My thoughts kept returning to the times when Mother and Mrs. Wicker were friends. I tried to recollect just when the change occurred. I believe it was near the time Seth died, but I could not determine if it was before or just after. Only Susannah was left at home. Zachary had gone to Ohio and had not yet returned for her. Lizzy had been gone from us three months.

Charlotte stopped cold. *Lizzy? Was that Eliza?* She knew that family names were repeated often in the nineteenth century even among immediate family members who were occasionally named for a sibling who had died. The Eliza Kendall whose grave had become a legend trip site could have been named for this Lizzy or vice versa. Or she could have come so much later that Jerusha's Lizzy was all but forgotten. She could also have been a cousin of Jerusha's, an aunt, a grandmother. If only Charlotte knew the dates on the gravestone.

She called Heidi to ask if she could arrange for her to talk to Angela. Her interest was piqued enough to want to know if this Lizzy could have been the same one or at least rule out the possibility. Clearly something odd had happened not long after Lizzy's death. Granted, whatever caused Jerusha's mother to have a falling out with her neighbor might not have anything to do with Lizzy, but Jerusha had mentioned in a previous entry that most of her family had died of consumption. Most so-called vampires as well as their victims had fallen prey to the same disease. Then there was the fact that Seth had died only months later, and something occurred between Jerusha's mother and Mrs. Wicker to destroy their friendship. In a time when community interdependence was a matter of survival it had to have been something drastic. Could digging up the body of your neighbor's dead daughter to see if it was playing host to an evil spirit who was feeding off of other family members have been drastic enough? Many considered it an actual remedy, if a last-ditch one. People generally went along with it, even exhumed their own family members, so would Jerusha's mother really have had such a dramatic reaction to it?

Charlotte picked up the diary again, reading with rapt attention, hoping for some clue.

A knock at the door interrupted Charlotte's reading. It was Heidi come to say that she'd just spoken to Angela.

"She said she would be happy to talk to you though she doesn't know if she'll be of much help. I asked her when Eliza Kendall died. She said she thought it was 1815, but she couldn't be sure.

1815. Too early to have been Jerusha's Lizzy, but not by that much. And Angela wasn't sure about the date. Still, Charlotte was eager to talk to Angela. Even if there was no connection, it would be interesting to learn how a legend regarding one of the so-called New England vampires was being spun today.

"Would you ask her if she will allow me to tape record her so that I can document what she says and not have to rely on my memory?"

"Sure. Angela and I work the same shifts. We're off this weekend. How about Saturday? We can go somewhere for lunch. I'll go call her back now."

Charlotte returned to the diary. Most entries focused on weather and the work Jerusha and her mother did in their dairy. Apparently, they kept their community supplied with milk, butter, and cheese in return for work done or goods made by others. Charlotte was struck again by the profound interdependence of their society. She reflected, too, that if Jerusha had been eight or nine when the rift occurred, her mother had held this grudge for an awfully long time. It had to have been something of great significance.

Charlotte tried to imagine what could have created such enmity. A sexual indiscretion, say, an affair between Mrs. Wicker and Jerusha's father might do it, but given the social mores of the time, it was unlikely. What could it be? Theft? A betrayal of some sort? Yet whatever it was, it had been kept a secret from Jerusha. An affair fit with that. Who'd want their daughter to know? Also, if Jerusha was remembering correctly, it occurred close to the time that Seth died. Perhaps it was the power of suggestion since Jerusha seemed to feel there was a connection, but Charlotte, too, felt it. But what? Maybe Seth didn't die of consumption. Maybe Mrs. Wicker accidentally caused his death in some way. But how would that have been hidden from Jerusha? Why would her mother be so adamant that she know nothing about it? It wasn't as though she'd been trying to prevent Jerusha from having ill will towards Mrs. Wicker. She seemed not to care about that, if not outright wanting it. If Mrs. Wicker had somehow been the cause of Seth's demise it was unlikely that Jerusha would not have known at least something about it. No. It was some big secret. One Charlotte hoped Jerusha figured out and explained in her diary.

Chapter 15

October 1831
Birch Falls, Vermont

The rest of the summer and into the fall was a time of relief for Jerusha. Lizzy had no more coughing fits and seemed to have returned to her healthy, buoyant self. Seth, who they'd worried over after the attack he'd had while mowing hay, had only suffered one more. That was on the day in August when they were harvesting rye. He'd been brought home early despite insisting that he could continue. After the first attack, their mother had finally prevailed in insisting Seth sleep in the house. Since he'd told her it was likely the hay making him cough, he had no recourse to object.

When Zachary left for Ohio shortly after the hay was in, Susannah moved back into the garret with Lizzy and Jerusha so that Seth could take the room that she and Zachary had used. Mother claimed she heard Seth coughing at night, but he insisted that was not so. Still, he appeared fine during the day no matter how strenuous his work.

Jerusha forgot to be worried over either of them as nothing seemed amiss anymore. Perhaps they'd been wrong. Perhaps something else had caused their coughing fits, after all. Lizzy assured her she felt fit as a fiddle. Her behavior did not indicate otherwise.

It was fortunate that all were in fine fettle come autumn. Once the flies that had multiplied all summer to the point of creating a constant buzzing drone throughout the house had died, it was time to reverse all the work they'd done in the spring. Jerusha, her mother, and sisters spent the days washing windows, removing fireboards, cleaning hearths of the assortment of birds and small creatures unfortunate enough to have fallen down the chimneys, whitewashing the kitchens and bedrooms, scouring the floors, and giving the dairy room a thorough cleaning.

The harvest was bountiful, a blessing for the coming winter, but a tremendous amount of work for the fall. The girls trudged from the kitchen garden to the root cellar filling it with winter squashes, potatoes, and root vegetables. Pumpkins were gathered from the cornfield and set to dry. Ripened ears of corn were picked and carted from the fields. The orchard had produced an abundance of apples, but they were behind on gathering them.

"The moon will be full tonight," Jerusha's father announced one October day at dinner. "We will finish in the orchard tonight."

"Are the Wickers going, too?" asked Jerusha.

"Yes. We will work together and get it all done."

Jerusha beamed. There was something enticing about gathering apples by moonlight.

"Oh, for the vigor of youth," said her mother, who Jerusha noticed, appeared very tired indeed.

Jerusha and Lizzy giggled all the way to the orchard. Once there, they set to work, enthusiastically filling their baskets with ripe fruit. The moonlight shone brightly enough that they could work without too much hindrance, yet still left enough darkness for bumping into one another and tripping over apple baskets. Jerusha slipped on a squashed apple, slid into Lizzy who tumbled over a full basket sending its contents cascading across the orchard. Both girls laughed until their sides hurt.

"See if you can pick them up now without stepping on them," said their mother.

"We are only gathering tonight, Little Ox," joked Seth. "You can make the applesauce later."

Jerusha heard something whiz past her ear followed by a thunk in the direction of Seth's voice and knew Lizzy had lobbed an apple at him.

"Enough horseplay," said their father. "We must get this done. I would like to sleep before the sun comes up."

Jerusha and Lizzy retrieved the spilled apples then set to work gathering more. The brisk night air coupled with the tangy scent of apples squashed underfoot proved too intoxicating to prevent more laughter and hijinks. The two youngest Wicker boys were as bad as Lizzy about treating the apples like snowballs until their own father put a stop to it.

The next several evenings were spent peeling the apples that would be preserved by drying or made into applesauce. Two days after the moonlight gathering, Jerusha's father readied a load to take to the cider mill.

"Can we go with you, Father, please?" Lizzy begged.

He glanced at his wife.

"I can spare them for a while" she said, smiling at the girls.

Jerusha and Lizzy grabbed their cloaks, squealing with delight. They jumped into the wagon next to their father as he set off for the cider mill.

It was a perfect October day, the sky a cloudless deep blue, the air crisp and chilly enough to redden their cheeks. Once they arrived at the mill, the girls jumped down from the wagon. She and Lizzy watched as their father loaded the apples into the nut mill. When he had a good pomace, he wrapped it in straw and the girls breathed in the tart scent as it was pressed so that the liquid oozed out into the tubs below.

After the barrels of fresh cider were loaded onto the wagon, they moved on to the blacksmith's shop where Isaac Ward was pounding a brightly glowing piece of metal on his anvil. He looked up when they entered.

"Good day to you, Isaac," said Eli. "I have a bit of work to discuss with you when you have a moment."

"Be with you shortly," he said.

Jerusha and Lizzy lingered in the doorway of the squat building. The girls had always liked the blacksmith's shop. They loved to see the sparks fly and watch Mr. Ward pull on the massive bellows.

When he was able to set aside the piece he was working on, Eli stepped closer so they could converse.

"Let's look," said Jerusha venturing further into the shop, sneezing as the smoke from his forge tickled her nose.

A few moments later male voices sounded behind her, and Jerusha turned to see that Mr. Ward's apprentice and the owner of the sawmill had come in together. They joined Mr. Ward and Jerusha's father in conversation.

Jerusha was surprised to see that Lizzy was still standing in the doorway.

"Lizzy?" she called.

As Jerusha moved closer, a chill crept up her spine. Lizzy was staring, transfixed at the anvil.

"Lizzy?" Jerusha said again, louder this time. Lizzy did not look away.

Jerusha reached for her arm, but Lizzy broke away. She ran from the blacksmith's shop and climbed into their father's wagon.

"What's wrong?" asked Lizzy, scrambling up beside her.

"I do not know." The words came out in a trembling whisper that frightened Jerusha.

"What do you mean? What were you staring at?"

"The anvil."

"But why? After Mr. Ward stopped hammering, there was nothing to see."

"I know. It was..." But here words failed her. She tried again. "The strangest feeling came over me while he was hammering. Something bad. Something that disturbed me as though he was pounding on my very heart. Even when he stopped, I could still feel it."

Jerusha's own heart was hammering now. Rarely had she seen Lizzy show fear. She was certainly not prone to being dramatic. The paleness in Lizzy's face and the trembling of her body beside Jerusha's on the wagon seat unnerved her.

"Have you pain in your heart? Jerusha asked.

"Not pain, but a queer feeling. It terrified me."

"Are you ill? Should I get Father?"

"No, though I do wish to go home. I daresay Father will be along soon enough."

It was only a few more minutes that they waited before their father returned. Lizzy improved as they rode home, though she remained more quiet than usual.

That night marked the return of her coughing fits with one so violent it woke Jerusha from a sound sleep.

Chapter 16

July 1973
Middlebury, Vermont

Charlotte and Heidi walked from the apartment house to the Cucumber Café on Merchant's Row where they met Angela.

"Thanks for agreeing to let me interview you," said Charlotte once Heidi had introduced them.

"I'll tell you what I can."

Angela was a short, slightly plump, curly-haired woman about the same age as Charlotte and Heidi.

Charlotte inserted a blank cassette tape into the tape recorder she'd set on the table. They had taken a booth in the back of the café where it was a bit quieter.

"I've never been interviewed before," said Angela, eying the recorder nervously.

"Standard procedure when a folklorist interviews an informant. It's just so I won't forget anything," Charlotte explained.

"Informant?" Angela asked, her eyes growing wide. "Makes me sound like I'm about to give evidence against a mobster or something." She grinned, then suddenly her expression changed to one of wariness. She glanced from Charlotte to Heidi. "Does this have anything to do with my telling you that Peggy's boyfriend dug up the grave? Because that was a long time ago, and probably not even true. I'm sure he was joking or trying to impress her."

"Don't worry," said Charlotte, grinning. "Informant is the word folklorists use to mean anybody who is telling their story."

"Oh, okay," said Angela, looking relieved. "Where should I start?"

"Can you tell me what the legend is concerning Eliza Kendall's grave?"

"The story that I've always heard is that Eliza Kendall is a vampire. She might be a ghost as well. She's supposed to rise out of her grave like a mist and chase people who come after dark. That's more like a ghost, right?"

"Are there any stories of her biting anyone and drinking their blood?" asked Charlotte.

"Maybe that's what she does if she catches you."

"Do you know how the term vampire came to be applied to her, then?"

Angela stared at a spot beyond Charlotte and Heidi, one finger twisting a light brown curl. She pursed her lips as she thought.

"I don't know. But everyone said she was a vampire. Kids used to leave plastic vampire teeth on her grave. Mostly boys. I think it was supposed to make her mad and then she'd rise up and go after them. The boys were always trying to prove how brave they were."

Charlotte smiled at the classic legend-tripping behavior.

"So, yeah, we all thought of her as a vampire. But I don't know how that got started."

"Heidi said you went to her grave. Was that with a group?"

"Yeah. I went a couple of times. The first time it was just me and the kid I was going out with at the time. He's the one who told me the story. I think he just wanted to make out and he thought if I was scared enough, I'd fall into his arms."

Another common use for legend trip sites, thought Charlotte.

"Did it work?" asked Heidi.

Angela gave a sheepish grin. "Kinda."

"What was the story he told you?" Charlotte asked.

"He said that Eliza was a vampire and if you read the inscription on her gravestone out loud, she would come after you."

"What does the inscription say?" asked Heidi.

"Something like, I will come for you. Isn't that a creepy thing to put on a gravestone?"

"Did he bring vampire teeth?" asked Charlotte.

"No. He didn't mention that. Just the stuff about reading the inscription. Like I said, he was only in it for a make-out session."

"How many other times did you go?"

"Just once. That was with a group of kids."

"Could you tell me about that?"

"There was a whole bunch of us. Um...let's see. There was me and my boyfriend."

"The same one?" asked Charlotte.

"No. This was a year later. Different guy."

"How old were you?"

"Almost seventeen. Anyway, I think there were three other couples. I remember Robin Donnelly was dating Freddy Cook. Freddy was older. Eighteen, I think. He drove."

"What time of year was it?" asked Charlotte.

"Around Halloween. We all piled into Freddy's car and drove out there. It's an old cemetery. Lots of gravestones are broken or leaning. The grass was overgrown in the section where Eliza's grave is, except there's hardly any on her grave. It was really strange to see that."

"Did a lot of kids visit her grave?"

"Probably. You see, I lived on the border of Vergennes and Birch Falls. I hung out with a lot of Birch Falls kids. They're the ones I went with that night. I think my friend, Robin, was the only one besides me from Vergennes. And that first time? That guy was a Birch Falls kid. I don't know if very many Vergennes kids went or had even heard of it. But it seemed like all the kids in Birch Falls went there or, at least, knew about it."

"What did you talk about on the way there?"

"Some kids talked about having gone there before. One guy said that when he went before, he put a pair of vampire teeth on the tombstone and he immediately heard a creepy voice saying, 'I'm coming for you.' Then a mist came up from the ground in front of the gravestone. He said he ran like hell, but he did turn back to look, and the mist was shaped like a woman in a long, flowing dress and she was floating towards him. He said he high tailed it back to his car and drove away."

"He was alone, then?" asked Charlotte.

"No. He was with others, but he said he was the only one brave enough to go right up to the grave."

"Did others tell their stories?"

"I think so. I don't remember everything. I know we were all talking about it. Some had never been before, but everyone at least knew someone who'd been out there and had a story about it. Everyone was pretty jumpy by the time we got there."

"What happened when you arrived?"

"Freddy parked in the church parking lot. The cemetery is next to a church. It used to be an old meetinghouse, but it's a Congregational church now. Eliza's grave is pretty far into the cemetery. Freddy and a couple of the other guys knew right where it was.

"We all got out of the car. A couple of girls were hanging back, like they were scared, but we got them to come. We walked to the grave. Once I got there, I remembered it from the last time. Still no grass on it. At least not much. Then all of the guys took their vampire teeth out of their pockets and put them on the gravestones. We all backed up. Oh, that's right. One of the guys, I forget which one, had said as soon as we put them on the gravestones, we should back up in case she started coming out of the grave. So that's what we did.

Then in unison, we all started chanting, 'Eliza are you coming for me?' three times.

"Then what happened?" asked Charlotte, when Angela paused.

"We waited, all huddled together. Then one of the guys said, 'Did you hear something?' Then another one said, 'I think I see the mist.' One of the girls screamed and started running. I think that spooked most of us, though at least one of the guys was laughing, probably Freddy. We all ran back to the car and drove back to Freddy's house."

"What did you do on the drive back?" asked Charlotte.

"Talked about what happened. Someone said they heard a voice saying, 'I'm coming for you.'"

"Did you hear it?"

"No. Probably no one really did. Either he made it up or imagined it. Same with seeing the mist. It seems silly now, but at the time we were scared to death."

"Scared in a fun way?" asked Charlotte.

"Well...yeah. It was kind of exhilarating. Like the way you're scared when you go to a horror movie. And afterwards we could all say we'd done it. We thought that was really cool."

"Did you ever do it again?"

"No. I've never gone back there. I graduated and left for nursing school. By then it didn't matter anymore."

"What's the story about the kid who claimed to have dug up the grave?" Charlotte asked. "And don't worry. I'm not going to the cops about it." She laughed.

"That was my friend, Peggy's boyfriend, Jimmy. All I remember is one time when I was telling Peggy about us going out there – she hadn't been with us – she told me that Jimmy had gone a few times. He wanted to find out if Eliza was really a vampire, so he went one night alone and dug up her grave. I asked Peggy what he found, but she said he wouldn't tell her because it was too gruesome and would terrify her. Honestly, I'm sure he didn't really do it. Jimmy liked to brag, and Peggy was one of the most gullible people I've ever known."

"You're right. He probably didn't. That would be a bit difficult to get away with," said Charlotte. "Makes a good story to tell his girlfriend, though. Do you remember what was on the gravestone besides that inscription?"

"The name and dates are all I remember."

"Eliza died in 1815?"

"I think so, but I might be wrong. I didn't pay that much attention to the dates."

"Do you know if kids still go there?"

"No idea. I suppose they might. I always thought we came up with it, but later I found out that Robin's dad had gone with his friends when he was a kid, so I guess it had been going on for a while. It wouldn't surprise me if kids are still doing it."

"Do you know anything about the Kendall family? They must have lived in Birch Falls."

"Yeah, I guess they must have, but I don't know about them. Some of the old timers up there might, though."

An idea was forming in Charlotte's mind. "Do you remember how to get to that cemetery?"

"Oh, sure. Finding the cemetery is easy. I could write down the directions if you want."

"That would be great."

When they had finished lunch, Charlotte thanked Angela for the interview. Angela promised to write the directions and give them to Heidi at work.

"Are you going to go?" Heidi asked as she and Charlotte walked back to the apartment house.

"I think it would be worth a trip. I'd like to check the dates for myself, maybe talk to someone at the local historical society. I'd love to know if Eliza was related to Jerusha. Even if she's not Jerusha's sister, Lizzy, she might still be my ancestor."

"Please don't go on a weekend I'm working. I'm dying to go with you. I might get some vibes from her gravestone."

"We'll find a Saturday when neither of us is working and take a drive up," said Charlotte. "Just promise me you won't bring any vampire teeth."

Chapter 17

October 1831
Birch Falls, Vermont

The coughing fit that awoke Jerusha on the night of their trip to the cider mill also woke Susannah.

"She's in fever," Susannah said. "Get Mother and bring a bowl of cold water and vinegar with a cloth," she instructed Jerusha.

Jerusha scrambled down the stairs, her feet cold on the wood floors. Her mother was in the hallway before Jerusha could reach her door.

"What is it?"

"Lizzy. She's coughing terribly and Susannah says she's in fever. She sent me for you and to get water and vinegar."

"Go quickly," her mother said, heading for the garret stairs.

The house was dark and chilly. There was just enough moonlight for Jerusha to make her way to the well, though she wished she'd taken time to slip on her shoes. Dry leaves crunched underfoot, and sharp twigs stabbed the soles of her feet.

By the time she returned to the garret with a basin of water and vinegar, Lizzy was sitting up in bed. At first Jerusha though this was a good sign until she realized that Susannah and her mother were holding her up. Jerusha could see just enough from the lit candle coupled with the moonlight streaming in from the window to know that Lizzy's eyes were closed. Her head lolled to one side, resting on Susannah's shoulder.

"Is she…" Jerusha couldn't finish her sentence, not wanting to speak the words she feared most.

"She had another coughing fit. A bad one," said Susannah.

"Bring the water," said her mother.

Jerusha set the basin on the bed, a cloth floating in the water. Her mother reached for the cloth, wrung it out, and began mopping Lizzy's brow. Jerusha could hear Lizzy's breathing, a harsh, rasping sound. Lizzy's body convulsed, her eyes flew open, her chest heaved and suddenly she was coughing again, choking and sputtering. The basin sloshed water over its sides onto the bed. Jerusha grabbed it before it was knocked to the floor. She stood away from the bed, holding the basin, watching Susannah and their mother support Lizzy while she coughed and retched. A sense of helplessness came over her when Susannah held a handkerchief to Lizzy's mouth. In the dim light, Jerusha caught sight of something viscous slide into the handkerchief. Jerusha had seen this before with Rebecca and Josie. She knew there was no turning back for Lizzy now. Jerusha could only wonder how long it would before Lizzy joined their sisters in the graveyard.

Lizzy remained in bed the whole of the next day. Her throat was sore, her head and body ached. Mother rarely left the garret. Jerusha and Susannah did all the day's chores and cooking. On their mother's instructions, Seth went for Mrs. Wicker and Caroline Cutting. Mrs. Wicker, being much closer, arrived first. A bit later, Mrs. Cutting appeared and joined the other two women in the garret. Jerusha was quiet as she went about every task Susannah set for her. She could not stand the thought of losing Lizzy, yet she was powerless to force her mind to cease thinking about it. She felt as though she were in a cocoon, though not a protective one. Rather, it was a suffocating feeling, as if she were hemmed in by invisible walls that grew smaller with every breath.

She kept herself focused on her work, trying vainly not to think of what might be happening in the garret or of her day without her sister by her side becoming a normal circumstance. Once or twice tears threatened. She was able to hold them at bay by watching Susannah going about her work with determined focus. If she broke down, Susannah would be left with all the day's work.

Jerusha's father and Seth returned to the house at dinnertime. Mrs. Wicker had returned home to feed her own brood. Jerusha was sent to fetch her mother from the garret to join them for the meal.

"Eat, Mary," Mrs. Cutting instructed when Jerusha's mother said she was not hungry. "You must keep up your strength. I will stay here until you return."

Reluctantly, she followed Jerusha downstairs.

"What does Caroline say?" asked Jerusha's father, once they'd seated themselves at the table.

"She cannot be sure. Lizzy has fever, sore throat, cough, but it could be a wracking cough, another lung illness, or even just catarrh." Her mother's voice was so low, Jerusha barely caught the words.

"She does not think it is…" he trailed off.

Mary stared at her plate; at the food she could not touch. "It could be that, too."

"I will go for Doctor Eacker," he said.

Her mother looked up. "Will he do more than Caroline? He could do nothing for the others."

Jerusha watched as her father's gaze dropped away. "Perhaps he can do something. We will let him try."

The rest of the meal was consumed in silence. A creak of footsteps sounded on the stairs as they were finishing. Caroline Cutting entered the kitchen.

"Her fever has broken," she announced. "She is greatly fatigued and needs rest, but I should like her to take a bit of broth first to see if she will regain some strength."

"Let me." Quickly filling a bowl, Mary left the room headed for the garret.

"What do you think, Caroline?" asked Eli. "Not what you told Mary. What do you honestly think?"

The woman bowed her head, sighing heavily. It was a moment before she spoke. Finally, in a weary voice she said, "I know you want an answer. The truth is that several ailments produce these signs. God alone knows which it is. I would not presume to make a pronouncement."

"You have many years of experience, though. Surely, you've at least a strong suspicion."

Jerusha stood by Susanna, both of them shifting their gaze from their father to Mrs. Cutting as each spoke. Jerusha could not stop herself from taking her sister's hand as she awaited Mrs. Cutting's answer.

"Given the coughing fits Lizzy has had in the past and the family history, I cannot rule out consumption," she said at last.

"Then we are to lose her, too?" This came from Susannah. Her voice was a frightened squeak, so unlike her that Jerusha glanced in surprise.

"I am afraid that is very possible," said Mrs. Cutting.

"However," she continued, "if it is that each case is different. Some pull out of its clutches for a long while before succumbing. There is no telling at this point what might come. We must keep Lizzy comfortable, feed her on the most nourishing diet possible, and, when she is able give her as much exercise and fresh air as she will tolerate."

"You think she will recover enough for that?" asked Seth.

"That is for God alone to know. But from my experience, I can say it is very possible."

It was several days before Lizzy was strong enough to rise from bed. Doctor Eacker had examined her but came to the same conclusion as Caroline. Jerusha, taxed from extra chores along with little sleep due to Lizzy's coughing, was exhausted. October had given way to November by the time Lizzy resumed her normal tasks. All were pleased to see her once again going about the house and yard. Though no one spoke of it, it was obvious to Jerusha that Lizzy's former vigor was gone. She remained pale except when fever crept up on her, turning her cheeks bright red and giving her eyes an unnatural brightness. She had lost weight during the time she'd remained bedridden but had not gained it back. Her appetite had decreased. Her constant sore throat made swallowing difficult. Though she did all the tasks expected of her, there was no buoyancy in her movements. No more did she ask to help Seth and their father, instead preferring the quiet tasks of spinning, sewing, and knitting.

Jerusha watched as Lizzy grew thinner and weaker. It had happened with Rebecca and Josie, but the disease had seemed to progress more slowly with them. Perhaps, she thought, because they had always been slight and delicate, it had not been as pronounced. They'd never had Lizzy's robust vitality. Now, Jerusha thought, as she looked up from her spinning, Lizzy seemed to be dissolving before her eyes.

Chapter 18

August 1973
Middlebury, Vermont

Charlotte had given up waiting for Brad to read her plan for the Halloween exhibit. His complete lack of response caused her to second guess herself. Wondering if it was really any good, she gave copies to Jonathan and Paul for their opinions.

"This is fantastic!" said Jonathan a few days later, coming into her office, her proposal in hand.

"You think so?" she asked eagerly.

"Yes, I do. Paul agrees."

"I wish I could get Brad to at least read it," said Charlotte. "I don't know what he's waiting for. I'm afraid to ask him again. I've asked so many times now, once more and I think he'll can me."

Jonathan gave her a perplexed look. "He has read it," he said.

"What? When? He never said anything to me."

"Paul asked him a few weeks ago if he'd read your proposal. We need to get going on whatever will be needed for the exhibit. Brad told him he'd read it and get back to us."

Dumbfounded, Charlotte gaped at Jonathan.

"Obviously, he hasn't said anything to you."

"No," said Charlotte, when she found her voice. "Did he tell Paul that we're going to do it? Did he say if he even thought it was a good idea?"

"I don't know. Paul just told me he said he'd get back to us. I figured Brad must have approved it. I thought that's why you gave us each a copy."

Jonathan had been out when Charlotte had brought the copies to the Curatorial Department. She'd given both to Paul asking that they read it and let her know what they thought. Apparently, Paul believed she meant what they thought about putting it into practice, not simply whether or was a good idea.

About an hour later, Brad returned from his meeting with the museum president and the board of directors. Charlotte knocked on his office door, took a deep, steadying breath when he said, "Come in," and pushed open the door trying not to let her stomach sink to the floor.

"Charlotte," he said, looking up from some papers on his desk.

"Hi, Brad. Sorry to disturb you, but I'd really like to know what you thought of the proposal for the Halloween exhibit I've been looking forward to hearing your opinion." That last sentence galled her a bit, but she decided stroking his ego was worth it if it got an answer.

"Glad you asked. Have a seat."

Charlotte sat in the chair across from his desk.

"I read your proposal. It's not too bad for a beginner."

His look of smugness turned her stomach. Forcing herself to remain calm, she asked, "What did you find lacking?"

"Well, it's just...you know...it doesn't have enough...punch."

"Punch? What do you mean?"

Brad drew himself up, squaring his shoulders. "It's not engaging enough."

"How so?"

The focus of her proposal was on the evolution of Halloween from its beginnings as the ancient pre-Christian Celtic festival of *Samhain* and moving through the folkways of later periods showing how each tradition came about and built on the one before it. Charlotte had included having visitors write their memories of their own Halloween folk traditions on index cards and post them on a bulletin board where they could compare their own to those of other visitors. Later, the cards would be collected and kept in the museum archives.

"It's hard to explain," said Brad. "I know it when I see it."

"I can work on it some more," she said, though she honestly wasn't sure what to improve.

"No, no. I realized I needed to take things in hand, so I've created a plan for the exhibit. In fact, I've just explained it to Henry and the board. They loved it. We'll meet with Jonathan and Paul tomorrow. I'll give you all copies. Then we can start implementing it."

Henry Shephard was the president of the museum. When Charlotte had first met him, he'd talked at length about how he wanted the New England Folklife Museum to progress. He wanted it to be a stellar example of what a museum dedicated to New England folkways should be. He'd said he hoped she would bring a fresh perspective on presenting it to the public.

"Oh," said Charlotte, taken aback.

If Charlotte thought she was stunned by what Brad said in his office, she was completely dumbfounded the next day. Brad's plan was almost exactly her own. How could he simply steal her idea?

Neither Jonathan nor Paul looked at her. It had to be obvious to them that this was her work rewritten. Did Brad think they were all fools? Then she remembered. Brad didn't know she'd given them her proposal.

"Let's get down to business," said Brad. "Jonathan? Paul? What are your thoughts on getting this up and running?"

The gall of the man. Not only had he stolen her idea, he was now shutting her out, turning to the other men. Feeling the heat rise in her face, Charlotte knew she must be turning scarlet. She wanted to scream at him, but she had to be professional. She half-heard the three men discussing logistics and making plans.

Jonathan and Paul mainly kept their eyes on the pads of paper before them or looked at each other. Neither said anything about having read Charlotte's proposal or about how closely Brad's resembled it, but both appeared uncomfortable.

"Brad," she began again. "You know the proposal I gave you?"

"Mm," he muttered, scribbling on his pad.

"A lot of what you've got in this is very similar." She forced herself to keep her voice steady, pleasant even.

He looked up. He stared at her, daring her to continue. She hesitated, knowing she needed to choose her words carefully.

Paul cleared his throat, breaking the silence. "If there's nothing else, we should head over to Collections and get started."

Brad continued to stare at Charlotte a moment longer, then turned back to them. "Go ahead."

Jonathan and Paul rose. Before leaving, Jonathan turned back, giving Charlotte a look that she interpreted as "be careful."

Once the curators had left, Charlotte took a deep breath.

"Brad, I don't understand. This is basically my idea. I should get credit for the stuff I came up with."

"It's not your proposal, Charlotte."

"It is, though. Look," she said, pointing to a section of the paper.

"Charlotte," he said, his large hand coming down on top of the paper, fingers spread wide.

Weren't you listening? I came up with this idea months ago. You really need to pay attention in meetings, Charlotte. You're supposed to be my assistant. Can't have you daydreaming."

Brad, do you realize that every time I try to say something in a meeting you cut me off?"

He rolled his eyes. "Don't go getting hysterical."

She felt her face flush with embarrassment.

"Why don't you go back to your office and pull yourself together. Then go meet up with Jonathan and Paul. They should be getting started." He gave her a pitying look. "If it makes you feel better, you can think of this as a 'great minds think alike' scenario."

Furious, Charlotte hurried from the room. She forced herself not to slam the door of her office. Throwing herself into the chair, she pulled a copy of her proposal from her desk drawer. Putting the two side-by-side she reread both trying to see if she was mistaken. She was not. Brad had lifted almost everything from her proposal. Considering he didn't know that Jonathan and Paul had read hers, she wondered why he bothered at the effort of rewording it. She wasn't sure which galled her more, the fact that he'd stolen her idea, or that there was nothing she could do about it.

As she sat fuming, she began to wonder if it was true that he really had thought of this months ago. He was right that they probably both knew the same things. That part wasn't a stretch. Still, if that were the case, after reading hers he could have said something about how interesting it was that their ideas were so closely related. Instead, he'd belittled her effort, calling it not bad for a beginner. As far as Brad was concerned, it now appeared to the curators that he had dismissed her proposal and that he alone had the idea they would use. And hadn't he said he'd told President Shepherd about it? And the board? Now they think this is entirely Brad's idea. That she had contributed nothing.

* * *

"The nerve of that man!" Charlotte slammed her fist on the kitchen counter as she finished relating the story to Heidi that evening.

"He really is a class-A jerk," said Heidi. "What happened when you went to the Curatorial Department? Did they say anything about it?"

"Neither of them was surprised. They said it was typical of him. He never has really good ideas of his own, so he steals other people's and passes them off as his. He changes them just enough that they aren't exactly the same."

"Can't anyone do anything about it? Could you tell the museum president?"

Charlotte sighed, wringing out the dish cloth after wiping down the counter. "I told Jonathan and Paul that I wanted to do that, but they talked me out of it. They said it probably wouldn't do any good. He's certainly not going to take my word over Brad's. I'll get labeled a troublemaker." She slapped down the damp dish cloth. "There's not a damn thing I can do about it."

"Charlotte, are you sure you want to keep this job? You're miserable."

"I'm furious. But I'll be damned if a male chauvinist pig like Brad Louden is going to drive me out. I've worked too hard to get this far."

Tears of rage and frustration stung Charlotte's eyes, making her even angrier. She refused to cry over work problems. Being too emotional was one of the criticisms lobbed at women by people who thought they didn't belong in the workplace. She drew a deep breath, tipped her head back to stare at the ceiling, forcing herself to suppress her tears.

"I'm so sorry, Charlotte," Heidi said. "Maybe he'll leave. Or better, get fired."

"Yeah. Maybe," she said when she could speak safely. "Meanwhile, I have to work on this project that I should have loved."

"At least Brad thought it was good enough to steal."

An idea I'll never get credit for, she thought, finding herself again unable to speak.

"Maybe this will make you feel better," Heidi said, pulling a note from her purple shoulder bag, layered with a mountain of fringe. "Angela gave it to me this morning." She unfolded it, laying it flat on the countertop. "It's the directions to the cemetery in Birch Falls."

Charlotte slid the paper closer. Angela had not only written the location of the cemetery but had also jotted down what she could remember about the location of Eliza's grave. It was at the far end of the cemetery near the woods, furthest away from the old meetinghouse.

"The easiest way to get to the grave is to drive around behind the meetinghouse and park as close to the trees as possible," Charlotte read aloud. "Follow along the line of trees into the graveyard until you're all the way to the back. Then look for a grave close to where the woods start. It will be the one with no grass on it. See back."

Charlotte flipped the paper over to find a drawing of a meeting house with a graveyard beside it and woods in the distance. Angela had drawn arrows showing where to park and, from there, where to walk.

"This is great. Please thank her for me," said Charlotte.

"I will. I'm off this weekend. You want to go?"

"I can't. It's the week my family is coming to visit my grandmother. They'll get here on Saturday, but I promised Grandma I'd come down Friday after work. I want to talk to her first anyway to see if I can find out more of the family history. When is your next free weekend?"

"In two weeks."

"Perfect. Let's go that Saturday."

"I can't wait. I just know I'm going to pick up some strong vibes from Eliza's grave, especially if she is related to you. Your being there should help her to come through."

Charlotte couldn't help a smile. She was grateful to have this diversion to take her mind off her problems at work. She hoped Eliza was her ancestor. And that she was the "vampire" in question. It would be so cool to have a folk legend in the family.

Chapter 19

November 1831
Birch Falls, Vermont

Mary opened the door to find Lavinia Wicker looking pale and alarmed. "What is it, Lavinia?" she asked, ushering her neighbor into the house?

"I just saw crows, six of them, fly over your house."

Relief flooded Mary. "They are gone now," she said. "May I take that from you?"

Lavinia was carrying the new coverlet she had woven for the Kendalls.

"But Mary, there were six," said Lavinia. "An even number. It is a bad sign. An even number of crows is very back luck. And they flew right over the house."

Mary sighed. "We've no need of crows to tell us that." She took the coverlet from Lavinia. Setting it on the table, she unfolded it. A pleasing pattern of tan, black, and brown squares in varying sizes embellished the linen and wool fabric. Long fringe tassels hung from the ends.

"This is lovely," said Mary. "You always do exceptional work, Lavinia."

"Thank you, Mary. What did you mean? Has something happened?"

Mary turned from her inspection of the coverlet. "Seth," she said. "He had a terrible coughing fit in the night. The first one since summer."

"No." Lavinia put a hand to her heart.

"Between Seth and Lizzy is it any wonder six crows would fly over this house?"

Lizzy had become subject to regular intermittent bouts of fever and wracking cough. She continued to lose weight and strength. Mary did not need Lavinia's superstitions to expound upon the ill fortune that had befallen them.

"Come with me to the parlor," said Mary, noting the balls of yarn and knitting needles Lavinia carried.

The two women sat together in the waning sunlight, knitting, and talking.

"What do you hear from Zachary?" asked Lavinia.

"He is well, thanks be to God. He has had no attacks since he left us. He believes he will travel home in the spring to fetch Susannah."

"That is welcome news."

"I suppose."

"You do not sound as though you think so."

Mary raised her head to look at her friend. "I was wrong to sound so. It is good news that Zachary is doing well and will likely make a good home for Susannah. I am just sorry to be losing her."

"Ah, yes. I do not blame you."

"I know it is God's will that they should go. I try to give Susannah willingly, but I have lost so many." Mary felt a catch in her throat.

Lavinia reached for Mary's hand. "God will give you strength if you but trust him. Remember that she goes to a life that will ease the suffering of her husband. She will have the chance to raise a family. Perhaps they will prosper. If they were to stay it is likely that she would become a widow far too soon."

"You are right, of course, Lavinia. I am being selfish."

"No, Mary. You are far too good for that. Your mother's heart is aching, is all."

Lavinia patted her hand then went back to knitting.

"Will your niece return?" Mary asked.

"I had hoped so, but it is not to be. Her mother has taken ill, and she is needed at home. I do not suppose one of your girls could be spared for the winter? I would have liked Lizzy as she has worked with me the most, but if her present condition forbids it..."

"I would prefer to keep Lizzy with me," said Mary.

"I would not ask to take Susannah just now as you will want to spend as much time as remains with her."

"Jerusha is but nine," said Mary. "Though were we in the warm months she would think it her fondest wish realized to move in with your loom."

Lavinia laughed. "I daresay the loom won't get much more use until spring. As yet, she is too young."

"I shall send whichever of my girls can go as they can be spared. Lizzy sometimes has good days. I will try to send her on those, and Jerusha can be of help with some things. I am not so selfish that I would not send Susannah from time to time as well."

"That is most kind, Mary. Until I can get a girl to board, that will have to do."

From the parlor, the women heard the kitchen door creak open. Men's voices filled the room. Mary and Lavinia gathered up their knitting. Back in the kitchen, Mary called to Jerusha to bring the cheese and butter for Lavinia in exchange for the coverlet. Jerusha emerged from the dairy, arms laden with the items.

"How are you, Seth?" Lavinia asked.

"Well enough, thank you, Mrs. Wicker," he answered without much energy in his voice.

"Your mother told me of the attack you suffered last night. I was very sorry to hear of it." She turned towards Mary's husband. "I trust Joseph has been of help to you, Eli?"

"Indeed, he has."

Joseph Wicker had been sent to help given Seth's diminished condition.

"I am glad of it," she said. "Let us go home for supper now, Joseph."

As they climbed into bed for the night, Mary asked, "Eli, how did Seth seem to you today?"

Hearing him sigh heavily, she reached for his hand under the covers.

"Seth is not well, Mary," he said, resignation obvious in his voice. "He tried as best he could, but it took much out of him. And work at this time of year is not as taxing as in the summer. I am of a mind to send him with Susannah when Zachary comes to fetch her."

Mary gasped. "Send him away? Our only son?"

"It does not please me to do it, Mary, but the boy's life could be at stake. You know this is recommended for men who suffer consumption. The long ride in the open air seems to have greatly benefited Zachary, though Doctor Eacker would have liked him to go further south. He says the cold weather breeds consumption. I fear it will be a difficult winter for Seth, but if he makes it through, we should consider having him go with them in the spring."

Mary lay on her back staring up into the darkness. She could form no words. Eli was right. That was the prevailing treatment for men who could undertake the journey. If it was necessary to save Seth's life, it would have to be done. Still, the thought of losing yet another of her children was more than she could bear at this moment. Tears sprang to her eyes when she realized that either way Seth was likely lost to her.

Chapter 20

August 1973
Bennington, Vermont

Charlotte leaned close to her grandmother, peering at the fragile page. They sat on the living room couch with the Bible open on Eloise's lap. Soon after she arrived on Friday evening, Charlotte related to her grandmother everything she'd learned about the Eliza buried in Birch Falls. When she'd asked if more information about Jerusha's family was known, her grandmother had taken the ancient family bible from a cabinet in the living room.

"Here it is," she said, opening to a family tree at the back. "I'd forgotten until recently that this was in here. Look, here you are," she said pointing to a line with Charlotte's name sitting low on a tree branch. "Here is your mother, Lois. And me." Eloise's finger traced the names upwards on the page. "My mother, Ida," she continued. "My grandmother, Eliza."

"Eliza?" asked Charlotte.

"Yes, but she certainly can't be the one. She died when I was very young, but I do vaguely remember her. I never heard any tales about her like what you've told me."

"But look at who her mother was," said Charlotte. "Jerusha."

"Yes, Jerusha Kendall. She married Nathan Halsey. She's the one who wrote the diary. Her mother was Mary Kendall.

"Nathan Halsey. Jerusha mentions a Nathan in her diary. He was a hired man who live with them. I wonder

142

if he's the Nathan she married. She doesn't mention his last name. At least I haven't come across it yet."

"Could be," said her grandmother. "It might be she named her daughter Eliza after her sister, Lizzy."

"I wish I knew when Lizzy died. If Angela is right about the date on the gravestone, it can't be her."

"You'll know that when you visit her grave."

"I'll bet when you gave me Jerusha's diary you never thought I'd be tracking down a vampire."

"If that's the case, I don't think Jerusha figured it out. My memory is failing these days, but I'm pretty sure I'd remember reading about one of my ancestors being called a vampire."

"Jerusha wouldn't have used that word."

"But you said they dug them up. That image would have stuck in my mind even without the word vampire."

"I suppose it would," Charlotte conceded.

"Are you hoping it was her?"

"Well, yeah. I am."

Her grandmother sat back, appraising her.

"I am a folklorist, Grandma. It would be really cool to have something like this in my own family."

"Cool, is it? Seems horrific to me for a family to have gone through something like that."

Charlotte felt her cheeks burn. "It was, I'm sure. I'm not wishing such tragedy on anyone. But it was over a hundred and fifty years ago. We can't undo anything that happened. I just mean that if it did happen, it would be amazing to study that in my own family."

Charlotte felt as though she was tripping over her own words. She hadn't meant to offend but didn't feel she was explaining very well.

"I'm thinking of it academically," she tried again, relieved when her grandmother's face broke out in a smile.

"I understand, Charlotte. You will keep me informed of the post-mortem escapades of our ancestors, won't you?"

"If there were any, I certainly will," she said, kissing her grandmother's cheek.

A tinny chime announced someone at the back door.

"Hi Charlotte," said Keith when she opened the sunporch door. "I thought that was your car in the driveway."

"Hi Keith. How's your summer going?" she asked, stepping back so he could enter the sunporch.

"Okay, I guess. It's pretty mellow at my grandparents' house but I don't mind."

"Did you take your brother on that legend trip yet?"

"Yeah. It was funny. After our talk, I noticed all three parts. I had to keep myself from critiquing everything as it was happening."

"Maybe you should have taken notes," Charlotte said, laughing.

"I told my brother about our conversation the next day. He was amazed that anyone else did that stuff. I tried to tell him the world is a lot bigger than his little corner of it. I'm not sure he can dig that yet."

"He will. Eventually."

"Keith, come in," said Charlotte's grandmother, joining them on the sunporch.

"Hi Mrs. Tessier. I just came to let you know that I'll mow the lawn tomorrow. Anything else you want me to do?"

"If you have a moment, the sash cord in one of the bedroom windows has broken."

"I can take a look at it," he said.

"Oh, thank you. I noticed it a while ago. Even bought a replacement cord, then promptly forgot about it." She tapped her head just above the temple. "The old memory's going, I'm afraid. My daughter and her family are coming up from Massachusetts tomorrow. She and her husband will be staying in that room. I'm sure they'd like to catch the evening breeze, but the window won't stay open."

"Where's the sash cord?"

Eloise opened the drawer of the Hoosier cabinet and removed a package.

"I'll show Keith to Mom's room," said Charlotte. "Follow me, Keith."

There were two side-by-side windows in the bedroom. Going to the one that was not open, Keith pulled a piece of wood from the inner left side of the window frame. Taking a screwdriver from the back pocket of his jeans, he started turning the screws behind the wood he'd removed.

"You look like you know what you're doing," said Charlotte, a bit surprised. He was only just out of high school, after all.

"My dad's a carpenter. He taught us all the basics and a little more besides. That's why I've got the screwdriver in my pocket. Never go anywhere without it. That and a jackknife."

He reached into the window frame and pulled out a long, cylindrical weight.

"I never knew those were in there," said Charlotte, picking it up. "Wow, that's heavy."

"Uh-huh," he said, turning to do the same thing on the other side of the window frame. "Runs on a pulley system. But the sash cords only last so long before they break."

"The ropes, you mean?"

"Ay-uh."

It was the first time Charlotte had heard Keith use the Vermont term for the word *yes*, almost more of a grunt than a word. *Like an old farmer*, her mother would have said, though she'd heard her grandmother and her Uncle Will use it often enough. On occasion, even her mother uttered it, probably without realizing it.

Keith pulled the broken cording out. Opening the package of new cording, he slipped the rope over the pulley at the top of the window frame and threaded it down.

"Grab it when it comes out down there, would you?" he asked.

"Sure."

It was no time before the new sash cord was in and the window was able to remain open rather than banging shut on its own.

"All set," he said. "So, it's your mom who's coming up?" he asked.

"Yeah. My parents, brother and sister. They're staying a week but leaving my sister to help Grandma for the rest of the summer. That's why I came down again."

"Nice," he said. "I'll try to get over here early and have the lawn done before they arrive."

"It's no bother if you're here when they are. I think my mom will be happy to know someone's helping Grandma take care of things. When do you leave for school?"

"End of next month. Your Gram might want to find someone after I leave, especially for the winter. Snow can get pretty heavy. I don't think she'll want to be shoveling it."

"To be honest, I'm worried about her. She's all alone here."

"My grandparents are just up the street. She can always call on them if she needs anything. 'Course they're no spring chickens either. There must be some kids in the neighborhood who'd be willing to shovel. I'll ask around."

"Thanks. I'd appreciate that."

"How's it going?" They turned to see Charlotte's grandmother coming down the hall towards them. The soft carpet on the stairs and hallway floor muffled her footsteps enough that they hadn't heard her. Charlotte hoped she hadn't overheard them talking about her. Her grandmother had her pride.

"All fixed," said Keith.

"Wonderful. Aren't you a treasure," she said, coming to inspect the window.

Keith chuckled.

"Did Charlotte tell you her recent discovery about one of our ancestors?"

"No."

"Well, you should hear it."

"Come back downstairs and I'll tell you all about it over a Coke," said Charlotte.

By the time she finished explaining about the diary and Eliza Kendall, it had grown dark.

"I hope I get to hear how it all turns out before I leave," he told her before heading out the door.

*　*　*

"Who is that?" asked Tracy the next day as she, along with Charlotte's parents and brother, Russ, trooped into the house. She nodded towards Keith who had just finished putting the lawn mower away in the shed.

"His name's Keith Perry. He's helping Grandma while he's staying with his grandparents for the summer," Charlotte told her.

"He's a real hunk!"

"Think so?" Charlotte asked, amused at the wide-eyed look Tracy was giving him. "A little too old for you. He's leaving for college in the fall."

"I can still look, can't I?"

"I suppose."

"Charlotte, come tell us all about your new job," her mother called from the kitchen.

Charlotte left Tracy staring out the screen door of the sunporch.

"It's okay. Busy. We're preparing a Halloween exhibit," she said. Charlotte had decided not to tell any of her family about her problems with Brad. She wanted to handle them on her own.

"Do you like your apartment?" asked her mother.

"I love it."

"I can't wait to have my own apartment," said Tracy, bounding in from the sunporch.

The kitchen had suddenly become a beehive of activity. Her mother had several plates, each with two slices of bread on them and an array of mustard, mayonnaise, cheese, and cold meats set out before her, knives dipping in and out of condiment jars and flashing across the slices of bread. Her dad was mixing drinks. A screwdriver for Mom, an old-fashioned for Grandma, and a highball for himself. Russ was in and out, hauling suitcases from the kitchen to the bedrooms. Tracy was a whirligig of constant motion. In the midst of it all, her grandmother sat, hands folded on the table before her, a beatific smile on her face.

"Sit still long enough to eat, would you," said Lois, sliding a plate with a sandwich, pickles, and potato chips in front of Tracy.

"Got any soda, Grandma?" asked Russ, returning from taking the last suitcase upstairs.

"In the fridge. I loaded up when I knew you were coming."

"Grab me one, Russ," said Tracy.

"Here." He tossed a can across the room which she deftly caught.

"Russel!" Lois admonished.

"What?" he grunted, picking up a sandwich.

Until this moment Charlotte had not realized how much she missed her boisterous family. She hadn't noticed it in college as there were always so many people around, so much going on. Now that she was on her own, she enjoyed the peace and quiet, but her family's descent upon her grandmother's house, bringing with it all its noise and commotion made her feel as though something had been missing from her life for the past three months.

"What's your apartment like?" asked Tracy, already half-way through her sandwich.

Tracy's ravenous appetite coupled with her svelte figure was a marvel to Charlotte. The kid must have the world's fastest metabolism. It was her gymnastics and perpetual motion, Charlotte assumed. Calories melted off her like butter on a hot griddle.

"It's small, but cute. I really like it."

"I hope I get to see it while I'm in Vermont."

"I'm sure that can be arranged," said their grandmother.

Lunch was spent with everyone catching up on each other's recent activities.

"I finally got my round-off back handspring, layout," Tracy told Charlotte. "I want to show it to you. I can do it on the lawn."

"Let your lunch digest first," her mother told her.

"That sounds like a lot of flipping," said her grandmother. "You're going to do that on my lawn? Don't you need a mat or something?"

"Nah. I do it on the lawn at home all the time."

"You let her do that, Lois?"

Charlotte's mother shrugged. "I gave up trying to stop her a long time ago."

"But isn't it dangerous?"

"Let's go outside, Charlotte," Tracy said, obviously wanting to absent herself from the turn the conversation had taken.

"If I get a bottle of hydrogen peroxide and wash my hair with it, will it turn blond?" Tracy asked.

Charlotte sat on the porch steps while Tracy dropped onto the grass facing her, sandals kicked off and tossed to the side.

"Why do you want blond hair?" Charlotte asked. Tracy's hair, a rich auburn which she wore in two pigtails, gleamed in the sunshine. "Your hair is a beautiful color."

"I want it to look like Cathy Rigby's. It curls enough if I use rollers, but if it was blond, it would be just like hers."

"Will that make you a better gymnast?" Charlotte felt a smile twitch at her mouth.

Tracy had begun a complex series of stretches. "No," she said, her face buried in her legs stretched out straight before her. "I just want to look like her."

"Does Mom know you want to go blond?"

"Yeah, she knows." Tracy had switched to a straddle position, almost a perfect split and was leaning her upper body sideways over one leg.

"And she said you could do it?"

"Are you kidding?" Tracy answered, coming back up to stretch over the other leg.

"Well, don't look at me to help you with something Mom will get mad about. And don't wash your hair with hydrogen peroxide. You'd ruin it doing that."

Tracy lay on her back, pushing herself up with hands and feet into a backbend. With legs together and straight, she shifted her weight over her arms until she was in a perfect arc, her head nearly touching her bottom.

"You really can turn yourself into a pretzel, can't you?" asked Charlotte. "Doesn't any of that stuff hurt?"

"No," she said, her voice muffled by her contorted position.

"Hurts me to watch," said Charlotte under her breath.

"You are so lucky," said Tracy, after she lowered herself back to the ground. "I can't wait to have a job and an apartment and no one telling me what to do."

"I do have a boss, you know," said Charlotte, thinking of how Tracy might change her mind if she knew what Brad was like.

"That's not the same. You don't live with your boss. You can go home and do whatever you want."

"It is good to be on my own, but it's not always all it's cracked up to be." Not wanting to get into the details of her work life, she added, "How about showing me your new flips."

That evening they all sat in the living room while Charlotte recounted the story about Jerusha's diary and Eliza Kendall.

"Cool!" said Russ when she finished. "We've got a vampire in the family. I love it."

"Can I go with you when you go to her grave?" asked Tracy.

"You're here to help your grandmother," said her dad.

"You know," said Charlotte's mother, head tipped back as she searched for a particular memory. "I think my grandmother mentioned something about it."

"She did?" asked Charlotte and her grandmother together.

"Yes. Well, not about a vampire per se, but something about an odd occurrence in the family from a few generations before."

Charlotte had the bible on her lap open to the family tree. "Your grandmother was Ida. Her mother was Eliza, Jerusha's daughter."

"I guess. I know my grandmother's name was Ida, but I never knew the names of anyone before her."

"What did she say?" asked Tracy.

"I'm trying to remember. It was a long time ago. I was younger than you are now. I think we were talking about family history. She said something about a house that had been in the family for a few generations that was supposed to be haunted."

"A vampire and a haunted house," said Russ. "Very cool!"

"I don't remember my mother ever saying anything like that," said Charlotte's grandmother. "What house was she talking about?"

"I think it was the one her mother grew up in, but I'm not certain."

"Was that in Birch Falls?" asked Charlotte's father.

"It must have been," said Charlotte's grandmother. She was sitting next to Charlotte on the sofa, peering at the bible. "It says that Eliza was born and died in Birch Falls. I wonder if the house is still standing."

Charlotte's mind was spinning with ideas to find out about the house. The tax assessment office, a search of the deeds at the county courthouse, the historical society. Her thoughts were interrupted by her father.

"Could you sink your teeth into this, Charlotte?"

She looked up at him.

"Sorry."

Charlotte knew from his smile and the gleam in his eyes that something was percolating in his mind.

"I definitely could," she said, smiling back at him.

"Is it dissertation worthy?" he asked. Her father had championed her continuing education more than anyone. He'd always been proud of her intelligence and told her she should use it to its fullest.

"A doctorate?" she asked.

"Why not? You've got the brains for it."

"For heavens sake, Dan," her mother interrupted. "She just finished her masters and started a new job. You want her to go back to school again? Whatever for?"

"She's got the mind for it," he said.

"But she doesn't need to. She's employed. What would she do with a doctorate anyway?"

"I could teach in a university," said Charlotte.

"Would you like to do that?" asked her father.

Charlotte thought of the few women professors she'd had, wondering if they were treated any better than what she was enduring.

"I might. I see my role at the museum as a form of teaching." At least that's what she'd expected it to be.

"Can you get ahead there?" he asked.

"Does she need to?" her mother asked. "What if she gets married and starts a family? What good will all the time, money, and effort that that goes into getting all those fancy degrees have been?"

"What if she doesn't get married?" asked Tracy. They all turned to look at her.

"Well, she doesn't have to, does she? I don't think I will."

"And what do you plan to do, Miss?" asked their mother.

"I don't know yet. But I know I want to do something besides clean a house and change diapers. I might major in journalism when I go to college. I think I'd like to be a reporter."

"You change your mind every other day about what you want to be," said her mother.

As the conversation turned to Tracy's inability to settle on a career choice at the tender age of fifteen, Charlotte turned the idea of going back for her Ph.D. and teaching folklore over in her mind, not for the first time. She remembered her conversation with Heidi who also though she should do it.

Later that night, as she lay next to Tracy in Aunt Beatrice's bed, she wondered if her grandmother giving her Jerusha's diary and finding out about Eliza Kendall's grave being a legend trip site were signs. She tried to figure how she could balance a full-time job with studies and writing a dissertation. She'd have to leave the museum to go somewhere with a good Ph.D. program. When she'd first taken the job, she'd have rejected the idea of leaving it right away, but with the way Brad was treating her, the position wasn't exactly working out as she'd imagined. She did enjoy having her own apartment. She'd have to find work of some sort near the university to support herself. It wouldn't be easy, but it might be worth it. Then another though struck her. Was she seriously considering it just to get away from the situation with Brad? Hadn't she insisted she would not let him drive her from her job?

The warm glow produced by the thought of a doctorate in folklore and teaching in a university warred all night with the galling sensation that doing so would be equivalent to running away like a coward.

Chapter 21

November 1831
Birch Falls, Vermont

Jerusha kept close to Lizzy in the Wicker's big barn, swamped in a sea of corn. Neighbors within a mile or so had gathered for a husking frolic. First came the work. Ears of corn lay in mountainous piles all over the barn floor. Everyone worked together stripping the husks and silk from each ear then throwing them into separate baskets. What husks weren't fed to the livestock would be used to replenish the filling in mattresses.

"Are you well?" Jerusha asked Lizzy for at least the fifth time.

"Yes. I have told you so already."

"Sorry," said Jerusha, noting the irritation in Lizzy's voice. Lizzy had been having a good spell all week, but Jerusha knew it could change at any time.

"You needn't fret over me." She patted Jerusha's hand.

"At least you felt well enough to come. I know you love frolics," said Jerusha.

"I may not be up to my usual. Even if I were, Mother would not allow me to do too much."

"Mother would be pleased to see you acting your old self."

"I should be pleased if I could," said Lizzy, giving Jerusha a wan smile.

Shouts and laughter filled the barn from the unmarried young men and ladies who made the most of frolics.

"Do you think Geneva Weir and Michael Arnold likely to marry soon?" Jerusha asked, noticing the young couple seated close together, seemingly oblivious to everyone else in the crowded barn.

"Indeed, yes," said Lizzy. "Susannah said they will marry at Thanksgiving of this year."

"How merry!" said Jerusha.

"A red ear! I've found a red ear!" called a youth, waving a half-husked ear over his head.

"Whom do you choose?" called another.

The young man with the red ear strode to the center of the barn, trying and nearly failing to keep his balance among copious ears strewn across the floor.

"I know exactly who," he said, making straight for a young lady, his lips already puckered for the kiss due the finder of a red ear of corn.

"You dare not do it, Amos Abbot," cried the girl, rising quickly, her lap full of ears bouncing to the floor.

She ran, or tried to, heading for the barn door, whooping all the way while Amos chased after her. She was a pretty girl, dark haired and rosy-cheeked. It was no wonder Amos had chosen her. Steps from the barn door, Amos caught up with her. Jerusha was certain she let herself be caught and, despite her protests, was not a bit sorry when he threw his arms around her and planted a kiss on her to the cheering of the onlookers.

Jerusha laughed along with the others. She expected Lizzy to be laughing, too, but a glance at her sister showed only a wistful expression. Jerusha caught herself before she could ask Lizzy again if she was well.

"Don't you find it amusing?" she asked instead.

"I suppose it is," said Lizzy. "I was just thinking, is all."

"Of what?"

Lizzy dropped her gaze to the ears of corn in her lap.

"Lizzy?" Jerusha asked when her sister didn't answer.

"That will never be me," she said, so quietly that Jerusha had to lean close to hear her.

"You want to kiss Amos Abbot?"

At that a laugh did escape Lizzy. "No!"

"What did you mean, then?"

"I will not reach the age for courting."

Jerusha felt a stab of fear. "You might live a great many years. No one can tell. Mrs. Cutting said so."

"Mrs. Cutting cannot feel what I feel inside. I am dying."

"Lizzy, please do not talk so."

"It is hard knowing I will not be in this life much longer."

Jerusha felt tears well in her eyes.

Hannah and Betsy dropped to the barn floor next to Jerusha and Lizzy. "Rose will be impossible to live with for at least a fortnight."

Jerusha glanced at Hannah's older sister, Rose, sitting in the midst of her friends across the barn. "She does not look perturbed."

"She would never let anyone know, but she has had a case for Amos Abbot for at least a year. I caught her one day when she thought she was alone. She looked all dreamy and was scribbling in her journal."

"So?"

"She closed the journal quickly and tried to act like nothing was out of the ordinary. Later, I found that she had been scribbling his name over and over in it."

"Hannah Small, you are incorrigible," said Betsy with a laugh.

Lizzy's friend, Annie Marsh, moved to sit next to Lizzy. As the two began their own gossip, Jerusha had no more opportunity to speak with her sister.

Once the corn was husked and twilight had descended, the group made their way into the Wicker home. Barrels of cider and beer, freshly baked biscuits, cheese, and pumpkin and apple pies were heartily consumed by the hungry crowd. Shortly after, a young man pulled out a concertina, another a fiddle, and another a flute. Two lines formed, one of young men the other of young ladies. When the music started, the dancers moved in unison towards then away from each other, breaking to spin with a partner in the opposite line then back again. The steps continued with turns and loops, while those watching clapped along in time to the music. As the dancing continued, the married couples and older people drifted closer to the fire to talk. Jerusha, Lizzy, and others their age sat on the floor watching and clapping. A few little girls attempted to imitate the dancers' steps in a corner of the room.

When the dancing concluded, everyone found seats whether on sofa, chairs, or the floor. Nuts were brought in for roasting. A whisper went round, begun by Sophia Wren, the same young lady who Amos Abbott had chosen to kiss. There was much giggling as they crept closer to the fire.

"What are they doing?" asked Jerusha, trying to peer over the hunched backs and bobbing heads in front of them.

"Telling fortunes," said Betsy.

"How?"

"Each girl writes the name of her sweetheart on the nut and puts it in the fire," Hannah explained. "If it burns steady, his love is true, but if it pops or jumps out of the fire, then he is a false lover."

"Do you suppose Rose wrote Amos Abbot's name on her nut?" asked Jerusha.

"Perhaps, but he is not her sweetheart. She only wishes he was."

Jerusha inched closer, hoping for a better view, but the group of older girls was bunched so tightly before the fire she could not break through. A great popping noise resounded, making the young ladies spring back as one. Jerusha was nearly bowled over by their sudden dispersal from the hearth. Hooting and giggling, they tripped away taking seats throughout the room.

Jerusha noted the satisfied look on Rose's face and assumed that the nut that had jumped was Sophia Wren's with Amos Abbot written upon it.

Chauncey Haskell set his chair close to the fire, facing the room. Voices hushed as the old storyteller settled himself. Jerusha watched the firelight flicker across the side of his face, lighting it up while the side furthest from the fire remained in shadow. He took his time, watching to see that he had the attention of the entire assembly before beginning.

"The dancing here tonight has put me in mind of some dancers I watched on a moonlit night long, long ago." His sonorous voice captivated young and old alike. "I was no more'n sixteen, but I remember it like it was yesterday. Ye see, the dancers were not in a house such as this. No, indeed. Where I laid eyes on 'em was in a graveyard." He leaned forward in his chair, his gaze slowly sweeping the room. "They were dancing on their graves."

A gasp escaped from the midst of the group. "Their own graves?" The question was asked by a timorous voice.

Chauncey Haskell nodded slowly.

"It was a chilly autumn night, late in October. I had been helping at a neighbor's farm and was walking home. It was still light when I set out and would have been nearly so still had I not dawdled on the way. I had to pass the home, you see, of Sarah Englund. A more comely creature you never did set eyes upon. There's some say she could cast spells. If that were so, she may have cast one over me as I was surely taken with her. She was just walking from the cow shed to the house as I passed by. I stopped to share a few words with the lady. Though it seemed I only spoke with her but a moment or two, I found it was quite dark when I left. Friends told me later that she must have bewitched me, and perhaps she had, given what I was about to encounter."

Jerusha caught sight of Lizzy leaning forward as though loathe to miss a word.

"I had to pass an old graveyard on my way home. The Morley family plot, it was. An old family that had been in these hills since long before the Revolution. It was overgrown, as the Morley's, by that time, had all died out and no one looked after it. You might not even notice the stones if you didn't know they were there as they were covered over by the tall grass. But we all knew, those of us who lived nearby, as we had been warned that it was a haunted place. We were told not to go near it, but that oft-repeated warning only drew us in. In the daylight, that is. None that I knew would dare to visit at night, though there were those who claimed to have done so.

"Now on this night as I walked home, I knew I would have to pass that graveyard. I don't mind telling ya, I shook a bit as I neared it. I thought mayhap I should retrace my steps, take another route, but I was sore hungry by then and doing so would have made me even later. I was determined to press on. As the moon was full, I could see well enough, and I thought I would go as quickly as I could past the graveyard. It was a small one, after all. It would only take but a few running steps."

Chauncey leaned further towards his spellbound audience. He swept his gaze right to left then back again, taking them all in. Jerusha, like all the others, hung on his every word.

"My heart hammered away in my chest as I approached that old boneyard. I could feel the blood rushing through my ears as I came even with the remnants of gateposts leading into it.

"'Just get by as swift as you can,' I told myself and forced my legs to pick up speed, despite they felt like lead weights were tied to 'em. I might have made it if not for the old maple tree just the other side of the gate. As I ran past, I tripped over an exposed root, or so I thought, and fell to the ground. It took me by surprise, you see, because I have walked by that tree many a time in the daylight. Never once do I remember any roots sticking up, but what else could it be, thought I.

"As I lay sprawled in the dirt and leaves, I thought I heard voices nearby, though I could not make out a word. It seemed there were many of them all talking, or rather, whispering at once and excitedly, too, as if about to embark on some great adventure. I knew this could not be and counseled myself I was only hearing the swish of the leaves or the wings of some night birds.

"I had determined to pass the graveyard without looking at it, but the fall had turned me 'round a bit so when I got to my feet, I was staring straight into it. And stare I did for a good while before my poor brain could take in what I was seeing."

His voice dropped to just above a whisper. The listeners inched closer.

"The sight before my eyes gave me such a turn it about froze me to the spot." He sat up straight in his chair, his gaze fixed on some point across the room as if watching his tale play out before him.

"There in the graveyard were the figures of a goodly amount of specters. I did not stop to count them, but I reckon they may have numbered ten or more. Men and women both, they were, dressed as in days gone by. They were mixing and mingling not unlike we here tonight, talking and gossiping for all the world like they were at a frolic. You might say, 'well, but mayhap that is what it was then.' Ah, but had there been a frolic would I not have known of it? And would it take place in such an odd location? Even were that so, at the bottoms where their legs should'a been was nothing but wisps like fog, yet it was a clear night. And when they began to move, it was like they were gliding on air.

"'Got him, I did,' I heard one of them say to his companions. 'Threw my boot in his way. That caught him up short.'

"I had no time to ponder these strange words before an eerie tune was struck up. It seemed to be coming through the bare tree branches, like they were making an unholy sound a rubbin' together. Then the hoot of an owl joined in keeping rhythm with the trees. The specters took up two lines, men on one side, ladies on the other and began to dance.

"Well, I could take no more of it. I turned and ran for home. My hunger forgotten, I shot straight to my bed and dove under the covers not so much as poking my head out until daylight.

"The next day I had about convinced myself it was all a dream, until on my way back to the neighboring farm, I passed that tree. There were no roots sticking, but an old boot was laying beside it. 'Twas then I remembered what the specter had said about catching someone up short by throwing his boot out in front of him. I knew in that moment, that someone was me. Whether he only meant it for a mischievous prank or had a more sinister plan in mind, I shall never know."

He leaned forward again, his forefinger extended, pointing at one and all in admonition.

"I warn you, when you walk home tonight, be sure not to go any stretch of the way alone. Take care not to tarry for you never know what lurks about after dark."

Jerusha was grateful to have her family with her as she made her way home late that night. Still, she could not help peering around cautiously as she walked. The hoot of an owl caused her to shriek and clutch Lizzy's hand.

Lizzy, who had been quiet all the way home, asked solemnly to no one in particular upon entering the house, "Do you think it is true that people can come back after they die? As specters, I mean. Like in Mr. Haskell's story."

"That story was nonsense," said her mother. "It was told for amusement, nothing more."

"I will try," Lizzy said, her voice earnest.

"Try what, Little Ox?" asked Seth as they made their way through the dark house to the stairs.

"To come back. Not to scare anyone, but to show that I am well. And to see you all again."

"Such talk!" their mother admonished. "No more of it."

No one spoke another word, but Jerusha was more unnerved than she had been on the walk home. She had noticed a strange quality in her mother's voice and could not decipher if it was anger or fear.

Chapter 22

August 1973
Birch Falls, Vermont

"I found it!"

Charlotte looked up from the gravestone she was reading when Heidi, a few yards ahead of her, called out. A couple of trees towered over her on either side only a few steps into the woods.

Charlotte dropped to her knees before the old gravestone.

Eliza Kendall
1817 – 1832
Daughter of Eli and Mary Kendall
Aged 15
I will come for you all

Charlotte pulled her camera from her backpack. She snapped a photo of the gravestone, then backed up and took several more photos of the area. Other gravestones stood nearby. She and Heidi read the names: Eli Kendall, Mary Kendall, Rebecca Kendall, Josephine Kendall, Seth Kendall.

Charlotte stopped when she found the stone bearing the name Jerusha Halsey. Next to it was a stone that read Nathan Halsey.

"This is it," she said. "These are my ancestors. This is Jerusha Kendall whose diary I'm reading."

"Far out!" said Heidi.

Charlotte slid her hand over the top of Jerusha's gravestone, feeling the smooth, time-worn marble.

"I feel like I know her," she said, her voice soft as if speaking to herself. She knelt before the stone, tracing the carved letters.

"It looks like the whole family is here," said Heidi.

"Not Susannah and her husband," said Charlotte. "They moved to Ohio. But the rest of these names are all in Grandma's bible." Straightening up she wandered among the stones noticing how much thinner were the older ones, especially those for Rebecca and Josephine, and how the carving in them was only partially legible.

She moved further into the woods to get a photo of the graves from the other direction. As she walked, her foot caught on something that almost sent her sprawling.

"What was that?" asked Heidi.

"I don't know." Kicking through the pile of leaves covering whatever had tripped her, Charlotte uncovered a small headstone with only one word on it. *Infant.*

"How sad," said Heidi coming up beside her.

"Yeah, but quite common at the time," said Charlotte. "Jerusha must have had a sibling who died very early on or was stillborn. Be careful. There may be others around."

Sure enough, Heidi's hiking boot soon came in contact with an identical stone not far from the first one. "Let's go back," she said. "These babies' stones are too sad for me."

They returned to the site of Eliza's grave on the border between the woods and the cemetery. Together they crouched before it.

"I wonder why Angela told us she died in 1815," said Heidi. "That's not the date.

"Probably they were too keyed up at the time to pay much attention. It says she was fifteen when she died. Angela probably conflated the age with a date. Doesn't matter, though. The names are all correct. This is my family."

"Look at these dates," Heidi said. "All the Kendall kids except Jerusha died young. And so close together. Only a year or two between each of them. And look, only three months between Eliza and Seth. But Jerusha lived into her seventies."

"Susannah lived a long life according to the dates in Grandma's bible, though her first husband died long before she did. She had a bunch of kids, too."

"She stayed in Ohio?"

"As far as I can tell."

"How sad it must have been to lose so many siblings," said Heidi. "Of course, I'm an only child so I don't even know what it's like to have siblings, never mind lose any of them. And the parents. All but Jerusha and Susannah went before them. You're not supposed to bury your kids."

"That's what people say now, but it was different back then. It was practically a miracle if you didn't. There are hardly any listings of families where some of the kids didn't die before the parents, often quite young."

They were silent for a moment, standing amongst the stillness of the graves. Charlotte thought of her own family, what would it be like to lose Russ or Tracy. She could barely fathom the pain of it. What must it have been like for Jerusha? As the youngest, she'd had a houseful of siblings from birth. The noise, the activity, the constant proximity of other people. Then to have it slowly wiped away, one by one until she was the only one left. How bereft she must have felt. That it was not uncommon did not mean it didn't hurt.

"What do you make of that?" asked Heidi, pointing to the inscription. "I will come for you all. That's kind of creepy."

"Not to them," said Charlotte. "They would have believed that when a family member died, those who had gone before would meet them to welcome them into heaven. It was a statement of faith that they'd be together again in paradise."

"Wow. I would have taken it to mean she was coming back to haunt them."

Charlotte smiled. "Yeah, that's undoubtedly what the legend trippers think, too. Look at this." She stretched out her arm to retrieve something laying in the shade of a nearby tree.

"Get out!" said Heidi as Charlotte held out her hand, a set of vampire teeth resting in her palm.

"They're still fairly clean. I guess the legend trippers have been here recently."

"I can't believe I never did that stuff when I was a kid," said Heidi.

"You did go to a cemetery to contact a spirit."

"That was different. I was by myself, and it wasn't because of any story I'd heard about that particular grave. That was my own connection to the spirit."

Charlotte nodded, unwilling to argue the point.

"I'd love to see if I get anything from Eliza," Heidi said. "Is it okay with you?"

"Sure," said Charlotte. "What do you have to do?"

"I need to put myself into a totally relaxed state so that I'm open to letting Eliza's spirit come through. Then I'll ask her if she wants to contact us. If she has any message for us."

Charlotte wasn't sure how she felt about this. She was skeptical of Heidi having any ability to contact the dead, but she was fascinated by the fact that Heidi believed she could.

"I'll get out of your way," she said, getting up from in front of the gravestone and brushing the dirt from her bare knees. "Angela was right about no grass growing here. We're only on the edge of the woods. The other graves have grass on them."

"Strange, isn't it?" asked Heidi, moving in to sit cross-legged in front of the stone.

"Not really. This grave probably attracts a lot of people. Legend trippers and others who just want a look at the infamous grave. With all that foot traffic, it's not surprising." She moved away to sit with her back against the nearest tree. "You know she's on the other side, right?"

"Of course. That's why I'm trying to contact her."

Charlotte laughed. "No, I mean where she's buried. They put the stone at the foot of the grave facing away from it. If you want to sit over her grave, you'll have to come around to the other side."

Heidi shrugged. "I didn't know that, but I don't think it matters."

"Okay. You're the medium. Do you mind if I take your picture while you're doing your thing?"

"Not at all."

Charlotte pulled a notebook and pencil from her backpack ready to jot down notes about what Heidi did and said. "Okay if I record you?" Charlotte's backpack was kept full of everything necessary for a folklore encounter which included a tape recorder and blank cassettes.

"I guess so, but I don't know if there will be anything to record."

Charlotte shrugged. "If not, no big deal." She snapped a tape into the machine checking first that the batteries were working and that she had extra just in case.

For several minutes both sat still and silent, Heidi in front of the stone, eyes closed, hands resting on her knees palms up, taking slow, deep breaths. Charlotte watched intently, ready to press 'record' should Heidi make a sound. She snapped a few photos, then leaned back against the tree and waited.

Eventually, Heidi stretched out her hands, resting them flat against the gravestone. Her head dropped forward. She appeared to be in a trance-like state though Charlotte was sure she was simply relaxed.

"Eliza, are you here?" Charlotte pressed the record button, pushing the recorder closer to Heidi with her foot.

"Charlotte Lajoie is here. She's a direct descendant of your sister, Jerusha. Do you have anything to tell her?"

Heidi fell silent. Charlotte snapped another picture then waited.

Finally, Heidi lifted her head, removed her hand from the stone, and looked towards Charlotte. "Sorry," she said. "There's nothing. Not even a vibration."

"That's okay. You tried," said Charlotte, slightly disappointed but more relieved that Heidi neither deluded herself nor resorted to fakery.

"I thought for sure I'd get something. I don't know why she won't come through." Heidi stared at the gravestone as if it could give her an answer.

"Maybe it's because I'm here," said Charlotte. "Should I leave you alone to try again?"

"Maybe, but I expected your being here to help."

Charlotte got up. "I'm going to walk around in the woods a bit. You can try again if you like."

Leaving her backpack, she strolled beyond the infants' graves, deeper into the woods. There were a few scattered, ancient-looking gravestones here and there, the writing on them barely legible. Glancing back, she saw that Heidi had moved around to the back of Eliza's grave, apparently deciding to see if being on top of the actual grave made a difference.

Leaves crunched underfoot. The scent of pine reminded her of Christmas despite the August heat. Following a well-worn path, she came to a clearing. Atop a small hill was a house. It looked old but seemed in decent repair. Sheets hung on the clothesline in the yard. A low fence surrounded a pat of garden. If it weren't for the chaise lounge and a few Adirondack chairs in the yard she might have felt as though she'd stepped through a portal in time.

The yard backed right up to the woods. Charlotte stared at the house wondering when it was built. It looked quite old. Could it have been here at the time of her ancestors?

"Charlotte?" Heidi's voice came from behind. She turned to see her friend coming towards her, a look of excitement on her face.

"Any luck?" Charlotte asked.

"Not with Eliza," said Heidi when she reached her. "But there sure was with Mary."

"Eliza's mother?"

"Yeah, I tried again with Eliza but got nothing. Her mom's grave is right next to hers. I put my hand on the stone as I was getting up. It felt like an electrical shock going right through me."

Heidi's face was flushed. Charlotte didn't think it was just from traipsing after her through the woods.

"What happened then?"

"I sat down at her stone and tried again, and I swear the ground practically vibrated. The woman is very upset about something."

"Did she say anything?" Charlotte wasn't sure if this was an odd question or not.

"Not exactly. I mean, I didn't hear actual words, but I did get a very strong sense of something. I'm not sure what. It was an emotion. Anger, but something else besides. Something like..." Heidi groped for a word. "Indignation, I think."

"Did you ask her anything like you did Eliza?"

"I asked her what was wrong. What I could do to help."

"And?"

The color suddenly draining from Heidi's face made Charlotte's stomach lurch. "What, Heidi?"

"I know you'll think this is crazy, but I tipped over."

"What do you mean?"

"I was kneeling with my hands just barely touching the stone. Suddenly, I lost my balance and tipped to the side. I fell towards Eliza's grave. I even grazed my arm on her stone." She turned sideways to show Charlotte the scrape down the side of one arm. "Then it all stopped. I didn't get anything else from Mary. Everything went back to normal. And I came to tell you."

"I'm sorry you got hurt," said Charlotte wishing she'd witnessed what happened.

"It's nothing. But I think Mary was telling me that whatever she's upset about has to do with Eliza."

Charlotte waited a second before speaking, not sure that she wanted to ask, but decided to, anyway. "You mean you think Mary pushed you?"

A pained look crossed Heidi's face. "Not literally, but in a way, yeah. I mean, I wasn't dizzy or off balance or anything. There's no reason I should have tipped over like that."

Charlotte doubted that but did not want to argue. Turning towards the house, she said, "Look. I was just wondering how old that house is. It might have been here when Jerusha was alive."

Heidi gazed at the house. "Do you know where your ancestors lived?"

"No, but I'd like to speak with someone at the town's historical society. Maybe there's a record of them."

Before leaving the cemetery, Charlotte looked again at all the gravestones. She put her hand on Mary's but felt nothing out of the ordinary. She noticed that Heidi avoided Mary's stone.

In the car on the way back, Heidi asked, "What are you going to do about Mary?"

"What do you mean?"

"She needs help. She wants something."

"But what?" asked Charlotte.

"I wish I knew."

"I am going to do some research on the Kendall family. Maybe something will come to light."

Chapter 23

"I have spoken with Lizzy about it," Mary told Lavinia. "I have been trying to prepare her as I did Rebecca and Josie, though it feels as if I would die of heartache each time."

"Poor dear," said Lavinia, patting Mary's shoulder.

The two women sat side-by-side on the settee in the Wicker's parlor. Mary had come to her friend to pour out her anguish. Lizzy had not let go of the notion that she would come back to them after she died. She seemed more intent on it than on preparing her soul for heaven. For Mary, this was a terrifying caprice. She feared her daughter, who could go from her at any time, might leave this life unready for the next.

"I have told her that she must pray and read the scriptures often. That she must ask the Lord to make her fit for heaven."

"She is not altogether wrong, though, Mary," said Lavinia, a reflective look on her face. "Surely, Rebecca and Josie will be there to meet her when she goes. As will your parents and Eli's. Perhaps she simply misunderstands the concept."

"I thought that at first, but upon much discussion I find that she understands well. Meeting us at our departures to welcome us into our heavenly home she surely plans to do if our Lord allows, but that is not what she means. She spoke quite plainly to me when I questioned her on it. She says she will come to us, not when we are ready to die, but before. As a ghost. That is what she said. As a ghost.”

“How does the child think such things?” asked Lavinia.

“It was Chauncey Haskell’s tale at the frolic that put this notion into her head. There are times I wish he would keep his frightening stories to himself, especially when there are young, impressionable ears to hear them.” Anger at Chauncey welled up in Mary, not for the first time since the frolic. His penchant for tales of hauntings, ghosts, and the like too often found fertile ground where they could cause the most trouble.

“But no one believes his tales to be true,” said Lavinia. “I would have thought Lizzy old enough and clever enough to recognize a fanciful yarn when she hears one.”

“Oh, she does not believe his story was any faithful account. Yet, it set her mind on things most peculiar. Now, the thought of returning to us has such a grip on her that she is fixated. Lavinia, what should I do? I cannot bear to think of my dear girl leaving this life unprepared for the next. What injury might this fancy wreak upon her soul?” Mary felt hysteria rising within her. She clutched the teacup with both hands to keep them from shaking.

“Have you spoken with Reverend Cobb? Perhaps he could speak with Lizzy.”

Mary stared into her teacup. “I have not,” she whispered. She had thought of doing so, but it felt like admitting that she had been remiss, had failed in her maternal duties. She knew she must now accept her own mortification for Lizzy’s sake. “You are right, of course. I will go.”

* * *

Mary was welcomed by Reverend Cobb’s wife, Althea. She had smiled upon answering the door, but her countenance quickly changed to a look of concern.

173

"Mary, what is wrong? Is it Eliza?" she asked, taking Mary's cloak, brushing the flakes of snow from it before hanging it on a peg just inside the parsonage door.

"Yes, it is. Is the Reverend here?"

"He is in his study. I will fetch him for you. Come, warm yourself by the fire." Althea led her to a small, cozy parlor. "Let me get you some tea," she said once she had Mary seated.

"Thank you. That is most kind." Mary suddenly realized she was shaking, though she knew it was not simply from the cold. She gratefully wrapped her hands around the steaming cup Althea brought her a few moments later as much to steady as to warm them.

"Is she quite unwell? Is it to be soon, then?" Althea had pulled a chair close to Mary's, her hand on Mary's arm, her face full of compassion.

Mary took a sip, then placed the cup on the tea table at her side. "No. You mistake me. Lizzy is well enough at present. It is another matter, though related, about which I wish to speak to the reverend."

Althea sat back in her chair. Her face relaxed. "I am relieved to hear it. But you appear so distressed. What has happened?"

Mary thought a moment. Perhaps it was as well to speak with Althea as with the minister. Althea was a mother, too. A mother who had lost two children. Perhaps she would understand.

"It is about Lizzy," she began. Without warning, tears stung her eyes. "Or, perhaps, it is about me." Althea, she was sure, had not experienced a similar dilemma. Her children, the children of the minister and his wife, would have been so thoroughly reared in the scriptures that such a thought as that which had taken hold of Lizzy would never have dared enter their heads. She wondered if Althea would understand after all.

Althea leaned forward again, taking Mary's hand gently in her own. "Are you concerned that Eliza is not adequately prepared to meet our Lord?" she asked.

Such tender feeling shone in the soft blue eyes searching hers that that Mary could not bear to hold the older woman's gaze. As she turned away, her face crumpled. A sob escaped her.

"Mary," said Althea, wrapping her arms around her. "Mary, my dear. This is so hard, I know. I felt the same way. It is a terrible, terrible burden."

"You did?" Mary asked, not without a little astonishment.

"Of course, I did. I believe all mothers do when they must endure such a thing. A good many have come here just as you are today."

Taking a deep breath, Mary wiped her eyes. "It was not so with Rebecca and Josie," she said.

"No?"

"Not the same," she amended. "I did my best to prepare them and left the rest to God. I was as sure as I could be that when the time came for each of them, they were ready. I have no doubt that they are with our Lord now awaiting the rest of us."

"What gives you greater concern for Eliza? Surely, you are doing your best to prepare her as well."

Mary nodded, staring at the handkerchief she twisted in her lap. "I have...I am doing my best, but..."

"She resists?" asked Althea. "Is she sore afraid?"

"No. It is not that."

Mary took a moment to gather her wits, to decide how to explain. Althea waited in patient silence.

"She has taken a strange notion into her head." Though the words came out barely above a whisper, they came with urgency making Mary realize how desperate she was for help.

"Lizzy was taken by Chauncey Haskell's tale of ghosts at the frolic. She is determined she will come back to us as a ghost. Not to haunt us, but to let us know she is well. She meant to reassure us, I know this, but it is not a sound Christian belief. I fear with her being so close to...to...death," the word hung in the air while Mary tried to compose herself. "I fear her mind is on this fancy more than on preparing herself to stand before the Lord as a good Christian ought to do."

Mary lifted her head, tilted it so that she looked Althea in the eye. "I fear for her soul."

Althea's brow knit. She appeared about to speak, then hesitated. *I have scandalized her.* Mary felt herself flush with shame at the thought.

"Mary," Althea's voice was no more than a whisper. "I believe it is merely a fancy of youth, but as it comes at such a time, it may be..." her voice trailed off and she glanced away. Then she closed her eyes, composing herself. "Let me fetch Jonas," she said with a reassuring pat on Mary's shoulder.

Mary waited only a few moments, though it felt much longer, before the Reverend Jonas Cobb entered the parlor.

"Mary," he said, holding out both hands to her.

Reverend Cobb's expression was a mix of concern and compassion. His blue eyes were rheumy. The top of his head was bald, but snowy white hair ringed it in a perfect semi-circle just above his ears. He held his head at a slight tilt as he greeted Mary who had jumped to her feet upon his entering the room.

"Please, Mary, sit down," he said. "Althea has told me why you have come." He took the chair vacated by his wife who had not rejoined them. "I am so sorry for your troubles. But do not fear, Mary. We will set dear Eliza on the right path. It is but a child's fancy as I am sure my good wife has told you."

"Yes, she has. What shall we do for Lizzy?"

"I should like to speak with her myself, if you and Eli would permit it."

"Of course. We would be most grateful."

He nodded, smiling benignly at her. "Once I have assessed her true thoughts I will know better how to proceed. The poor child is likely frightened and scarce knows what she is saying.”

Mary had doubts about that. Lizzy was frightened of very little, though impending death might scare even such an intrepid soul as she. She did, however, seem quite certain of what she intended. Mary hoped Reverend Cobb would get through to her.

“She means no harm, I am sure,” Mary stated, eager that the minister not think ill of Lizzy. “She is not a bad child. She is confused, though we have tried very hard to set her right.”

“Of course, you have,” he said, his white head bobbing in agreement. “Eliza is a good child, raised well by you and Eli as have been all your children. But she is understandably frightened. I believe she is looking for a way to stem that fear, yet she is going in the wrong direction. Our duty is to set her on the right path.”

It was Mary’s turn to nod now. “Yes. Thank you, Reverend. Perhaps if you speak to her, she will understand.”

“May I call upon you tomorrow?”

“I would be so grateful.” Mary felt a weight lift from her. To have this burden moved from her shoulders to those of one trained to bear it was like being set free from torturous captivity.

As they rose from their chairs, Althea Cobb returned to the parlor clutching a handful of pamphlets.

“These may be of help,” she said, holding them out to Mary. “They proved quite valuable to us when we were losing our boys.”

Mary took the pamphlets all of which bore the title, *The Youth’s Companion.*

“You will find,” continued Althea, “that along with amusing and cautionary tales, they also contain sound advice for young people, including how to prepare for a good death.”

“Thank you, Althea. I will give these to Lizzy.”

"Perhaps she and Jerusha might read them together," said Althea.

Mary felt her stomach lurch. Of course, the minister's wife only meant that they were appropriate for both girls. Still, the thought that Jerusha, who at present showed no sign of illness of any sort, might, too, fall sick with a deadly disease was almost more than she could bear. As it was, Seth, who had not shown signs of illness for months, had begun to cough and complain of an aching head and sore throat again.

Mary's gaze dropped to the floor. Mary, who had carried eight children in her womb, had buried four of them and would likely bury two more before she herself was taken from this world, and who would lose one to Ohio, would be bereft of all but Jerusha. And if Jerusha should succumb as well? How could she endure the loss of all her children?"

Chapter 24

January 1832
Birch Falls, Vermont

Jerusha awoke to find herself clinging to Susannah, her arms wrapped tightly around her sister. It was Susannah's hands gently tugging at Jerusha's arms, trying to free herself that woke her. A low, unplaceable hum seemed to fill the garret. Even awake, Jerusha could not let go at first, as if her arms were not in communion with the rest of her body and would not obey any thought of letting go. Something in Jerusha's mind dimly connected this situation to the hum.

"Jerusha, please," Susannah said. "It is time to rise."

Susannah's voice broke whatever was making Jerusha's embrace so relentless. Her arms went slack long enough for Susannah to slip from the bed.

"Dress quickly. It is unbearable cold," Susannah counseled.

The noise in the room rose from a hum to a sigh to a howl. The garret window rattled. Jerusha, now more fully awake, understood it to be a fierce wind. She pulled the covers up over her head.

"No, silly goose," said Susannah. "Get up. We must help Mother."

Then she remembered. Sleep and cold had dulled her thinking, but the relative warmth of being curled into a ball beneath a mountain of blankets and quilts had begun to thaw her mind. Mother did need their help. Lizzy was in the chamber off the kitchen now, had been for a fortnight, the room in which Rebecca and Josie had died. In the past few days, she'd grown so gaunt, so skeletal, it was obvious she would not be with them much longer. Mother rarely left her side. Susannah and Jerusha did most of the work in the home. For the past two nights neighbors had come to watch at Lizzy's bedside. Some were likely still there. It was like the last days for Rebecca and Josie. Hopes that Lizzy would rally again had been extinguished.

Ever since their mother had brought home a stack of the *Youth's Companion* followed the next day by a long visit from Reverend Cobb, Jerusha and Lizzy had been tasked daily with at least an hour's reading and discussion on preparing for a good death. Reverend Cobb had come several times to detail for them the delights of eternal life with Jesus and to remind them that they would only know such a destiny if they left this world properly disposed for the next.

Lizzy stopped talking about returning to them as a ghost. At first Jerusha thought it was the influence of Reverend Cobb and the stories and obituaries in the *Youth's Companion* that had wrought the change. Lizzy dutifully prayed, read, and studied the Scriptures. She was indeed sincere. But only one week ago when she and Jerusha had been left alone, Lizzy had confided in her that she had not given up the belief in her ghostly return.

"I have upset Mother, though I did not mean to. I had thought to console her, to console you all by saying that I would come back to let you know all was well for me. But I see that Mother has taken my meaning wrong. There is naught I can do to change her mind, so I speak of it no more," she'd told Jerusha. "I believe I am prepared for death. How could I not think on it? How could I not pray and do all I can to ready myself to come face to face with our Lord? But if the Lord allows, I still intend to come back, if but only for a moment so that you will know and can be at peace about me."

Jerusha had not known what to say so she'd said nothing.

"Please do not speak of this to anyone. Mother is more settled now that she sees I am on the right path. I just want you to know so you will look for me."

Now Lizzy lay in bed two floors below Jerusha, burning up with fever, coughing hard and long enough to crack her ribs. Jerusha thought of what it would be like to see her sister's ghost. She wondered if it would frighten or comfort her.

She hadn't long to think about it. Suddenly, the covers were whisked from her curled up form. A blast of cold air set her immediately to shivering.

"Up. Now!" Susannah dropped Jerusha's woolen frock onto the bed next to her.

All day the wind howled at the windows, down the chimneys, and through the chinks in the walls. At times it returned to the low hum Jerusha had heard when she'd first awoken, but then it would build up to a rousing crescendo, once blasting into the kitchen along with a miniature cyclone of snow when the door opened to admit their father returning from the barn.

That evening Jerusha stood by the bed staring down at Lizzy. She barely recognized her sister anymore. Lizzy had grown rail thin, her concave stomach causing her ribs to jut out.

Lizzy's eyes were open; her gaze unfixed. Her visage would have been the picture of health with her rosy cheeks and brightly gleaming eyes if those attributes were not caused by a raging fever and those cheeks and eyes not sunken into a skeletal face. She was nearing the end. Jerusha had seen this twice before.

Also now familiar was the gathering. Just as with Rebecca and Josie, she did not stand alone at Lizzy's bedside. The remaining members of the Kendall family, Caroline Cutting, Mrs. Wicker, and several other neighbors were here as well. Mother sat at Lizzy's side, holding, and kissing, her hands while Mrs. Cutting and Susannah took turns replacing the cold compresses on her forehead.

In the past month Lizzy had rapidly declined. It seemed to come on so quickly. She'd awakened one night, coughing, and choking so loudly it had brought Mother running to the garret. When they saw the blobs of green and yellow mucous on the coverlet, they knew the end was near. Mother moved Lizzy to the first-floor bedchamber the next morning. Jerusha had prayed it would stop. She knew Lizzy would never fully recover, but she could get better, at least for a while.

It was not to be. Lizzy progressed rapidly from expelling yellow, then green mucous, and finally blood. Just spots of it at first, but in no time, it became great clots. Young though she was, Jerusha already had enough experience with the disease to know there was no going back now.

"Mother." The barely audible word coming from Lizzy sounded cracked and hoarse to Jerusha's ears.

"Yes, my darling," said their mother as she brushed a few wayward strands of hair from Lizzy's eyes.

It seemed as though the room held its breath. Everyone leaned in close. It was difficult for Lizzy to talk so her words would be few, but no one wanted to miss them as they might be her last.

"I have made my peace with God. I am ready."

Mrs. Wicker put a hand on their mother's shoulder. A tear dropped onto the coverlet.

A movement near the doorway caught Jerusha's attention. Seth had come in from the barn, a dusting of snow on his shoulders. He, too, had lost weight, begun to cough more, and grew tired easily. Yet he could still work with their father at times. Whenever he was well enough, he threw himself into the work so fully he had to be reminded not to overtax himself. Like Lizzy, he fought the illness with all he had. Yet Jerusha no longer held any doubts as to which one would win.

Seth's appearance in the doorway caught Lizzy's eye, too. With effort she lifted her hand towards her brother. Jerusha saw the tears glisten in Seth's eyes, something she'd never seen before.

"What is it, Little Ox?" His words, barely above a whisper, sounded strangled.

"I will come for you," Lizzy said, her voice equally strained, though with hoarseness from coughing. "I will come for you all," she said, her gaze sweeping the faces encircling her bed.

Jerusha's mother took Lizzy's outstretched hand, held it against her own cheek. "We know, my darling daughter. And we will rejoice when we meet you at the gates of heaven." Like Seth, tears choked her words, but she made no effort to restrain them.

A great gust of wind howled around the cracks and crevices of the house, rattling the window so hard Jerusha feared it would shatter. Everyone in the room responded. Some gasped while others pulled their shawls and cloaks more tightly around themselves or shifted away from the window. Everyone except Lizzy. Within the span of time it took for the wind to rattle through the house, she had taken her final breath.

Chapter 25

August 1973
Middlebury, Vermont

"I'll try to carve a few real ones just before the exhibit opens," Jonathan said, handing Charlotte a wooden turnip. "I've preserved Jack-O'-lanterns with petroleum jelly, but I've never tried it on a turnip before. I suppose it will work, though."

Charlotte and the two curators had been going through collections all morning, making lists of artifacts and reproductions so they could write up information to mount next to them once they moved everything into the exhibit site.

"What? Oh, yeah. Good idea," she mumbled.

"You okay? You seem a million miles away."

"I'm fine. Just thinking."

Charlotte's mind was on Eliza Kendall more than the job at hand. She was grateful for the distraction given that focusing too much on the exhibit only reminded her that she was helping to implement her idea for which Brad would get all the credit.

"I don't blame you for being upset about Brad stealing your idea, Charlotte," Paul told her, obviously assuming that's where her thoughts were. "If it makes you feel any better, you're not the first person he's done this to, and you probably won't be the last."

"I don't know if that makes me feel better or not," she said. "I'm just so angry. It's not fair."

"You're right. It's not," Jonathan agreed. "But it's the way it goes around here."

"Why?" asked Charlotte. "I still don't get why I can't go to President Shepherd. If Brad has a history of doing this, shouldn't he know about it?"

"What makes you think he doesn't?"

Charlotte stared at him. "What do you mean?"

Paul sniggered. "Maybe we're just old and cynical, but we think he knows what Brad's like. He just doesn't care. Besides, it makes for a good puppet."

Charlotte sat on the floor of the Curatorial Department, mouth hanging open.

"Brad thinks he's putting one over on everybody," Jonathan explained. "Heck, for all I know maybe he convinces himself that the ideas he steals are really his own. Shepherd's no dummy. He's got to know what's going on, but as long as the work gets done, the museum's admissions are good, the visitors like the experience they have here, and we stay in good standing with AAM, he's not about to rock the boat."

"That's absurd!" Charlotte's cheeks grew hot. "Why wouldn't he care about how the museum he's in charge of is run?"

"It's no skin off his nose what goes on between department members. He assumes if there's a problem the department heads will take care of it."

"In this case the department head is the problem!"

Both men laughed.

"You got that right," said Paul. "Just don't expect it to change. Shepherd doesn't want to go through the hassle of a search for a new director. The last person who tried to call out Brad on something got fired within a week. That's why we told you not to go to Shepherd about it."

"So, we're all supposed to work our tails off and let Brad take the credit. He's not even helping with any of this." She gestured at the boxes of artifacts and reproductions pulled from the shelves and the mountain of paper covered with scribbled notes about each one.

"It used to bother me a lot," said Jonathan. "Things were different before Brad was hired and Shepherd became President. But I'm only a few years from retirement so I don't worry about it. My time here is almost done."

"I started looking at this as a job with a paycheck, albeit not a very big one, not long after Brad arrived," said Paul. "I show up, do my job, get my pay, such as it is, and go home."

Charlotte stared at him. "But you studied for years, got an advanced degree for this. It's not just a job. It's your profession."

Paul snickered. "That's how it was when I started. After Brad came, my perspective changed. It had to for self-preservation."

"You could look for another job," said Jonathan glancing over at Paul who shrugged.

Another job. Charlotte had just started here. She'd had such high hopes. She thought of her grandmother's pride in her. Jobs like this in her field weren't easy to come by. If she left, what would she do? But could she put up with the way she, and apparently others, were treated?

"If you think Brad should be helping us, don't worry," said Jonathan. "He'll show up when we start putting everything into the exhibit. Just like he did with the Fourth of July. Remember?"

Charlotte thought of all the work they'd done preparing for that exhibit, and it dawned on her that Brad hadn't shown his face until they actually began setting it up. Then he strutted around the exhibit space, making declarations about where and how everything should be placed, though that had already been decided. He'd simply acted as though he was making the decisions on the spot. At the time, she'd thought he was a bit showy but as it was the first exhibit she'd worked on with them she hadn't given it much thought.

"Personally, I'm just as glad he stays out of our way as much as he does," said Jonathan. "I'd much rather do more of the work than have to deal with him."

Charlotte sighed again. She had to admit she did enjoy working on exhibits with Paul and Jonathan. She'd just have to keep thoughts of Brad stealing her idea at bay and focus on the project or ruminate instead on Eliza Kendall.

After her visit to the cemetery, Charlotte had called the Birch Falls Town Hall asking how to contact the town's historical society. She was told there was no official historical society or commission, but when she mentioned that she was interested in information about an ancestor who had lived in Birch Falls she was instructed to contact a Mrs. Edna Marner. Apparently, Mrs. Marner was the town's unofficial historian. Upon telephoning the woman, Charlotte got the distinct impression that the elderly lady did indeed have a vast knowledge of the town's former inhabitants.

* * *

"Thank you for agreeing to meet with me," Charlotte said as Mrs. Marner opened the door and ushered her into her home. On the drive up, Charlotte had passed the Congregational Church and the cemetery where her ancestors were buried. Following the road that swung up behind it, she realized Mrs. Marner's home was probably close to the house she'd spied from beyond the graveyard. It might even be the same one.

Once inside, Charlotte couldn't help but gaze around her. The parlor was filled with antiques, a tall case clock, and old secretary desk, a high boy cupboard, a sofa and matching chairs with carved mahogany backs and arms, and a round tea table.

"Please have a seat," said Mrs. Marner. "I've made lemonade. Would you like some? I make it the old-fashioned way with real lemons, not that powdered stuff they're selling nowadays."

"Thank you," said, Charlotte, accepting a glass.

"Now," said Mrs. Marner, settling herself in her chair. "What do you want to know about the Kendall family?"

Charlotte sipped her lemonade, fighting a delicious pucker, then set the glass down on a coaster. She looked at the woman across from her. Edna Marner was likely in her mid-seventies or early eighties, a bit heavy-set with short, wavy, gunmetal gray hair. She had a wide face with chubby cheeks. Charlotte thought that when Mrs. Marner was younger, they were probably what her mother would have called "apple cheeks," but now the skin sagged a bit. She moved slowly, but her blue eyes sparkled with intelligence and zest.

"As I mentioned on the phone, I recently discovered that the Kendalls are my ancestors. My grandmother gave me Jerusha Kendall's diary. I'd like to learn more about them.

"If you have Jerusha's diary, you've got one of the best sources for information. That's called a primary source. That means it comes directly from the time period being studied, don'tcha know."

Charlotte smiled. "I do know. I'm a folklorist."

Mrs. Marner clapped her hands together. "Oh, that's right. You did tell me that on the phone." She tapped her temple. "My memory isn't what it used to be." She smiled and her eyes twinkled. Charlotte noticed that they almost matched the blue of her dress. "But I still remember everything about the history of Birch Falls. That's stuck right in here." She jabbed a stubby index finger in the center of her forehead. "Just don't ask me what I had for breakfast or what someone told me yesterday."

Charlotte laughed. "What can you tell me about the Kendalls?"

"If you're going back to Jerusha, then you'll want to start with her parents, Eli and Mary, I expect."

"Yes," said Charlotte. She flipped open the flap of her leather shoulder bag. Withdrawing a paper, she said, "I have their names from my grandmother's family bible. The dates show that many of Mary and Eli's kids died young. Do you know what happened to them?"

Mrs. Marner nodded. "As I understand it, consumption. It took a lot of people in those days. May I see that?" she asked, holding her hand out for the paper.

She looked it over, nodded once or twice. Without looking up, she said, "There were also the two babies. Their stones just say 'infant' on them."

"Yes, I saw them in the cemetery."

Mrs. Marner nodded. "Rebecca, Josephine, Eliza, and Seth were all taken off by consumption. A terrible scourge it was. Sometimes it wiped out whole families."

"I know. It was awful. They were farmers, weren't they?"

"Oh, indeed. They had a place out on what's now Farm Hill Road. Don't know what they called it in their day, if anything."

"Is the house still there?"

"It is. Still in pretty good shape, too. 'Course it's been added on to and kept up. New folks just bought it. A young couple. The last folks that had it, the Ketchums – well Henry Ketchum died nigh on ten years ago and his wife, Millie, is in the old folks home now. She won't be coming back to it, so she told her kids to sell it for her. I expect the money from the sale pays her way at the Home. It's terrible what it costs to be cared for in your old age, don'tcha know. Back in the old days, folks took care of their elders at home, but times change, I guess. But that's not why you're here, is it? Forgive me if I get off the subject. Just scoot me back onto it if I do. Can't help it. It's part of growing old."

Charlotte felt herself quickly warming to this lady. "Do you know the new people?" she asked.

"I've met them a time or two. Can't say as I really know them. Knowing a body takes a while. Can't be done just meeting 'em once or twice."

"Of course. I just wondered if you thought they might let me see the house."

"Now, that I can't say. But I can tell you how to get out there and at least take a look at it from the road."

"Do you know their names?"

"Paquette, I believe. She's Julie and I think he's Andrew. Or was it Arnold? No, Andrew. Andrew and Julie Paquette."

"Do you have a phone number for them?"

"No, I don't, and they haven't been here long enough to be in the phone book, yet. But I can give you their address. Eighteen Farm Hill Road. Drop them a line. Best to write to them. That way they can make up their minds how they want to answer. Folks don't like being put on the spot."

Charlotte felt herself blush. Should she have written to Mrs. Marner rather than called her?"

"You're right," she said. "I suppose I should have written to you."

Mrs. Marner shrugged. "Don't make no never mind to me. I'm always happy to talk about Birch Falls history. I just know how most folks feel, though them being a young couple and all, maybe they don't hold to such old-fashioned notions."

"Still, I'll write first," said Charlotte. "What do you know about Eliza and her family?"

"Don't know how much there is to say. You know they were farmers. That's a hard life. Constant work. 'Course in those days most people farmed even if the menfolk worked a profession alongside it. And life was hard for everybody. They all worked sun-up to sun-down no matter whether they lived on a farm in the country or in town. Still, I think the farmers worked 'round the clock. Don't know when they slept." She chuckled softly.

"Mrs. Marner, have you ever heard of kids going in a group out to Eliza's grave at night expecting to see her ghost?"

The woman's eyes widened as she straightened up in her chair. "Don't tell me that's still going on. Young 'uns were doing that when I was a girl. I never would have believed they're still at it."

"It seems they are. Did you do it?"

The elderly woman pursed her lips. "I've been to her grave. We all have. I didn't go the way you're talking about, though. My friends, Maryanne, Eva, and I walked over there one afternoon when we were about, oh, I'd say fifteen or sixteen, just to see what all the fuss was about. We went on a summer afternoon, though. My sisters and I didn't go out of the house much at night, you understand. My parents wouldn't allow it. But one day the three of us got to talking about what some of the neighbor boys had said they'd done one night so we decided to take ourselves on over there and see."

"Did anything happen?" If Mrs. Marner started describing a legend trip, Charlotte was ready to pull out her tape recorder.

"'Course not," she said. "That was all nonsense those boys were going on about. Just trying to make themselves look brave." She chuckled at the memory.

"Some things never change," said Charlotte. "Do you remember the stories about why kids went to the grave at night? Was there a legend about Eliza?"

"Oh, my, yes. Quite a thrilling one, don'tcha know. Folks said she was a vampire."

"Do you remember the story behind it?"

Mrs. Marner leaned back in her chair, her gaze cast upwards, searching for the memory. "Well, now it was an awfully long time ago," she said, after a moment. "I couldn't tell you exactly what those boys tried to make us believe. All I remember was that Eliza Kendall was

191

supposed to have been a vampire, and if you went to her grave at night, you might see her rise from it as some sort of vapor. Then she'd come after you, so you had better scram. She was supposed to have said something, too. Now what was it?"

"Something about her coming for them?"

"Yes," said Mrs. Marner, drawing out the word. "Yes, that was it. 'Course I can tell you where that came from. Something to that effect is right there on her gravestone, after all. Now, as you might know, in Eliza's day that wasn't unusual. They put all sorts of things on gravestones that were perfectly ordinary to them but that later folks thought odd. But that's just because they don't understand the time period."

Charlotte nodded.

You read it, I'm sure?"

"Yes," said Charlotte. "'I will come for you all.' I'm familiar with the sentiment as one common for the time period. But I understand how easily later generations would find it strange, spooky even."

Mrs. Marner laughed. "Makes me wonder what things we do and say now that will seem strange to our descendants or that they'll completely misunderstand."

"Probably, plenty," Charlotte agreed. "But if we could get back to Eliza."

"Of course. What were we saying? Oh, the boys going to her grave, right? And kids today are still doing it. My, my. I never would have believed it."

"What I'm really interested in, Mrs. Marner, is why people thought she was a vampire. Other than the inscription on her stone, I mean. That inscription, odd though it may seem to people today, doesn't have a thing to do with vampirism. So where did that belief come from?"

Charlotte was pretty sure she knew. If Eliza had died of consumption, it was quite possible she'd been exhumed, but she wanted to know what people said was the reason.

"You know, I'm not sure. It's a legend that's been handed down for generations. You're right about the epitaph having nothing to do with vampires. I could see folks thinking she might be a ghost. That would make more sense, seems to me. But a vampire? Can't rightly say what led to that idea. Maybe it's got something to do with the house, but I can't think what."

"Eliza's house?" asked Charlotte, remembering her mother saying something about there being a haunted house in the family.

"Well, her father's house, yes. The house where Eliza lived."

"What about the house?"

"Folks say it's haunted."

"By Eliza?"

"I suppose. To be honest, I'm more interested in solid history than in things like ghosts and goblins. I don't believe in such things, so I never paid much mind to those stories."

"Do people still think it's haunted?" asked Charlotte, trying not to show her disappointment.

"Oh, I suppose some do. Every so often you'll hear tell of a story or two about it."

"You knew the people who lived there before the current owners, Mr. and Mrs. Ketchum. Did they ever say anything about it being haunted?"

Mrs. Marner thought a moment. "You know, Henry Ketchum was a stern old Yankee. He wouldn'ta been afraid of ghosts. If anything, they'd be afraid of him. But I do remember one time Millie told me – this was after Henry died – that she heard the sound of a woman crying at night. I told her it was probably the wind. She said something, too, about footsteps coming down from the garret. Now, you've got to understand, Millie had married Henry when she was nineteen years old. She'd lived with her parents up until then. After Henry died, it was the first time in all her life that Millie had lived alone. Plus, she was grieving for Henry. Put it all together and, well, you can see where her imagination might be playing tricks on her. I told her as much. She didn't say anything to me about it after that."

"What about the new people? Have they had any strange experiences in the house?"

"I wouldn't know. As I've said I've only met them once or twice. It's not likely they'd tell me such things so early on."

"Of course. Mrs. Marner, when I was at the cemetery, I walked a ways into the wood and came out in the backyard of a house that was probably quite close to this one. Maybe it was this one. Does your house abut the back of the cemetery?"

"Sure does. Come, look."

Mrs. Marner brought Charlotte through the kitchen and out the back door. Recognizing the Adirondack chairs and the placement of the clothesline Charlotte smiled. "Yes, this is the yard I saw. So that's where the woods lead to the cemetery?" she asked, pointing to the approximate location of where she'd stepped out of the tree line.

"That's right."

"How far is the Kendall house from here?"

"As the crow flies, you'd go through the woods that way." Mrs. Marner pointed to the right of the spot Charlotte had just indicated. "Cross over New Haven Road then up. The Kendall place is about halfway up the hill. There are two old houses up there. One's the Kendall place and the other belonged to a family named Wicker."

"The Wicker house is still there, too?" asked Charlotte. "Jerusha mentions the Wickers in her diary."

"Oh, yes, it's still there. Earl and Sadie Ormsbee live there. Been there a long time. Earl inherited it from his parents."

"Are the houses next door to each other?"

"No, not next door. There are quite a few houses between them, but none are as old as those two. People didn't live so close together back in those days. They had their farms and all, so they were more spread out. Developers have come in and built several houses between them. The Wicker house is higher up the hill."

"Do you think the Ormsbees would talk to me?"

Mrs. Marner chuckled. "Sadie Ormsbee will talk your ear off. If you want to hear ghost stories, she's the one to go to. She believes in all that hogwash. I mean no disrespect, you understand. Sadie's a good woman and a friend. It's just that some folks believe in ghosts, and some don't. She's one who does."

Charlotte could hardly contain her excitement. "Would she know the stories behind the rumors of the Kendall house being haunted?"

"If anyone knows, it would be Sadie. In fact, I was surprised Millie even told me what she did about hearing sounds. She knows I don't believe in that stuff. But she's friends with Sadie, too. Could be she's told her a lot more."

"Maybe Mrs. Ketchum was unnerved enough to want reassurance and figured you'd have a plausible explanation."

Mrs. Marner smiled at Charlotte. "You're a smart young lady. You're probably right. Anyhow, if you'd like, I could call Sadie and see if they'd be willing to talk to you."

"That would be wonderful. I'd really appreciate it."

"Then let's do it."

Back inside the house, Charlotte snacked on cookies and lemonade while Mrs. Marner phoned her friend. A few minutes later she rejoined Charlotte in the parlor.

"Good news. She'd be happy to talk with you. I knew she would. She wants to know could you come by next Saturday afternoon around two?"

"That would work fine."

"I'll let her know." Mrs. Marner went back to the kitchen. A moment later she returned with a piece of paper on which she'd written the Ormsbees' address and phone number and handed it to Charlotte.

"Thank you so much, Mrs. Marner. I can hardly wait to see the houses I've been reading about in Jerusha's diary. I'd like to drive by them when I leave here just to get a look at them. Could you give me directions, please?"

After her interview with Mrs. Marner concluded, Charlotte drove to the Ormsbee house. It sat atop a hill at the end of a long driveway. Not wanting to intrude, she contented herself with a long-distance view from the street. Continuing on, she came to 18 Farm Hill Road, the house where Jerusha had lived. It was down the hill from the Ormsbee place, situated much closer to the street. It was a two-story, red clapboard house with a sloping black roof. An addition jutted out from the side. She wondered if that had been added on during Jerusha's lifetime. There was only a small front yard, but a good-sized yard on one side, though only a tiny strip of grass on the other side between that house and the neighbor.

Charlotte tried to picture what it might have looked like in Jerusha's time. None of the other houses between this one and the Ormsbees had existed, nor had the road on which she was driving. Or, if it did, it was simply a dirt path. Charlotte figured out the way the family would have walked to get to the cemetery. If she had her geography right, they would have crossed what was now Farm Hill Road, walked up the hill, and gone about two blocks in today's landscape.

Charlotte would have liked to linger, but she didn't want to look suspicious so decided to move on. She would go home and write the letter to the current owners of Jerusha's home. She hoped they would agree to meet with her. How she would love to go inside the house, to walk the floors Jerusha and her family walked, to picture the things she was reading about in Jerusha's diary in their actual setting. She felt it was the closest she could ever come to meeting her ancestors.

Chapter 26

Late March 1832
Birch Falls, Vermont

Mud stuck to Mary's shoes as she trudged with Eli, Seth, Susannah, and Jerusha to the graveyard.

"No point in taking the cart. The wheels will only get stuck," Eli had said just before they set out.

Instead, Mary's shoes grew more mired with every step sucking her into the earth. She wished she could let the mud have its way. The snow had turned to slush in mid-March. Now at the end of the month, a few warm days had thawed the ground enough to change the dirt to an oozing muck threatening to swallow her with every step.

Mary could not have cared less about the fate of her shoes. It was the task at hand that caused her reluctance. When Lizzy had died on that brutally cold, snowy day in January the ground had been frozen solid. The funeral was held quickly, and the body removed to the graveyard's vault to await the spring when the earth would yield enough for a grave to be dug. At the time, Mary had wished they hadn't needed to put Lizzy in the vault. It felt like they were leaving her in a sort of limbo, yet the frozen ground and several inches of snow offered no other option. Now that the ground was pliable, Eli seemed in a hurry to have it done. Though Mary knew it was right and fitting to see that Lizzy was properly buried, it felt like experiencing her daughter's death all over again.

They were met at the vault by the entire Wicker family. Mary, Susannah, and Jerusha waited outside with Lavinia Wicker while the men went inside. The vault was dug into the side of a small hill leading up to the graveyard proper. From above, only a gently rolling mound in the earth signaled anything lay within the little hillside. In front, the vault had a double door set inside a marble façade. As she watched Eli and Seth enter with the Wickers, Mary shivered with the feeling that the temporary grave was swallowing them.

A few moments later, they all emerged, Eli and Seth, and Phineas and Joseph Wicker carrying Lizzy's coffin. As they climbed the hill, Seth's foot skidded on the muddy slope. The coffin dipped as he let go to steady himself. Asa Wicker, a year younger than Seth, stepped in to take his place. Watching Seth relinquish his spot without protest caused a squeezing sensation in Mary's chest. A sense of foreboding rooted her feet.

"Mother," Susannah whispered. "What is it?"

"Nothing," said Mary, not wanting to reveal her thoughts.

Seth's health had been deteriorating even before Lizzy's death. It had gone downhill rapidly ever since. Mary was surprised that Seth was able to join them today. He had barely risen from bed for several days at the start of the week. Yesterday, he did only a half-day's work. She'd urged him to stay home today, but Seth was adamant. Despite their bickering Seth and Lizzy had been close. Each adored the other though they'd never have admitted it aloud. Mary knew. She saw it in the way they looked at each other, in the hidden admiration of their teasing words. On her last day of life, Lizzy had known Seth would not be long in joining her. He was the one she reached out for. Despite his ill health, Seth would not absent himself from the duty of seeing Lizzy to her final resting place. That was why when he so easily yielded his place to Asa Wicker, Mary knew.

"Seth?" she asked, searching his face.

He kept his gaze downward.

"Tired," he said.

"It is hard to do this again," she said, understanding how sensitive Seth was to his loss of strength and vitality. Let him believe she thought his actions only reflected his sadness over the task at hand.

He glanced at her then. It was not a reproachful look, but one of resignation. She would have preferred the former. She could not hold his gaze knowing that before long she would make the trek to the graveyard again for him. Instead, she put her arm around his waist.

"This hill is difficult. Help me, please, son."

His arm went round her to assist, but it was Mary who supported him, clinging tightly, loathe to let go.

The grave had been dug the day before. All that was left was to set the coffin in and bury it. After saying a prayer, the men began shoveling the dirt onto the coffin, filling up the grave.

Eli had told Mary she needn't come. They'd had a funeral service right after Lizzy died. It wasn't necessary to endure this all over again. But she had insisted. It seemed wrong somehow not to be with Lizzy as she was finally laid to rest. Susannah and Jerusha had come, as had Lavinia Wicker. As Mary watched the clods of thick, muddy dirt fly from the shovels into the grave, heard the *thomp, thomp* as they hit the coffin, she wished she had taken Eli's advice. Her legs felt weak. She almost welcomed the thought of them giving way, sending her into the grave to be suffocated by the soil.

"There's no more for us to do here." It was Lavinia, her dear friend and neighbor, taking her arm, turning her, pulling her along on her numb legs. "Let them finish their work." Susannah and Jerusha followed.

They did not speak until they were out of the graveyard and on the road towards home. Then, in a forced casual tone, Lavinia stated, "Nan will arrive at the start of the week. It will be good to have a girl in the house to help again."

"Nan?" asked Mary. She felt as though she were floating outside her own body.

"Phineas's cousin's daughter, Nan. She is coming to stay with us for a while."

"Oh."

"She is fifteen. Sixteen before the summer ends. She will be of great help to me, I am sure. Her family is from Woodstock. Her father will bring her. He will stay a few days with us. Nan will stay a long while, I hope."

Lavinia's chatter slowly brought Mary back to the here and now.

"I hope she is a clever girl."

"Martha, her mother, says so. She has four other daughters so she can part with Nan for a while. Five girls and three boys all told." Lavinia sighed. "Oh, to have a mix of them. One cannot set a son to do a daughter's work or a daughter to do a son's. I am grateful for relatives who have a spare or two." Lavinia chuckled.

A spare or two. Suddenly the thought of no children, of all of them being gone, flashed through Mary's mind. First the babies that barely took breaths, then Rebecca, then Josie, then Lizzy, and soon Seth. Susannah would go to her husband in Ohio. She turned toward Jerusha who was walking behind her next to Susannah. Mary stopped. She stared into Jerusha's face. Her cheeks were red, but it was from the brisk March air, not fever. Her hazel eyes were the same. Wisps of dark brown hair escaped from beneath the sides of her bonnet.

"Mother?" asked Susannah.

Mary glanced at her oldest daughter. Seeing the questioning look on her face, she realized she had stopped them in the middle of the muddy road simply to stare at Jerusha.

"Mary?" This time it was Lavinia. "Are you quite well?"

"Yes," she said. She had returned her gaze to Jerusha. The girl looked as healthy as could be. She had shown no signs of any illness. For that matter, neither had Susannah. The doctors said they believed consumption to run in families, but that did not mean that every family member would succumb to it. Caroline Cutting had told her that no one, not even the trained physicians, really understood the disease. They were all guessing. Neither she nor Eli had ever suffered from consumption, though both had family members who had died from it. *Please, God, keep it from these two at least*, she prayed, before turning back to continue the trek home.

Mary had expected Lavinia to part from them when they reached the Wicker house, but instead she continued down the hill towards the Kendall home. Upon entering the house, Lavinia moved swiftly to the cookfire.

"What are you doing?" Mary asked.

"Making a cup of tea for you. Sit down, Mary."

Though she had work to do and no time to dawdle over tea, her wobbly legs made her grateful to sit. She watched as Lavinia busied herself with cups, saucers, and tea leaves. No need to tell here where to find what she needed. Lavinia and Mary knew each other's homes. What would she do without this kind, generous soul who always seemed to know what to do?

Chapter 27

April 1832
Birch Falls, Vermont

Jerusha wasn't sure what to make of Nan. The girl had been at the Wickers' for a few weeks now. Mrs. Wicker seemed pleased with her work. It was for certain she was industrious. Her energy reminded Jerusha of Lizzy in her healthy days, but in other ways she was quite different. Where Lizzy had had sparkling blue eyes, rosy cheeks, and a wide, almost ever-present smile, Nan was brown-eyed, thin-faced, and serious. Like Lizzy, Nan was strong and self-assured, but she had none of Lizzy's playfulness or sense of adventure. She went about her work with a single-minded determination. She was pleasant enough, but Jerusha found it difficult to warm up to her.

"She is not Lizzy and is not meant to be," Susannah told her one night as they lay in bed after Jerusha had poured out her heart. "You cannot replace Lizzy with Nan or anyone else." Her tone was not harsh. "You must let Nan be who she is. Besides, she has come to help Mrs. Wicker, not to be your playmate."

"I know that," said Jerusha. "It is just that I wanted to like her. We have lost so many. And you will leave when Zachary comes from Ohio to claim you. Then I will be alone. I had hoped Nan would be a sister to me." Try as she might, Jerusha could not hold back a sniffle.

Susannah folded Jerusha into her arms. "You are too young to bear this. Only nine and you have already lost so many."

The words of understanding broke whatever held back the floodgates in Jerusha. She soaked the front of

Susannah's shift with her tears. Susannah held her tightly, caressing her hair.

"Will you write to me often after you leave?" Jerusha asked once she could speak.

"As often as I am able," Susannah promised.

"And tell me all about Ohio and your home and Zachary and your new friends and neighbors. I want to know everything so I can picture you and feel as though I am there with you."

"And you must write to me, as well," said Susannah. "You must tell me how you are getting on at home and school and how Mother and Father and Seth are doing. I will count on you to keep me held fast to my family at home."

"I promise," said Jerusha.

The next morning Jerusha went to the Wickers with a wheel of cheese that was owed to them. Nan let her in, taking the cheese to place in the pantry. The clacking of the loom drew Jerusha further into the house.

"You have begun!" she exclaimed.

Mrs. Wicker looked up. "Oh, Jerusha," she said. "I have just started on a coverlet for Mrs. Cutting. Nan is setting up the dye pots in the dooryard."

"But the sheep are not sheared yet," said Jerusha, confused.

"This is what is left of last year's wool." She indicated a pile of skeins on the table. "I want to use that up and the weather is mild. I will work on Mrs. Cutting's coverlet while Nan dyes the wool for this year's orders."

Jerusha looked beyond her to the two dishes sitting on a table near the door. She crossed the room to peek into them. Mrs. Wicker rose from her bench to stand beside her.

"I know this is indigo," said Jerusha, pointing to the small bowl filled with deep blue chips. "Mother uses that to dye some of our clothes."

"Indigo does not fade with washing like some others do," explained Mrs. Wicker, "so we use it often for our most common clothes. But this is the one I am looking forward to using." She held up the dish containing what appeared to be tiny pebbles.

"What is it?" asked Jerusha.

"Cochineal. I was delighted to find it the last time I went to Mr. Hapgood's store."

"I have never heard of it," said Jerusha, reaching in to scoop up a small handful. "Where does it come from?"

"Mexico. They grind up the cochineal beetles to be used in dye."

"Ew!" Quickly, Jerusha slide back into the bowl. "I thought dyes were made from plants."

"Most are, but cochineal makes a wonderful scarlet dye."

"If Mother will allow it, may I help with the dyeing?" Jerusha had been nearly transfixed last year when she beheld the strands of wool in a variety of colors after they had been dyed. She longed to be part of the magic of turning plain white wool into a rainbow of colors.

"Your mother may need you for other things. Besides, I would like to get as much done today as possible. This warmth is uncommon for April, and I daresay it won't hold for long. I have had many requests from neighbors this year. There are only so many hours in a day."

"I wish Mother was a weaver" said Jerusha. "I would rather do this than make butter and cheese."

"Dairying is needed work, Jerusha. Your mother is a fine hand at it. Susannah has learned well from her and so will you."

"But I would prefer to weave." Movement outside the window caught Jerusha's eye. Nan was bustling about the dooryard, stoking fires beneath two large black pots hanging from trestles. She'd be setting up the dyes soon.

"May I help if Mother allows?" I will run home now and ask her."

"If she is agreeable."

That was all the encouragement Jerusha needed. She ran down the hill and burst through the door calling, "Mother! Mother!"

"What is it, Jerusha?" Her mother hurried to the kitchen.

Nearly breathless, Jerusha said, "Mrs. Wicker is dyeing wool today. She said I may help if you will allow it. May I, please?"

"I thought Nan was helping her."

"Yes, but she said I could help, too."

"Jerusha, there is but a month before Zachary returns to collect Susannah and you have much to learn. There will be a good many things Susannah can do that you will not be able to yet, but I need you learn as much as you can so that you will be of help to me once she has gone."

"But Mother—"

"I am sorry. Now run upstairs and help Susannah."

Dejected, Jerusha started across the kitchen for the stairs when the door burst open making her spin around to see her father supporting Seth.

"What happened?" asked her mother, hurrying to them.

"A fit came upon him in the barn so bad he could not catch his breath. I had him sit until it calmed. Then he thought to get back to work, but once he stood it began again."

Two of the Wicker boys came often to help but knowing others were doing his work brought such a melancholy upon Seth that it was decided to let him do what he could.

"Come. Sit at the table," said her mother to Seth. "I will get you some water."

He sat, quiet for a moment. But when he tried to speak, he was again wracked with coughing. Jerusha did not hear her sister come up behind her until Susannah gasped making Jerusha jump. All eyes turned towards her then back to Seth at whom Susannah was staring in horror.

It was then that Jerusha noticed the flecks of blood on his shirt front. Jerusha felt a familiar sinking in the pit of her stomach. Her mother, setting down the cup of water, took Seth's face in her hands.

"He is burning up," she said.

"I will go for Doctor Eacker," said their father hurrying out the door.

Jerusha's mother looked over Jerusha's head to Susannah.

"Mrs. Cutting?" asked Susannah.

"Quickly," said her mother.

Susannah rushed from the house.

Then Jerusha's mother turned to her. "Pull back the covers on the bed," she said with a wave of her hand toward the next room.

Jerusha went at once to do her mother's bidding, but it took all her courage. She'd hated the downstairs bedchamber since Rebecca had died there. Now that it was also the site of Josie's and Lizzy's deaths, she avoided it as though it was cursed.

Quickly, she turned down the coverlet, blanket, and sheet. She backed out of the room as her mother brushed by her helping Seth into bed.

Jerusha stood on the threshold watching as her mother pressed a cold, wet cloth to his forehead. She remembered standing in just this place, watching the same scene play out three times before. She knew how it ended.

A knock sounded at the door.

"See to that, please," her mother directed, never glancing up from her ministrations.

Jerusha opened the door to find Chauncey Haskell peering down at her.

"Good day, Mr. Haskell," she said.

"Good day to you, young miss. I have come to see your father about an important matter. I did not spy him in the fields nor was he about in the yard or the barns."

"He went for the doctor."

Mr. Haskell's eyes widened. "Your brother, then?" he asked.

Jerusha nodded.

Her mother called from the next room, inquiring who was at the door.

"Mr. Haskell," she called back.

Jerusha's mother appeared on the threshold of the kitchen. "Well, do not leave Mr. Haskell standing in the doorway, child.

"You are welcome to wait for Eli to return, sir."

Coughing erupted from the bedchamber. Mary's head turned in that direction.

"I need to see Phineas as well. I will take myself to the Wickers and return later."

Mary nodded. "Jerusha, show Mr. Haskell out," she said, hurrying back to Seth.

He turned to her before leaving. "God be with the poor lad," he said as he exited the house.

Jerusha felt like a shadow as she stood in the bedchamber doorway watching her mother, Susannah, and Mrs. Cutting fuss over Seth. When her father returned with Doctor Eacker and the usual squabbling began between him and Mrs. Cutting, she took herself to the garret. She knew there were chores she should be doing but she hadn't the energy for them. Instead, she huddled on the floor by the window staring up at the handful of puffy clouds floating across the sky. Jerusha wished she could float away like the clouds, away from the constant illness and death, away from arguing adults, away from the scourge of consumption.

She had no idea how long she sat there willing herself away. It was the tapping of footsteps on the garret stairs that pulled her back to herself.

"There you are," said Susannah settling down next to her. "We wondered where you went. What are you doing up here?"

She had no answer. She just wanted to escape the sick room. "Is the doctor still here?"

"No. He gave Seth cod liver oil but said there wasn't much more he could do. Mrs. Cutting is rubbing him with vinegar water while a simple is brewing."

"Will that help?" Jerusha asked, but she knew the answer.

Susannah shrugged. "He is quieter now. Perhaps he will get some sleep. Come downstairs. We have much work to catch up on. I need you to help me. I think Mother will want to stay with Seth as much as she can."

When Jerusha was on her way to the well, she saw Mr. Haskell and her father talking just outside the barn. Something about the look on her father's face made her stop. She was too far away to hear them. Mr. Haskell's back was to her, he rocked forward, his arms gesticulating rapidly. Her father noticed her.

"What is it, Jerusha? Is something wrong?"

"No, Father," she called back.

Mr. Haskell followed him, grabbing his arm. Her father paid him no mind, pulling away and striding forward. All of his attention was focused on Jerusha. Was he angry with her?

But his voice was gentle. Where are you going?"

"To the well to fetch water."

"I will go with you."

How odd, thought Jerusha. Why would he do that?

"Eli, you have got to listen to me." Mr. Haskell had just reached them.

Her father turned. "I have heard what you have to say, Chauncey. You need say no more."

That was the tone of voice that matched the expression Jerusha had seen on his face. Perhaps it was Mr. Haskell who was in trouble. But why?

Jerusha's father abruptly turned his back on Mr. Haskell. The peculiar actions of adults this day made her feel as though the world were spinning out of control.

"Think on what I said. That is all I ask. It cannot do harm and may be the only thing that saves you. But do not let time run out," Mr. Haskell stated before sauntering away.

His words sent a shiver down Jerusha's spine.

"What did he mean, Father?" she asked, not sure she wanted to know.

He glanced down at her, his face enraged. It frightened her more than Mr. Haskell's confusing words.

"Nothing you need to worry about," he said. His tone was quiet, but Jerusha sensed that he was working hard to control his voice.

Chapter 28

August 1973
Middlebury, Vermont

Charlotte had been coming home exhausted every night, partly from the actual work, but, she was sure, more from the emotional drain of putting her heart and soul into a project that had been stolen out from under her.

Work nights usually saw her fall into bed not long after cleaning up from supper. Upon returning from her visit with Mrs. Marner in Birch Falls, she felt reenergized. She was nearly finished reading Jerusha's diary. She'd been deliberately slow with it, trying to piece things together as she went along. Nonetheless, she would have finished it a long time ago if she hadn't been so wiped out after work every night.

Upon returning to her apartment from Birch Falls, she immediately slipped on her cotton gloves, grabbed the diary, and plopped down in the beanbag chair to read. Like so many entries, most of what she read was a mere recounting of weather, chores, and random details of daily life. As she neared the end of the diary she began to wonder if Jerusha had written anything more of interest. Stifling a yawn, she turned the page. The next entry was dated the eighth of September in 1839. What followed made Charlotte sit as upright as one could in a beanbag chair.

While cleaning the parlor today, I accidentally knocked Father's account book from his desk. He must have forgotten to put it away last night, so I opened the drawer to set it in its place. In the drawer was an old letter written in Mother's hand, but it was not her usual careful script. It looked wild. Perhaps it was wrong of me to do so, but I could not help myself. I read it.

It was addressed to her sister, my Aunt Helen. The date was the first of May 1832, the day after we buried Seth. She wrote that her dearest ones had betrayed her; her neighbors and friends had become her enemies. I could scarcely believe it when I read, 'even Eli whose loyal helpmeet I have been for more than a quarter of a century has taken sides against me, wounding me to my heart's core. How could he do this? How could they all do such an abominable thing to our dear Lizzy. I can never fathom nor forgive.'

I stood frozen at these words. The letter was never concluded but left off in the middle of a sentence. I searched the drawer but found no sign of the rest. It was only the sound of approaching footsteps that forced me to hastily replace it in the drawer.

I know it is wrong and I should not have read it, but Mother will never tell me and after all these years I must know. I only wish she had finished the letter so that I could learn what I have wanted to know for so long, though had she finished and posted it, I would not have seen it at all. It left me all the more confused. How could anyone have done anything to Lizzy? She had been gone from us for three months. Had mother meant to write Seth? And what had anyone done to him? I feel, as I write this, just as I did upon reading those words, completely bereft of understanding. No one we know, and certainly not Father, would ever have harmed Lizzy or Seth. It is beyond my comprehension what Mother could have meant, but I feel certain it is the key to learning what has led her down the path she has trod since Seth died.

I have made up my mind and have laid a plan. Tomorrow I will

"What? Tomorrow you will what?" Charlotte nearly yelled.

The diary ended without completing the sentence. Jerusha had run out of room on the last page. There had to have been another diary at hand where she'd continued.

The phone rang and Charlotte fought her way out of the beanbag chair to answer it.

"Hi, Charlotte," her sister's voice chirped over the line.

"Tracy. Is Grandma okay?"

"She's fine. Hey, there are only two weeks left before Dad comes to pick me up. Gram thought it would be fun for me to spend my last weekend in Vermont with you. Mom said it was okay. She's already mailed a check to you. She wants you to take me shopping for new school clothes. Can I come up next weekend?"

"Um. I guess. I'll come Friday after work to get you. But we'll only have Saturday. I'll have to get you back to Grandma's on Sunday. I've got work Monday morning."

Charlotte picked up the envelope sitting on the kitchen counter, a letter addressed to the Paquettes, the people who now owned what was once the Kendall home. She had hoped to visit them on Saturday, fitting it in before or after she met with Sadie Ormsbee. Well, it could wait, she supposed.

"Listen," Tracy interrupted her thoughts. "You don't have to get me. Keith is going home this weekend. He's got to get ready to leave for UVM and said he'd give me a ride."

"Oh," said Charlotte, noting the excitement in Tracy's voice. Her sister's crush on their grandmother's helper had been flourishing all summer.

"He can bring me up on Friday, before you get home from work, but I guess I can hang around your neighborhood until you get home."

"No way. Mom would kill us both. I'll ask my neighbor, Mrs. Pleasant, if you can stay at her place until I get home."

"Cool. I can't wait. What do you want to do? Besides buying boring school clothes, I mean."

"We'll figure it out. Hey, don't run up Grandma's phone bill. This is long-distance. I'll see you Friday."

After hanging up, Charlotte tapped the letter against the countertop, lost in thought. Now that Jerusha's diary had left her hanging, she was more eager than ever to see her home. Plus she had the feeling that Sadie Ormsbee would be full of stories about Eliza's legend and any hauntings of the Kendall house. Maybe she could take Tracy with her. They could do clothes shopping in on Friday night after grabbing a pizza.

Charlotte walked across the hall to knock on Iris Pleasant's door. Heidi opened it.

"Hey, I was on my way to your place to ask if you want to try candle making with me."

"Um. Sure. Is your aunt home?"

Charlotte quickly got permission from Mrs. Pleasant to have Tracy stay with her on Friday afternoon until Charlotte got home from work, then she and Heidi decided to walk out to the mailbox.

"So the diary just ends there? In the middle of a sentence?" asked Heidi when Charlotte finished telling her everything she'd read.

"Yeah."

"Man! Just when it was getting good."

"Tell me about it," said Charlotte. "It's so frustrating."

"Are you still going back up there on the weekend? What about your sister?"

Charlotte explained her plan.

"I know," said Heidi. "I'll see if Kate can swap weekends with me. She owes me for taking one of hers last month. I'll come with you. I'd love to get inside those two houses and see if I pick up any vibes. Maybe we could hit the cemetery again, too. Do you think the Paquettes would let us hold a séance at their house? Then we could ask Jerusha if there's another diary and where it is."

"Maybe we should just see how things go before we start asking for favors," Charlotte answered, hoping to rein in some of Heidi's enthusiasm.

Charlotte was delighted to answer the phone on Thursday evening and find Julie Paquette on the other line.

"Andy and I would really like to have you come up on Saturday if you can fit it in around your other visit," Julie told her.

Charlotte had to force herself not to squeal in delight. "I could definitely do that. I won't be alone, though. My sister will be with me for the weekend and a friend really wants to come, too."

"That's fine. I just...I want to know if..." Julie seemed to be having trouble finding the words.

"Is something wrong?" Charlotte asked. "Would a different weekend work better?"

"No. It's not that. You said you're a folklorist, right?"

"Yes."

"I'm not really sure what a folklorist does, but would you know anything about strange occurrences?"

Charlotte felt the hair on the back of her neck stand up.

"Strange occurrences?" she asked. "Like what?"

"Oh, it's probably nothing. Andy thinks I have an over-active imagination, but I think...well, I don't really know how to explain it. I'm alone right now. I don't want to talk about it over the phone. I'll tell you when you get here."

After hanging up the phone, Charlotte bolted across the hall. Mrs. Pleasant answered the door, informing her that Heidi was working the night shift and wouldn't be home until late. Charlotte returned to her apartment so wound up she barely knew what to do with herself. Finally, she decided on writing out a list of questions for both Sadie Ormsbee and Julie Paquette.

Feeling a little sheepish, she lit the candle inside the holder she'd made with Heidi, the one with the decoupaged magazine images of Halloween. Every time she looked at it, she remembered how Heidi had tried to convince her that she should go back to school for her doctorate. Maybe it was silly to want to use it now, but as she worked, she found her thoughts drifting towards the formation of a dissertation. The candleholder gave her some weird confidence that it could actually happen someday. If only she had the rest of Jerusha's writings. More than ever, she needed to know what had happened.

Chapter 29

April 1832
Birch Falls, Vermont

Lavinia leaned toward Mary across the kitchen table. "It's the only way, Mary. I would not suggest it if I did not believe that to be so."

"I will not have it."

"Mary, I understand that it is hard for you. I would feel the same. But I would do it to save the rest of my family."

Mary drew a sharp breath. She could scarcely accept that she was hearing such things from Lavinia. Part of her half-believed she was dreaming. She hoped she would awaken soon to laugh at herself for entertaining such ridiculous fancies even in sleep. But this was all too real.

"It is absurd, Lavinia."

"Chauncey Haskell has read about it in the papers. They have done it in other places."

Mary let out a laugh that was anything but amused. "Chauncey Haskell. I should have known he was the source of this nonsense. I want no part of whatever mischief he is brewing. The nerve of him to suggest such horrid things."

Lavinia shook her head, reaching across the table to take Mary's hand.

"No, Mary. This was not one of the tales he tells by the fireside. I assure you he was in earnest. He knows this has been done before. He said–"

"I will hear no more of this!" Mary pulled her hand from Lavinia's. "Now, if you please, I have much work to do as I am sure you do." She rose from her chair.

"Susannah and Jerusha are in the dairy. I have left them long enough."

Lavinia rose, nodded, and headed towards the door. Just before letting herself out, she turned back. "You may have no choice, Mary," she murmured.

Mary remained staring at the closed door after she left. Her feet were frozen to the floor, though her heart pounded as if she was running for her life. She knew Chauncey had not concocted what Lavinia came to propose. Seth had read it aloud to all of them from the newspaper the first night they had put Josie in the downstairs bedchamber. She remembered being horror struck by the tale to the point of throwing the paper into the fire after the others had left the room. To think it should be proposed to her. And by her most cherished friend.

Though Eli had blown out the candle once they'd climbed into bed that night, Mary could see by the moonlight that he remained sitting up.

"Is something the matter?" she asked.

"You tell me."

Mary pushed herself up to sit beside him. "What do you mean?"

"You have been uneasy all evening. And do not say it is worry over Seth. I know what worry over sick children looks like upon you. This is different. Something else is troubling you. I assumed you would not want to speak of it before others, but now that we are alone, I hope you will feel able to unburden yourself."

"Am I so transparent to you then?" she asked, almost smiling despite herself.

A subtle laugh escaped him. "My darling, by now I should think we can read one another without any words at all. I am certain you are able to do so with me."

Mary's eyes closed as Eli's finger gently traced the outline of her jaw, stopping to rest at her chin. "So, my dear Mary, what is it that troubles you?"

Mary sighed. She hadn't wanted to burden Eli with Chauncey and Lavinia's foolishness.

"Lavinia came by today to propose a – dare I say it – a very unseemly suggestion regarding a cure for Seth.

Eli snickered. "Ah, more of Lavinia's superstitions?"

"I suppose it is a superstition, though this one came from Chauncey Haskell."

Mary felt Eli stiffen next to her. In the near-dark she thought she saw his jaw clench. His voice, that by turns had been gentle and amused, grew stern. "Chauncey Haskell? What did he propose?"

Mary's heart began to race at the sudden change in Eli. "It was a half-witted notion no sane person would countenance and not worth repeating."

"Mary, tell me." He sat up straighter, leaning towards her. "Chauncey cornered me yesterday and urged me to do something I found repulsive. I told him so. I believe he went to Lavinia, encouraging her to talk you into it."

Mary gasped. "What? What did he say?" She could barely get the words out.

"I had not thought to disturb you with it. I had hoped my refusal had put an end to it, but I see that I was wrong. Do you remember the night Seth read to us from the newspaper the account of people in Woodstock who dug up the bodies of a family to learn if one was coming back to sicken the others?"

"Yes," Mary whispered. She was shaking now. "It is what Lavinia proposed. Eli, we cannot do it." Tears sprang to her eyes. "We cannot." She fell forward into his arms. "How could they ask it of us? They are our friends."

"They mean well, I suppose," he said, holding her close. "But no. Of course, we will never do such an abominable thing."

The next afternoon Lavinia returned, Nan in tow. Mary, Susannah, and Jerusha were busy in the kitchen.

"Mary, may we speak with you alone?" Lavinia asked.

Mary nodded, wondering at Nan's presence. She led them into the parlor.

"I want you to hear what Nan has to say."

Mary looked at the girl. What might she say that could not be said in front of others? Nan's doe-brown eyes looked directly into Mary's, but her face held no emotion Mary could discern. "What is this about?" she asked.

"It is about our discussion yesterday," said Lavinia.

At that Mary took a step back. "I thought I made it clear that I will hear no more on that subject."

"You must hear what Nan has to say. She has knowledge of it. You do remember the girl is from Woodstock. They have done it there twice. Go on, Nan. Tell her."

Mary glanced back at Nan who continued to look her in the eye.

"It is true, Mrs. Kendall," the girl said. "I saw it myself."

"What?" Mary gasped.

"The Piersons live nearby my family. My father was among those who helped with the digging. First it was Ellen, but she showed no signs. Isaac, now he was different. He was turned on his side."

"I do not suppose a corpse goes about changing position on its own," Lavinia interrupted. "It goes against the natural way of things." She gave a sharp nod of her head as if that settled the matter.

"There was more, though," Nan continued. "When they brought him up out of the grave, there was blood at his mouth. I saw it myself."

"You were there? You watched this?" Mary was aghast. Nan would have been about thirteen at the time. How could her family have allowed it?

"I was indeed. We were all there. The whole town turned out."

"Go on," urged Lavinia. "Tell what happened next. Tell about the doctors."

"Doctors Blake and Merriman were there. They examined the body, cut open the chest and took out the heart."

Mary clapped a hand over her mouth. "The young man's family?" she whispered. "Were they there?"

"They were. Most interested of all they were, of course, it being of such importance for them to know the truth of it. Benjamin was sick. He was the only one left. He was there, as well. They hoped to cure him by finding who was causing his illness."

Mary could not believe what she was hearing. "People do not come back from the dead to do harm to their family."

"But they do," Nan insisted. "We saw the corpse. We saw how it was not as it should be. Surely, that cannot be natural."

"Something evil must have taken possession of it, Mary," said Lavinia. "How else do you explain what was found when they opened that grave?"

"I am sure I do not know. I am equally sure you do not know either. Neither of you."

"But Mrs. Kendall, the cure worked. That must prove it to be true."

"What do you mean it worked? What cure?"

"They took the heart straight to the blacksmith's shop, burned it on Mr. Horton's forge. Benjamin was brought right to it while it burned and told to breathe deeply. That was two years ago, and he lives still."

"That means nothing," said Mary. "Consumptive people can live a very long time with the disease. It often comes and goes and sometimes it goes for a very long while. Years even."

"But the others, Isaac and Ellen. They went so quickly. It does seem that if Benjamin were to die of it, he would have gone soon, too."

"Ask Mrs. Cutting," said Mary. "She will tell you that is not always the way. It is different for everyone. None of this makes any sense. It is appalling." Mary turned her attention back to Lavinia. "I will have no more talk of it. No one is going to dig up my children. Do you understand?"

A gasp came from the parlor doorway. Susannah stood on the threshold. All heads turned in her direction.

"Mother?" she asked. Her face had gone white.

"Excuse me," Mary said to Lavinia and Nan. She went to Susannah, leading her from the parlor.

"Mother, what was that about digging up your children?"

"Nothing, Susannah. What did you want to tell me?"

"I...has that been suggested? Like what Seth read to us in the paper when Josie took ill?"

Mary pulled Susannah close. "It has been proposed and denied," she whispered. "Say nothing of this to anyone, especially Jerusha."

The same warning was given to Lavinia and Nan. Nan looked sufficiently alarmed when Mary sternly warned them, "Never speak a word of this foolishness to or in front of Jerusha. You will give the child night terrors. She has had enough to contend with in her nine years. Do you understand?" Having obtained promises from both Lavinia and Nan to keep Jerusha in the dark, she saw them out.

Mary prayed Lavinia would respect her feelings and relinquish the whole idea. She felt torn apart by the anger and resentment she experienced toward her dearest friend. There was almost nothing she wished for more than for both of them to forget the whole subject and return to their normal accord.

That evening she related to Eli how Lavinia had brought Nan to convince her. "We must put a stop to this, Eli," she begged.

"I will speak to Phineas in the morning. He will tell Lavinia not to bother you with such notions again."

As she began to drift off to sleep, a crash resounded from the floor below. Mary and Eli were out of bed and racing down the stairs as fast as the light from one candle allowed. Upon entering the bedchamber, they found Seth on the floor, the bedside table overturned, and the floor wet from a spilled pitcher of water. Susannah, who had been sitting vigil with Seth, was attempting to help him back into bed. It was obvious what caused the crash, but the din continued as Seth's body shook with a horrid wracking cough.

"What happened?" asked Eli.

"Seth began to cough," Susannah explained. "I tried to give him a drink, but his coughing worsened. It got so bad he began to shake. When it slowed down a bit he tried to stand, but then it came on him again, worse than before. He lost his balance. He fell over before I could catch him and knocked over the table.

The three of them worked to get Seth back to bed, right the table, and wipe up the spilled water. Once Seth was somewhat quieted, Susannah told them, "He had been sleeping. Just before he started coughing, he awoke. He kept saying someone was sitting on his chest. I told him he must have dreamed it, but he was insistent. Then the horrible coughing started."

Mary reached out a hand to Seth's face. "He's a bit feverish," she said. "We will give him willow bark before it gets any worse," she said, going out to the kitchen for the remedy.

Upon returning, she found Seth propped up with pillows, his breathing ragged.

"I saw her," he said, between panting breaths. "She was here."

"Saw who?" asked Mary, handing him the cup.

Seth was about to answer when his strength gave out. He lay back on the pillows, nearly dropping the cup. Mary grabbed it, held it to his lips as he drank.

Once Seth was asleep, she turned to Eli and Susannah. "Who was he talking about?" she asked.

Eli and Susannah exchanged glances.

"Lizzy," Susannah said. "He said she had come for him."

Chapter 30

August 1973
Middlebury, Vermont

"Keith, I didn't expect you to still be here." Charlotte arrived at Iris Pleasant's apartment to collect Tracy before going across the hall to her own.

"We got a later start than I expected. I had a bunch of last-minute things I wanted to finish up for my grandparents before we left."

"They've been here less than an hour," said Mrs. Pleasant. "I invited Keith to rest for a bit before continuing on."

"That was very nice," said Charlotte as Keith lifted his glass of iced tea.

"He's been telling me all about his preparations to go off to college," Mrs. Pleasant continued. "I told him I hope he finds a nice girl while he's there."

Charlotte fought the urge to roll her eyes.

"I'm taking Tracy out for pizza before we go clothes shopping. Would you like to come?" she asked Keith.

Tracy perked up. "You are? Cool! I love pizza."

Charlotte noticed that Tracy's curly pigtails showed streaks of blond. Apparently, she'd decided to go for the Cathy Rigby look.

"I won't say no to pizza, either," said Keith.

"Why are we going shopping tonight?" Tracy asked as they slid into the booth at the pizza parlor. "Wouldn't you rather go tomorrow?"

"Nope," said Charlotte. "We've got something else to do tomorrow."

"What?"

"We are going to Birch Falls."

"The town where the family vampire lived?" Tracy asked, eyes widening.

"That's right. Eliza, or Lizzy I guess is what Jerusha called her."

"I thought you already went." Charlotte had kept up a correspondence with her sister and their grandmother all summer, updating them on her progress with Jerusha's diary and her trip with Heidi to the cemetery. She hadn't yet told them about her visit to Mrs. Marner, though.

"Tomorrow we are going to visit Jerusha's house."

"Is that the one Mom says is haunted?"

"Haunted?" asked Keith. "You've got vampires and a haunted house?"

Charlotte explained everything from her mother's revelation that there was rumored to be a haunted house owned by one of their ancestors and her visit with Mrs. Marner.

"That is so cool!" said Tracy. "I can't wait to see it."

"I wish I was going with you," said Keith.

"Can't you come?" asked Tracy.

"My mom will flip if I don't get home so she can supervise my preparations to leave for college," he said.

Their pizza, covered in onions, mushrooms, and green peppers, arrived just then. Talking stopped briefly while they each lifted steaming slices onto their plates.

"I hope you'll let me know how it goes." said Keith.

"Can I have your address?" Tracy asked. "I'll write to you and tell you everything."

Charlotte couldn't help a smile. Tracy's crush on Keith was obviously still at full strength.

"Um, sure," he said. "But I won't be at home that long before I leave for UVM."

"You can send me that address when you know it," she told him, beaming.

"Yeah. Okay, I guess."

Noticing the look of mild embarrassment on Keith's face, Charlotte decided to change the subject.

"I've been wondering if there might be another diary in the house. It's driving me crazy the way it just ended in the middle of a sentence. There has to be another one that picks up where Jerusha left off."

"Wouldn't someone have found it by now?" asked Keith.

"I suppose. You know, I've never thought to ask my grandmother where the one I've got came from. I think her mother gave it to her, but I wonder if she told her how she came by it."

"Can't hurt to ask."

When they finished eating, Keith said goodbye and continued north. Tracy hopped into Charlotte's car. "He is so cute," she gushed.

"Forget it," Charlotte said, laughing. "He's way too old for you."

"I can still look, can't I?"

A few hours later, they returned to Charlotte's apartment laden with shopping bags full of school clothes.

"Got any chips?" Tracy asked after she stashed the bags in a corner of the living room.

"You can still eat?" asked Charlotte. They had stopped for hot fudge sundaes after shopping.

"Yeah. Why?"

"Because I'm stuffed. But, yeah, here you go," she said, tossing a bag of potato chips to her sister who had bounced down on the couch. After grabbing an Orange Crush for each of them, Charlotte joined her.

"Where am I sleeping?" Tracy asked.

"With me, I guess. There's only one bedroom. Unless you want to sleep on the couch."

"Got another beanbag chair?"

"No. Why?"

"If you push two together you can sleep on them like a bed."

"Hmm. Heidi has one. I'll go ask her. By the way, she's coming with us tomorrow. Did you meet her?"

"Nope. She was still working while I was at Mrs. Pleasant's."

"She should be home by now. I'll go see."

A few moments later Charlotte returned with Heidi and the extra beanbag chair. After they set it down next to Charlotte's, Tracy plopped onto them, stretched out full.

"See?" she said. "I do this all the time when I sleep at my friend, Debbie's house."

"If you say so," said Charlotte.

After Charlotte grabbed another soda for Heidi, the three of them started talking about their plans for the next day.

"Can you really talk to ghosts?" Tracy asked Heidi.

"Sort of. It's not quite like we're doing now. I just get some really strong vibes, you know? It's hard to explain, but it's kind of like I can sense when they're present."

"What if you sense them in Jerusha's old house? I mean, do they ever say anything to you?"

"In a way. I get a sense of what they're trying to say."

"That is so cool. I hope you hear some when we get there."

After Heidi left, Charlotte and Tracy changed into their nightgowns.

"Need a pillow?" Charlotte asked as Tracy stretched out on the beanbags beneath the open window. A soft summer breeze lifted the curtains.

"Nope."

"Blanket?"

"It's pretty warm."

"Here, take this anyway," she said, tossing the red and brown crocheted afghan from the couch to Tracy. "You can use it if the temperature drops."

Climbing into her own bed, Charlotte's thoughts drifted to her one ghostly experience from her childhood. She still only half-believed it was real. Yet, she couldn't shake a shadow of the fear she remembered from that time. She wasn't sure what she was hoping for from tomorrow's visit to the old Kendall and Wicker homesteads. There was something tugging at her, something she could not put a name to. It was as though something otherworldly was calling to her, pulling her towards this adventure for its own purposes.

That's ridiculous, she berated herself. *This is research. It might turn into a dissertation.* Trying to force her thoughts towards the purely academic, she finally fell asleep and dreamed she was conducting an interview with a ghost who was sitting in a mountain of fake vampire teeth.

Chapter 31

Late April 1832
Birch Falls, Vermont

"You could not stop them?" Mary was dumbfounded.

Eli had just come into the kitchen. Susannah and Jerusha had gone to bed. Mary had been sitting up with Seth who slept fitfully awaiting Eli's return.

He dropped into a chair before the kitchen fire. "I tried, Mary. I offered every argument."

Mary sat next to him, her face in her hands. She felt stunned, as though her brain was surrounded by a thick fog.

For the past two weeks Lavinia Wicker and Chauncey Haskell had been stirring up their neighbors, Lavinia talking to all the women and Chauncey loitering at the country store accosting everyone who entered. Eli's request to Phineas that he insist his wife refrain from such talk had either fallen on deaf ears or he had no ability or desire to restrain her. Many people refused to believe that a spirit had invaded the corpse of one of the deceased Kendall children, but they were able to convince a sufficient number. Chauncey, with his long years of honing his story-telling skills held enough folks enthralled. And Lavinia, so convinced of her dearly held superstitions as to be persuasive by pure force, had succeeded in gathering enough adherents to increase the pressure on Mary and Eli to accede to their wishes.

Mary had been so vigorous in her refusal that horrible quarrels followed. Finally, an assemblage of

Lavinia and Chauncey's convert, or mob, as Mary now thought of them, had taken it upon themselves to go as a body to the town selectmen to force the issue. Eli had gotten wind of their plan and set out to join them with every intention of putting an end to this foolishness. The selectmen, after all, were reasonable men. Surely, they would see the madness of what was being proposed.

"The selectmen agreed?" Mary asked.

"Whether they believe or not is questionable, but they were persuaded that letting this rabble have their way was in the best interests of all."

"What could have made them think so?"

"When Chauncey put forth his argument, they scoffed at first. Then others insisted. They claimed it has been done in other places. That we know is true."

"And how much good did it do in those other places? Did anyone think to ask that?"

"The notion of its effectiveness did not seem to be in question."

Mary huffed.

Eli continued. "I thought they were ready to dismiss the idea when Benjamin Hawn spoke up. He said Lavinia told his wife that if something was not done to put an end to it then once our family is gone the spirit that is taking their lives will move on to others. It will go to all the families, taking all their loved ones, perhaps even spawning more of its kind. The assemblage was nearly hysterical upon hearing of such a possibility. Benjamin swore Nan assured them that is why it was done in Woodstock, to stop not only the taking of that one family, but to spare the whole town."

"The selectmen gave credence to such wild imaginings?" Mary's breath caught in her chest so that she almost couldn't speak the next words. "And so it is to be, and there is naught we can do to stop it?"

Eli dropped his gaze. He looked tired, beaten. "Yes," was all he said.

Mary and Eli sat side-by-side, silent, staring into the fire. Finally, Mary gathered enough courage to ask, "When?"

"Saturday next. The selectmen insisted that the Regulator of Funerals be present."

"Mr. Jackman? Why?"

"It is his job to see that burials are done properly. He is to oversee it."

"This is not a burial, but the opposite," she whispered. "Which of our children will they..." she couldn't say the words.

"All of them. Until they find the one they think responsible."

Mary felt her face crumple. Anger stirred like a whirlwind within her. "And when they find all of them to be in the normal state of the dead? What then?"

"Then they will owe us a tremendous apology."

She lifted her chin. "They owe us that now," she said, nearly spitting out the words. "There is truly naught we can do?" she asked. "Was Mr. Jackman at the meeting?"

"No."

"Then how do you know he will agree?"

"I suppose the selectmen will simply insist he do it."

"What of your good Doctor Eacker? He could not agree to this, could he?"

"I doubt if he would, but he was not present, and I do not know if his opinion would sway them."

"Ask him," she said. "And I will seek out Reverend Cobb on the morrow. He would never agree to this. They must listen to him."

"He is away, Mary. He will not be back before the Sabbath."

Mary groaned. She had forgotten that Reverend and Mrs. Cobb had gone off to visit their daughter and baptize their newest grandchild.

"The doctor then. And I know Caroline Cutting is against it. Perhaps they can make them see reason."

Eli drew a deep breath. "They are frightened, Mary. They believe this. You did not see them tonight. It was as though the devil himself was hounding them. They fear for the lives of their own families. We can try, but I doubt there will be any way to stop them."

On the following evening, Mary looked up from her place by Seth's bedside to see Lavinia enter the bedchamber. Eli was in the barn and Jerusha had gone to bed. Only Susannah and Caroline Cutting were with her.

"Why are you here?"

Susannah gasped at the sharpness of her mother's voice.

Lavinia looked as though she had been slapped. "I have come to sit with you," she said.

But now Mary could barely stand the sight of her closest friend.

"I should think you would be ashamed to show your face in this house." Mary rose from her chair, starting towards Lavinia. Caroline put a hand on Mary's arm, but Mary shook her off.

Inches from Lavinia's face, Mary's words exploded. "You started this trouble. You and Chauncey Haskell. You and your foolish superstitions. And now, because of you, my children are not to be allowed to rest in peace. You must have them dug up and heaven knows what done to them. Why? How could you hurt us like this? I thought we were friends."

Lavinia stood, mouth agape. Mary felt an arm go around her shoulders and realized that Susannah was beside her. "Mother," she whispered, tugging her gently, trying to coax her away. But Mary would not budge. She stared hard at Lavinia awaiting an explanation that could never be satisfactory.

"Hurt you?" Lavinia gasped out the words. "The doctors cannot help nor can Caroline. What else is left to us?"

"So, you picked a time when Reverend Cobb was away to go to the selectmen. I suppose you must know he would not approve and would have spoken against it."

"We did not go because the Reverend is away. We went because time is running out. Look at Seth. Do you not want him to live, Mary? There is nothing else that can help him."

"You truly believe that unearthing his sisters will save him?" Mary could not fathom how Lavinia saw any sense in such actions.

"It has been done elsewhere. There are many who think it a good remedy, perhaps the only remedy. Nan says—"

"Nan is but a child!" Mary exploded. "How can you countenance taking such drastic steps on the advice of a mere girl? Have you lost your senses?"

"Chauncey—"

"And Chauncey Haskell is an old fool too fond of his tales!"

"We are not the only ones. I know you are distraught, Mary, but you must think of others. It is not only your family at risk. Once yours is gone it will come after the rest of us. You must not be selfish."

Mary's mind raced for words, but frustration fogged her brain, and she could only stand dumbfounded.

A noise from behind her drew her attention. She turned to see Seth's scrawny arms thrashing as though trying to push something off himself. Mary, Susannah, and Lavinia all hurried to the bed.

"His fever is rising," said Caroline, pressing a cold compress to his forehead.

"Off," Seth rasped, the word barely understandable. "Off me."

"What is he saying?" asked Lavinia.

"Off. Get off me!" Seth's arms pushed at something invisible on his chest. The air expelled to force out the words brought on a frightful coughing fit.

"Help me," said Caroline to Susannah. Together they pulled him to a sitting position. The coughing became more violent, expelling blood and mucous.

"Why does he not want the cloth on his face?" Lavinia asked.

"It is not the cloth," Caroline answered. "He feels as though something is on his chest. He wants to push it off."

The fit subsided and Seth, worn from the force of it, laid his head back upon the propped-up pillows.

"You are fine now, Seth," Mary cooed. "There is nothing on your chest."

Seth opened his eyes for a moment, seeming to focus on something at the foot of the bed where no one stood.

"She..." he whispered. "She comes..." Speaking was torture for him. They tried to hush him, but he paid them no mind. "...every night." Exhausted, his eyes closed again, and he fell back into a fitful sleep.

"She comes every night," Lavinia repeated. She turned to Mary. "Do you see? It is so. He has said it himself."

"He is in fever," Mary insisted. "He does not know what he says."

Lavinia shook her head. "No. I am more certain now than ever. One of those girls has come back. She will take him. And then she will take the rest of you. Susannah may escape as she is leaving soon, but the rest of you will fall one by one. And then she will come for us. And all the others. You must see it now, Mary."

Mary's heart felt like lead in her chest. She could not believe she was living this nightmare. When she spoke, her words came out in a low, whispered voice. They were simple words, but they closed an iron door on her life-long friendship with Lavinia Wicker.

"I would ask you to leave us now."

Chapter 32

August 1973
Birch Falls, Vermont

"Come in, come in," Sadie Orsmbee held wide the door, ushering Charlotte, Tracy, and Heidi into her home, or as Charlotte thought of it, the Wicker House.

Crossing the threshold, Charlotte tried to imagine the house as it would have been when the Wicker family lived here. It wasn't as easy as she'd hoped. The living room, with its couch, easy chairs, television, and wall-to-wall carpeting hindered her imagination. Still, it had been their home. Jerusha had come to visit this house often, at least before her mother and Mrs. Wicker had a falling out. Settled on the couch, sodas in hand, and a big plate of freshly baked chocolate chip cookies on the coffee table in front of them, Charlotte turned her full attention to Sadie Ormsbee.

"Thank you for agreeing to meet with us, Mrs. Ormsbee," she said.

"Oh, I'm delighted." The woman's round face smiled at her. She was a large woman with curly white-blond hair and dancing blue eyes. She wore a green housedress covered in a paisley pattern. "What can I tell you?"

"Well for one, we know this was once the home of Phineas and Lavinia Wicker. Do you know much about them?"

"Only that they lived here and handed the house down to one of their sons. He married and worked the farm and eventually passed it on to one of his sons. It was sold out of the family before we bought it. Edna Marner knows as much or more about them as I do,

237

and you've already spoken with her. She's the keeper of the town's history."

A door opened in the adjacent room, most likely the kitchen, Charlotte thought.

"That's my husband," said Mrs. Ormsbee. "Earl, come meet the young ladies," she called.

A tall, lanky man entered the living room. His thin hair, what there was of it, was combed to one side and a long nose dominated his face. They exchanged pleasantries, then Charlotte said to both of them, "My grandmother gave me a diary that belonged to my ancestor, Jerusha Halsey, only she was Jerusha Kendall when she wrote it. The Kendalls and Wickers were neighbors and had been good friends until something happened that ended their friendship. I don't know what it was. Apparently, Jerusha was trying to figure it out, but the diary ends before she could say if she did or not. We were hoping to find out what it was all about."

"Ay-uh," he said. "Heard all about your mission up here. Edna's been over a few times since you saw her. She and Sadie been talking non-stop about it. She couldn't hardly wait for you to get here. Suppose I'll leave you ladies to it," he said, giving them a lopsided smile and returning to the kitchen.

Charlotte turned her attention back to Mrs. Ormsbee. "Edna said you were interested in the ghost stories," Sadie said.

At her words, Heidi leaned forward. "I'm very interested in them."

"I am, too," said Charlotte, "though I'm even more interested in the legends about Eliza Kendall. Do you know why people think she was a vampire?"

Mrs. Ormsbee laughed. "Not was. Still is, as I understand it. I wasn't half as surprised as Edna was to find out that kids are still going to her grave. I suppose it has to do with what's written on her gravestone. You've seen it?"

"Yes. 'I will come for you.' But that wasn't unusual for the time period," said Charlotte. "And even at a later date, when people might no longer have understood its original meaning, don't you think it would have made them think of a ghost rather than a vampire?"

Mrs. Ormsbee nodded. "That legend goes way back, though. Now the fella we bought this house from, he bought it from a Wicker descendent. And that fella told him that Eliza was thought to have been a vampire in her own time."

"How did you know that?" asked Heidi.

"I suppose it was handed down in the family."

"But Eliza was a Kendall, not a Wicker," said Charlotte.

"Hm-hm, but as you know, the Wickers and Kendalls were close. He said it had something to do with his old Wicker ancestor calling Eliza a vampire and Eliza's mother not taking kindly to it. Seems maybe she spread the word about the girl after she died. Can't say why, especially if she'd been friends with Eliza's mother. Seems a vicious thing to do to a woman who's lost her child, even if she weren't a friend. But that's the story of it. At least what I heard."

Here was a bit of information that helped explain why Mary Kendall would have ended her friendship with Lavinia Wicker.

"They wouldn't have used the term 'vampire' in those days, though," said Charlotte.

"Well, whatever they would have called her, that's the family lore that got handed down."

"Have you ever heard any stories about them digging up Eliza's grave to see if she was a vampire?" she asked.

"Oh, there's all sorts of tales. I couldn't tell which are true. I can't imagine a family unearthing one of their own dead. It's too gruesome."

"It would seem so, but some did do it." Seeing Sadie Ormsbee's shocked expression, Charlotte launched into a full explanation of the nineteenth century's occasional practice of disinterring suspected vampires.

"Well, I'll be," said Mrs. Ormsbee when she was finished. "You could knock me over with a feather. I thought that talk of digging her up was a lot of fairytale hogwash."

"So there are stories about her having been disinterred?" asked Charlotte. "Do they say who did it?"

"Well, now. I've got to go back a long ways in my memory. I haven't thought about that in years." Sadie leaned back casting her eyes towards the ceiling in an attempt to extract long-forgotten information.

While his wife was thinking, Earl Ormsbee reentered the room.

"If you want to know all that old-time stuff who you really should talk to is Alvin Stankard."

"What!" exclaimed Mrs. Ormsbee, nearly jumping from her chair. "You wouldn't send these girls off to that old swamp Yankee?"

"Well, he'd be the one to ask. He knows all those stories."

"He's a crazy old coot is what he is. Besides, they got anywhere near his property, and he's as soon shoot 'em as look at 'em."

"He ain't as bad as all that."

"Well, I wouldn't trust him as far as I could throw him."

"Who is Alvin Stankard?" Charlotte asked.

"What's a swamp Yankee?" Tracy inquired at almost the same moment.

Mr. Ormsbee chuckled. "Alvin Stankard is a fella that lives on the other side of Birch Falls. He's a bit of a character."

"Hmph! That's putting it mildly," said Sadie. She sat with her arms folded and lips pursed.

Earl lowered himself into a wingback chair. Dressed in work clothes that looked as though he'd been puttering in a workshop or garage before he arrived, Charlotte couldn't help but wonder if he would leave a stain on the chair. Her mother would have freaked out if it had been her furniture, but Sadie didn't say a word.

Earl Ormsbee leaned towards the sofa. "Are you girls really interested in finding out about this stuff?"

"We certainly are," Charlotte affirmed.

"Then old Alvin is the guy to ask. Now, Sadie's right about him being more than just a character, but he ain't as bad as some people make him out to be. Problem is, he don't like strangers. And he definitely don't like them on his property. He knows me well enough, though. I'll vouch for you. If I talk to him first, maybe I can wrangle a meeting with him for you. Won't be at his house, though, I can tell you that."

"It won't be at my house, either," said Sadie, raising her eyebrows at her husband. "I'm not having that swamp Yankee in my clean house."

"If I can get him to do it, I'll set up a neutral location."

"And you'll go with them. You're not sending these young girls off to meet with Alvin Stankard alone."

Charlotte felt her heart begin to beat harder and wasn't sure if it was from excitement or trepidation.

"Oh, for heaven's sake, it ain't like he's a murderer or anything," said Earl.

"Wouldn't surprise me if he was," Sadie replied, half under her breath.

"But, yeah, I'll go with 'em," Earl conceded.

"Does he really live in a swamp?" asked Tracy.

Earl chuckled and leaned back in his chair. "No, no. A swamp Yankee is what you call a New Englander who lives in a house that's been in his family for generations, usually a farm family. The good land the family owned has all been sold off over the years to other farmers. What they got left for land's not truly a swamp, but it's called that 'cause it's no good for farming, although in Alvin's case, I hear tell it may be a bit swampy in places out his way. Never been to his house, myself. I just run into him in town from time to time. Swamp Yankees may or may not have much money, but they tend to be frugal and keep the old ways. I hear Alvin's got no electricity. Not sure about indoor plumbing. Maybe, maybe not. Whatever, he likes the old ways."

"Tighter than the paper on the wall, you mean," said Sadie.

Earl chuckled. "That, too, I 'spect."

"Would he really shoot us?" asked Tracy.

"Well, I don't know about that, but I wouldn't show up on his property uninvited. He's really out in the sticks, so you're not likely to just happen onto it, and he's got No Trespassing signs all over the place. If he saw you, he'd run you off for sure, but shooting you might be a bit of a stretch."

"I wouldn't put it past him," said Sadie, her mouth still in a pucker as though she'd just eaten a whole lemon.

"You said a swamp Yankee's family has been in the same house for generations. Does that mean his family goes back as far as the Kendall and Wicker families?" asked Charlotte.

"Oh, I 'spect it does, maybe even further. He could tell you. I'll bet he knows every one of his ancestors back to Adam and Eve. He's a keeper of his own family history kind of in the way Edna Marner is a keeper of the town's history."

Sadie Ormsbee's eyes popped wide open. "I'll thank you not to compare Alvin Stankard with my friend Edna." Then she turned her attention to the girls seated on the sofa. "And mind you, if you do go to meet with him, bring clothes pins."

"Clothes pins?" asked Heidi.

"For your noses. I don't think that man has taken a bath in years. He may not live in an actual swamp, but he sure smells like one."

"Eeww!" Tracy squealed. "I'm glad I won't be here."

Charlotte wasn't sure how Heidi felt about meeting this Alvin Stankard, but she believed he would probably prove to be a folklore goldmine.

"Please set up a meeting for us, if you can, Mr. Ormsbee," she said. "I'd love to meet him."

"I'll do my best. We'll give you call if it's a go. I suppose weekends are best for you?"

"Yes."

"Okay, then. I guess I'll get on back to the shed. Been trying to fix my lawnmower. I'd only come in for a drink of water. I'll let you ladies get on with your ghost stories."

Once Earl had left, they turned their attention back to Sadie.

"The ghost stories are about Eliza Kendall's house?" asked Charlotte. "Or I guess I should say the Paquette's house."

Sadie nodded. "Folks here still call it the old Kendall place no matter who's living there. It was Millie Ketchum and her husband, Henry, lived there before the Paquettes who told me about it. She couldn't speak to Henry on the subject. He didn't believe in ghosts and wouldn't hear a word about it. Imagine living in the same house with a ghost and not believing in it."

"Some people are more sensitive than others," Heidi explained.

"Oh, I believe that," said Sadie. "Take me and Earl. I've had my share of odd experiences. But him?" she jerked her thumb in the general direction of the back yard. "He wouldn't know a ghost if one bit him on the nose. Though unlike Henry, he does enjoy a good ghost story now and then."

"So, what did Mrs. Ketchum tell you?" asked Charlotte. "And may I record you?" she asked, pulling her tape recorder from her bag. "I don't want to forget anything."

"Oh." Sadie looked a bit taken aback, but quickly recovered. "I guess that would be alright. You can plug it in over there." She indicated an outlet.

"Thanks. Folklorists prefer to record what people tell them. That way we don't lose or forget anything. Of course, that's only as long as the...subject...agrees." She decided not to refer to Sadie as an informant.

"I see. Well, I don't see any harm as long as it's only for you."

"It is," she assured her.

Once the recorder was set up, Charlotte asked. "When did Mrs. Ketchum first tell you about the ghosts in her house?"

"Well, that was a long time ago. We were young then. We'd both only been married a few years. We moved in right about the same time, too. My Joey was only two and Millie still had her first on the way." Sadie nodded vigorously. "That's right! I remember now. That's how it started. Millie was visiting over here one afternoon, and we got talking about the odd things that happen when one is expecting. You know, the weird food cravings and the like. Well, she asked me if when I was pregnant with Joey, did I ever have unusual experiences. I didn't know what she was getting at, so she had to come right out and tell me that she'd been hearing strange noises in the house like someone walking down the stairs from the garret. Then there was the den on the first floor just off the kitchen. She said she had an awfully strange feeling whenever she went in there and it had gotten to the point where she could barely stand to go in at all. Hated to clean that room. She just wanted to stay out of it."

"We'll definitely have to check that room out when we visit," Heidi interjected. "It must have a lot of spirit energy."

Charlotte gave her a quick nod, then turned back to Mrs. Ormsbee, who continued with her story.

"Millie said she'd told Henry about it, and he said she was just overly sensitive because she was expecting. But he didn't mean sensitive in the way you meant it," she said looking at Heidi. "He meant it was all in her head due to being pregnant." Sadie's pursed lips and arched eyebrow indicated what she thought of Henry's idea.

"I remember a time – now this was long after she'd had the baby – that she came over here, little Joanie, a toddler then, in her arms, all panicked, saying there was someone in her house.

"It was afternoon and Henry was at work. I tried to get her to call the police, but she said she couldn't because it wasn't a real person. It took a while to get the story out of her, but she finally told me she'd been in the kitchen making lunch when she heard a noise coming from the den. Joanie was in her highchair in the kitchen and no one else was in the house. She claimed it sounded like something had fallen over. It gave her the creepy-crawlies, but she went to check anyway.

"At first, she didn't see anything out of place, but then she noticed a wet spot on the floor. She knew she hadn't spilled anything. She stayed away from that room as much as possible. If Henry had spilled something, he wasn't the type to have left it. He'd have cleaned it up immediately. It didn't make sense. Then she said that awful feeling she got from that room came over her again. The next thing she knew the door to the den slammed shut and a split second later she heard a door upstairs, likely the door to the garret, slam shut, too. She was so startled she just flew out of that room, grabbed Joanie and ran to my house.

"We had lunch here. She was afraid to go back, but she didn't want Henry to come home to an empty house and no supper on the table so, later, when she had calmed down, I went back with her and the baby."

"What happened then?" Charlotte asked.

"As I recall, everything seemed calm in the house when we got there. I wiped up the water for her. I went upstairs, too, but not a single door was shut, so I can't say what it was she heard. I stayed until Henry came home. I don't know if she told him or not. She may have mentioned it to me, but if she did, I don't remember. It was a long time ago."

"That's okay," said Charlotte. "You've remembered a lot already."

"That's not the kind of thing you tend to forget."

"Did anything ever happen when you were at her house? Tracy asked.

Sadie drew a long breath. "There was one incident. I'll try to relate it to you, but it gives me the shudders just to think of it."

Chapter 33

Late April 1832
Birch Falls, Vermont

"Up, up. No time to dawdle." Susannah tugged at Jerusha's arm. She had fallen asleep face down on the sofa, exhausted from the day's work. Not only were they in the midst of spring cleaning, but the next day was the Lord's Day and Jerusha's mother held to as little work being done on that day as possible, so extra was done the day before.

"I am so tired," Jerusha complained, pushing herself up. She had only meant to lay down for a moment, to simply rest her eyes, but had fallen asleep before she knew what she was about. Her mother had kept her up later than usual the night before insisting she practice her mending until Jerusha almost fell asleep over her needle and thread. Then she'd been awakened just before dawn and immediately set her to work. It was most unusual, but her mother only said they had much work to do and needed to get an early start.

"You will sleep well tonight," said Susannah. Jerusha caught the sideways glance and knitted brows of her sister who looked towards the kitchen where their mother was cooking and wondered what Susannah knew that she didn't.

Their mother had been behaving strangely all day. While it was true that Seth's rapidly deteriorating condition had them all feeling anxious, her mother was acting especially frantic today. She tore through the house like a cyclone, speaking little other than to issue orders for work to be done. Now she was cooking enough for tomorrow's dinner as well as todays. Between tasks, she would stop into the room where Seth lay abed. He slept off-and-on all day, awakening only when the coughing wracked his body too violently to allow for sleep.

Caroline Cutting had stopped by twice already to look in on him and was expected to return at dusk to wait throughout the night with the family.

It struck Jerusha as odd that the Wickers had not spent much time sitting with Seth. For that matter, very few neighbors had come by. Those who did had not stayed long. Her mother's chilly manner seemed to drive them away. Harsh-sounding words were often whispered between them, sometimes accompanied by a furtive glance in Jerusha's direction. It was obvious something was afoot that she was not to be a part of.

"Susannah," she said, picking up her dust cloth, "why have so few people come to sit with us by Seth's bedside? They came for the others."

"They will come. It is just that this time of year is so busy for everyone. Now, go on child. Finish your chores." With that, Susannah abruptly left the room.

Dinner had been a hurried affair, and supper was served earlier than usual. Jerusha had barely finished when her plate was whisked away.

"Get the milking done quickly girls," said her mother as she cleared the rest of the table.

"Why is everything so rushed today?" Jerusha asked as she and Susannah set up the milking stools in the cow shed.

"Tomorrow is for church and prayer, not work. We must get everything done today."

"But we do that every week and it is not like today."

"There is always more work at this time of year. You know that."

"But not like this." The odd feeling of something being wrong had plagued Jerusha all day.

Before Susannah could sit down to milk, Jerusha grabbed hold of her. "What are you not telling me?"

"Nothing," she said, avoiding Jerusha's eyes. "It is just that there are fewer of us to do the work this year so it seems more tasking than before. Now, please, Jerusha, get to your milking. Susannah dropped onto the milking stool, her forehead against the cow's side, and went to work.

Realizing she would get nothing more from her sister, Jerusha, too, set to her own task.

Once they had completed everything, Jerusha was told to go straight to bed. The sun had only just begun to set. There would be no mending or knitting by the fire tonight. She was so exhausted she hadn't the energy to complain. Rather, she was grateful to turn in early.

Alone in the garret, she stripped to her shift and climbed into bed. Susannah was to sit up with their parents and Mrs. Cutting in Seth's room. It was rare that Jerusha should have the bed to herself. Burrowing under the covers, she quickly fell asleep.

It was dark when she awoke to the sound of angry voices. The moon glowed through the garret window, throwing a patch of soft light across the coverlet. The voices, though muffled, gave the impression of a rather great crowd of people. Had the Wickers and the other neighbors finally come? Did this mean that Seth had died or was close to death?"

Jerusha flung off the coverlet and crept to the door. In the dark, she felt her way down the garret stairs to the second floor. A crash sounded from the floor below followed by shouts and gasps. She tried to hurry, but in almost complete darkness, could not go as fast as she wanted to.

"What has happened?" she called.

Within seconds Susannah appeared on the stairs, a lit candle in hand.

"Jerusha, go back."

"Why? I heard a crash. What is happening? Has Seth..." she couldn't finish the sentence.

"Seth is with us yet. The table by his bed was knocked over. That is all. Now, go back to bed."

In the dim light from below, Jerusha caught the silhouette of Mrs. Wicker seemingly being chased by her mother and Mrs. Cutting.

"Why is Mother–"

She got no further for Susannah forcibly turned her around, nearly carrying her back up the stairs.

Back in the garret, Jerusha climbed into bed. Suddenly, without realizing she was going to, she began to cry. Nothing made sense. Her brother was about to die. Those watching in the room where he lay should have been keeping a peaceful vigil in prayer. Friends and neighbors should be bringing comfort to her parents. Instead, there were noisy crashes and her mother chasing her dearest friend from the house. Feeling the bed spin beneath her, Jerusha grabbed a fist full of the blankets to steady the world that careened around her.

Slowly, she registered the feel of Susannah's hands stroking her hair, her soft voice crooning a lullaby. Darkness enveloped her, drawing her into its depths. The last sound she heard before sleep claimed her again was the catch in Susannah's voice.

Chapter 34

August 1973
Birch Falls, Vermont

Charlotte leaned in close eager for Sadie Ormsbee to relate her story.

"Well," Sadie began. "As I recall, it was springtime. April, I think." She tilted her head to the side as she tried to picture the long-ago event. "Millie and Henry had gone out for the evening. I can't remember where. But I do remember they couldn't get a sitter so I said I'd stay with the kids. They had three by then. Earl was home so he stayed with ours.

"Everything started out fine. I fed them supper, cleaned up, and got them all into bed with no trouble. I was sitting in the parlor reading a book when I heard a noise from upstairs like a door opening and closing and footsteps in the upstairs hallway. I assumed one of the kids had gotten up to use the bathroom or something, so I didn't give it much thought at first.

"The staircase comes down into the parlor, you see, and I heard the stairs creak. I looked up expecting to see one of the children, but no one was there."

"Are you sure it was on the stairs?" Heidi asked.

"That's what it sounded like. I decided to go up and see what was going on. Couldn't have one of those little ones wandering the house in the dark after all."

"How old were the children then?" asked Charlotte.

"Oh, let's see. Joanie was about eight, I think. So that would have made Jack six and Marlene four." Her brow furrowed and she put a finger to her chin as she questioned her own math. "Yes. Yes, I believe that's right. Or close to it, anyway.

"So, I went upstairs to see who the little wanderer was, but when I got there all three kids were in their beds fast asleep. I thought it was strange that if one had just been up, they would be back in bed and sound asleep so fast, but I had no other explanation. As for the noise on the stairs, I figured it must have been the house settling as old houses do. I know that from living in this one." She chuckled. "It makes some strange noises from time to time, but I'm used to them. I was used to them by that time, too, but I really didn't think the noise I heard was like them at all, but then, I figured, well, maybe different houses make different noises. Who knows?

"I was about to head back downstairs when the door that leads up to the garret opened. Now, that door is at the end of the hallway. I had my back to it, but I heard it creak open. I can tell you I don't care how many years are put between me and that door opening, I will never forget the feeling it gave me. Made every hair stand on end."

"Can't things like that happen in old houses?" asked Charlotte. "Just like the house settling?"

"That's just the thing," Sadie said. "It can and does. It's happened here. The floorboards are a bit warped. There are drafts. Some latches don't quite catch anymore. So you'd think it wouldn't have had such an effect on me. It probably wouldn't have, either, if it hadn't been for the feeling it."

"What do you mean by that?" asked Tracy who had inched a bit closer to Charlotte.

"That's what's hard to explain. I suddenly had the feeling that someone was standing behind me. I thought for sure when I turned around there would be someone right there. I'd never had a feeling like that before. Certainly not in this house and its as old as the Kendall place."

"What did happen when you turned around?" asked Heidi. "Was anyone there?"

"No. At least not anyone I could see. I told myself it was the machinations of an old house, but to be honest, I wasn't believing myself at all. Still, I forced myself to go shut the door. If one of the kids did wake up during the night, I didn't want them to find it open and wander up there."

Sadie stopped talking. She lay both palms on her lap, fingers splayed, and stared at them. She seemed a little spooked by the memory, and Charlotte thought she was trying to regain her composure.

"Mrs. Ormsbee?" she prompted. "Did something happen when you went to shut the door?"

Sadie drew a deep breath.

"I put my hand on the doorknob and started to close it." As she spoke, she reached out her right hand, miming the gesture. "I got it about half-way shut when I heard footsteps again. This time, they were going up the garret stairs. There was no mistaking it. They were footsteps moving deliberately up the stairs. There weren't loud, more like the steps of a child, but they were there for certain."

Charlotte glanced at Heidi who had leaned forward. Her eyes were wide as she took in the story. Tracy, who was now pushed right up beside Charlotte, went rigid.

"What did you do?" asked Charlotte.

"I almost screamed, but caught myself in time so as not to wake the kids. I didn't want to frighten them. There was a nightlight on in the hallway, but it didn't cast enough light to see much and, frankly, whoever was walking up those stairs wasn't anybody I wanted to see. More than anything, I wanted to get out of there, but I couldn't leave those kids. What if it was an intruder? I'd no idea how anyone could have gotten in, but I couldn't take the chance."

"Did you get the kids out of the house?" Tracy asked.

"No. I was afraid if I woke them up, they'd make noise and if someone was in the garret, they might come back down. But I couldn't just walk away, either. I figured my job at the moment was to protect those kids so I went into Millie and Henry's bedroom, grabbed the heaviest object I could find – I think it was a table lamp – and stood right outside that door ready to whack anybody who might come down the garret stairs."

"And you just stayed there like that?" How long?" asked Tracy.

"Don't know for sure. It felt like hours, but it couldn't have been. Millie and Henry came home before too much longer. When I heard them come in, I went to the top of the stairs and called down to them. Henry got a flashlight and went up to the garret. There was no one there. He didn't say much, but I suspect he thought it was my imagination. Millie didn't though. She'd heard it before. She told me many times that the garret and the room between the kitchen and parlor were haunted and I don't doubt her for a minute."

Chapter 35

Late April 1832
Birch Falls, Vermont

Mary stared out the window of the chamber where Seth lay sleeping fitfully. She felt guilty for keeping Jerusha up late the night before then waking her up extra early and working her so hard all day, but it had been necessary. The townspeople, her neighbors, her friends, were set to exhume the graves of her children late this afternoon. They would come to the house afterwards; she was sure of it. She wanted Jerusha to have no part in this horror. She was not even to know. Powerless to stop them, Mary was able to force one concession. She had gone that morning to the Wicker house to confront Lavinia and extract a promise that Jerusha was never, ever to know of what was to take place that afternoon.

"How can I promise that?" Lavinia had asked. "Everyone knows of it. People talk."

"Then you had better talk to them first. You did a perfectly good job of convincing them to go along with this, so you had better do just as good a job at convincing them never to speak of it. Jerusha is the only one not touched by what is happening and is to stay that way. She is the only child left that I can protect." Mary fell apart on those last words.

"Mary, please," Lavinia cooed, putting her arms around her. "I know this is awful for you, but it will work. It will save Seth. I am certain of it. And that means it will save Jerusha, too. And Susannah and Eli and you and all of us."

The scents of bread dough and wool clung to Lavinia. Mary inhaled them, blindly searching for solace.

"Once it is over, we can put this all behind us," Lavinia said.

At these words, Mary pulled back, forcefully breaking free from Lavinia's embrace. She stared at her friend, blurred through her tears. "This will never be behind me."

"Come now, Mary. When all are well in your household you will be grateful for it, though it will never be a pleasant memory."

"How?" she asked. "How can you truly believe that one of my children is returning to take the lives of the others? Why do you not understand that it is not possible? Why must you put us through this?"

"But it is true, Mary. Why do you think they did it in Woodstock? And Chauncey says they've done it in other places as well. You speak as though I fabricated the idea out of whole cloth."

Mary wiped her eyes. Lavinia's superstitions had always somewhat annoyed her, but at times, also amused her. Occasionally, over the years, she had tried to talk sense into Lavinia, but as the woman refused to relinquish her tightly-held beliefs, Mary gave up trying. They were only harmless fancies of an otherwise good woman, after all. Until now. Fueled by Chauncey Haskell's imagination they had fed off the fears of their neighbors, stirring them into a mob that would look for any safeguard against the dreaded disease of consumption.

Lavinia stretched out her hands towards Mary, but Mary stepped away. Straightening to her full height, she glared at Lavinia.

"If there was any way I could put a stop to this I would do it. But as you have turned even the minds of our selectmen to sawdust with your abominable beliefs, I am helpless to stop you."

She raised a hand, pointing a finger straight at Lavinia. "But I promise you, if this ever becomes known to Jerusha, I will come here in the night and I will burn your house and everyone in it to the ground and so much for saving your own family by refusing to let my children rest in peace."

The words had spilled from her mouth likes sparks shooting from a blacksmith's hammer. She could not believe she was speaking such violent, hateful utterances, unaware until they poured forth from her that she was even thinking them. Did she mean it? Would she ever be capable of such behavior? At the moment, she was not certain.

Mary flushed with a moment of satisfaction as the color drained from Lavinia's face. She thought the words, "she will never know," came from Lavinia in a barely audible tone, though she might have imagined them.

Later, she could not remember leaving Lavinia's kitchen and walking down the hill to her own home. The day had been a flurry of spring cleaning, commanding Jerusha to the hardest, most tiring tasks the child could accomplish in order to exhaust her to an early bedtime.

Now, as Mary stood by the window watching the sun sink over the horizon, she was glad she had done it. Jerusha had willingly gone to bed early. That the child would miss whatever might come was the only small blessing Mary could find in the sordid affair.

Eli stepped into the room. His face looked as grim as Mary felt.

"I have decided to go with them," he said.

Stunned, Mary could only gape at him.

He shook his head. "If this thing is to be done, I want to make sure it is done with as much respect as can be had. And if they say they found something, I want to see it with my own eyes. They will not get away with spreading falsehoods about any of our girls."

Mary crossed the room and fell into Eli's arms, not caring that both Susannah and Caroline Cutting were present.

"Oh, Eli. I could never have asked it of you, but I do thank you. I pray that you will be able to bear it."

Once Eli left, Mary busied herself as much as she could in a useless effort to keep from thinking about what was happening in the graveyard.

Seth slept fitfully, waking on occasion from a bout of coughing. Talk in the sick room was quiet, mostly whispered words about Seth or softly spoken instructions from Caroline when his fever rose, or he seemed to gag on blood and mucous spewing up from his lungs.

All three women sat alternately praying and knitting during the time when Seth slept more or less peacefully. Occasionally, Mary glanced at her daughter or her friend. Usually, their faces were focused on their work or turned towards Seth, but a few times she caught them looking at her. She was not sure of the expression they held. Pity? Anguish?

After the sun had set and the room had grown dark but for the fire they kept stoked in the room's small fireplace, Mary could stand her silent thoughts no longer.

"Why must it take so long?"

No one answered. "They should be done by now. There was nothing to find. What could they be doing?"

A rustle of skirts and she found Caroline had come to sit beside her.

"Mary," Caroline spoke softly. "Do not torment yourself. You did all you could to stop them. Now you must leave it to be as it will."

"How can I?"

"Mother, it cannot be much longer," Susannah's voice came from the shadows on the other side of Seth's bed. "It will be over soon."

"I do not feel as though it can ever be over." Turning towards Caroline, she added in a subdued tone, "I pray about it, but I do not believe I will ever be able to forgive. I thank God that you do not believe as they do, Caroline."

"Of course, I do not. It is all foolish superstition. Did not Doctor Eacker tell them so as well?"

"He did, but they would not listen to him. They will not listen to anyone but themselves."

Mary put her head in her hands, willing the nightmare to end. Her heart nearly stopped when her wish was realized, and excited voiced were heard outside the house.

"I will go," said Caroline, getting up and heading for the door.

"Hush!" Mary heard her command as the voices increased in volume when Caroline opened the door. The talking ceased, but the sound of so many footsteps made Mary think the entire town was parading into the kitchen.

Before Mary could make her way towards them, they entered the sick room, Lavinia Wicker and Chauncey Haskell in the lead, Lavinia carrying a mug. The entire hoard moved as one straight for the bed where Seth lay. Their crowding presence pushed Mary aside. Susannah rose to her feet, leaning protectively over her brother as if sensing something ominous in their advance.

"Sit him up." It was Lavinia's voice.

"Why?" asked Susannah. "What are you giving him?"

"The cure," said Lavinia.

They seemed to swarm around the bed, these people who had been their friends, their neighbors, but now looked to Mary like a throng of demons descending on her son. She heard the bed creak and knew they were sitting him up. A groan escaped him. She pushed forward, elbowing between the backs that seemed intent upon shutting her out.

"Let me through. Let me through!" Mary pushed with her hands, shoulders, even stomped on the foot of a man blocking her way until she reached the bed.

Holding the earthenware mug to Seth's lips, Lavinia tipped it forcing him to drink while the others held him upright. A wet, blackish stream trickled down his chin.

"Good, Seth. You are doing well, Drink it all." Lavinia's voice was like a gentle mother feeding a young child.

"What is that? What are you giving him?" Mary grabbed the mug from Lavinia. A sooty mess sloshed onto the coverlet. "What is this?" asked Mary, staring into the half-drained mug.

"Give it to me. He must finish," said Lavinia, grabbing for the mug.

"Mistress Wicker is right." Mary glanced up to see the face of Chauncey Haskell, fiendish in the winking firelight. He was the one holding Seth up, having usurped the place where Susannah had been. "It is the heart of the one who has been tormenting him. Once he drinks her ashes, she will have no more power over him."

At first, Mary could not grasp the meaning of his words. They seemed so much nonsense. Then, staring at the slick, ashy trail rolling from the sides of Seth's mouth, the realization struck her, and she screamed. Blinded by fury and revulsion, her hand let go of the mug as if it was on fire.

Lavinia grabbed for it, but Mary slapped her hand away, and, snatching it up, hurled it to the floor with all the strength she possessed. Then, staring Lavinia in the eye she yelled, "Get out! Leave this house and never return!"

Lavinia took a half step back, as far as she could move with the crowd hovering close behind her. "You do not understand, Mary," she hissed. "It was Lizzy.

She has been coming back for Seth. We saw the evidence ourselves."

"Get out!" Mary screamed again.

Behind Lavinia, Mary caught sight of another neighbor who suddenly jerked back as though pulled roughly from her feet. Caroline Cutting had yanked the woman away and was roughly pushing her towards the door. Others began to follow.

"We may as well go," said Chauncey, glancing at Lavinia. "He drank enough I hope and, if not, it is all he will get. The deed is done. Lizzy can do no more. We have seen to that."

One by one, the crowd dispersed, melting into the darkness of the hallway, but Lavinia remained staring at Mary.

"You go from this house, now." Mary's voice rasped out the words. In the quiet she heard Susannah's choked sob from the other side of the bed.

Caroline, having dispatched the others, took hold of Lavinia's arm to pull her away. Mary walked with them, close to Lavinia, wanting to be sure she left. As they moved from the room, she heard the creak of the stairs and a voice call out, "What is happening?"

Jerusha.

Spinning around, she called for Susannah who hurried from the room to ward off her sister while Caroline and Mary continued to escort Lavinia towards the door.

"We did what was right, Mary," Lavinia said. "Ask Eli. He saw. He will tell you." With that Lavinia departed.

Chapter 36

August 1973
Birch Falls, Vermont

After lunch at the Ormsbee's, which Mrs. Ormsbee had insisted on feeding them, the three girls decided to kill some time by visiting the cemetery before heading to the Paquettes' house.

"Okay, that's just plain creepy," said Tracy, kneeling before Lizzy's gravestone to read the inscription. "Even knowing what you told me about what the people back then meant by it, seeing 'I am coming for you' on a gravestone still gives me the creeps."

Charlotte laughed. "That's why it's such a magnet for legend trippers, especially since most of them don't know what it really means."

"I'd like to try again to see if I can pick up any vibes," said Heidi, placing her hands on Lizzy's stone.

Charlotte and Tracy moved away so Heidi could kneel by the grave. She closed her eyes and took several deep breaths. "Lizzy, we are going to visit the house you grew up in. Is there anything you want us to know?"

Tracy glanced at Charlotte, lifting her eyebrows. Charlotte just smiled.

"Anything?" Charlotte asked after a moment.

Heidi dropped her hands from the gravestone, sighing. "Nothing. I can't understand why I don't get anything from her. You'd think the vibes would be flying from her gravestone."

"I guess she doesn't have anything to say," said Tracy.

"We should head to the Paquettes' house. I don't want to be late," said Charlotte.

As they started to move away, Heidi suddenly gasped and fell to the ground.

"Are you okay?" Charlotte asked, bending to help her friend.

"Yeah. I'm fine," said Heidi. "That was weird, though. It felt like someone grabbed my ankle."

"Cut it out," said Tracy. "That's not even possible. We were in front of you and no one else is even in the cemetery."

Charlotte glanced at her sister. Tracy's face had gone pale.

"You must have tripped over something," Charlotte said to Heidi.

They looked, felt through the grass with their hands. There was nothing.

"Oh!" Heidi exclaimed. "It's her."

"Who?" asked Tracy.

"Mary," said Charlotte, looking to where Heidi was pointing at a gravestone. "She was Lizzy's mother."

"The last time we were here, she's the one who came through to me," said Heidi. "Remember, Charlotte? I told you it felt like someone pushed me when I was sitting by her stone. That was right here. Right in the same spot where I just fell."

The three of them stood together, staring down at the stone.

"I'm sure she's trying to tell us something," said Heidi.

"Maybe she wants you to leave her daughter alone," Tracy offered.

"Maybe we'll find out when we get to her old house," Heidi countered.

* * *

Charlotte entered the home where Jerusha and her family had once lived with a feeling akin to what she experienced when she visited any historic landmark only this time it took on a personal, more intense aspect. Her own ancestors had lived in this house. They had experienced life with all its joys, sorrows, worries, and celebrations within these walls. And several of them had died here as well.

Once they'd been greeted and ushered in by Julie Paquette, Charlotte couldn't keep from looking in every direction. She tried to picture Jerusha and her family moving through these rooms while going about their daily tasks, walking across the very floor she now walked on.

"This was the home of your ancestors?" Julie asked. "Would you like a tour of the house?"

"We'd love it," Charlotte answered for all of them.

They started in the kitchen, the room that undoubtedly looked the least like it did in Jerusha's time. It had been updated with all the modern conveniences and a linoleum floor. In the living room there were now a television and a stereo, but Charlotte could picture Jerusha and her family gathered around the fireplace in the evenings.

There was a small room to the left, just beyond the kitchen as you stepped into the living room. It was currently being used as a study with a desk and several bookshelves. Upstairs were two bedrooms and a bathroom, something that had obviously been added after indoor plumbing became common. Two more bedrooms occupied a space in a newer section of the house that most likely hadn't existed in Jerusha's time.

"Where does that go?" asked Heidi, pointing to a door at the end of the upstairs hallway.

"That leads to the garret," said Julie.

"May we see it?" Charlotte asked.

"There's not much to see. We just use it for storage."

"It's where Jerusha and her sisters slept," Charlotte explained. "It probably hasn't changed much."

"Well, I guess it would be okay," said Julie, though Charlotte didn't miss the uncomfortable look that crossed her face.

"Don't worry," she said. "Our attic is a mess. We don't care about that. I'd just like to see the place where they slept."

"It's not that," said Julie. "It's just...oh, well, let's go up."

She opened the door and flipped a switch just inside to reveal a narrow staircase. A wall of heat and a musty odor hit them full force.

"Sorry," said Julie. "I know I should keep the door open in the summer. That's what the last owner said to do, but I just don't like to. We don't come up here much anyway."

Following Julie up the stairs, they came out into a room with unfinished wood plank floors and sloping walls. The space was separated into three compartments, doorways without doors leading to each one.

"They slept up here?" Tracy asked, her tone incredulous.

"Yup," said Charlotte. "It was common for the kids to sleep in the garret. They also dried herbs up here and stored stuff like squash and pumpkins. They used it for storage, too, just like we store stuff in our attics."

"I would be totally creeped out sleeping in an attic," said Tracy.

"Oh, I don't know," said Charlotte. "If you cleaned it up and put up some nice wallpaper, I'll bet it could be quite cozy."

"Yeah, but they didn't. It looked just like this, right?"

"It did," Charlotte conceded.

"Well, there's no way I could do it," said Tracy. "I mean I'd be afraid there were ghosts up here. Or at least, spiders. Besides, it's wicked hot up here. They must have sweltered."

Charlotte laughed. "Yeah, and froze in the winter, but it's how life was, so I guess they didn't question it."

"We should go back down now," said Julie.

Her voice sounded shaky, and Charlotte saw that her face had drained of color.

"Are you okay?" she asked.

"Honestly, I'm not comfortable being up here." Julie crossed her arms over her chest like she was hugging herself.

"Alright. Let's go back down," said Charlotte.

They started towards the stairs when Charlotte realized that Heidi wasn't with them. She turned back to see her friend standing near the window in the farthest section of the garret.

"Heidi," she called. "We're going downstairs."

Heidi turned towards her, a look on her face Charlotte couldn't quite interpret. "What?" she asked as she walked towards Heidi.

"There's something here," Heidi whispered when Charlotte got close. "I can feel it."

A chill ran through Charlotte despite the sweat dripping down her back.

"I think Julie can, too," she said. "She doesn't like being up here. We need to go back down."

Once back on the first floor, they settled in the living room.

"It must be really cool to be able to see the house where your ancestors lived," said Julie, kicking off her sandals and tucking her bare feet underneath her on the easy chair. She tossed her long brown hair over her shoulder. "I don't know anything about my ancestors."

"I didn't know much about mine either until my grandmother gave me Jerusha's diary," said Charlotte. "It's been fascinating to learn about her life through reading it."

"Yeah, and apparently, her sister, Eliza, was a vampire," said Tracy. "That's pretty cool. How many people can say they have a vampire in their family?"

"A vampire?" asked Julie.

Charlotte threw Tracy what she hoped was a withering look. She'd wanted to ease into that subject. But since Tracy had brought it up, Charlotte related everything she knew about Eliza's legend and the history of alleged vampirism in New England.

"I've never heard of any of that," said Julie when she finished. "Andy and I are from Connecticut. We just moved up here."

"Lots of places have legends," said Charlotte, watching as Julie bit her lip. It looked as though she was debating about whether or not to say something.

"On the phone you mentioned something about strange things happening in this house," Charlotte ventured. "What did you mean?"

"Yeah, our mom said there was supposed to be a haunted house in our family, too, so we kind of figured it must be this one," Tracy added.

Charlotte wished she was sitting next to Tracy instead of Heidi so she could nudge her in the ribs. Instead, she made do with a glare that Tracy didn't even seem to notice.

"Really?" asked Julie. "Your family thinks this house is haunted?" Her voice shook a little.

"We don't actually know if it's this house or not," said Charlotte. "My mom didn't know which house it was."

"What did she say happened?"

"She didn't know. Some house in our family from way back is supposed to be haunted. That's all she knows."

"Yeah, but we were just talking to Mrs. Ormsbee up the hill," said Tracy. "She's friends with the lady who lived her before you and she said this house is haunted. She's heard footsteps on the garret stairs and there was something weird about a room. That one, I guess." She pointed toward the study near the kitchen.

The color drained from Julie's face.

"Are you okay?" asked Charlotte.

"Those are the places I hear things," Julie said, though her words came out in a strained whisper.

"I definitely felt some vibes up in the garret," said Heidi, leaning towards Julie. "Can you tell me what you've experienced?"

"I hear footsteps on the garret stairs," she said. "Mostly at night. Andy works a part-time job at the grocery store along with his regular job. That's where he is right now. Sometimes he gets home late on Friday and Saturday evenings. I won't even go upstairs until he gets home."

"Has he heard it, too?" Charlotte asked.

"No. He thinks I'm imagining it. But I know I've heard footsteps on those stairs. That's why I don't like to keep the door open. I know that's silly. A ghost, if there is such a thing, could probably walk right through the door, but it makes me feel better to keep it shut."

"Do you hear someone walking in the garret or any other sounds coming from up there?" asked Heidi.

"No, not up there. It's just the footsteps coming down the stairs. They aren't loud. More like a kid's. That's why it unnerved me when you said the kids slept up there. I didn't know anyone ever slept up there. Next time I hear it, it's really going to freak me out."

"What about that other room?" asked Tracy.

Julie glanced toward the study. "Andy uses that room. He's got his books and desk in there. I stay out of it as much as possible. I don't like it because more than once I've heard a crash in there like something got knocked over, but when I go in to check, nothing's been moved. The weirdest thing was when I walked in one time and found a wet spot on the floor."

Charlotte felt a chill run down her spine. Hadn't that been something Mrs. Ormsbee had mentioned?

"What caused that?" asked Tracy.

"I don't know. I thought either Andy spilled something the last time he was in there or he had left behind a glass of water that had somehow got tipped over, but I couldn't find a glass or anything. I told him about it when he got home. He said he hadn't brought anything to drink in there recently. He did check all the pipes to be sure we didn't have a leak, but he couldn't find anything."

"You should tell him the same stuff happened to the lady who was here before you. Maybe he'll believe you then," said Tracy.

"Do you mind if I go into that room?" asked Heidi. "We just glanced in when you were showing us the house. I promise I won't bother any of your husband's stuff."

"Sure. Go ahead," said Julie.

Charlotte followed Heidi into the room while Tracy and Julie hung back in the doorway.

Oh, yeah," said Heidi, walking slowly around the room, arms outstretched but not touching anything. "There are definitely some strong vibes in here. A lot of them. I think from more than one person."

"Charlotte, what would this room have been used for when Jerusha lived here?" asked Tracy.

"I'm not sure," said Charlotte. She looked around the room taking in the desk, bookcases, the wing-back chair in the corner, the boarded-up fireplace.

"It's close to the kitchen, but it's not very big. I know the family did a lot of dairying, but I don't think it would have been here."

"I was told the dairy was off the kitchen," said Julie. "I can show you where the door was that led to it, but the dairy was dismantled years ago. The barn that used to be on the property was taken down, too. Could this have been a pantry?"

"Possibly. It could also have been used as a bedchamber. Or a borning room."

"You mean a room where the mother had babies?" asked Tracy.

"Yeah. It could also have been the room where they put family members who were sick. That way the mother could keep an eye on them while she was cooking and doing housework.”

“Didn’t several of Jerusha’s sisters die of tuberculosis?” Heidi asked.

“Yeah. Her brother died from it, too.”

“So a lot of people could have died in this room?” asked Tracy.

“Possibly,” said Charlotte.

“You know, it’s kind of an odd thing, but I sometimes get a weird feeling just standing on the threshold of this room, even more so than actually being in it,” said Julie who had moved even further away than Tracy. “I can’t stand in the doorway for more than a few seconds without getting chills.”

Charlotte moved to the doorway. “Hmm...it’s a threshold. That’s a liminal space,” she said, more to herself than aloud. She moved back into the room as Heidi approached the doorway.

“Oh, wow. You’re right. This spot has some incredibly strong vibes. Something definitely went on here,” she said. “I wonder...”

Heidi moved to stand just outside the room facing into it. “This is it. Right here,” she said. “I feel fear and sadness. I think it’s someone’s energy that got trapped here.”

“You mean you think someone watched something bad from that spot?” asked Tracy.

“I think so, or something like that,” said Heidi. Turning to Julie, she asked, “Would you let me hold a séance here?”

Julie took a step back. “No,” she said. “I’m sorry, but there’s enough weird stuff going on in this house. I don’t want any more. I have to live here. Besides, Andy would never allow it.”

“But if there are spirits trapped here maybe it could help them move on. Then you wouldn’t have any more problems with them,” Heidi explained.

"Or it could make things worse. I've heard of that happening," said Julie. "I'm sorry, but no. I just can't risk it."

Charlotte noticed that Julie was beginning to tremble a little.

"I'm sorry if we've upset you," she said. "Let's go back to the living room."

Charlotte felt that they should be going but didn't want to leave Julie in a frightened state. "Will Andy be home soon?" she asked.

"Yeah. He's not working late today. He should be home in a few hours."

"Will you be okay then? We've taken up enough of your time, but I don't want to leave you if you're afraid to be alone."

"It's okay. I'll go into town and do some shopping. I'll just stay out until it's time for Andy to come home."

"Okay. Then I guess we should be going. Thank you for letting us come and look around," said Charlotte. "You can't imagine what it's like for me to be able to walk through the house where my ancestors lived."

"I'm glad you came," said Julie. "And I'm glad you told me about the last owner having similar experiences to mine here. At least I know I'm not crazy."

Just as they rose to leave, there was a loud thud in the study. Charlotte froze, as did Tracy and Julie. Only Heidi seemed unfazed.

"May I go look?" asked Heidi.

Julie nodded.

Charlotte regained her composure enough to follow Heidi into the small room.

"I'm not going back in there," said Tracy who remained with Julie in the living room.

Charlotte let Heidi go ahead of her into the study. As Heidi walked slowly around the room, Charlotte eased towards the desk wanting to see what would happen while staying out of the way. As she stepped towards the edge of the desk, the shag rug beneath her sandaled foot squished. Looking down she saw dirty water squeeze out from under her foot leaving a tinge of wetness on the hem of her denim maxi skirt.

"What was it?" asked Julie from just beyond the doorway.

"I don't see anything that could have fallen," said Charlotte, but the floor is wet."

Julie looked about to pass out. "Where?" she asked.

"Here." Charlotte moved away and pointed.

"That's where I found the water," said Julie.

Heidi came over and knelt down, pressing her hand into the water spot. Wetness squeezed up around her hand with what appeared to be small flakes of soot floating among the pile of the white rug.

"What do you think? Charlotte asked.

Heidi quickly pulled her hand back as though the water had turned hot. "Something bad happened here, but I don't know what." Getting to her feet, she added, "I wish you could find the rest of Jerusha's diary. Maybe it tells."

"You mean there's more?" asked Julie.

"The diary stops on the last page mid-sentence," Charlotte explained. "I figure she must have continued in another diary."

"Do you think it could be in this house?" asked Tracy.

They all looked at each other.

"I suppose it could be," said Charlotte. "It's more likely than anywhere else. That is if it still exists. I'm guessing the garret would be the best place to look since that was, for lack of a better word, her bedroom."

"Can we look around up there, Julie?" asked Heidi. "You don't have to go up if you don't want to."

"I'll go with you. It's better than being down here alone."

"We should bring some flashlights," said Charlotte.

"Once back in the garret, Charlotte asked, "Is all the stuff up here yours?"

"Yes," said Julie. "It was empty when we moved in."

"Then where do we look?" asked Tracy.

"It's a long shot, but look for a loose floorboard or any nooks and crannies where something could be hidden. Diaries are supposed to be private. I suppose she might have hidden it."

"Wasn't the diary you have found up here?" asked Julie.

"Probably. Or at least somewhere in this house."

"If there was another one, wouldn't it have been found at the same time?"

"That depends on how well Jerusha hid it," Charlotte answered. "I doubt we'll find anything, but it can't hurt to look."

They played their lights across the floorboards, nudging any that seemed loose with their feet, but nothing budged. Glancing up, Charlotte noticed Heidi at the window where she had been the first time they came up to the garret.

"What is it?" she asked, going over to her.

"I don't know. I just keep feeling really drawn to this area. There must be a reason."

Julie and Tracy joined them, scouring the floorboards near the window.

"It's so hot up here," Tracy complained. "Can we at least open the window?"

Julie moved to slide the window upwards, but it wouldn't budge. "Heaven knows when was the last time it was opened," she said through gritted teeth. "I can't do it."

"I'll help," said Tracy. Together they pushed, both groaning with the effort. Finally, it began to give with a screech.

"I don't think we'll get it much further," said Julie, looking at the few inches between the pane and the sill. "This will have to do."

"Those old windows can be tough," said Charlotte. "I watched someone fix one in my grandmother's house. Yes, it was Keith," she added with a wink at Tracy. "Do you know that inside here there are weights and pulleys?" She ran her hand over the window casing. "The rope was broken and the window wouldn't stay open. He had to replace the rope. It was quite a production."

"Something seems to be sticking this one," said Julie.

Heidi reached up to touch the casing. "This opens?" she asked. "How?"

"You have to remove this part first," Charlotte said, clinking her fingernail against the glass of the sash. "Then remove these sides. Keith did it with a screwdriver, but this appears to have nails."

"Do you have a hammer with a claw?" Heidi asked Julie.

"You want to fix the window now?" Julie asked, looking incredulous.

"Not fix it. I want to get inside."

"If you think the diary is hidden in there, I can tell you it's not wide enough for that. It would never fit," said Charlotte.

"Well, I'm telling you that something is powerfully drawing me to this window. I think we should check."

Charlotte gave Julie a questioning look.

Julie sighed. "I'll get the hammer. I just hope we can put it back together with no problem or Andy will not be happy."

When she returned with the tool, Charlotte tried her best to remember how Keith had removed the various parts of the window in her grandmother's house. They got the sash down then pried loose the door to expose the weights on the right side of the window. Reaching in, she pulled out the long, heavy weight. Then she stuck her hand in, gingerly at first, not sure what might be hiding inside. Mice maybe? Or bugs.

“Nothing in here,” she said, then replaced the weight and housing.

She did the same on the left side. Once the door was off the casing of the window and the weight removed, Heidi held her flashlight over the opening. Again, Charlotte reached in. Almost immediately, her fingers brushed something papery. Fearing that it was a nest, she quickly pulled her hand out. “There's something in there,” she said.

“I knew it,” said Heidi.

“It's not a diary. I think it might be a hornet's nest. It feels like thin paper.”

While the others backed away, Heidi moved closer, maneuvering the flashlight for the best view.

“I don't think it's a nest,” she said. “It looks like an old piece of paper. I'm going to try to get it out without tearing it. Charlotte, could you hold my flashlight?”

Charlotte took the flashlight while Heidi reached in and slowly extracted the paper.

“What is it?” asked Tracy once the paper was out.

Heidi handed the folded paper to Charlotte who in turn handed it to Julie. “It's your house,” she said.

“But your ancestor. You look first.”

Wishing she had her gloves, Charlotte carefully unfolded the brittle, yellowed paper. Heidi held the flashlight over it so she could get a better look. Charlotte's heart beat faster the moment she saw the faded writing at the top of the paper. *My dearest Jerusha* it began.

“It's a letter to Jerusha,” she said. Flipping it over to look for the sender, she found the name Susannah at the bottom. It's from her sister. The one who moved to Ohio.”

“She was Jerusha's only surviving sibling, wasn't she?” asked Heidi.

“Yes. I can't wait to read it.”

“How do you suppose it ended up in there?” asked Julie.

"She must have hidden it for some reason," said Charlotte. "She certainly went to a lot of trouble to hide it well. Maybe once we read it, we'll understand why."

Chapter 37

April 1832
Birch Falls, Vermont

"What did she mean by that?" Mary asked, turning on Eli. She had not seen him come in with the others. He hadn't helped disperse the crowd, hadn't moved to stop them from forcing their awful potion down Seth's throat.

Eli stood in a corner of the kitchen, in shadow. Mary moved towards him. "What did she mean?"

Lavinia's parting words: *Ask Eli, He saw. He will tell you*, coupled with his odd behavior threw an unfamiliar feeling of betrayal across her heart. "You went with them to make sure they did not dishonor the remains of our children." She heard her own voice shaking. "How is it they came here with Lizzy's heart..." She could not finish the sentence. All the air seemed to have been sucked from her body.

She fell forward, but arms caught her. Caroline's arms. She guided Mary to a chair. A cup of cold water was placed in her hand. "Drink this," Caroline commanded.

Mary drank, then leaned forward against the kitchen table, letting it hold her up.

"Eli, what did happen?" Caroline's asked.

"It was not what I had expected." Eli's voice came from the corner of the room. He was still in shadow, furthest from the light of the kitchen fire. Mary's back was to him. It was just as well. She did not think she could face him.

"Start from the beginning," she heard Caroline say.

Mary glanced up at Caroline who was now rubbing Mary's hands. Caroline's face was turned towards Eli, her eyes hard in the firelight. "What happened when you first got to the graveyard?"

"There was a crowd. Everyone seemed to get there at once. Mr. Jackman gave the orders for the first grave to be opened. They began with Rebecca she having been the first to go. They made quick work of it, pulled up the coffin, and opened it. She was..." Here his voice faltered. He had to stop a moment. "She was as you would expect."

Mary's body tensed at the thought of what her child, dead more than a year, must look like now. She closed her eyes trying to shut out the image.

"Go on," said Caroline.

"They reburied her and moved to Josie. She, too, was as would be expected. Then they turned to Lizzy."

He grew silent again. There was a shuffle of feet as he crossed the room. A chair scraped the floor as he pulled it away from the table and seated himself opposite Mary and Caroline.

"I cannot describe what it feels like to see one's own children in the state they were in. I was beside myself already. All I could do was steal myself for a similar sight with Lizzy and then it would be over. They would be proven wrong, and we could all move on from this. But when they opened her coffin..."

Again, his voice trailed off. Mary looked up, though she didn't want to. Eli's eyes were shut tight. Both hands lay on the table in fists. His mouth was working as though he fought to spew out the words that would not come. Caroline's grip on her hand tightened.

"What about Lizzy?" asked Caroline.

"She was...not as you would expect," he finally said.

"How was she, then?" Mary found her voice, rough though it was, long enough to ask.

Eli swallowed hard. He rubbed a hand down his face. "She had turned. She was laying on her side."

"Is that all?" asked Mary. "That could have happened when her coffin was carried from the vault to her grave. Seth nearly dropped his end. It was jostled. It does not prove anything."

Eli looked away from the two women, his gaze fixed on the fire crackling in the hearth. "That was not all," he said to the fire.

Turning back, he looked Mary in the eye for the first time since he'd returned to the house. "They turned her on her back. Her hair and fingernails had grown longer. Mary, she had become…" He searched for a word. "Unnatural."

Mary looked to Caroline.

"Perhaps your Doctor Eacker can explain why that might be," said Caroline. For the first time her voice held a hint of a tremor.

"Perhaps," Eli allowed. "But there is more. There was blood at her mouth. Fresh blood."

"No!" Mary slammed her palm on the table. "That is not possible."

Susannah appeared in the doorway, a hand clutching the throat of her dress.

"I am sorry, Susannah," Eli said, his voice lowered again.

Susannah came to stand behind Mary, her hands on her mother's shoulders. "Seth is sleeping," she said. "Was it then that they cut her heart from her?" she asked. Mary wondered how Susannah was able to speak the words.

He lowered his gaze to the table. "Yes. And it, too, was filled with fresh blood."

Mary felt her own blood drain from her face.

Eli went on, his words pushing out into the room. "They set her heart aside, cut her head from her body and placed it between her legs. They said it was so she would be unable to rise again. They reburied her body but took her heart to Isaac Ward's shop. He burned it to ashes on his forge.

"It was that girl, Nan, who said Seth should be there, that he was supposed to breathe in the smoke while the heart burned. It is how it was done in Woodstock. They asked me to fetch him, but I told them he was too ill to leave his bed. Chauncey said we would bring it to him, and he could drink the ashes and it would do just as well."

As Eli spoke Mary stared at him feeling as though she did not know him, as though the twenty-five years they had been married and the eight children she had borne him were of no consequence. She was looking at a stranger. Susannah's gasp from behind her made Mary jump.

"Sit down, Susannah," said Caroline.

"Come. Sit next to me," said Mary. She took Susannah's hand in her own. Then she remembered Jerusha's footsteps on the stairs as she and Caroline forced Lavinia from the house telling Susannah to see to her.

"Did you send Jerusha back to bed? Did she see anything?" Mary asked.

"She did not. At least nothing of consequence. She knows there were people in the house. That is all. I brought her back to the garret. She was quite concerned that Seth was near death and wanted to be with him, but I assured her it was not yet time."

Mary nodded. At least Jerusha was spared this nightmare. Mary glared hard at Eli, catching his eye, almost daring him to look away. "And she will never know of this. Any of it."

Eli nodded. "Of course," he agreed.

The sound of coughing drew their attention to Seth's room. Upon returning to his bedside, Mary nearly slipped in the ashy water that still pooled on the floor by his bed. Caroline bent to retrieve the mug that had rolled under the bedside table. "I will get a cloth to clean that up," she said, leaving the room.

Seth coughed harder, expelling a large mouthful of blood. It landed in a clot on the coverlet. Trying to wipe it away with a cloth, Susannah only succeeded in mixing the blood with watery ashes making and ugly smear on the fabric. And odd fury rose in Mary as she realized the stain would never come out. She could not bear the thought of it being a constant reminder. Yet she could not afford to dispose of the coverlet, and she could not conceive at that moment of ever taking another one from the hands of Lavinia Wicker.

Caroline returned to the room with a cloth to wipe the puddle from the floor and a fresh cup of clean water for Seth. When his coughing subsided, Mary helped him to drink. He lay on the bed, his breathing ragged.

All night, they sat with him, no one speaking a word. At dawn, Jerusha appeared in the doorway.

"Come," said Mary, taking the child upon her lap. "Pray with us for your brother."

They had just finished their prayer when Seth took his final breath.

Chapter 38

August 1973
Middlebury, Vermont

Charlotte grabbed the wire handles of the flimsy frying pan of popcorn, dumping it into a bowl, taking care not to burn herself on the puffed-up foil, then carried it to the coffee table in her living room. She, Heidi, and Tracy had stopped for supper on the way back from Birch Falls. Julie had been kind enough to let her take Jerusha's letter from Susannah with her. She'd read it aloud before leaving Julie's home but wanted to study it more carefully.

"Not yet," she admonished as Heidi and Tracy's hands lunged towards the popcorn. "It's too hot. I want to read the letter again while we're waiting because no one can touch it with buttery fingers once we start eating the popcorn."

She went back to the kitchen, washed and dried her hands, then returned with the cotton gloves she wore when handling the diary. She had refused to reread the letter in the restaurant despite the fact that they all wanted to peruse it again for fear of getting any food stains on it.

"Read it out loud again," said Tracy. "I can't remember everything."

Sitting on the floor, Charlotte carefully unfolded the delicate missive.

"My dearest Jerusha," she began. "You have asked me to tell you of something about which I am not at liberty to divulge. I understand that you are curious to know why Mother and Mrs. Wicker had a falling out

282

when they had previously been such loyal and steadfast friends. You ask if it had something to do with Lizzy or Seth and why Mother was angry with Father shortly after Seth died. I will not say anything false to you. So, as you have asked if I know what it is all about, I must say that I do know. However, I am solemnly bound to not ever discuss the matter. If you are determined to know the circumstances of the contention between Mother and Mrs. Wicker, then I suggest you go to Mother with the letter you found and beg pardon for having read it. Only be prepared to be scolded for prying among property not your own.

"If you do this, you may still be disappointed as I do not believe Mother will tell you anything. Had she wanted you to know, she would have told you by now. I agree that it is very sad that such a sweet friendship as that which she shared with Mrs. Wicker was ruined, but I assure you Mother had good cause for the ill will she bears her neighbor. I had always hoped that as time went by, the rent in their friendship would somehow be repaired. Your letter acknowledges that it is not to be. Despite your longings, you cannot make it so, though your desire to heal past hurts is laudable.

"Better advice than going to Mother with the letter is to pray that the demon Curiosity will let you be so that you no longer brood over this matter. Plan instead for your own future rather than worry over what has gone on in the pasts of others.

"I thank the good Lord that you, Mother, and Father are well and that Nathan proves to be a useful and congenial hand. We, too, are well. Zachary does a good business with his store. Daisy and Jonathan keep me busy running after them, and I am grateful that Maria is now old enough to start being of some help. She is a good-natured soul and will make a sound role model for her younger brother and sister. Please give my love to all.

Your affectionate sister,

Susannah"

Charlotte set the letter down on the coffee table far away from the bowl of popcorn that the others were now greedily digging into.

"I wish we had Jerusha's letter to Susannah so we'd know what she asked her," Tracy said. "Got any ice cream?"

"How can you eat so much and stay so skinny?" Heidi marveled at her.

Tracy shrugged. "Gymnastics, I guess."

"She never stops moving, in case you haven't noticed," Charlotte said. "There's a box of Neapolitan in the freezer. Help yourself."

Tracy headed towards the kitchen doing a series of one-armed front walk-overs rather than walking. Charlotte chuckled. "Don't do that with a dish of ice cream in your hand on the way back."

Instead, when she returned, Tracy flew over the coffee table in a split leap, bowl held safely in one hand, though the spoon sailed through the air and she came dangerously close to hitting her head on the ceiling.

"I'd love to watch you perform some day," said Heidi as Tracy plopped back down on the couch next to her.

"I think you just did," said Charlotte. "I wonder why Jerusha hid this in the window casing."

"She probably didn't want her mom to know she'd asked her sister to tell her what happened."

"Well, yeah," said Charlotte. "But the window casing? She'd have to take it apart to get it in there. There had to be easier places to hide it than that."

"We may never know why she put it there," said Heidi.

"Probably not," Charlotte agreed. "The real question is, what did happen? Obviously, Susannah knew the story, but was sworn to secrecy, I'm guessing, by their mother.

"Do you think it has to do with Lizzy being a vampire?" asked Tracy.

"I'm almost certain of it," said Charlotte.

"I get why Jerusha asked about Lizzy having something to do with it, but why Seth? He wasn't thought to be a vampire, too, was he?" asked Heidi.

"Not likely or his grave would probably be a legend trip site, too. But if you remember, that letter Jerusha wrote about in her diary, the one her mom started but never finished. Jerusha seemed to think whatever happened had to do with both of them."

"I wish her mom had finished that letter. Then we'd know what it was all about," said Tracy.

"If she'd finished it, she probably would have mailed it. Then we'd never know," Heidi answered.

Charlotte stared at Susannah's letter to Jerusha. "Hold on a minute," she said, getting up and going off to her bedroom. She returned with Jerusha's diary. Finding the page where Jerusha had written about finding her mother's letter, she read it aloud, ending with Jerusha's unfinished sentence, "I have made up my mind and have laid a plan. Tomorrow I will"

"Will what?" asked Tracy.

Charlotte shrugged. "That's where it ends. She ran out of pages in this diary. She must have had another one and gone right on to it. She wouldn't have just left it in the middle of a sentence. I'll bet she had decided to write to her sister."

"I really wish Julie would have let us hold a séance in the house. Then we could ask her," said Heidi.

Charlotte, wanting concrete answers, shrugged again. "I can understand why she wouldn't. I can't imagine living in a house where she's scared all the time, especially when her husband doesn't notice anything."

"Why don't you hold the séance in the cemetery?" Tracy offered. "Right at Jerusha's grave."

Charlotte was not inclined to drive all the way back to Birch Falls for that. Hoping Heidi wouldn't be disappointed, she asked, "Don't there need to be more people? I have to take Tracy back to Grandma's tomorrow and I don't know of anyone else offhand who would go."

Heidi looked lost in thought. "I don't think that would work," she said, much to Charlotte's relief. "Both times we've been there I get nothing from Lizzy's grave. Granted, I haven't tried Jerusha's but it's always their mother who seems to come through to me so she might get in the way."

"But she knows what happened," Tracy argued. "Just ask her. She obviously wants to tell you something."

"I don't know," said Heidi. "I got a feeling of hostility from her. It might not be a good idea."

"Let's work with what we have," said Charlotte. "Here's what we know for sure. Jerusha's brother and her sisters, except for Susannah, all died before her, probably from tuberculosis. Lizzy's grave has become a legend trip site because she was believed to be a vampire. The inscription on her gravestone contributes to the legend tripping lore, but it doesn't explain why they think she's a vampire. My guess is she was one of the people who were thought to be coming back and killing off the rest of the family. They probably dug her up to find out and that's how the rumor got started. What I don't get is why wouldn't Jerusha know that? It seems like it would be a difficult thing to conceal especially considering how closely-knit communities were at that time."

"True," said Heidi, "but there was obviously some big family secret that was bothering Jerusha because she didn't know what it was. It had something to do with her mother, Mrs. Wicker, and, apparently, Lizzy, Seth, and maybe even their dad. What could all that have been about?"

"I wish I knew," said Charlotte. "It's entirely possible that it has nothing to do with Lizzy having been thought to be a vampire, but I have a strong feeling that it is connected." She chuckled to herself. "Maybe it's wishful thinking. I'm in love with the idea of there being this great legend in our family history."

"Hey," said Tracy, jumping up as though a sudden thought had propelled her from the couch. "Maybe that swamp guy will know something about it. Mr. Ormsbee said he might."

"Swamp Yankee and, yeah, if he'll even agree to talk to me. He might be a folklorist's dream, but I'm not sure how much he knows about our family's history."

"Are you going to meet with him if Mr. Ormsbee can set it up?" Heidi asked.

"Sure. Why not?"

"He didn't sound like the most savory character."

"Does that mean you don't want to come with me?" Charlotte grinned at her friend.

"I didn't say that." Heidi's voice was apprehensive sounding. "I don't think you should go alone."

"I won't. Mr. Ormsbee said he'd be there, too, remember. I think his wife would kill him if he didn't come with me."

"Do you want me to shut the window?" Tracy asked. Rain had started to fall, and a streak of lightening flashed across the sky.

"I guess you'd better," said Charlotte, chagrined because even with the windows open the apartment was stiflingly hot.

"I'd better go," said Heidi. "My aunt doesn't like thunderstorms. She won't want to be alone."

Having said goodbye to Heidi and closed all the windows, the two sisters sat side-by-side on the couch.

"I wish I wasn't going back tomorrow," Tracy said. "This is just getting exciting. I want to stay and see how it turns out."

"I have to go to work tomorrow and school starts for you in a week. When's Mom picking you up at Grandma's?"

"Wednesday. She wants me home for a few days before school starts. I'm going to be dying of curiosity after I leave so you've got to promise to write and tell me everything you find out."

"I will."

Lightning flashed followed immediately by a clap of thunder.

"Charlotte?"

"Mm."

"Do you believe in vampires and ghosts?"

"Vampires, no. Ghosts? Well, I'm not sure. Do you?"

"I liked Barnabas Collins in Dark Shadows. I kind of wish he was real, but no, I don't believe vampires really exist. I do think I believe in ghosts, though. I think Julie's house is definitely haunted. Don't you?"

"There is certainly something unusual going on there."

"What about Heidi? Do you think she can really contact dead people?"

"I don't know. Probably not, but I won't say that to her."

"It is weird about the stuff that happened at Jerusha's mother's grave. What if her mother is trying to tell Heidi something? Maybe she's trying to tell us all something. Maybe she wants us to know about whatever happened. I think she's really upset."

Charlotte was about to reply when a flash of lightning lit up the entire room followed so closely by a crashing peal of thunder it made them both jump. Instantly, the lights went out and they were plunged into a world of darkness.

Chapter 39

April 1832
Birch Falls, Vermont

Sitting on her mother's lap, Jerusha stared at Seth. She knew he was gone. His ragged, struggling breaths had ceased. Mrs. Cutting pressed her fingertips to his neck then looked at Jerusha's mother, shaking her head slightly. She felt her mother's arms tighten around her, pulling her close. Her body trembled against Jerusha's back. A sob from the other side of the bed caught her attention. She looked up to see Susannah wipe away a tear as Mrs. Cutting folded her into her arms. Her father stood at the foot of the bed staring at Seth. The odd look on his face startled her. It was different from the one he'd worn when her sisters had died. There was grief to be sure, but something else Jerusha could not name.

She felt herself slide to a stand as her mother rose then stepped in front of Jerusha to bend over Seth's still form and kiss his cheek. Then her mother turned toward her father and glared at him in a way that truly frightened Jerusha. Her father left the room in silence. Her mother followed.

Jerusha stepped closer to the bed. "Goodbye, Seth," she whispered as she leaned in to kiss his cheek. Her hand on the bedsheet came away wet, and she wiped it on her skirt. Looking down at the bed, she saw the large damp spot near his pillow. Something must have spilled, she thought. But all down the side of the bed was a water stain with flecks of some gritty substance. Jerusha was about to ask what it was when her mother's voice from the kitchen arrested her.

"Go!" she heard her mother shout.

All heads turned towards the sound. Jerusha sidled towards the doorway. She who had stood on the threshold of the sick room so often not wanting to enter now felt fear of leaving it. But she peeked around the corner towards the kitchen. Her parents were standing near the door. Her mother's voice was lower now, but she heard the words just the same.

"Go and tell Lavinia and Chauncey that Seth is dead. Tell them their foolishness has done no good. Tell them never to step foot in this house again."

Jerusha's heart hammered in her chest as she remembered her nocturnal descent of the staircase the night before, Susannah meeting her halfway and ushering her back to her room. Then she remembered the crowd. It was the many voices that had awakened her. Before Susannah had turned her around, she had caught sight of her mother and Mrs. Wicker who seemed to be arguing and Mrs. Cutting who Jerusha thought had been pressing Mrs. Wicker towards the door. Where had all the people gone? Why had they not stayed to pray over Seth? Why, especially, had Mrs. Wicker left? Wouldn't her mother have wanted her dearest friend with her then? But now she seemed angry with Mrs. Wicker. Was it because she had not stayed?

As Jerusha watched from the edge of the kitchen, her father dropped his gaze to the floor. He turned, opened the door, and walked out into the breaking dawn. Jerusha shrank back before her mother turned around and returned to the sick room where Susannah and Mrs. Cutting were already preparing to ready Seth's body for burial.

Two days later Jerusha stood quietly in the parlor as Reverend Cobb offered prayers of comfort and warning to those gathered in the parlor where Seth's coffin stood. Only her parents, Susannah, Mrs. Cutting, and the minister's wife were present. Her mother seemed to want it over with quickly. Once the simple service had ended, Jerusha made ready to leave for the walk to the graveyard, but her mother held her back.

"I am not going, Jerusha. I want you to stay home with me."

This perplexed Jerusha, but something in her mother's face forbade any questioning.

The two of them were left alone in the house. They worked in near silence preparing the day's dinner. There were so many things Jerusha did not understand about all that had happened, so many questions she longed to ask but did not dare. It was as if a forbidding atmosphere had permeated the air around them, invisible, but almost tangible.

Days went by without this oppressive element in the home lifting. The family seemed to go about their business in a sort of trance. A crushing silence filled the house, only occasionally broken by a necessary word or two. There were no visitors bringing condolences other than Mrs. Cutting and the Reverend and Mrs. Cobb who came to check on the family from time to time.

Days turned to weeks with little change in Jerusha's mother, though her father and Susannah seemed to come back to themselves. Jerusha had tried to ask Susannah for an explanation, but her sister had put her off first saying it was the grief of so much loss, then, after Jerusha pushed, telling her there were things she was too young to understand and must not try to fathom.

Once when Jerusha proposed visiting with Hannah or Betsy, her mother refused to allow her to leave the house. In a curt tone, she told Jerusha that she was needed at home more than ever and could expect to spend much less time cavorting with friends.

"Give it time, Jerusha," Susannah had told her then. "Mother is still very upset over the loss of Seth. She will come 'round, but it may take a while. Be patient."

But Jerusha was missing her friends terribly. She had lost all but Susannah. Home felt oppressive. While going about her chores, she daydreamed of picking blueberries with Hannah and Betsy and laughing in the schoolyard with them and her other school chums. Sometimes it felt as though she might never set eyes on them again.

Though many years apart in age, she was at least comforted by the companionship of Susannah. Their mother had decided that Jerusha was no longer to attend the district school and insisted that Susannah give her lessons at home. She was a patient teacher, and Jerusha progressed in her studies, but she dearly missed the company of her fellow students. If it weren't for Susannah, Jerusha would have felt completely lost in an abys of loneliness.

On a bright day in May, Jerusha and Susannah were working in the garden. A gentle breeze played with the strings of their bonnets, and Jerusha finally began to feel a lessening of the anguish that had consumed them. For the first time in many weeks, she and her sister fell into a benign merriment, even laughing together while they worked. Not that things would be as they were before, but that some light might come back into their lives.

She was on the point of asking Susannah if she thought their mother might consent to a visit from Hannah or Betsy when the sound of wagon wheels coming up the road made them both turn to see who approached.

Susannah dropped her hoe. "Zachary!" she exclaimed.

As Jerusha watched her sister run from the garden toward the wagon that carried her husband, she knew things were about to change indeed. Zachary had returned from Ohio. He was back to claim Susannah and take her with him to their new home.

Chapter 40

August 1973
Birch Falls, Vermont

Charlotte had been at her desk all morning writing text for exhibit signs. When her phone rang, she grabbed the receiver without even looking up. "Assistant Director of Programs, Charlotte Lajoie speaking," she said, while continuing to write.

"Charlotte, dear, I'm sorry to trouble you at work, but I need to tell you something important."

Charlotte put down her pen. "What's wrong, Grandma?"

"It's my sister, your Great Aunt Lorraine. She passed away. My brother just called to tell me."

"Oh, Grandma, I'm so sorry. What happened?"

"Heart attack, they think. She died in her sleep as far as we know. She lived alone so no one's really sure what happened. A neighbor who looked in on her from time to time hadn't seen her in a day or two. She went to check and found her."

"She was older than you, wasn't she?" Charlotte had only met her great aunt once or twice when she was little and barely remembered her.

"Yes, by a few years. Anyway, I wanted to let you know, in case you had any plans for coming down, that I'll be away for a bit. Armand is coming to pick me up this afternoon. He's only in Weston, you know."

That would be Charlotte's Great Uncle Armand. Another relative she barely knew.

"He'll drive us up to Peacham. He's already been on the phone with the funeral parlor making arrangements. It's not fair to leave it all to him, though.

I want to help. Afterwards we'll need to clean out her house."

"She never married, did she?" asked Charlotte.

"No, which is why it's up to Armand and me. No husband or kids to do it. I doubt there will be many people at the funeral. Just Armand, me, and probably a few neighbors."

"How long will you be gone?"

"At least a week, I expect. Maybe longer. We'll stay at her house until we've got it cleaned out. Then Armand will put it on the market. She did have a will. She told Armand she was leaving it to us, so we've agreed to sell it and split the money. I'll call you when I get back."

"Okay, Grandma. I'm really very sorry." Charlotte wished she could think of something better to say. Her grandmother had just lost her sister. I'm sorry seemed inadequate.

"Thank you, dear. She had a good life, and it seems she went peacefully. There's not much more we could ask."

Charlotte had just hung up when Brad showed up in her office doorway. She glanced up to see him leaning against the doorframe, arms crossed, a lit cigarette between two fingers. He took a long drag and blew the smoke towards her. Was he trying to look sexy? She wanted to gag. Instead, she said, "Hi, Brad. Did you want something?"

"I've got some news to tell you," he said, strolling into her office. He pulled out a chair across from her, putting one foot on her desk.

"What is it?" she asked, fighting the urge to shove his foot back to the floor.

"Shepherd is so impressed with my idea for the Halloween exhibit that he wants me to do the same for Thanksgiving and Christmas."

His idea. The one he stole from her. Her hands gripped the edge of her desk to keep from slapping the smug look off his face.

"Of course, Thanksgiving and Christmas are coming right up, so I've got to give them my full attention right away, which means I'll have to leave the rest of the Halloween exhibit to you. Do you think you can handle it?"

Charlotte's grip on the edge of her desk relaxed. Finally, she could take charge of this exhibit and make *her* idea a reality. Granted, President Shepherd wouldn't know it was her idea, but she could still do a great job of it, and he'd know it was under her direction.

"Of course," she said, her tone a bit more clipped than she'd meant it to be. She purposely softened her voice at the look of irritation flashing across Brad's face. "Thank you for trusting me with it."

Charlotte's emotions bounced from vexation with Brad to joy and excitement over taking charge of the Halloween exhibit.

"It's not like I have much choice," he said. "You'll need to put in some extra hours. Can you work this Saturday?"

At that her heart sank. Just last evening Charlotte had received a phone call from Earl Ormsbee. He'd finally talked Alvin Stankard into meeting with her about her ancestors. It seemed he did know about the origins of Eliza Kendall's supposed vampirism. Mr. Ormsbee had set up the meeting for this Saturday. He'd been clear about how difficult it was to talk Mr. Stankard into it. He didn't like or trust anybody he hadn't known most of his life and certainly not a newcomer. It was only because she was a descendant of a family who had lived in Birch Falls as long as his own that he'd finally agreed. She feared that if she canceled, he would never reschedule.

"This Saturday isn't good. I've agreed to meet a man in Birch Falls on Saturday, but I can work any other weekend after that. I'll work late, too, if needed to make up any time."

Brad removed his foot from her desk and leaned forward in his chair.

"Are you saying you won't put in the extra time this Saturday because you have a date?"

"What? No! It's not a—"

"Ah, Brad, there you are." President Shepherd appeared in her doorway. "I'm sorry. I didn't mean to interrupt. Good morning, Charlotte. I suppose Brad has given you the good news. Brad, come see me when you're finished here. I've a few things to discuss with you."

Brad stood, turning towards President Shepherd. "Sir, I was just telling Charlotte that she'll be overseeing the installation of my Halloween exhibit."

"Excited to take charge?" he asked. "Brad has assured me he's arranged everything so all you'll have to do is follow the instructions he's laid out."

Charlotte pried her gritted teeth apart to say, "I'm sure it will all run smoothly."

"If you don't fall behind," said Brad.

"I'm sure Charlotte won't mind putting in some extra hours, if need be," said President Shepherd giving Charlotte a pointed look.

"Of course, I won't mind," she said.

"As long as it doesn't interfere with her love life," said Brad with a little laugh. Charlotte felt her cheeks burn.

"What does that mean?" asked President Shepherd.

"Only that I just asked her to work this Saturday, but she says she can't because she has a date."

"It's not a date," said Charlotte, her voice rising a notch.

"You said you were meeting a man in Birch Falls, didn't you? Sounds like a date to me."

"He's an informant. It's folklore related."

President Shepherd left the doorway to stand in the middle of Charlotte's office. "Museum business?" Looking to Brad, he added, "That you don't know about?"

"No," said Charlotte, standing now, too. "Not museum business. It's personal."

An inkling of suspicion shown in President Shepherd's eyes. "Not museum business, but folklore-related? There wouldn't be a conflict of interest, would there?"

"No, no. It's nothing like that." Charlotte sighed. She would have to explain it all to prevent any misgivings on the part of the museum president about her loyalty to the museum.

"It's actually an interesting story that has to do with one of my ancestors."

As Charlotte related the story, she watched President Shepherd grow more and more intrigued. He took a seat and motioned for her to sit, too. Brad interrupted to ask, "President Shepherd, didn't you want to see me about something?"

"It can wait. We'll meet after lunch. Right now, I want to hear the rest of this."

Charlotte was aware that President Shepherd's degrees were in education, not folklore. He'd taught high school history for a while before becoming involved in the museum field. But he was an administrator much more than a historian or a folklorist. Nonetheless, he obviously had a strong interest.

Brad dropped into his chair, this time keeping both feet on the floor.

"Tell me more about this belief in vampires. I had no idea. Witches, of course, I knew about, but not vampires."

Warming to her subject, Charlotte regaled him with her knowledge of the odd phenomenon.

"And your ancestors were involved in this?"

"It appears so. A legend of vampirism is attached to Eliza's grave. It still attracts legend trippers to this day."

"Legend trippers?"

As Charlotte began an explanation of legend tripping, Brad let out a heavy sigh. He leaned back in his chair and rolled his eyes. As much as Charlotte wished she could tell him that if he wasn't interested, he could leave, she knew it would not only be rude but detrimental to her career at the museum. He was still her direct supervisor.

"Is there anything about this vampire belief or legend tripping in the exhibit?" the president asked.

"No," said Charlotte.

"Why not? I think people would be very interested in it."

"It doesn't fit with the rest of the exhibit," said Brad. "Which we should probably let Charlotte get back to work on. If she's not going to put in any time on Saturday, then we shouldn't be taking up what time she has today."

Charlotte decided to take a chance. Who knew when she'd get another opportunity. She'd be risking Brad's ire, but at least he wouldn't be able to say she'd done anything behind his back.

"President Shepherd, I agree with Brad that it doesn't work with the current exhibit. We're showing the progression of Halloween from its beginnings as the Celtic festival of *Samhain* to what we know of it today. The vampire belief was in no way connected to Halloween. They didn't even use the word 'vampire.' Besides, it's late now to begin adding to the exhibit.

"However, I also agree with you that it is a fascinating topic and one most people don't know about and would probably be very interested in. Perhaps we could make it its own exhibit in the future. I'd be more than happy to handle the research on it. I'm doing it anyway for my family."

The contrast between the two faces before Charlotte could not have been more pronounced. President Shepherd's eyes lit up as his face broke into a huge grin at the same time that Brad's face showed barely controlled rage.

"That's a fantastic idea, Charlotte. As soon as you're done working on the Halloween exhibit you can get started on coming up with ideas for how to present it. And, of course, you must go to meet with this Alvin Stankard on Saturday. I hope you get some good information from him." Turning towards Brad, he added, "You've picked a winner in this young lady. Good job!"

President Shepherd took his leave followed quickly by Brad who only turned to glare at Charlotte before heading out the door.

Charlotte sat back in her chair and drew a deep breath. Two emotions warred within her – exhilaration at securing her own exhibit and trepidation at how Brad might choose to make her life hell for doing so.

Chapter 41

June 1832
Birch Falls, Vermont

Mary walked alone to the burying ground. She had not gone when they buried Seth. She could not bear the sight of the freshly dug up graves of her daughters. She averted her gaze whenever she came and went from Sunday meeting or had any other occasion to pass. Her family's graves were not close to the meetinghouse itself, so it was not hard to do, but it was not a large burying ground. Despite their relative distance from the meetinghouse, she would have been able to see them if she'd tried.

Enough time had gone by, she thought, and she felt the need to visit Seth's final resting place. Something inside her also wanted to be near her girls. She ached for having allowed the desecration of their graves and Lizzy's very body. There was probably nothing more she could have done to prevent it, but still, she was their mother. Perhaps she should have fought harder, physically stood in the way even. But she had trusted Eli to ensure their children's bodies were treated with respect. How could she have known he'd allow what they had done to Lizzy? She did not care that the child's corpse had not been as one would have expected. She did not care if Lizzy had been found sitting upright eating a pumpkin pie. Had she been present, they would never have done what they did. Never.

As she crested the hill upon which sat the meetinghouse and burying ground, sweat rolled in rivulets down her back. It was a warm day. She wiped her forehead with the back of her hand, nearly knocking the straw bonnet from her head.

As she neared the graves, Mary slowed her pace, then stopped completely only a few feet away. A wave of grief overtook her as she gazed towards them. As yet only Rebecca's and Josie's graves had stones. There had been so little time between moving Lizzy from the vault to her grave and Seth's rapid decline and death in April, then all that had happened afterwards, that they had not yet attended to it. Eli had mentioned last night that he had spoken with Edward Turner about inscribing and setting the stones. It was his speaking of it, a subject rarely broached in their now fragile relationship, that determined Mary on visiting the graves.

Taking a deep breath, Mary pushed on until she reached the graves of her children. She lowered herself to the ground at the spot where she knew Seth and Lizzy lay. Her gaze traveled to the gravestones of Rebecca and Josie and to the tiny markers of her infants.

"My children," she whispered, running a hand gently over the grass. "I am so sorry. So deeply sorry." Anything else she had thought to say vanished. All the misery she'd locked inside spilled forth in a flood of tears. She made no effort to hold them back. She was alone in the burying ground. There was no one to hear or see her. When she had cried all she could, she felt almost cleansed. Still, something nagged at her. There was something still needed, but she was uncertain what.

After wiping her eyes, she sat staring at the stones of the other graves and the bareness of the two newest ones. Her gaze traveled beyond them to the other graves in the burying ground. It was then that she noticed the difference in the grass. It was longer on the other graves. It had been a rainy spring allowing for abundant growth for undisturbed grass. But for her children who had been dug up and for Seth newly buried in April, the rain had inhibited such rapid growth. The realization that the evidence of what had occurred here was still visible if one knew how to see it, felt like a stab to her heart.

"I will mend it for you, Lizzy," she said aloud, her voice strong, though still rough from crying. "They will always be reminded of how they have wronged you."

With energy born of new-found determination, Mary rose, trudged down the hill, heading for the farm of Edward Turner.

"Mr. Turner," she called, upon catching sight of him in his field.

He straightened up as she strode towards him. He began to tip his tall, straw hat but stuttered the movement for a second when he realized who had hailed him. The reaction was not unusual. Nearly everyone in Birch Falls was wary around her, treating her as if she had gone mad. At times, she wondered if she had. Still, it was reassuring in a way. As long as they were cautious, they would remember to keep quiet about what had happened. No one was to speak of it so that it would never get back to Jerusha. Mary's threat to burn down the Wicker house with all of them inside had become well-known, and her anger was such that no one was quite certain whether or not she had been serious. In any case, none wished to be responsible for so much as a whiff of a rumor finding its way to Jerusha's ears. Mary believed that their own sense of guilt should be enough to seal their mouths, but if being thought mad helped, she could tolerate it for Jerusha's sake.

"Good day, Mrs. Kendall," said Edward Turner, now standing fully upright and clutching his straw hat in his hands.

"Good day, sir. I understand that my husband spoke with you yesterday about carving the stones for Seth's and Lizzy's graves."

"Indeed, he did." Mr. Turner tilted his head seeming to appraise her for signs of lunacy.

"I want you to add a line to Eliza's gravestone."

"What would you like on it?" he asked.

"Her final words before she left us. Please listen carefully so you do not forget."

"I will remember. What were they?"

"Just before Lizzy drew her last breath, her thoughts were for her family and friends gathered at her deathbed. She said, 'I will come for you all.' I want that on her stone so that all who see it will know and remember that her final thoughts were for the salvation of us all, that she looked forward to our heavenly reunion."

Mr. Turner stared down at the rock he was edging from the ground with his toe. "I will do that for you, Ma'am," he said without looking up.

Before the month was out, two new gravestones graced the final resting places of Seth and Lizzy. The words *I will come for you all* were etched deeply at the bottom of Lizzy's stone. Standing alone at the grave, taking in the two new stones, Mary whispered, "There now, my Lizzy, all who read this will know you were never capable of causing harm to anyone."

Chapter 42

September 1839
Birch Falls, Vermont

Jerusha sat by the garret window. After Susannah had left with Zachary for Ohio seven years ago, Jerusha had moved to the chamber on the second floor rather than continue to sleep in the garret. But now she wanted utter privacy or at least as close as she could come to it. The sun had set, and Jerusha worked at the small table by candle and moonlight to carry out the plan she had decided on and written in her second diary just yesterday.

Dearest Susannah, her letter began.

She went on to explain how she had found her mother's unfinished letter to their Aunt Helen and what it contained. She related how she had asked Mrs. Wicker, but she had refused to tell her anything.

I believe, dear sister, that you must know what occurred to turn Mother and Mrs. Wicker from cherished friends to bitter foes. You may say that it is not my concern, and perhaps you would be right. But I remember days when our family and the Wickers were close and felt much affection for one another. Those were good days. It was the way Christian neighbors ought to behave towards one another. Do you not remember the corn husking frolics? Those were my favorite. My most comforting memories are of Mother and Mrs. Wicker baking together in a warm kitchen on frosty days. They would talk and laugh and fill the room with love.

Mother has not traded with Mrs. Wicker for any of her weaving in years. Instead, she gets what we need from Mr. Hapgood's store, or we go without. I am only allowed to enter the Wicker home when we owe them work time for what Joseph or Asa do on our farm. Mother is like a thundercloud on those days. She says now that we have Nathan we can do without the Wicker boys, but there are still times when more help is needed.

Please, Susannah, tell me what you know. Tell me what Mother meant by someone harming Lizzy and Seth. I am not simply prying. I want to help rectify the situation if I can. And, I admit, I want to know what secret has been kept from me all these years. I, too, am a member of this family. No longer a child, I have a right to know.

* * *

A few days later, Nathan Halsey announced that he was going to Mr. Hapgood's store for a few needed items. Jerusha asked if he would mind her accompanying him as she needed some sewing supplies. In truth, she wanted to post her letter to Susannah without anyone knowing. They took the wagon as Eli wanted Nathan to bring the plow to the blacksmith for repair.

"I keep thinking about why Chauncey Haskell would say we had something in common," Nathan told her as they sat side-by-side on the wagon.

Jerusha thought back to their conversation on the Fourth of July when he had mentioned Mr. Haskell's comment.

"Have you deciphered it then?" she asked.

"No, other than we have both lost family members, but that could be said of most anyone. Truthfully, I hadn't though much on it since we spoke of it in July, but recently I saw Mr. Haskell and so had occasion to ask him."

305

"What did he say?"

"He did not tell me the reason which I thought was odd, but he did say we both have a dark secret."

Jerusha felt as though her stomach flipped over. Her palms turned sweaty. She had tucked her letter up her sleeve to keep it out of sight. Now its corner dug into the soft flesh of her arm.

"Why would he say such a thing?" she asked. Even to her own ears her voice sounded frightened.

Nathan glanced at her, a look of concern on his face.

"I did not mean to alarm you," he said. "You know Chauncey Haskell even better than I. You know that old goat likes to tell wild stories and stir up everyone's imagination."

Jerusha nodded. Certainly, this was true. He'd been telling them all chilling tales for as long as she could remember. Still, she had never fully understood what connection Nathan had to the old storyteller. "How did you come to know him?" she asked.

"He knew my uncle so when I left Connecticut, I was told to go to him. I stayed with him when I first arrived in Birch Falls. He told me to see your father as he needed help on the farm. He said I would likely find a welcome because I am not from Birch Falls. I thought that odd but as he would not explain, I did not pry."

A flush of shame spread through Jerusha. It was well-known that her mother had become cold and distant towards many of the inhabitants of Birch Falls. Only Mrs. Cutting and her family and the minister and his wife seemed immune from her disdain. Jerusha and her father did not feel the same way, but her mother would be out of sorts for days if either of them seemed too friendly with others. Jerusha barely saw Hannah and Betsy anymore nor any of her school friends. After Susannah left, she did her lessons with her mother and sometimes Mrs. Cutting. She missed walking to and from school with a group of friends, sitting with them in the classroom, visiting at each other's homes, and being part of gatherings. Often the loneliness weighed heavily on her.

Her mother had, however, readily welcomed Nathan when he appeared at their farm looking for work. In fact, she seemed relieved that he had come. It meant that despite the Wicker boys being close by and willing to lend a hand to Father whenever needed, they would have much less occasion to set foot on Kendall property.

"I remember that he had me meet with the minister first and spend time doing chores at the parsonage. It was Reverend Cobb who gave me the reference for your father. Mr. Haskell said not to mention his name, that the good word of the Reverend would do well enough. I followed his advice, but never understood why he did not want me to mention him."

Jerusha fought back tears. She had been living with her mother's unexplained anger and growing reclusiveness for so long that she had not realized how deeply it affected her until she heard it put into words by an outsider. The unexpected reaction it provoked surprised her. She quickly wiped her eyes.

Nathan brought the wagon to a stop.

"Jerusha?" he asked. "Are you well? Have I offended you?"

His voice held such a strong note of concern that she could not keep from glancing up at him. Dark brown eyes held hers, his curly dark hair lifting gently in the breeze.

"No, you have not offended me." She dropped her gaze to her hands folded in her lap. "There is a secret in my family," she said. "But I do not know what it is. It seems all of Birch Falls knows but me."

"How do you know there is one?" he asked. "It seems odd that an entire town would conspire to keep a secret from you."

She looked up at him again, searching his face to judge if he thought her mad or simply silly. His countenance held no trace of disbelief, and his tone had been sincere. She took a deep breath, deciding to trust him. If his family had a secret, too, perhaps he would understand.

"Until my brother Seth died, my mother and Mrs. Wicker were the dearest of friends. And Mother had no foe in all of Birch Falls. Something happened about the same time as we lost Seth. I do not know what it was, but ever since then she has behaved as though she hates Mrs. Wicker and barely speaks to most people other than the Cuttings and Reverend and Mrs. Cobb."

"Have you asked her what it was?"

"Of course, but she becomes angry at the mention of it and will never tell."

"What about Mrs. Wicker? I suppose she knows what happened."

"I asked her once and she told me that it was for Mother to say. Now it seems that Mr. Haskell must know all about it as well. I suppose everyone does but me."

"Is there on one you can ask?"

Slowly, Jerusha withdrew the letter from her sleeve. "My sister, Susannah. This is why I wanted to come with you today. I want to post this letter without anyone knowing."

"Ah, so you were not simply desirous of my company."

Surprised, she glanced at him, uncertain whether or not he was teasing. "I always enjoy your company," she said.

Nathan let out a hearty laugh. "And I yours." He flicked the reigns setting the cart in motion again.

At the store, Jerusha gave the envelope to Mr. Hapgood who marked the number 25 in the upper right corner. Jerusha hoped Susannah would not mind paying the postage for a letter that came only from her without including the greetings and messages of their parents as well. Though she wasn't truly low on them, she picked up a few sewing notions so as not to arouse suspicion by returning home empty-handed.

"So, you think your sister knows, then?" asked Nathan on the ride home.

"I suppose she must. I was only nine when Seth died, but Susannah was already married. She was just waiting for Zachary to fetch her from Ohio."

Jerusha had been turning something over in her mind since her earlier conversation with Nathan. Finally deciding to ask, she said, "Mr. Haskell told you we both have a dark secret, but I do not have a secret. I am the one who the secret is being kept from. What of you? What is your secret?"

Nathan stared off into the distance not answering.

"I apologize," she said quickly. "I should not have pried."

"No," he said. "You are not prying, just trying to understand. It is only that mine is not so much a secret as a memory of something rather unpleasant."

The grim set of his mouth told her it must be something unpleasant indeed. She resolved to speak of it no more.

After a moment, Nathan asked, "Jerusha, what did Seth die from?"

"Consumption."

"And the others? Did they die of consumption, too?"

"Yes. All of them."

"Hmm..." He seemed to be mulling something over.

"Consumption is what carried off some of my brothers and sister before I left as well. Tell me, do you remember any talk of your sisters coming back?"

Confused, she asked, "Coming back? How?"

He looked down at her, seeming to gauge his next words.

"From the dead," he said finally.

"What?" The word came out in a gasp. "What do you mean?"

Nathan straightened up, eyes on the road before them. "I will tell you my so-called secret. Perhaps it will shed light on yours. Perhaps not. But I must warn you, it is a bit of a ghastly tale. One, in fact, that would be worthy of Chauncey Haskell."

Chapter 43

September 1973
Birch Falls, Vermont

Charlotte tried making conversation with Mr. Ormsbee as he drove them to meet Alvin Stankard, but her nerves kept getting the best of her. She'd driven up to the Ormsbee's house as they'd arranged on the phone, then gotten into Mr. Ormsbee's car. When she'd asked where they were meeting Alvin Stankard, he'd told her, "There's an old greasy spoon place called Jack's Kitchen on Route 7, not far. It's a favorite with truckers. Stankard likes it, too. He figures if he's gonna do this, he should get a free lunch out of it."

"I hope I have enough on me. I had no idea."

"No, no. I've got it covered. Besides you might not have much of an appetite once you sit down with him. My wife's right about him being a bit odiferous."

Charlotte started wondering about what folklore truckers carried with them. Most occupations had some – common beliefs, rituals, legends, and so on. It would make a great study, she thought. She didn't linger on the idea, though. She was too excited over the prospect of conversing with a real honest-to-goodness swamp Yankee, especially one who might have knowledge of her family history. She sincerely hoped he did, but even if he couldn't tell her more than she already knew, he was most likely a folklorist's dream informant. He must have a mountain of stories to tell.

"Do you think Mr. Stankard will let me record him?" she asked as Mr. Ormsbee pulled into the parking lot of Jack's Kitchen. Rigs of various sizes crowded the lot, and gas pumps took up one side.

"You can ask, but I'd bet my house he'll say no. He's not the kind of guy who's going to want his words recorded. Might make him suspicious."

Charlotte decided right then to leave the tape recorder in the car. The last thing she wanted was to give him a reason to hold anything back.

"I'll just take notes, then," she said.

"Ask about that first, too," he told her.

As they walked into the diner, Charlotte was immediately hit with a mix of aromas. The scent of hamburgers, French fries, and old grease mixed with diesel fuel and sweat. A middle-aged waitress in a stained pink and white uniform approached.

"We're meeting Alvin Stankard here," Mr. Ormsbee told her.

"Back there," she said, jerking her thumb towards a corner table at the end of the aisle.

Charlotte followed Mr. Ormsbee to a square, wooden table that could seat four. As they approached, the food and diesel smell mixed with another, even less inviting one. A large man was seated there, the back of his chair against the wall. He wore a dark jacket over a pullover shirt that was so stained and faded Charlotte had no idea what its original color might have been. He was clean-shaven, a surprise, as she'd pictured him with a bushy beard, but his face did not appear as though he'd washed it all that recently. It was fleshy and his head seemed to sit on his shoulders without benefit of a neck. His hair was dark, lank, and thin. His eyes, she thought, might be a bluish gray, but it was hard to tell as he squinted at her.

"Alvin," said Mr. Ormsbee. "This is Charlotte Lajoie, the girl I told you about."

"Hello, Mr. Stankard," said Charlotte. "Thank you for agreeing to meet with me."

The man gave her a sideways glance and a half-nod but didn't speak.

"Have a seat," said Mr. Ormsbee, holding out a chair for her.

She slid in opposite Mr. Stankard while Mr. Ormsbee took the seat next to her on the aisle.

"I hope you weren't waiting long," said Charlotte.

"Nah." It was more of a grunt than a word.

After the waitress took their orders, Alvin Stankard turned towards Charlotte and asked, "So, what do you want to ask me?"

As he turned, even just that slight bit, a wave of body odor washed over her. A glance at his hand as he picked up his water glass showed deeply encrusted dirt inching up his wrist. The rest was hidden under the sleeve of his jacket, but Charlotte just knew the rest of him was even worse.

Resting her elbow on the table, she placed her chin in her hand so that her palm covered her mouth, and her forefinger was in front of her nose. She hoped she conveyed a look of deep thought, though she was really trying to block the smell. Mr. Ormsbee was right. She doubted she'd be able to eat the grilled cheese she'd just ordered.

"Well," she said. "I understand that your family has lived in Birch Falls for many generations and that you might know something about my ancestors, the Kendalls. I know that there is a legend about Eliza Kendall and that kids have been visiting her grave for decades because they think she's a vampire. I was hoping you could tell me why they think that."

"Ay-uh," he said. "I know all about that. But why do you want to know?"

Charlotte was taken aback. "She's my ancestor. Her sister, Jerusha, was my great grandmother going back six generations. I'm a folklorist and I have a strong interest in legends. I only recently found out that I have such an interesting one in my own family. I'd like to know more about it."

"I told you all this, Alvin. Don't you remember?" asked Mr. Ormsbee.

"Yeah, I know. I wanted to hear it from her." He gave Mr. Ormsbee an annoyed look, then turned his attention back to Charlotte.

"Weren't no legend. They thought she was a vampire because all her family was dying from consumption. The neighbors got the idea in their heads that one of the kids that had already died was causing it all, so they went on out and dug up the graves. When they got to hers, they found her looking like she'd just drunk a gallon of blood. She had it dripping all over the place, I'm told. Then they cut her open and found her heart was full of fresh blood, too. So, they figured she was the one causing all the trouble. They took her heart out and burned it. Messed up her bones and such so she couldn't get out of the grave no more for good measure. Then they reburied her. I 'spect she left them alone after that, but folks don't forget something like that, so the story stuck around. What her family had writ on her gravestone, something about her coming after everyone, probably just encouraged it. Though I 'spect at the time, they was just trying to warn folks away. Funny that it had the opposite effect."

Charlotte decided against correcting his misunderstanding about the purpose of the inscription. Instead, she asked, "Was the story passed down in your family, then?"

"Ay-uh. My family goes back in Birch Falls at least as far as the Kendalls, maybe further. My ancestor, Chauncey Haskell, was around the same time as your Jerusha and Eliza. They'd a known each other, though they'd a been kids and he was getting on towards old age at the time."

Charlotte remembered the name Chauncey Haskell from Jerusha's diary. He had told Nathan that he shared something in common with Jerusha's family.

"Would he have been a neighbor to the Kendalls?" she asked.

"Ay-uh. From what I know, he was a real storyteller. Kind of an informal town historian. But I guess he liked to spin a good yarn now and then, too, or so my granny said her granny told her."

The waitress arrived with their lunches. As her plate was slipped in front of her, the aroma of melted cheddar cheese wafted to Charlotte's nose. She breathed deeply of the welcome scent. She thought if she held it close to her face the whole time, she might be able to get through eating it. Normally, she'd consider that rude table manners, but in this instance, she assumed Mr. Ormsbee would understand, and Mr. Stankard would never notice.

In between bites, they resumed their conversation. "The few people I've talked to who've gone to Eliza's grave know that the legend is that she was a vampire, but no one seems to know why a vampire and not simply a ghost," said Charlotte. "Your explanation fits with the legend, but apparently, the actual events that created the vampire legend have been lost."

"'Spect so," said Alvin Stankard. "I went to her grave back when I was a kid. We all did."

"What happened?" asked Charlotte.

"Nothing much. We scared ourselves and went home."

Charlotte couldn't suppress a smile. He'd said it as though simply scaring themselves was all they'd set out to do, and, though most wouldn't admit it at the time, it was the truth for all legend trippers.

"Did your ancestor know the Wicker family?"

"'Course he did. Small town. More of a village, I guess, at that time. Everybody knew everybody."

"According to Jerusha's diary, her mother had once been very close friends with Lavinia Wicker, but later had a falling out and they no longer spoke to each other. Jerusha seemed to be trying to figure out what happened. Do you know anything about it?"

Alvin Stankard tilted his head back and stroked his chin. "Hmm…I'm not sure about that. All I know is that

Chauncey was friendly with the Wickers, but not so much with the Kendalls. What went on between them two ladies, I couldn't tell ya."

"Do you know if Chauncey was present at the disinterment?"

"Now, that I do know. That story's been handed down in the family. Makes for quite a tale, you understand, so's we like telling it."

Charlotte leaned in closer despite the smell, ready to hang on every word, wishing she could have recorded it. As it was, she'd decided against even taking notes so as not to spook him out of telling her everything.

"Seems Chauncey Haskell was behind the whole thing. It was his idea to dig up the girls. He'd heard about it being done other places and figured it was worth a try to see if it would stop the sickness. I guess folks believed that sort of stuff back then. Anyway, he talked the rest of the Birch Falls folks into it. I think that's the reason he wasn't so friendly with the Kendalls. They probably didn't cotton to the idea of having their dead kids dug up and examined, especially when taking their hearts out and burning them could be the result. Though, I 'spect they might a been grateful once they found the culprit."

Mr. Ormsbee chuckled. "You sound like you believe in that stuff, too, Alvin," he said.

Alvin Stankard eyed him sideways. "I ain't saying I believe it. I'm saying they did."

"But according to the dates in my grandmother's bible, Seth died not long after Eliza. So, it didn't work," Charlotte told him.

Alvin Stankard pointed a French fry in Charlotte's direction. "But he was the last one, wasn't he? He probably was too far gone by the time they thought of digging up those kids. But the others didn't catch it, did they?"

"I suppose not," Charlotte agreed. "Or if they did, it wasn't until much later. I don't actually know what Jerusha and her parents died from. Her sister, Susannah, moved to Ohio, but lived many years after that."

"That's what I'm saying. In their eyes you'd think they'd believe it worked."

"Then what caused the rift between Mary Kendall and Lavinia Wicker?"

"Don't rightly know 'bout that. Probably just some dust up between womenfolk."

Charlotte felt a twinge of annoyance at the remark and dismissive wave of his hand.

"Mr. Stankard," she said, "how do you know so much about what happened with Eliza? My own family had no knowledge of it. It happened so many generations in the past. How do you know it?"

He gave her what started out as a glare that quickly moved to a self-satisfied smirk. "Ay-uh, that's the problem with most folks nowadays. You don't pass on the stories, and they get lost. In my family, we told the stories. Not to outsiders, you understand," he gave her a look that said she was more than lucky and had better be grateful for his willingness to divulge what he knew of the Kendalls, "but within the family they were told over and over again so as not to forget them. They got passed down from one generation to the next."

"But the Kendalls weren't your family. Were they?" The sudden thought that she might be related to Alvin Stankard, no matter how remotely, was a bit off-putting.

"Nope. No relation. But folks back in those days relied on one another a lot more than they do today. You didn't have to be related to know what was going on. Besides, if Chauncey Haskell was behind it all, of course he'd tell the story." He gave a laugh that was more of a snort. "Even if he didn't instigate it, it was too good a story not to tell."

Charlotte was confused. He was obviously correct that a story like that would likely get passed down, yet it was her own family, and it hadn't been known to her mother or her grandmother. Given what Jerusha had written, whatever happened between Mary Kendall and Lavinia Wicker had occurred around the same time as the exhumations, yet she never mentions them and even questions what her mother could have meant about people causing harm to Seth and the already dead Lizzy. That thought – *the already dead Lizzy* – suddenly made everything begin to fall into place. Charlotte related to the two men what Jerusha had written in her diary and how Susannah had answered her letter inquiring about what had happened. "Then she asked, "Is it possible Jerusha didn't know?"

"It doesn't seem as though something like that could be kept a secret," said Mr. Ormsbee.

"She was only nine at the time," said Charlotte. "She was so young. Maybe they didn't want her to know."

"Maybe they kept her out of it at the time," he agreed. "But you'd think she'd have caught wind of it at some point."

"Whatever it was," said Charlotte, "her mother certainly did not want to tell her."

Charlotte glanced at Mr. Stankard, ready to ask his opinion, and noticed that his brow had furrowed, one eye almost completely shut as though he was in deep thought. She waited, not wanting to disturb him.

"You know," he finally said, "I remember my cousins being surprised when they heard about that story. They were down visiting, oh, I guess this was ten, fifteen years ago. We were telling the family stories, like we do, and when I brought up that one, they just looked at me like I'd suddenly grown feathers or something. They'd never heard of it. I was confounded as all get out as to how they'd missed that one. 'Course we don't see

318

them often, but still, their folks had passed on what seemed to be all the same stories.”

“So, how come you knew it and they didn’t?” asked Charlotte.

“All I can think is it came down through my branch of the family but not theirs. Chauncey Haskell was ancestor to the lot of us, but I come from the line descending from his son, Silas who lived up to Cornwall for a while whereas his other sons stayed in Birch Falls. If there was some reason why it wasn’t being talked about in Birch Falls, which don’t make much sense to me, but if that’s so, then he might have told the son that lived in Cornwall. ‘Course Silas didn’t stay there. After his wife died, she being the one from Cornwall, he moved back and remarried. I guess he never shared it with his brothers, though I’m supposing his own kids knew of it. Hard to believe given the way our family has always talked about the goings on, but possible.”

Charlotte felt excitement building inside her. She was beginning to piece together what might have happened. She couldn’t wait to get home, write down everything Mr. Stankard had said, reread the diary, and try putting it all together to see if it fit.

“One last thing,” she asked after draining her glass of ginger ale. “Have you ever heard any stories of the house the Kendalls used to live in being haunted?”

Cocking his head towards Earl Ormsbee, he said, “He could tell you that better than I. His wife was friendly with the Ketchum woman who lived there for years. But, yeah, I’ve heard the stories.”

“How old are the stories you know? Do they go back from before the Ketchums?”

He shrugged. “Some might, I suppose. It’s all the same, though. Footsteps in the garret or coming down the garret stairs. One of the rooms downstairs is supposed to be haunted, too, I guess. I doubt I’ve heard anything different from what you already know.”

“Do you know who the ghost is supposed to be?”

"I 'spect folks think it's Eliza since she's got the legend about her and all. Truth be told, plenty of people died in that house. Could be any of them. If you believe in that sort of thing, that is."

Despite Alvin Stankard's inability to shed any light on the haunting of the Kendall house, Charlotte was ecstatic over the information she'd gained about the disinterment of the Kendall daughters. It upheld her hypothesis that Eliza was considered by the people of her own time to have been a vampire. She thanked Mr. Stankard profusely, then walked with Mr. Ormsbee back to her car. The feeling of anticipation with which she'd entered the diner had become elation on the way out. It was, she hoped, worth whatever Brad would do to make her pay for getting an exhibit of her own.

Chapter 44

September 1839
Birch Falls, Vermont

Jerusha stared down at her lap as Nathan told his tale, never daring to look at him. His voice, which cracked now and then, told her that he was not making this up, though she wished he were. She wanted to shut out his words but could not. Nor could she ask him to stop. Though the story was ghastly, a part of her needed to hear it. Her mind took in the images of his brother Isaac, dead three months at the time Nathan's tale took place. The townspeople had dug up Isaac's grave thinking he was responsible for the ill health of Nathan's other siblings.

"When they opened his coffin, they found he had blood in his mouth. Fresh blood. Like he'd been drinking it," he told her.

"Drinking it?" Jerusha could not help asking. The notion was appalling.

Nathan glanced down at her. "I should not be telling this to you."

"No," said Jerusha. "I want to know. But how could he have been drinking blood? He had been dead and in his grave three months."

"That is true. But it was the very sign they were looking for. They said it proved he was coming back. Feeding off the rest of us. My sister, Catherine, was ill. My brother, Francis, had died but two weeks earlier. They claimed Isaac was causing it and this was the proof."

"I do not see how. A dead person cannot come back. Even if he could, why would he harm his own family?"

"They claimed it was not Isaac harming us. It was something evil that was using him, living in him during the day and coming at night in his form to each of us in turn to drain the life from us."

Nathan brought the wagon to a stop by the roadside. "Think of it, Jerusha. The victims of consumption slowly fade away. They become like the dead while still alive, like skeletons with only a thin layer of skin. Do they not seem to worsen at night? Francis and Catherine both complained that someone was sitting on their chests at night. They did not say this during the day."

Jerusha felt the blood drain from her face. She stared into Nathan's troubled eyes. "But that is from the illness." Her words were barely a whisper.

"And what causes the illness?"

"I...I do not know. No one knows. The doctors seem to think it comes from being closed in too much or the prolonged cold of the winter."

"They think, but they do not know. The best they can do is guess at the cause. Others think it is caused by an evil seeking its prey."

"Surely, the doctors know better." Jerusha could scarce comprehend the idea. Yet a thought wiggled far back in her mind. Some memory from long ago was trying to force its way out.

"Perhaps they do," said Nathan. "Perhaps someday they will know for certain the cause as well as the cure. I pray it is so. In the meantime, when nothing else is of any use, people look for answers of their own."

Jerusha tried to take it in, but it was almost too much for her. She could not believe that anything like what Nathan was relating to her could have occurred in her family. Her parents would never have countenanced it, and, surely, she would have heard of it.

"What did they do after they dug him up?" she asked, not sure she wanted the answer, but resolved to hear the story to the end.

Nathan exhaled in a long sigh. "In order to make it stop, they cut his heart from his chest and burned it. Catherine was made to stand beside it and breathe it in as it burned."

Jerusha gasped. "She was there?"

"Not at first. She was too unwell to stand about while they dug. If they'd found nothing, they would have taxed her strength for no reason. When they were convinced, though, they sent me to fetch her."

"You were there? You watched it all?"

Nathan nodded. "I did. I can attest to what I saw. There was fresh blood in Isaac's mouth and in his heart." He gazed at her, a look of pleading in his eyes. "Jerusha, I cannot explain why Isaac was in such a state. It does not seem that he should have been so. Yet, I have doubts that he was truly possessed by anything evil. Still, having seen what I saw..." Nathan stared off in the distance shaking his head.

"What happened to Catherine? Was she cured?"

"It seemed so at first. She was better for several months afterwards and we all thought, perhaps, it had worked. Then she relapsed and died."

"I am so sorry." Jerusha put a hand on Nathan's arm. "I know how it feels to lose so many."

Nathan held her gaze. "I know you do," he said, softly, before once again putting the wagon into motion.

Jerusha mulled over all she had been told. As her family's farm came into view, she finally asked, "Do you think that is what happened in my family?"

"Possibly, though I could not say for certain. Can you not ask either of your parents?"

"I told you I have asked Mother, and she will not speak of it."

"You asked her what happened. Now could you ask her if it was the same as what happened in my family?"

"Does Mother know about your family?"

"Not about that. I do not speak of it if I can help it. It is not a pleasant memory. In fact, it is the reason I left home. I wanted to be away from all that reminded me of it."

Jerusha felt her heart sink. "And now you have come here to face it again. I am sorry."

He gave her a weak smile. "You have no reason to be sorry. If my telling you brings you the answers you seek, then I am glad of it."

For the rest of the day Jerusha ruminated on what Nathan had told her. Mentioning her deceased siblings at all to her mother was difficult enough. Doing so by connecting them with such a grisly affair as the one suffered by Nathan's family was unthinkable. Perhaps she could speak to her father of it. She might simply tell him what Nathan had told her and gauge his reaction. But would her father be angry that Nathan had burdened her with such a horrid remembrance? She did not want to get him into trouble. She would have to think carefully on how to go about this. Meanwhile, she hoped Susannah would answer her letter with a satisfying explanation.

It was not until Jerusha lay in bed on the verge of sleep that the memory that had been eluding her all day suddenly sprang to mind making her sit bolt upright in bed. Towards the end, like Nathan's siblings, Seth had complained that someone was sitting on his chest. But Seth had named that person. Lizzy.

Once the memory was let loose others followed in quick succession. Lizzy had wanted to come back to let her family know she was alright. Reverend Cobb had spoken to her about that, telling her it was not a proper Christian belief. Could Lizzy have unwittingly called forth some evil presence? Was any of this even real?

The remembrance of the crowd of neighbors in the house the night before Seth died, Susannah's refusal to let her join them and her insistence that Jerusha return to her bed, then her mother's astonishing change in behavior towards everyone, especially Mrs. Wicker and her father, from that time on all came rushing back on her. Seth himself had read aloud from the newspaper about such an event in Woodstock the night Josie fell so ill. Could it be that Lizzy had been thought to have been like Nathan's brother, Isaac? Had she been?

Sleep eluded Jerusha for much of the night as she turned these thoughts over again and again, praying that such a gruesome ordeal had not befallen her family. Now it seemed more important to her to find out for sure that this was *not* the secret that had been kept from her than to uncover what the secret actually was.

Chapter 45

September 1973
Middlebury, Vermont

Once Charlotte returned home from her meeting with Alvin Stankard, she immediately lit the candle in her decoupaged candleholder and wrote down everything he'd said. Then she grabbed the diary and made notes. Putting everything together, she was as sure as she could be that Eliza Kendall had indeed been believed to have come back from the dead to feed off her living family members.

Heidi had been disappointed that Charlotte's meeting with Stankard was on a weekend she had to work, so as soon as Charlotte heard Heidi coming up the stairs, she ran into the hallway to meet her. They'd agreed that Heidi would pick up a pizza on her way home for them to share.

"Come in, come in," Charlotte said, bouncing on her toes as Heidi reached the top of the stairs. "You have to hear all about what I found out," she told her, ushering her directly into the apartment.

While they ate, Charlotte told Heidi everything about her meeting with Alvin Stankard and what she had figured out after combining what he'd told her with what was written in Jerusha's diary.

"You know," said Heidi, when Charlotte had finished. "I think I've been trying to contact the wrong person."

Charlotte cocked her head. "What do you mean?"

"At the cemetery. I was trying to pick up vibes from Eliza and getting nothing."

"You think you should have tried Jerusha instead?"

"Maybe. But I was thinking of their mother."

"Mary? Why?"

"She's the one who's been trying to get through to us. Well, me anyway. The more I think about it the more I think she did push me over the first time and trip me up the second time."

"Seems a little menacing, don't you think? Are you sure you want to mess with her?" asked Charlotte, suppressing a laugh.

"She's trying to get my attention. She knows I can communicate with her. Let's go back up there and try it again at her grave."

Charlotte let out a sigh. "Sounds great, but I'm out straight at work. I don't dare take a weekend off until the Halloween exhibit is up. We're starting to install it now. It's all hands on deck. Except for Brad, that is."

Heidi smirked. "You don't want *his* hands on anything."

Just as they finished eating, the phone rang. Charlotte picked it up to hear her grandmother's voice on the line.

"Hi, Grandma. Are you back already? I thought you'd be gone longer."

"No. I'm still at my sister's house. I had to call you because Armand and I were cleaning out Lorraine's bedroom and you will never guess what we found on her closet shelf."

"I don't know. What?"

"A diary."

Her grandmother's voice held a tone of self-satisfaction. This was a long-distance phone call, and she would not have made it if she didn't have earth-shattering news. Charlotte's heart began to race. "Oh?" she said, almost afraid to hope. "Whose diary?"

"Jerusha Kendall's."

Charlotte gasped. Heidi turned a questioning look on her. "What's wrong?" she mouthed.

Charlotte covered the mouthpiece of the receiver. "Grandma found Jerusha's other diary when she was cleaning out her sister's closet."

Both women squealed with delight.

"Oh, Grandma," she said, returning to her phone call. "That is out of sight!"

"Well, it was out of sight. It was so far back on the shelf I almost didn't see it."

"No, that's not...never mind. That's fantastic. I can hardly believe it!"

"I nearly dropped my teeth when I opened it and realized what it was. I didn't even know there was another one. My mother must have given it to Lorraine around the same time she gave the other one to me. Lorraine never was much for history or family beyond those she knew personally. She probably shoved it in her closet and forgot all about it. I'll bet she never even opened it."

"Have you read it, Grandma? What does it say?"

"I tried to read some of it, but you know my old eyes aren't what they used to be. I couldn't make out most of it. I expect to be home by the middle of next week. You can come pick it up whenever you'd like."

Charlotte's elation suddenly plummeted. "I can't come before October. I can't take any time off from work until we finish installing the exhibit."

Heidi grabbed Charlotte's arm and tugged.

"Hold on a minute, Grandma," she said.

"If it's okay with your grandmother, I could drive down to Bennington and pick it up," Heidi offered.

"Grandma," she said. "Could my friend, Heidi, come down and get it next weekend?"

"Of course, Charlotte. I'd be happy to have her."

"Thanks, Grandma."

After she hung up, Charlotte and Heidi sat in the living room talking over this latest development.

"I can't believe it," Charlotte kept repeating.

"I hope Jerusha found the answer and wrote about it in that diary," said Heidi.

"Me too. Now that I'm getting to put together my own exhibit on it, it would be fantastic to use the information from my own family."

"Maybe it will give you enough for a good foundation for a doctoral dissertation." She eyed the glow from the candleholder.

"I've been thinking about that more and more. Wouldn't that be the coolest thing? I've got to write to Tracy. She'll want to know all about this."

Later that night Charlotte lay in bed unable to sleep. She kept turning over in her mind all that had happened that day. She couldn't wait to get her hands on Jerusha's other diary. No matter whether or not she was right in her assumptions, it was still a privilege to have the insight into the lives of people long gone, especially when they were members of her own family.

The more she thought about it the more she wanted to be sure to honor her ancestors and those of others who lived through similar experiences. She realized she would need to be very careful as to how she presented it in her exhibit. *Her* exhibit. Just the thought of it made a warm glow course through her.

People today would think digging up your dead family members, cutting out and burning their hearts was barbaric and disgusting. She would need to present it as the folk remedy that it was, highlighting the fact that people were dropping like flies from consumption, a disease no one then understood. People became desperate for any way to stop it. Looking to their own ancestors' beliefs and folkways from their old countries seemed as viable as anything else, but it didn't mean they didn't find it a grisly and repellant thing to do. Just a necessary one to save lives.

Charlotte turned over in bed as thoughts continued to course through her mind. What must it have been like to live with such a familiarity with death? Few families of Jerusha's time did not experience the loss of at least a few of their members. How would she handle the death of her sister or brother? Would it be harder for her since it wasn't as common? But what of the families who had sons in the war? Many would never be coming home. That thought led to Keith. She wondered how he was faring at UVM and whether there had been any word from his brother in Vietnam.

Perhaps people would understand the desperation of trying to save family members. Combat troops had only come home six months ago. It was still a fresh wound. What wouldn't families have done to bring their sons and brothers home safely? Perhaps that was the link to help museum visitors understand.

No matter what the exhibit entailed, Charlotte vowed to herself that it would not be sensationalistic. She would create it with sensitivity. She felt as if Jerusha had handed her the way forward in her career, and she was determined to honor her.

Chapter 46

October 1839
Birch Falls, Vermont

"Jerusha, what ails you, child?" Mary could not keep the note of impatience from her voice. She'd been asking Jerusha that question for days. Something was wrong with the girl, but she could get no true answer.

"Nothing, Mother. I am fine."

"You are not." Mary put down the mending. "For the past several days you could not have followed me more closely were you my shadow, and cling like a bur. With this entire room to ourselves you sit so close you are practically in my lap. It is not like you."

She reached a hand to Jerusha's forehead. "You are not ill?"

"No, Mother," said Jerusha, taking her mother's hand. "I am quite well."

Mary eyed her, relieved that no sickness was upon her, but still confounded by Jerusha's odd behavior. Before she could recommence her questioning, the kitchen door opened. Eli strode in.

"Mary, can you spare Jerusha tomorrow? There was extra work this week. Asa was a great help to us. He says his mother could use some assistance."

"Why is Nathan's help not enough?" she asked.

"I had to send him to pick up the mended plow. While he was gone two of the pigs got loose, and I lost time rounding them up. I found a break in the fence that had to be mended. The harvest is ready. We needed extra help." There was exasperation in Eli's voice. Mary knew he was tired of explaining why he sometimes had to accept help from one of the Wicker boys.

"Very well. I can do without Jerusha for part of the day tomorrow." Glancing at her daughter, she saw a flash of excitement in her eyes. She also saw it quickly doused when Jerusha realized her mother had seen it. Jerusha still harbored a love for the loom. The look of sorrowful resignation on Jerusha's face gave her another twinge of guilt.

Perhaps she should relent.

In seven years, no one had uttered a word about what had happened. But every time she was ready to yield, a wall went up barricading her mouth.

After Eli left the room, Jerusha turned to her mother. "If I am to be gone tomorrow, I should do extra today. This mending can wait." With that, Jerusha got up and quickly exited the parlor.

While she sewed, Mary's thoughts kept returning to how, after all these years, she might consider allowing Lavinia to teach Jerusha to weave. One moment her heart swelled to imagine Jerusha's face. Hard on the heels was the memory of the night Lavinia and the others had crowded into Seth's sick room trying to make him drink their awful potion.

She remonstrated with herself for allowing vengeance on Lavinia to prevent her from bringing joy to Jerusha. And, really, what good had her so-called vengeance done? She no longer traded clothing or bedclothes made by Lavinia for her butter, milk, or cheese. Both families had to go elsewhere for those needs. She did not speak to Lavinia nor acknowledge her presence even at Sunday meeting. At first, that had given her a measure of satisfaction, but over time it began to weigh on her soul.

Her bond with Eli had eventually begun to mend. He had apologized repeatedly, and she truly tried to forgive. It took time, but she was finally able to listen, to hear him with her heart, when he told her how aghast he had been upon the unexpected condition of Lizzy's body, how his mind had turned somersaults trying to fathom it, and how, in the moment, with the fervor of the crowd, he had found himself unable to do aught but step back and let them have their way. He had not encouraged what they did, but his stunned brain gave no command to his tongue to make them stop.

It took him a very long time to reconcile his inaction. At times, he said, he still wondered how he could have let them do it. He had felt as though he'd stepped out of his own body and was watching it all as some detached entity.

It had taken more than a year, but Mary had finally been able to recognize the trauma Eli had suffered. She was then overcome with anguish that she had let him suffer alone. But her new awareness had only fueled more anger towards Lavinia, Chauncey and the others, blaming them for that as well.

Always practical, Eli had understood the necessity of continued ties with the community. But of all the reciprocity required for life to go on, it was hardest when it came to the Wickers. Lavinia's actions felt like the worst betrayal. There was only a cold, empty space where once there'd been friendship.

She could not sort out her feelings on her own. Rising from the settee, she sought out Jerusha.

"I am going to call on Caroline," she told her daughter. "There are some simples we need. A household should never be without all the proper medicines, as one never knows when they will be needed. Remember that for when you have a home of your own."

With that, she left the house heading for the Cutting farm.

* * *

Caroline was setting herbs to dry when Mary arrived.

"Ah, Mary, it is good to see you," said Caroline, ushering her into her kitchen. "You look as though something troubles you," she continued, pulling out a chair at the table for Mary."

"I need a wiser heart than my own to make sense of it."

Caroline lay aside the bundle of sage she was tying and took a seat next to Mary.

"We can work while we talk. I did not mean to interrupt your tasks."

Mary poured out her heart to the older woman, releasing thoughts and feelings she had held inside for years. A few times she felt tears prick her eyes but was surprised that they never developed further. Perhaps she had cried herself out over the years or perhaps it was Caroline's calming presence that assuaged them.

"Mary," said Caroline, taking her hand. "You know the answer. Your love for Jerusha is greater than your anger. It is the very reason you have protected her all these years from learning the truth."

"And in doing so, I have closed the world in on her."

"Open it again. Jerusha was so young when it happened. Now she is nearly grown. She needs to renew attachments beyond you and Eli. There can be no harm in letting her learn to weave. Lavinia will never breathe a word of that night to her. No one in Birch Falls would dare."

Mary tried to prevent the sheepish smile threatening to spread across her face. "Am I still so terrifying?"

Caroline sat up straight in her chair. "Oh, Mary Kendall. You are ferocious when riled."

Caroline had been her staunchest ally through it all while managing to maintain a certain professional distance as she continued carrying out her healing services to the community.

"Very well, then," said Mary. "For Jerusha's sake, I will consider relenting on this point."

Mary finished tying the last bundle of herbs and prepared to take her leave. Yet there was one thing still niggling at her.

"Caroline do you think I am wrong about how I feel? And to still feel after all these years?"

Caroline set the armful of bundled herbs on the table. She took Mary's hands in her own. "Mary," she said. "What you endured that day should never have happened. But I will tell you something I have never told anyone. A few months later, Lavinia came to me asking if she had done wrong."

Mary's eyes widened. She had never considered that Lavinia might have questioned her own actions.

"She was at once devastated at losing your friendship, yet still convinced that they had acted fittingly. She said that, in your position, she would likely have felt the same. That, she said, is why she and Chauncey Haskell took control. She honestly believed that once it was over, Seth would be saved, and you would then understand."

"How could she believe it?" Mary's words tumbled out through her tears. "How could they all believe it?"

"It has been done before. You know Lavinia's gullibility for superstition. Though most others do not believe in such things as a rule, when desperate, people will come to believe almost anything if it will give them a measure of control. Or at least, if they think it will."

"Seth died."

"That is why Lavinia was so distraught, but she assumed it was because he was too far gone. None of the rest of you have succumbed. So, in her mind, it did work."

"But we were never sick."

"That is irrelevant to a mind that wants to believe."

Mary wiped her eyes, took a deep breath. "What did you tell her when she asked you if she'd done wrong?"

"I told her I believed she had but that I understood she acted out of concern for your family and for others. Remember they all believed that once your family was gone, theirs would be next. I said I comprehended her fear but could not condone her actions. She was deeply grieved and wanted to make amends with you but did not know how. I told her it may not be possible, but if it might someday happen, it would take much time."

Time thought Mary. Was that why she was beginning to feel a softening, simply the passage of time?"

"What do you plan to do now, Mary?" Caroline asked.

"I will pray and think much on what you have said. I do hope my feelings will allow me to give Jerusha what she desires. It is hard, Caroline, so hard. A memory steals upon me of baking with Lavinia or sewing together or of laughing together over the antics of our children when they were babes. I have to banish the memories from my thoughts because it hurts too much to remember. She took that from me, too."

The wrenching sobs that Mary thought were behind her now gushed forth. Caroline took her in her arms, holding her tightly.

"She took them from herself as well, Mary. And she also suffers greatly because of it," she whispered.

Chapter 47

September 1973
Middlebury, Vermont

Charlotte and Jonathan walked together into the exhibit area. It was nearly finished, but they still had some work to do on it. Paul, the other curator, had gone to other museums to pick up some artifacts they had agreed to loan to them for the exhibit and was stopping at the home of a private collector in Randolph on the way back for some other items.

They had set up the exhibit in two parts, each following a path so that visitors would experience the evolution of the holiday. The first section showed the ancient European origins of Halloween long before it was ever called by that name.

Charlotte and Jonathan examined the first stop in the exhibit, the section depicting *Samhain*, the ancient Celtic festival. Charlotte cast a critical eye over the masks she and curators had made to represent those used by early Celts in the *Samhain* festival. They were crudely sewn out of cloth with sheep's wool and straw for facial hair. They had followed pictures from a museum in Ireland to create them, though she was nervous about how authentic they appeared. The note cards placed next to them identified them as recreations. They weren't trying to fool the public, but she was anxious that everything in the exhibit be as perfect as possible.

A giggle escaped Charlotte as it always did when she looked at Jonathan's wooden carving of a turnip lantern. She pointed at it. "I just love that."

Jonathan folded his arms in mock disdain. "Then why are you acting like it's an adorable kitten? It's not supposed to be cute. It's supposed to be scary."

"It is scary," Charlotte assured him, though to her, there was something captivating about it as well. Jonathan had done a remarkable job making it look like the one in the book from the Irish Folk Museum. He'd carved slitted eyes and a leering mouth complete with teeth. It actually looked more like a real face than those of today's Jack-O'-lanterns, albeit a creepy one.

Other representations of festivities celebrating the abundance of the harvest were depicted through baskets of nuts and fruits, necklaces made from rosehips and chestnuts, and a replica of an apple corer made from bone.

Even more important to Charlotte was the Celtic belief of the soul's journey to a world they call *Tir na tSamhraidh*, Land of Summer, and that the doors between our world and that one opened one night a year on *Samhain*. On that night, the dead were able to return to the world of the living and the *sidh*, or fairies, crossed over to torment humans.

Charlotte had paid special attention to this section of the exhibit because it spoke to one of her favorite elements in folklore – liminality. She was fascinated by liminal times and places where people were between two important points, just leaving one and moving on to the next. Liminal times are important and often marked by folk rituals, which, in turn, help the person performing them to make a successful transition.

Samhain marked a very liminal time – the harvest completed in preparation for the long winter ahead and the dying of the year itself. It was no wonder the Celtic people believed that the veil between the two worlds was rent asunder on this night.

Here she had portrayed the ancient Celtic belief that because the veil was so thin at *Samhain* signs from the other world could more easily come through, making fortunetelling a popular pastime.

"I am so glad you and Paul are as good as you are at making things look real. If we had to use real bread for that *bairnín breac* we'd have to replace it every few days."

"You've got Paul to thank for that one," said Jonathan.

"Well, if it were just me trying to do it, we'd be in big trouble. My talent with that kind of stuff ends at the rings," she said, pointing to the woven straw rings next to the pretend loaf of Irish raisin bread. A sign beside it told of baking a ring into the bread. Whoever got the piece with the ring in it took it as a sign that they'd be married within the year.

"I assume you'll want to include something about liminality when you do your exhibit about the vampire lore from the nineteenth century," said Jonathan.

"Oh, definitely, especially with the legend-tripping angle. It marks a rite of passage from youth to adulthood, especially for boys. Mostly they do it around age sixteen. And it almost always involves a car."

"Will we need to put a car in the exhibit?"

"If we can, it would be very cool."

Jonathan laughed. "I'll see if Paul and I can build one for you."

"I know you're joking, but the car is very important. Legend tripping takes place when kids are moving from their teens into adulthood but aren't quite there yet. They have just embarked on a new sense of freedom with the ability to drive and move further from parental control. They go in groups to do something they see as scary and dangerous because it involves a death or a tragedy and something of the supernatural. In an almost literal sense, they face death, but come away unscathed, even though in most cases, they're never in any real danger."

"I suppose that depends on how much beer they've been drinking before they get behind the wheel."

"You do have a point," said Charlotte as they moved along the exhibit space.

The next section detailed the transition from the three days of *Samhain* to the three days of All Hallows Eve, All Saints Day, and All Souls Day once the Celtic lands had been Christianized. Charlotte had obtained a few poster-sized copies of images created by artists shortly after the Black Death in late medieval Europe. Signage explained that the horrific plague had changed the popular culture of the time creating an obsession with death depicted in much of the artwork. During this same period, the printing press was invented allowing for such images to be mass produced. Two images of the Dance Macabre hung on the exhibit wall showing skeletons in burial wrappings and the Grim Reaper dancing with living people. A scythe had been placed next to the images.

"Should we add text explaining the blending of the culture of the time with the belief that the dead crossed into the living world on that one night?" she asked Jonathan.

"I don't think we need it," he said. "You've done a great job with the objects in the display and the way everything is laid out. I think most people will see the connection."

"Are you sure? Because I could create more text. There's room for it."

"Charlotte, calm down," he said, an indulgent smile lighting up his face. He really did remind her a lot of her father. "You need to learn to trust yourself. You don't need to do all the work for the visitors. In a good exhibit, which this is, they should be able to connect the dots on their own."

"You're right, of course. I'm just so nervous. I want it to be perfect."

"It will be. Don't worry so much. You've done an excellent job."

"No small thanks to you and Paul for that."

He shrugged. "That's our job. Now look how it flows from the Black Death images to the 1480s witch hunts. Visitors will have no problem connecting all this with the images they see at Halloween all the time. They'll get the progression."

"I must say, Jerry Soder really knocked himself out with this stuff," said Charlotte. Jerry Soder was a local artist who was often hired to do artwork for the museum's exhibits. For this he had created a large painting of an old woman tied to a stake, a pile of kindling at her feet which was about to be lit as a crowd looked on. The text Charlotte had written made note of the sweeping witch hunts in Europe at the time as witches were blamed for creating and spreading the plague. Jerry had also created a tableau of a witch stirring a cauldron with a black cat at her feet and a corn broom against the wall beside her. On the other side of the tableau was another of Jerry's paintings in which he depicted a midnight gathering of witches over which the devil himself presided.

They walked on to the next installation with a sign reading "European Origins of Trick or Treating" hanging above it. Silhouette cut images showed a group of young boys in seventeenth century Britain going house to house collecting for fuel for Bonfire Night and Guy Fawkes Day, both closely associated with Halloween. In dialogue bubbles above the heads of some of the silhouettes were the words, "A penny for the Guy."

On a huge board in the next section hung the entire poem "Hallow'en" by Robert Burns, all 252 lines of it. On the floor beneath it rested a mock-up of a fireplace with nuts roasting in it. Charlotte had stenciled a line from the poem next to it –"Two hazel-nuts I threw into the flame and to each I gave a sweetheart's name." A placard told how fortune-telling games continued to be popular, but instead of rings baked into bread, two nuts represented two possible lovers. The one blazing the brightest and longest represented the person whose love was truest.

"I love how so many folk traditions carried over from the ancient festival," said Charlotte.

"And later arrived on our shores," Jonathan agreed. "That thing with the nuts was done here well into the nineteenth century."

"This is one of my favorite parts of the exhibit," said Charlotte as they moved to the next section which focused on Cabbage Night. Her research had uncovered even more connections between cabbages and Halloween than she'd previously known. One of her favorites, Burning the Reekie Mehr, came from Scotland. It was represented in the exhibit with a hollowed-out cabbage stalk filled with tow, and a description of how when lit it produced long flames that were blown through keyholes.

"When I found out about kids tying strings to cabbages in a field so that to passersby it looked like they were flying, I had to call my dad and tell him. He said he wished he'd known about that when he was a kid."

Jonathan laughed. "I thought the same thing. What a hoot that would have been."

They were just about to enter the next room which housed the second half of the exhibit when they both turned at the sound of hurried footsteps behind them.

"Charlotte, I've been looking for you. I've got some great news." It was Brad.

"What is it?" she asked.

"I just spoke with a friend of mine over at WVMB. He owes me a favor and has agreed to do an interview about the exhibit."

"WVMB?" she asked.

"Local TV news station," said Jonathan.

"Sorry," said Brad. "I forgot you haven't lived here that long. Anyway, they'll tape it, and it will air in early October, just after we've opened the exhibit."

"That's wonderful!" said Charlotte.

"It will be great exposure," Jonathan agreed.

"When will you do the interview?" Charlotte asked.

"That's what I came to tell you. He's going to interview you."

"Me? Why me?"

"You've taken over the work on this exhibit. Also, I mentioned to him what little I know about your other project with your ancestor. He'd like to include that in the interview, too."

"Really? Nothing's fleshed out on that yet. I'm still digging."

"Oh, he knows. He just wants you to talk about how they dug up bodies looking for signs of vampirism and what they did when they found them. I know it's not really connected to Halloween in the historical sense, but it's got a creepy enough vibe to make it a good fit for the interview. Besides, most of the interview will be about the current exhibit. He'll just tuck a bit about that other stuff in along with it. It will be great for drumming up some early interest in you coming exhibit."

Excitement welled in Charlotte while Brad spoke. She could hardly believe Brad was actually giving her this opportunity. She wondered if maybe he felt bad about stealing her idea after all.

"I told Shepherd about it," he added. "He's thrilled."

"When is the interview?" she asked.

"Next Thursday. Will everything be ready so they can film some of the exhibit?"

"Sure. We're close to ready now," she said.

"Great." He chucked her on the shoulder before leaving the exhibit space.

Charlotte stood staring after him and blinking her eyes several times as if trying to wake herself up from a dream. "I can hardly believe it," she said, turning to Jonathan. "I'm amazed he gave this interview to me."

Something in Jonathan's face took the wind out of her sails. "What?" she asked, suddenly feeling wary.

"Nothing," he said. "It's a great opportunity." He smiled, but she sensed it was forced.

"You think something's wrong?"

Jonathan dropped his gaze to the floor. "It's just that Brad giving you the interview is really out of character for him." Then he shrugged. "I guess he's just too busy to do it himself. We'll, we'd better make sure everything is ready in time. Let's keep going."

Jonathan's explanation of Brad's being too overworked did not placate Charlotte. As they entered the second part of the exhibit, it kept nagging at her. She forced herself to focus on the exhibit, though her eyes only skimmed over the image of nineteenth century Irish and Scottish immigrants that would welcome visitors to the "Halloween in America" section of the exhibit, they being the folks who brought the holiday to the United States. On a table under plexiglass sat a copy of an account of Queen Victoria's 1869 Halloween visit to Balmoral Castle in Scotland with its description of the large bonfire and the explanation that it, like anything to do with the queen, was devoured by the American public. Not long after its publication, the first written mentions of the holiday in the States began to appear.

"I'll bet your father would like this part of the exhibit," said Jonathan.

"Huh? Yeah, he would." *Focus* she reprimanded herself.

"More like what he remembers?" Jonathan nudged.

The section they were in now portrayed Cabbage Night in its American guise, celebrated on October 30th, a night for boys to play all sorts of pranks.

"Yes," said Charlotte. "I drew on my dad's stories for some of this." She'd obtained permission from a magazine for enlarged photographs of farm wagons atop house and barn roofs and a pig painted red, white, and blue. The curators had created the façade of a housefront, soaped its windows and placed a fake cow on the front porch. A roll of toilet paper, a carton of eggs, and a can of shaving cream at the end of the section would convey to visitors that Cabbage Night mischief lives on.

They next walked into an array of cornstalks in the center of which was an empty space awaiting a copy of Winslow Homer's woodcut, "Husking the Corn in New England" which Paul would bring back from his rounds this afternoon. Corn husking parties, or frolics, as they were called in the nineteenth century, generally included food, drink, music, games, and dancing once the work was done. A table laden with wax apples and assorted fake popcorn balls, nuts, pumpkin pie, and doughnuts showed the refreshments served at such a gathering, as well as at many a modern-day Halloween party.

A few steps away stood a space almost completely empty save for wooden pillars of varying heights. Each one would be topped with a carved pumpkin or turnip, but since they would not last throughout the entire exhibit despite being treated with petroleum jelly, they would not be put up until opening day.

"I figure I'll carve them all on the last day of this month," said Jonathan. "That way I can set them out just before we open. I'll have to check on them every so often. I expected I'll have to make a second set of everything after a few weeks. I may even need a third set towards the end of October. They've got to look good for Halloween."

"I can't wait to see them. I've heard you carve a mean pumpkin," said Charlotte. "Sorry about all the extra ones you'll have to carve this year.

"No problem. How are you at carving pumpkins?"

Charlotte shrugged. "Okay, I guess. My dad always did them at home, but sometimes I helped. I'd be happy to help you carve pumpkins, but I'm not so sure about turnips."

"They're done the same way as pumpkins just on a smaller scale. And use a tealight for a candle rather than a taper."

Charlotte laughed. "I'll take your word for it. Let's get Paul to help, too. We'll get it done a lot faster."

"You don't want to ask Brad for help?" he asked, a hint of sarcasm in his tone.

Charlotte rolled her eyes. "I'm sure carving pumpkins is beneath him. I'm looking forward to the painting Paul is bringing back from the collector." One of the items Paul was borrowing from Tynan O'Hearn, a local collector of Halloween memorabilia, was an 1858 painting of the headless horseman chasing Ichabod Crane in "The Legend of Sleepy Hollow." O'Hearn had said that the horseman was holding a Jack-o'-lantern like he was about to throw it at Crane.

"I'm looking forward to seeing that, too. The fact that they were making art from that story shows how popular it was. It should be a perfect addition to this section of the exhibit."

Charlotte looked over the area. A large sheaf of paper hung from the wall with John Greenleaf Whittier's poem, "The Pumpkin" written in calligraphy on it. "Susan did a remarkable job on that," said Charlotte, pointing to the scroll-like paper that Susan Moreno, the museum's publicity director had made to look aged by tea staining. "I love how people from different departments help out to make it all come together. And Susan is so talented. I wish I was half as artistic as she is."

"She's a wiz alright. You should see some of the things she's done for past exhibits. We still have most of her work in storage. I'll show it to you sometime."

"I'd love to see it. I think this should be close to the ropes when we put them up," she said, indicating a stand with a pamphlet on it under a plexiglass cover.

"Visitors won't be able to read it if it's too far away." She peered down at the 1898 pamphlet by Martha Russell, "Hallowe'en: How to Celebrate It," open to the section stating that a Halloween party should be "grotesquely decorated with Jack-o'-lanterns made of apples, cucumbers, squashes, pumpkins, etc."

"I'm just glad you didn't ask me to carve cucumbers," said Jonathan.

"Could you?" The question earned Charlotte a sideways look from Jonathan that made her laugh.

"Have we decided who will do the recording?" she asked. The legend of Jack the Blacksmith for whom the Jack-o'-lantern was named was to be recorded and played on a continuous loop through speakers that Paul would set up in this section of the display.

"I asked Malcolm. He said he'd do it," Jonathan told her, referring to one of the security guards.

"Oh, that's great! He's got the perfect voice for it. I hope he doesn't mind. It's not exactly in his job description."

"He seemed excited about it."

"Good."

As the exhibit progressed into the end of the nineteenth century and the beginning of the twentieth, the focus turned to the remedy for the pranking that had gone to such extremes it had become out-and-out vandalism and nearly got Halloween banned in the United States by the 1930s. To prevent that from happening, towns turned to organizing Halloween parties, parades, costuming, and contests, and the practice of neighbors pooling resources to create parties in which groups of children were led house-to-house, each home hosting a different activity – the precursor to trick-or-treat.

"I'm not happy with the arrangement of the Bogie books," said Charlotte. "And the postcards need to be displayed better."

To work in this section, Charlotte and Jonathan stepped into a scene with a table and chairs that could have been in any early twentieth century kitchen. On the table was a set of Bogie books, the annual Halloween decorating guides put out by the Dennison Company in the earliest decades of the twentieth century. Next to them were several craft items. At the other end of the table was a stack of turn-of-the-century picture postcards with colorful and fantastical depictions of Jack-o'-lanterns, witches, ghosts, and black cats, all of which solidified these images forever as icons of Halloween.

"I want this section to look like someone has just stepped away from creating some of the decorations described in the books and another person is about to start writing out postcards. But everything is too neat."

"Well, let's mess it up, then," said Jonathan. "I'll take the postcards."

Charlotte gathered up the Bogie books that were neatly fanned out on the table. She opened a couple to random pages and haphazardly stacked the others off to the side. Then she cut into some orange crepe paper, leaving the vintage scissors atop it so that they appeared to have been set down in mid-cut next to the rubber-tipped glue bottle.

While she was doing that, Jonathan shuffled the stack of postcards, flipped a few onto their backs and laid the fountain pen atop one of them, moving the dip pen, ink jar, and metal nibs just off to the side.

They stepped back to take in the scene.

"That's better, don't you think?" asked Charlotte.

"Much," he agreed.

They moved on to the final section of the exhibit, showing how the post-World War II years, when the boom in suburban development increased safe neighborhoods, ushered in Halloween as it is now known. Halloween costumes from the 1940s and '50s in their deep boxes and cellophane-windowed tops were stacked on the floor.

"Let's put a few out," said Charlotte. Opening the box on top, she pulled out a mask – a garish green witch's face. Beneath the mask was a black cape with yellow outlines of owls, cats, and a crescent moon. She draped the cape over a chair and hung the mask from the top by its elastic band.

"We need a dress form for this," she said, picking up a paper packet from the Dennison Company which held a crepe paper Dutch Girl costume. "Otherwise, it will just look like wads of paper to the visitors."

"My wife has a dress form," said Jonathan. "I'll see if she'd be willing to loan it to us for the exhibit."

"Tell her I'd be very grateful," said Charlotte, setting the packet aside to focus on an assortment of ghost, mummy, and vampire costumes.

"My son wore something like this one year," said Jonathan, holding up a cowboy costume.

"Very popular in the fifties with all those cowboy TV shows," said Charlotte.

The very end of the exhibit had one wall covered with corkboard. A small table held several large piles of index cards, a tray of pens, and a container of thumbtacks. A sign told visitors they were welcome to write down their own memories of past Halloweens along with an approximate date and pin them to the corkboard. After the exhibit closed, the cards would all be collected, read by the staff, and kept in the museum archives. There were a few school desks and chairs in the room so that people could sit to write. Next to the door leading out of the exhibit area was a large bowl of individually wrapped candies with a sign that read, "Help yourself. One per person, please. Happy Halloween!"

"Do you think we'll need to post a guard by the candy dish?" Jonathan asked, only half joking.

"We might have to," said Charlotte. "I was just thinking that I could go for the candy bar I've got stashed in my desk drawer right now."

"Well, I think we're done here until Paul gets back."

"I'm going back to my office," said Charlotte. "Let me know as soon as he's here. I can't wait to see everything he's bringing back."

As Charlotte sat at her desk nibbling on her chocolate bar, Brad's announcement about the interview played over in her head. She kept trying to figure out how his letting her do the interview could be a bad thing. She replayed everything he'd said to her in her mind looking for how it could be a trap, but there was nothing she could pinpoint. *Oh well,* she thought tossing the empty candy wrapper in the wastebasket. *I'll just do the interview and not worry about it. What could possibly go wrong?*

Chapter 48

November 1839
Birch Falls, Vermont

"Jerusha!" She heard Nathan call her name as she herded the cows into the barn. "I have something for you."

He entered the barn, reaching into his coat pocket.

"Here it is," he said, handing her an envelope. "I picked it up at the store when I was in town this morning, but I figured since you do not wish for anyone to know, I would wait until I saw you alone to give it to you."

"Thank you," she said, taking the letter. It was from Susannah. She thought of bringing it inside to read, but Nathan already knew what she had asked her sister and was now a co-conspirator with her in learning the truth, so instead she opened it there in the barn.

The letter was not terribly long. Susannah came right to the point, that being that if their mother wanted her to know she would tell her, and that Jerusha had transgressed in reading their mother's correspondence.

"What does she say?" asked Nathan.

"Apparently, she knows the truth but refused to share it with me." Jerusha refolded the missive.

"I am sorry. You must be disappointed."

"I am, but it now makes me think that you may be correct about the secret our families share."

"Why do you say that?"

"Because it must be something horrendous if they all insist upon keeping it from me even after all this time. If we consider that Mr. Haskell implies we have a secret in common but will not tell what it is, I am becoming convinced it must be the same one."

"What will you do now?"

"I do not know yet."

"Perhaps you should do nothing. Try to forget it."

Jerusha had been staring at the barn floor. At this remark she looked up at him. "Perhaps I should, but I am not certain I can. It is difficult to know that my whole family, the whole town," her voice rose along with the frustration welling inside her, "has a secret they are determined to keep from me. I am no longer a child. I do not see why I should not know."

"I suppose they keep it from you so as not to distress you. Can you accept that is so, assume it is what we think, and simply go on with your life?"

Jerusha sighed. "It is difficult. I may not be able to explain why exactly, but I need to know. I feel left out." Her voice was almost a whisper on that last sentence. She dropped her gaze to the barn floor again, realizing how small admitting that made her sound.

Nathan was quiet for a moment. Finally, he put his hand on her shoulder and spoke in a soft, compassionate tone. "Jerusha, I do not know if there is anything I can do to help, but I am happy to listen. Sometimes that is the best help of all."

She looked up at him, at the serenity of his dark brown eyes, suddenly feeling that if she could gaze into them forever nothing else would matter. His hand on her shoulder was warm in the chilly November air.

"Thank you, Nathan," she said. "You are a good and kind friend."

He smiled, still holding her gaze. "It is easy to be good and kind to someone with such a warm heart."

The heat where his hand rested on her shoulder spread throughout her body. She leaned towards him barely realizing she was doing so when a gust of wind blew through the barn so hard it flung the door against the wall and sent hay flying through the air. Jerusha gasped, jumping at the noise.

Nathan propped the door open with a barrel then looked at the sky. "A storm is coming," he said. "I had best hurry with the rest of my chores."

Jerusha tucked the letter into her sleeve and set about gathering firewood and collecting the last of the pumpkins. As she worked, the wind picked up so that the bare tree branches scraped the sky like frenzied broomsticks. By the time she returned to the house, the day had grown darker. Rain mixed with snow began to fall. Upon entering the house, she was sent immediately by her mother to the garret to bring down three quilts from the chest for they would surely need them tonight.

The limbs of a tall, ancient tree scraped against the window in the garret. Hearing a crack, Jerusha stepped closer. The wind pushed the branches against the window making it rattle. She jumped back when a gust of wind smacked the branch hard against the house.

She set Susannah's letter aside, opened the chest, and pulled out three quilts, one for her parents' bed, one for her own and one to give to Nathan. Arms laden with quilts, she descended the stairs.

"Jerusha," her mother called. "As soon as you finish, come help me, please."

She hurried down the stairs having deposited two of the quilts on the beds and carrying the last one with her. She set it on a chair to give to Nathan. Her mother was busy in the kitchen preparing supper.

"I think this is going to be a bad storm," said her mother. "I will have Nathan sleep in the house tonight. Please make up the bed."

A flash of fear struck her as it always did whenever she had to enter the room where Seth and her sisters had died. She had grown to hate that room, but she could not refuse her mother's request and so, taking up the quilt, she forced herself to go into it.

She had just finished making up the bed when she heard the kitchen door open and close and the voices of her father and Nathan talking about the storm.

"The wind is bending the trees over," said her father, as Jerusha returned to the kitchen. "We will be fortunate if we do not lose any."

"It is sleeting now," added Nathan. "The ice will make the branches heavier. We will probably lose some limbs at the very least."

"We are all safe inside now," said Jerusha's mother, as she placed cornbread, pie, and tea on the table. "Nathan, you will sleep in the house tonight. I will feel better knowing we are all under one roof. Jerusha has already made up your bed."

Nathan smiled at Jerusha. "Thank you," he said.

As the evening wore on, the storm worsened, the wind roaring past the windows, the sleet making pinging noises against the panes.

Jerusha slept poorly. It wasn't just the storm that kept her awake. She toyed with the idea of writing to Susannah what Nathan had told her about his own family and asking outright if the same thing had occurred in theirs. Yet she could not justify the postage expense when she knew Susannah was not likely to be any more forthcoming. She thought about asking her father, trying Mrs. Wicker again, perhaps even going to old Mr. Haskell, but she knew they'd all say the same. It was for her mother alone to tell her and if she would not, neither would they.

She thought of Nathan's question about why she had such a strong need to know. She did not know how to explain that she could not trust her memories and that that was deeply disturbing to her. She remembered just enough of the night before Seth died to know that some event changed everything. She walked through that night again in her memory.

She'd awakened alone in the garret, moonlight shining through the window. Voices, lots of them, muffled from being two floors below her, nonetheless wafted up to her garret room, too loud for a gathering at Seth's sickbed. She'd crept down the garret stairs then started down the stairs leading to the main floor of the house. A glimpse of her mother, Mrs. Cutting, and Mrs. Wicker bunched together heading for the door was all she'd seen when suddenly Susannah was before her on the stairs, turning her around, ushering her back up. She must have asked Susannah what was happening but had no memory of her sister's reply. She only remembered the frustration of not understanding what was going on and the feeling that something was terribly wrong.

She tried putting together what she remembered with what Nathan had told her of his own family's experience. Could they have come to get Seth so he could breathe in the ashes as they burned his sister's heart?

The thought chilled her. It was understandable that her mother would not want her to know. She'd been thinking about how her mother would have felt ever since Nathan had related his family's story. It had affected her so strongly that she could not help but stay close to her mother, trying to offer her the solace of her presence. She had only succeeded in making her mother wonder what was wrong with her.

If she was correct, her mother had surely been against it. It must be why she was so angry with those who insisted on it. Jerusha, having been only nine at the time, was too young to have been involved and her mother would have been trying to protect her. It made sense.

Then another thought struck her, one that left her gasping for breath. What of her father? Could he have sanctioned it? How could he? It did not fit with the father she knew and loved.

She thought of Nathan. How had his parents felt? Had they been willing participants? Nathan himself had been there. He was the one sent to fetch his invalid sister. Had his parents believed in it? Had he?

Jerusha's feelings for Nathan had been changing of late. Their friendship seemed to be ripening into something more. She thought now of his soft brown eyes as he gazed at her and the way his dark curls lifted slightly when caught by a breeze. Lingering on this image dispelled the unease her previous thoughts had brought her. She felt relaxed and excited at the same time. It was a new sensation that had only recently been creeping up on her and taking her by surprise. She rather liked it.

Jerusha hadn't realized she'd finally fallen asleep until her mother's knock at her door pulled her reluctantly from her slumber.

"Jerusha you are needed," her mother called. "We have damage from the storm."

She rolled from the bed, dressed hurriedly in the chilly room, and went downstairs to find her parents and Nathan gathered in the kitchen. The sun was barely up, yet Nathan and her father were sweating as though they'd already put in several hours of work.

"What happened?" she asked.

"The storm sent a tree limb straight through the garret window."

"I cannot understand how we did not hear it," said her mother who was bustling about the kitchen. "Jerusha, gather the eggs, please."

Jerusha threw on her cloak, grabbed a basket, and headed out the door. Before going to the barn, she went to survey the damage. The tree was bent, most of its branches encased in ice. The garret window was smashed. A large hunk of a branch lay on the ground at her feet.

After collecting the eggs and milking the cows, Jerusha ate a hurried breakfast with her mother. Nathan and her father had gobbled down bread and jam, not waiting for anything else. Her father was in the garret, having sent Nathan to the store for a windowpane and supplies.

After helping her mother clean up the kitchen, Jerusha ran upstairs to assess the damage for herself. Upon entering the garret room, she spied a folded piece of paper on the floor. Susannah's letter. She had set it aside to get the quilts and forgotten to retrieve it.

Her father was obviously too concerned about the window to have noticed. Her parents would want to see any letter from Susannah and would not understand why she'd kept it from them. Until they read it.

Her father's back was to her as he worked at the broken window. All of the glass had been removed. He took apart the side casing where the weights and pulleys ran inside to check their condition. She picked up the letter, meaning to take it immediately to her chamber and return, but her father turned towards her.

"Jerusha, can you believe this mess?" he said indicating the shards of glass all over the floor. "Come here. Take a look."

She walked to the window, cold air making her shiver. She crossed her arms, hugging herself tight with her hands tucked beneath her elbows as much to hide the letter as to warm herself. There was a scrape mark on the sill.

"That wind was howling like a pack of wolves last night," he said. "That is the only reason I can figure that we did not hear it break."

"Yes, Father," she said, her mind searching for an excuse to get away with her secret missive.

Just then her mother appeared at the top of the garret stairs with a broom and dustpan in her hands. "We will get that glass cleaned up before anyone gets cut," she said.

The sound of a wagon drifted up to them.

"Nathan has returned," said her father, peering down to the yard below. "I will help him."

As her father left the garret, her mother handed her the broom. "I will gather the larger pieces while you sweep up the rest."

Her mother set the dustpan on the floor and bent over it. Panic overtook Jerusha. As soon as her mother's back was turned, she stuffed the letter inside the window casing. They had just finished cleaning up the glass when Nathan and her father returned.

Before Jerusha knew it, her father had replaced the casing, and the two men began work on installing the new pane. She stared at the window with Susannah's letter now sealed up inside.

"Come, Jerusha," said her mother. "No sense gawking. We have much work to do."

She left the garret, her dustpan heavy with shards.

Chapter 49

September 1973
Middlebury, Vermont

"Ta da!" Heidi delivered the diary to her with a flourish. "Your grandmother is a sweetheart. I almost didn't want to leave."

"See why I love her?"

They both bounced onto the sofa. Charlotte had donned her cotton gloves the moment she'd heard Heidi in the hallway.

"Read it out loud. I'm dying to know what she wrote," said Heidi.

"You didn't read it?"

"Of course not. You should be the first. But the curiosity is killing me."

Charlotte laughed. "Okay, then, let see what she had to say."

Carefully, Charlotte opened the diary. Just as she'd hoped, it picked up where the last one left off. She brought the first diary from the coffee table and began with the start of its last sentence.

"I have made up my mind and have laid a plan. Tomorrow I will...write to Susannah and ask her to tell me."

"I'll bet the letter we found was Susannah's answer to her," said Heidi.

"I'm sure that's what it is."

"Will she ever say if she found out what happened?"

"Let me see." Charlotte skimmed the pages, turning them carefully, looking among the entries of weather, household chores, the changing of the year from 1839 to 1840, and other mundane musings that seemed to fill a good portion of the diary. At the entry for the fifteenth of March in 1840, Charlotte let out a gasp.

"What?" asked Heidi, nearly bounding off the sofa with barely contained excitement.

"Listen to this. 'Mother astonished me today by saying that I may go to Mrs. Wicker this year to learn to weave. I was not sure I had heard correctly and asked her to repeat what she had said. She smiled, then, something I have missed seeing, and said she had decided it was a skill I should have. I do not know what truly changed her mind, but I am so delighted I cannot find words to express it.'"

"What changed her mind? asked Heidi. "Well, I'm happy for Jerusha."

"Listen to this entry. It's from April twenty-eighth. 'Today I have taken the seat at the loom, pressed the treadles and passed the shuttle. It was glorious as I knew it would be.'"

"Oh, good for her!"

Several days were skipped and the following entries consisted of more lists of springtime housekeeping tasks.

"Does she ever say if she found out what her mother had against Mrs. Wicker?"

"I'm looking. So far, it's mostly everyday stuff."

Charlotte took great care in turning the fragile pages. "Oh no!"

"What?" asked Heidi.

"Look," She tipped the book so that Heidi could see the damage starting just over a third of the way through the diary. "It must have gotten wet. The writing is blurred and there's mold. I can barely read it. Damn!"

"That's awful. Is all the rest of it like that?"

Charlotte opened to the back of the book which was even worse. "I'll bet someone dropped it in a puddle.

Maybe Grandma's sister. She didn't care much about this type of thing."

"Can you read it at all?"

Charlotte squinted at the pages. "Barely. Hold on. Let me get my magnifying glass." She retrieved the magnifier from a kitchen drawer and returned to the couch. Holding it over the words, she struggled to read.

"Ugh. This is terrible," she said, closing the book and setting it on the coffee table. "I'll take it to work with me tomorrow and ask Danny Melaney if he can do anything about it. He's the museum conservator."

"What's that?"

"He restores damaged artifacts and ensures that what we have is stored and maintained properly."

"I hope he can fix it."

"If anyone can, it's Danny. Since we can't do anything more with the diary right now, let me fill you in on what just happened at work."

Charlotte launched into the story of Brad's magnanimous arrangement for her to do an interview with the local TV station and her worries that he was up to something.

Later that evening as they sat together on Heidi's couch waiting for the Battle of the Sexes to begin, Heidi asked, "Did you ever find out Brad's birthday?"

Charlotte gaped at Heidi. "What?"

"I would really like to know his sign," Heidi explained. "I've thought all along that he's probably an Aries, but now I'm starting to think he might be a Gemini."

"If he's up to something, what difference does his sign make?"

"That's exactly why it would be good to know. When Geminis lie, they're usually very careful about their words. Now with an Aries you know they're lying when they become extra calm. They go overboard trying to appear like everything is on the up-and-up, so you don't suspect them. Seriously, when an Aries acts like that, that's when you should be suspicious."

"I don't think Brad is lying. I know the interview is for real because I got a call from the TV station that afternoon. What I'm concerned about is his motive for letting me do the interview. It's out of character. You know how he's treated me ever since I started working there – like I'm incompetent. He's always belittling me. I can't figure out why he's suddenly giving me the prestige of being interviewed on TV."

"Maybe he feels bad about how he's treated you, but he's too proud to apologize so he's doing this for you instead."

"I don't know. His attitude toward me hasn't changed. He still refers to my future exhibit as 'Charlotte's little vampire exhibit.' Besides, Jonathan thinks it's very out of character for him, too."

"What could he get out of letting you do the interview that would hurt you or benefit him?" Heidi asked. "Whether he wants to admit it or not, he knows you'll be very professional and do a great job. Nothing about that will be negative for you."

"I don't see where anything could go wrong, but it keeps nagging at me that something is off."

Heidi's brow furrowed as she thought. "Oh, look. It's starting."

She rose to turn up the volume on the television. Returning to the couch, she put the bowl of popcorn between them.

As the match began, Charlotte's heart beat faster. She wasn't a big tennis fan, but she very much wanted Billie Jean King to win. There had been so much hype leading up to this match. She was sick to death of hearing men talking about how King would lose and how no woman could ever beat a man at any sport. The first set ended with King winning six to four.

When the show went to commercial, Charlotte turned to Heidi. "Do you think he might be going to pull me from the interview at the last minute and do it himself?"

"Why would he do that?"

"To get me excited about it only to have it ripped away from me."

"That's petty," said Heidi.

"We are talking about Brad, here," Charlotte reminded her.

"Still, wouldn't that make him look bad to the others?"

Charlotte thought about that. "Maybe," she said. "I suppose that depends on what he gives them for a reason."

"Stop worrying about it," Heidi told her. "If he has an ulterior motive, we're not likely to figure it out. Just prepare for the interview and do your best. I can't wait to see you on TV."

Charlotte smiled at her. "You're right. I'm probably getting worked up over nothing. He's got me paranoid."

"What are you girls watching?" asked Iris Pleasant as she came down the hall from her bedroom.

"The Battle of the Sexes, Aunt Iris," Heidi told her.

"What on earth is that?"

"Bobby Riggs and Billie Jean King are playing tennis against each other."

"Oh, yes, I heard. I didn't know it was on TV tonight. Honestly, I can't understand a girl trying to play a sport against a man. She can't hope to win."

"She just beat him in the first set," said Charlotte. "And why couldn't she win? She's a great tennis player."

"Amongst girls, sure. But she can't beat a man."

"She's a woman, not a girl. And I'll bet she'll win."

"Well, if she does it will only be because he was gentleman enough to let her win. I don't know what kind of woman would want to show herself to be more athletic than a man," said Iris. "It's not very feminine and men don't like it. She'll never find a husband that way."

Charlotte could not stop herself from rolling her eyes.

"She already has a husband," said Heidi. "She's married to her coach, Larry King."

"And he lets her do this?"

Charlotte was about to retort when Heidi nudged her. Once Iris went into the kitchen, Charlotte said, "Sorry. I don't mean to be disrespectful to your aunt, but she can really get under my skin. She's like a female version of Brad."

Heidi chuckled. "You know that generation. That's how they think."

"I don't get it. How can she demean other women? It's bad enough hearing that stuff from guys. From another woman it feels like a betrayal.

"She thinks Billie Jean King is betraying other women by being unfeminine."

"I'm glad it's you who lives with her and not me."

Heidi laughed. "I love her so I let what she says roll off my back."

"I'm glad you can do that. I couldn't. Just look at what she implied. If Riggs wins it's because he's a man and, therefore, a better athlete. If King wins it's because he was a gentleman and let her win. Whether she wins or not, she loses."

Heidi shrugged. "Yup. You won't change her mind. But it doesn't matter. If Billie Jean King wins it might change other people's minds. That's what matters. Look, it's back on."

They turned their attention to the television.

"He finally took off his warm-up jacket," said Charlotte. "Maybe this isn't as easy as he thought it would be. Male chauvinist pig!" Iris's comments had fueled her anger. She wished she had Heidi's ability to not let it get to her.

"Wow! Did you see that?" Heidi asked, leaning towards the TV.

"Cool!" Charlotte exclaimed.

"Yes!"

They both jumped off the couch. The match had suddenly become intense, both players moving at high speed on the court returning volleys that looked like they should have been unhittable. The crowd in the Astrodome roared.

"She's giving the old man a workout," said Heidi, laughing.

As the game progressed, they left the couch to sit on the floor in front of the TV set like a couple of kids. Heidi's aunt had gone back to her room.

"If Aunt Iris comes out again, she'll tell us not to sit so close to the television or we'll ruin our eyesight," Heidi said and Charlotte laughed.

"My mother always said that, too."

Charlotte let out a whoop when Howard Cosell announced that Billie Jean King was running Bobby Riggs all over the court. "Yes, she is!" she agreed. "And I am loving every minute of it."

"If she wins, I think it will be very cathartic for you," Heidi said, tossing a piece of popcorn in the air and catching it in her mouth.

"Man, I want her to win so bad," said Charlotte, realizing that watching Billie Jean King beat Bobby Riggs felt like she was besting Brad. It was the release she needed after the months of putting up with his chauvinism and now worrying about why he had set her up for the interview instead of taking it himself.

"No!" said Charlotte as Billie Jean made her third error in a row in the second set. Charlotte was close to biting her nails.

"Don't worry, she'll come back," said Heidi. But Heidi's face looked as nervous as Charlotte felt.

"Wow, look at that crowd," said Heidi as the camera pulled back to pan the packed Astrodome, every so often focusing on the many celebrities in the crowd.

"Alright, she's got it back," said Charlotte as Billie Jean picked up several points one after the other.

Moments later, she and Heidi erupted in shouts as Billie Jean took the second set.

They used the commercial break to grab more sodas and talk about the banners and posters put up by the Astrodome crowd. This was unlike any tennis match ever. The quiet reserve was completely missing. Cheers, whistles, and catcalls continued non-stop. The arena was filled with banners supporting one player or the other.

"It's back on," said Charlotte, feeling all the more like a kid as she and Heidi dropped to the floor in front of the TV.

"It's a five-set game, but if she wins this one it's over. I so hope she skunks him. It would serve him right," said Charlotte.

"I hope she does, too, just to see you doing cartwheels all over the room," said Heidi.

"If I could, I would. Oh, please!" said Charlotte as Riggs called a time out claiming an injury to his hand. "He just wants a rest because she's kicking his ass all over the court."

"His hand probably does hurt. Maybe her returns are so hard they've broken it," Heidi joked.

They waited as the game came to a halt while Riggs took his ten-minute break. Once back on the court, the announcers claimed that Riggs may have taken the time out to throw Billie Jean's rhythm off. If that was the case, it didn't work. By the time she was one point away from winning the set and the entire match, Charlotte and Heidi were rocking back and forth with anticipation, eyes glued to the TV set.

"Come on, come on," said Charlotte.

At match point, Riggs couldn't return King's volley. Billie Jean had won the match, and the entire Astrodome erupted. Charlotte and Heidi fell into each other's arms screaming and whooping.

"What's happening?" asked Heidi's aunt as she hurried into the living room.

"She won, Aunt Iris! She won!"

"Go on."

"She beat him in three straight sets," said Charlotte who just realized that tears of joy were streaming down her face.

Charlotte and Heidi collapsed on the floor in delighted exhaustion. Even Iris couldn't help grinning at their exuberance.

Later, when Charlotte crawled into bed, the last thought she had before falling asleep was *bring it on, Brad. I'm ready for you.*

Chapter 50

Late April 1840
Birch Falls, Vermont

Though early May, the air was still chilly and damp. Nonetheless, Lavinia had decided it was time to start weaving. She had more requests than usual. Jerusha was so excited that she was finally going to learn to weave. She'd been utterly stunned when her mother had announced, "It is a skill you should learn." Jerusha knew this was hardly the case since textile mills were becoming more numerous. Home weaving was becoming a thing of the past. Her mother knew this, but Jerusha chose not to question. Instead, she threw her arms around her mother and thanked her. Then she ran to tell Mrs. Wicker the good news.

Lavinia had been taken aback by Jerusha's announcement.

"Are you certain you heard correctly?" she'd asked. Jerusha assured her she had, that she'd no idea what changed her mother's mind, but she was ready as soon as Mrs. Wicker began the year's weaving.

That had been in March. It was still too cold then to sit in the room without a fireplace. They would never be able to stay there long enough to get much done. The time between then and the end of felt interminable. When it finally arrived, Jerusha could barely contain her excitement. Once out of the house, she ran up the hill, her bonnet flying. Held on only by the ribbons tied beneath her chin, it bounced along behind her.

Jerusha sat on the loom before the bench feeling as though a new world was about to open.

"We will start with a plain weave as that is the easiest."

At Mrs. Wicker's direction, Jerusha passed the shuttle back and forth pushing down with her foot on the treadles. Each treadle having its own harness, she took care to get the right ones. She soon fell into an easy rhythm, taking to weaving as quickly and joyously as she'd always known she would.

"You have a natural ability, Jerusha," said Mrs. Wicker. "I had a feeling you would be good at this."

When, at the end of the day, Jerusha's face ached, she realized it was from smiling all day. "May I come back tomorrow?" she asked.

"That is up to your mother. She may need you at home. But you may come as often as she will allow."

"How was your first weaving lesson?" asked her mother when Jerusha returned.

"As wonderful as I always knew it would be!"

"I am glad you enjoyed it."

"I would love to have a loom of my own."

"That is a great expense, Jerusha. I believe Lavinia's loom belonged to her mother and before that, to her grandmother."

"It is only a dream. But I am so grateful to be able to learn and to weave on Mrs. Wicker's loom."

Jerusha longed to ask what had changed her mind but was afraid that asking might break whatever spell had come over her. Jerusha had noticed a change in her mother of late, a gradual releasing of the anger that had taken over her life since Seth died. She did not want to disturb whatever healing might be taking place. So, instead she asked, "When may I go back?"

"We will see. I will need you in the dairy tomorrow to make butter. If the weather is fine, Nathan will prepare the soil for the garden. Then we will have to start planting. There is much to do here."

The disappointment must have shown on Jerusha's face because her mother added, "Do not fret. You will go back soon enough."

After cleaning up from supper, Jerusha went for a walk with Nathan telling him all about her first day of weaving.

"I have never seen you so happy," he said.

"I never thought I would get the chance to learn to weave. I wish I knew what changed my mother's mind."

"Does it matter?"

"I think so. She was so adamant until now that I have nothing to do with Mrs. Wicker beyond what was absolutely necessary. If I knew why she now feels differently, perhaps I could find a way to bring them together again. I do so wish they could be friends."

"This is a good beginning. Let it happen as it will."

"You are right, of course. Our families were once so close."

When they reached the orchard, Nathan stopped under an apple tree that was just beginning to unfurl small pink blossoms. With one finger, he tilted Jerusha's chin up towards his face. Gazing into her eyes, he said, "It pleases me more than you can imagine to see you so cheerful. I hope to see your radiant smile and twinkling eyes more often."

Jerusha's breath caught in her throat causing her to blink several times. It was not only the weaving that had caused her jubilant mood. The more time she spent with Nathan, the more she grew to like and trust him. Sometimes, at night before she fell asleep, she would imagine what it would be like to have his strong arms around her, to feel his lips on hers. She hoped he felt the same.

"Maybe one day I will be able to make you as happy as weaving does," he said with a slightly embarrassed laugh.

Jerusha had no experience in the art of courting. Susannah was too far away to enlighten her and there was no one else with whom to discuss her feelings. She had never been allowed to resume her friendship with Hannah and Besty nor any other friends. How should she respond?

Nathan dropped his hand from her face and turned away, apparently taking her silence for rejection.

"I am sorry," he said, staring up at the apple tree. "I hope I have not offended you."

"No," she said. "No, you have not. Not at all. I just…I did not expect it."

She put her hand on his shoulder, turning him back to her. "I am glad of it," she said.

"Then you do feel as I do?"

"Yes. I do."

A smile spread across Nathan's face. Taking both her hands in his own, he leaned down and touched his lips to hers. It was a modest, chaste kiss, but it sent sparks shooting through Jerusha's whole being. She was full to the brim with happiness, a feeling she had not experienced in a very long time.

Nathan glanced toward the sky. "The sun is setting. We should go back." There was a reluctance to his voice, yet he meant it. He was a decent man and she understood that he would not compromise her in any way, knowing her parents expected her back before nightfall.

"Jerusha?" asked her mother, as she entered the house, Nathan having gone to the barn loft.

"Yes." She still felt as though she was walking on clouds.

Her mother looked at her with her head tilted to one side as if trying to decipher some riddle.

"Did you enjoy your walk with Nathan?"

"Yes."

"Good." Jerusha saw her mother bite her lip and turn away in an attempt to hide a knowing smile.

She knows. And she is pleased.

Jerusha fell asleep that night believing that it had been the best day of her life thus far.

Chapter 51

Late September 1973
Middlebury, Vermont

Charlotte surprised herself by not feeling jittery when Tony Armano arrived from WVMB along with a cameraman for her interview. She'd been preparing what to say for days and was ready.

"Hey, Tony, good to see you, man," said Brad as his friend entered the exhibit.

They had agreed to meet in the exhibit space after hours. Brad got there just ahead of her with President Shepherd arriving moments later.

"You aren't nervous, are you?" Brad had asked.

"Not at all," she told him.

Once the WVMB people arrived, Brad introduced Tony to Charlotte and President Shepherd while the cameraman set up lighting and looked for good angles.

"I'm sorry I can't stay," President Shepherd said to the others. "have a prior engagement. Best of luck to you, Charlotte," he said, turning to her. "It was good of Brad to give you this opportunity."

"Yes," Charlotte agreed. "I am grateful." *I think.*

"It's my pleasure," said Brad. "Charlotte's truly up-and-coming in the field of folklore. WVMB is lucky to be getting her first interview. Someday she'll be a revered name in our profession. Tony, be sure to ask her about the exhibit she'll be doing that involves her ancestors."

Charlotte had all she could do not to gape at Brad. She wanted to ask if aliens had snatched the real Brad and replaced him with a look-alike.

"I remember," said Tony. "I'll be sure to get it in."

"Great. Well, good luck, Charlotte. We'll talk tomorrow," said Brad.

"You aren't staying?" Charlotte asked. Truthfully, she thought not having Brad hanging around would be less intimidating, but she had expected him to stay.

"You don't need me. Knock 'em dead, kid," he said, chucking her on the shoulder before turning to accompany President Shepherd to the door.

"Okay, Charlotte," said Tony. "As soon as Joe is ready, we can get started.

"All set, here," said the cameraman.

"Solid. Why don't we walk through the exhibit from beginning to end. You can tell me about it as we go. Joe can follow us with the camera."

"I'm not sure we want to show the entire exhibit," Charlotte said. "Don't we just want to whet the viewers' appetites, so they'll want to come?"

"Absolutely. We'll be taking a lot more footage than we'll actually use. That's how we work. We get more than we need. When we go back to the studio, we'll edit it down to the best parts for the amount of time allotted for airing it."

"I see. That makes sense."

"Shall we get started?"

Charlotte walked them through the exhibit, stopping to talk about the items in each area as if she were giving a guided tour. When they finished, Tony said, "That was great. Now let's do some interview questions."

Tony positioned her in front of the entrance to the "Halloween in America" section of the exhibit. "Charlotte," he said, "What do you find most interesting about the history of Halloween?"

"Several things. I'm fascinated with how it evolved over time from the ancient Pagan festival of *Samhain*, celebrated mainly by adults, to the kids' holiday that it's become. I think it's connection with religion, first Druid then Christian, is an important aspect, especially that it held onto that aspect for so long. It's really the key to why it stayed alive all this time. When Christianity overtook Paganism, it evolved from its roots in the *Samhain* festival to being the eve of the Feast of All Saints. If it weren't for that, it might have died out. Finally, as a folklorist, I am deeply interested in understanding what it means to the people who participate in it, both now and in the past."

"Has the way people understand it changed greatly over time?"

"On some levels. For example, who today would think of Halloween as a religious holiday? But until the not-so-distant past, that's what it was, whether Pagan or Christian."

"And the Druids? How did they celebrate Halloween?"

"They didn't call it Halloween, but rather *Samhain*, a Celtic word that means 'summers' end'."

"Oh? I read somewhere that *Samhain* was the name of a Celtic god."

"You must have been reading the work of Charles Vallancey or someone who was relying on his research. Vallancey was an eighteenth-century British military engineer who like to dabble in history and linguistics. He became obsessed with the lore of ancient Ireland and wrote extensively on it. Unfortunately, most of what he wrote was inaccurate, but because his writing was popular, much of it became accepted and carried on by the general public despite it being denounced by experts of his own time."

The interview continued for much longer than she knew could possibly be allotted for the segment, with Tony asking lots of questions about different stages in the holiday's progression. She wondered what they'd keep and what they'd cut.

After Tony seemed to have exhausted all the questions he could think of about the exhibit and the history of Halloween, he said, "I understand that you will be spearheading a future exhibit that has something to do with your own ancestors and, of all things, vampires. Could you tell us something about what we can expect from that?"

"I can't say what will be in the exhibit itself. We haven't gotten that far yet. But it is a topic that fascinates me. I'm very excited about it."

"I'm sure our viewers are wondering what your ancestors had to do with vampires. Were they vampire hunters?"

Charlotte laughed. "Not exactly. You see, during the nineteenth century, tuberculosis, or consumption as they called it, was epidemic. There was rarely a family who wasn't touched by it. They didn't understand what it was or how it spread. Doctors attempted to treat it, but certainly couldn't cure it. Many families lost multiple members to it. People became desperate to save their loved ones. They would try anything, including, a folk remedy that came from Europe with their own ancestors."

"What was the remedy?"

"The folklore around it said that one of the family members who had died was coming back at night and feeding off the others. You have to realize that towards the end, a person suffering from consumption starts to look like a walking skeleton. They appear to others as if they are being consumed by some unseen entity. Hence the term 'consumption.' They also cough up a lot of blood, usually at night, so upon awakening they often have blood on them. Their chests felt heavy as if there was a weight on them. In their fever deliriums, they would sometimes hallucinate someone sitting on their chest."

"Let me guess. Sometimes that someone was one of their deceased family members?"

"You got it. Even if they didn't hallucinate, there was enough knowledge of this folklore that others began to assume that's what was going on."

"So, they thought the dead family member was a vampire who was coming back to drink their blood?"

"Not exactly. They never used the word 'vampire' and they didn't think of it in the way we think of vampires. They thought some sort of evil entity was using the dead person's body as a host during the day and coming out of the grave at night to feed off the living. There's no indication of the so-called vampire biting their victim on the neck and drinking their blood, but blood definitely played an important role."

"What did they do about the vampire?"

"They dug up the graves of the deceased family members to see if they could discern which of them was the culprit. They were looking for anomalies in the deceased's body. They didn't embalm during most of the time this was happening, so they expected a body to be in a specific state of decomposition depending on how long the person had been dead. If it wasn't as they expected, for instance, if they detected fresh blood in the heart or at the mouth, then they assumed they had found the offender."

"They actually found some of those things? How could that be?"

"Everything they found can now be explained scientifically, but they didn't understand any of that. They got bodies into the ground quickly. They weren't keeping them around to experiment on what happens during decomposition. They just knew what they were seeing wasn't as they thought it should be. It seemed completely unnatural. Supernatural, actually."

"When they found the one they thought was a vampire, did they drive a stake through his heart?"

"There were variations on what they did, but, more often than not, they cut out the heart and burned it. Sometimes they burned the whole body. Occasionally, they rearranged body parts thinking that would make it impossible for the deceased to get up and move around. In some cases, when they burned the heart, or it might be the liver, or both, they made the sick family members breathe it in as it burned. That was supposed to cure them."

"How often did this happen?"

"It's not known for certain. It's not like every family was doing this. But we know it happened because there were newspaper accounts of it that are still available in library archives. Henry David Thoreau even mentioned it in one of his diaries. Not everyone believed in it, of course. Most people probably didn't, but for those who did, it was seen as a viable option for a cure."

"That's amazing. So, if they didn't use the word 'vampire,' the so-called vampire wasn't biting people on the neck and drinking their blood, and they weren't driving stakes through their hearts, why do we refer to them as vampires?"

"It has a lot to do with Bram Stoker's *Dracula*. After his death, a newspaper clipping detailing one of these cases in New England was found in his notebook. It seems likely that he took what he learned from that newspaper account and let his imagination run wild. But his book, *Dracula*, was such a big hit that it became the basis for modern-day vampire lore. There are enough similarities for people to tack the word 'vampire' onto what our New England ancestors were doing."

"Speaking of ancestors, are you saying that one of yours was dug up?"

"It appears so. From my research so far, it seems that Eliza Kendall may have been exhumed and thought to be what we are now calling a vampire. Her grave has been a legend-tripping site for several generations."

"What is legend tripping?"

"It's when teens, usually boys, go together to a site with a spooky legend attached to it."

Charlotte launched into an explanation of legend tripping despite knowing a lot, if not all, of it would be cut. Still, they might keep just enough for people to get the idea.

"The legend attached to Eliza's grave is that she is a vampire. Given what I've been able to deduce thus far, the reason for it is probably that her body was exhumed for the purpose of applying this folk remedy."

"What happens when kids do this legend tripping to her grave?"

"I'm told they put plastic vampire teeth on her grave expecting her to rise out of it as a mist and come after them. Of course, no such thing happens, but once the kids have worked themselves up, their imaginations do the rest. It's really all just good fun as long as they don't engage in any vandalism or dangerous behavior like drunk driving, and it can be an important rite of passage for teens who engage in it. I plan to include a section on legend tripping in the exhibit."

"Sounds like it will be fascinating. I wish you all the best with it and with the current exhibit."

"Thank you," said Charlotte.

Tony turned away as the cameraman moved to the side. Looking into the camera, he said, "The Evolution of Halloween exhibit at the New England Folklife Museum in Middlebury is open through the end of October. Be sure to bring the whole family and learn some spellbinding facts about how Halloween came to be the holiday we celebrate today."

As Joe started packing up his lights and camera, Tony shook hands with Charlotte. "We got plenty of stuff to work with," he told her. "It will be great."

"I can't wait to see it. When will it air?"

"It's scheduled for October fifth. I know your exhibit opens on the first, but the fifth is the Friday leading into Columbus Day weekend, so we thought it would be good for people who might be looking for something to do that weekend."

"Great idea," Charlotte said.

On the way home, she kept going over the interview in her mind. Everything seemed to have gone well. The sense that Brad was somehow sabotaging her began to drain away. Maybe he really did feel bad about stealing her idea and this was his way of making up for it. Or maybe he was just plain weird. In any case, since it was after 7:00 p.m., the rates were down, and she couldn't wait to get home to call her parents and tell them all about it.

Chapter 52

October 1973
Middlebury and Bennington, Vermont

Charlotte left work early on the day her interview was scheduled to air. She'd packed the night before to travel to her grandmother's house as soon as she left work. Her parents were excited about her being interviewed on TV and, since they couldn't get the local Vermont station in Massachusetts, they decided to drive to Bennington so they could watch it. Her father had taken the afternoon off, too, and as soon as Tracy's school day ended, they headed north.

When Charlotte returned to her apartment to grab her suitcase, she found a note taped to the door.

Have fun watching your interview tonight! I wish we could watch it together, but I'm glad your family will get to see it with you. Aunt Iris and I will be watching. I can't wait to celebrate with you when you get back!
Love ya!
Heidi

Charlotte grinned reading the note. She wished she could have taken Heidi with her, but Heidi was on duty at the hospital all weekend.

When Charlotte arrived in Bennington, her parents and Tracy were already there helping to prepare supper.

"It smells so good in here," said Charlotte as she stepped into the kitchen. Her grandmother's homemade baked macaroni and cheese was bubbling away in the oven. Her mother and Tracy were chopping vegetables for a salad.

"There's our star," said her father.

"Charlotte!" Tracy dropped her knife and ran to her sister, throwing her arms around her. "I can't wait to see you on TV tonight. What was it like being interviewed? Russ is going to be disappointed that he's away at college and won't get to see it."

"Let her get in the door, Tracy," said their mother.

Charlotte dropped her bags and draped her jacket over the back of a chair then hugged each one in turn. Then she picked up her father's red and black hunting jacket. "I can't resist," she said, burying her nose in it. Her father had owned the jacket for at least twenty years, maybe more. It was worn to a cozy softness and smelled deeply of burning autumn leaves and pipe tobacco. Her father laughed watching her inhale its aroma.

"If there's anything in this world that makes me think of home and Dad, it's the smell of this jacket," she said, returning it to the chair back.

"I swear you're like a bloodhound, Charlotte," said Tracy. Then to the others she added, "Do you know that every time she goes into Aunt Beatrice's old bedroom, she smells an empty perfume bottle in the bureau drawer?"

"I can't help it," said Charlotte. "Certain scents remind me of people and places. "It's like this breadbox," she said, opening the creamy white enamel box on the counter and taking a deep breath. "I can't smell fresh bread without thinking of Grandma."

"I'm not sure how I feel about being remembered as a loaf of bread, but I guess there are worse smells," said her grandmother with a laugh.

"What reminds you of me?" asked Tracy.

"Hmm...I'm not sure I have a scent associated with you yet."

"You might, now. Take a whiff." Tracy held her wrist under Charlotte's nose.

"Nice," said Charlotte. "What is it?"

"Sweet Honesty."

"It's new," said her mother. "Avon just started putting it out."

"I got it for my birthday," Tracy told her.

"I can't believe you're sixteen now," Charlotte said, picking up a colander filled with freshly washed lettuce. "How was your party?" she asked, placing the lettuce in the salad bowl and adding the cucumbers and tomatoes Tracy and her mother had just cut up.

"Great, but I didn't do the Sweet Sixteen thing you did. I'm not into all the folklore-y stuff. I had a pizza party sleepover with a bunch of friends."

"Sounds fun."

"It was, especially when Heather Noronski and I – she's on the gymnastics team with me – had a handstand contest to see who could hold it the longest. I won. We did them on the deck railing. Susan Castor took pictures. I brought them."

"Oh, dear Lord," said their mother. "I'm glad I didn't know that was happening. You kids are going to break your necks one of these days and then you won't be doing gymnastics or anything else. It's a wonder we haven't been sued yet."

"Oh, Mom, the deck railing is wider than the balance beam. It's no big deal. Heather can do a back handspring on the beam, so it was wicked easy for her to do one in the railing."

Charlotte bit her lip to keep from laughing.

"Oh, Charlotte, I almost forgot to tell you, I can now do a side aerial on the balance beam and a wrap half twist with a mixed grip catch on the uneven bars."

"Sounds impressive," said Charlotte, not exactly sure what that entailed but certain she would be very impressed.

"My hardest vault is still a Yamashita. My coach wants me to start adding a twist to it."

"Enough with the stuff that gives your mother nightmares," said their father. "Charlotte, tell us more about the vampires and haunted houses."

"I think you know most of what I've found out so far."

"Did you learn anything new from the second diary?" asked her grandmother.

"So far only that Jerusha's mother finally let her take weaving lessons from Mrs. Wicker and she was totally gassed about it."

"That means she was wicked excited about it, Grandma," said Tracy.

"I figured that. Nothing else, Charlotte?"

"A lot of the pages appear to be water damaged. I can barely read them. I gave it to our museum conservator. He's going to see what he can do with it."

"I hope he can make it legible. It would be a shame if you couldn't read it."

"I'm not giving up hope yet. Danny's a wiz."

"I'm certainly looking forward to watching you on TV tonight," said her grandmother. "I'd never have dreamed any one in our own family would be on TV."

"Well, I'm looking forward to *that*," said Charlotte pointing to the casserole dish of baked macaroni and cheese covered with golden breadcrumbs that her mother was pulling from the oven.

After dinner, the family settled in the living room. There was a hush, an almost tangible sense of something akin to reverence as they crowded together on the couch while Charlotte's grandmother turned the station to WVMB. It took a bit of antenna adjusting, but finally the station came into focus.

They sat through the news program waiting for Charlotte's segment to start. It seemed to take forever, but finally the anchor said, "And now we turn to Anthony Armano at the New England Folklife Museum in Middlebury with a report on an exhibit just opened on the history of Halloween."

Excited squeals from Tracy were quickly hushed by the others as the camera cut to Tony standing just outside the museum entrance.

"I'm here at the New England Folklife Museum in Middlebury to take a look at the Evolution of Halloween exhibit. Assistant Director of Programs, Charlotte Lajoie will take us on a guided tour of a bit of the exhibit and tell us about how Halloween came to be the holiday as we know it today."

The shot then cut to Charlotte standing at the beginning of the exhibit.

Now not just Tracy, but the whole family made sounds of delight. Tracy, sitting next to Charlotte, grabbed her arm and exclaimed, "Charlotte, you're really on TV!"

Even Charlotte, who had earlier decided that she would watch with professional decorum as if being interviewed on television was a normal, run-of-the-mill occurrence, could not stop herself from grinning.

"Shh!" their father admonished.

As Tony had told her it would, the film had been edited so that only a few sections of the exhibit were shown. Charlotte thought it was well done, enough to whet the visitors' appetites, but not show so much they had no reason to go. It would help bring in lots of visitors who otherwise might not even know about it, she thought.

Then it cut to the interview part where Tony had asked her questions about how Halloween had evolved. Again, it was edited, but Charlotte found no fault with what had been kept and what had been cut.

Finally, Tony brought the interview around to Eliza Kendall and Charlotte's preparation for her future exhibit.

"Wow!" Charlotte heard her mother exclaim in a hushed voice as Tony began his questions about their ancestors' connection to vampires. "This is the last thing I thought I'd be seeing on TV."

A glance at her mother's rapt expression sent Charlotte's heart soaring. Every one of her family members leaned forward, eyes glued to the television, drinking in every word. It was the proudest moment of her life, not just for the fact of being on TV, but because all her years of study and hard work were being validated amongst the people she cared about most.

Tony had just asked her if her ancestors were vampire hunters. She remembered answering that question with an explanation about how people didn't understand consumption and looked for a folk remedy when nothing else worked. She watched in dismay as she heard herself say, *"Not exactly. One of the family members who had died was coming back at night and feeding off the other family members."*

"What?" she asked aloud. "They cut the explanation. Now it doesn't sound right."

"So, they thought the dead family member was a vampire and was coming back to drink their blood?" Tony asked.

"They thought some sort of evil entity was using the dead person's body as a host during the day and coming out of the grave at night to feed off the living, biting their victim on the neck and drinking their blood."

"What?" she exclaimed, louder this time. "That's not what I said."

"Shh," her father hushed her.

Mouth hanging open and palms squeezing her cheeks, Charlotte gaped at the TV as she watched herself say, *"They dug up the graves of the deceased family members to see if they could discern which of them was the culprit. They were looking for anomalies in the deceased's body. If it wasn't as they expected, for instance if they thought they detected fresh blood in the heart or at the mouth, then they assumed they had found the offender."*

"How could that be?" asked Tony.

"Supernatural, actually," was her reply.

"Oh, my God! I can't believe this." Charlotte shot up from the couch and began pacing the room, never taking her eyes off the TV set.

"So, when they found the one they thought was the vampire, they drove a stake through his heart?"

"There were variations on what they did, but more often than not, they cut out the heart and burned it. Sometimes they burned the whole body. In other cases, they rearranged body parts thinking that would make it impossible for the deceased to get up and move around. In some cases, when they burned the heart, or it might be the liver, or both, they made the sick family members breathe it in as it burned."

"How often did this happen?"

"Every family was doing this."

"No, no,no," Charlotte cried, tears streaming down her face. "How could they do this?"

Dumbfounded, she gazed at her own image on the television, seeing how she held herself so assured and professional with a poise she'd been so proud of when the segment had first started. Now, it simply appeared that she was self-assured while being completely wrong and possibly a bit unbalanced.

She heard herself continue, *"It seems to have a lot to do with Bram Stoker's* Dracula. *His book was such a big hit that it became the basis for what our New England ancestors were doing."*

"Speaking of ancestors, are you saying that one of yours was dug up?"

"It appears so. It seems that Eliza Kendall may have been exhumed and thought to be a vampire. Her grave has been a legend-tripping site for several generations."

"What is legend tripping?"

"It's where teens, usually boys, go together to a site with a spooky legend attached to it. The legend attached to Eliza's grave is that she was a vampire.

Given what I've been able to deduce thus far, the reason for it is probably that her body was exhumed."

"So, what happens when kids do this legend tripping to her grave?"

"I'm told they go to her grave expecting her to rise out of it as a mist and come after them. It's really all just good fun. They engage in vandalism or dangerous behavior like drunk driving, and it can be an important rite of passage for teens who engage in it.

At that, Tony turned from Charlotte to give the date and place of the Halloween exhibit and signed off.

"Charlotte!" her mother exclaimed. "How could you call that good fun?"

"That's not what I said."

"What do you mean? We just heard and saw you!"

"You don't understand. That whole last section was edited to the point where it sounds like I'm saying things I didn't say. It's all wrong." She was sobbing now. Her father got up, put an arm around her and drew her back to the sofa.

"Why on earth would they do such a thing?" asked her grandmother.

"It makes no sense," said her mother. "I know you said they had to edit for time, but didn't they realize how it would sound? Better to leave out that whole section."

"What jerks!" said Tracy.

"I've a good mind to call that station right now and give them what for," said her father, his arms tight around Charlotte. "Eloise, where's your phone book?"

Charlotte heard her grandmother walk out of the room and return a moment later.

"Wait," she said, wiping her eyes. She put a hand on the page to stop her father from flipping through the white pages, making him look up.

"Thank you, Dad, but don't. Please."

"Why not?" asked her mother. "They shouldn't get away with this."

"You're right. They shouldn't," she agreed. "But I need to handle it myself." She took her father's hands. "It was my interview. It will be my exhibit. And it's my job. I have to be professional enough to handle this on my own. And I will."

A smile spread across her father's face. "Charlotte, I'm proud of you," he said.

"What are you going to do?" asked her mother. "They probably won't give you the time of day. I think you should have your father call."

"No, Mom," she said, turning towards her mother. "I'm a grown woman. I can't have my dad fighting my battles for me."

"I wish I could be there when you tell them off," said Tracy. "You'll be like Billie Jean King, and they'll be like Bobby Riggs."

Charlotte couldn't help but laugh at that image.

"You know, Charlotte," said her grandmother. "You did an outstanding job in that interview. Your Aunt Beatrice would have been proud."

"Thank you, Grandma."

"She would also have been after them in short order for what they did. You can be like her and straighten them out." She ended the sentence with a resolute nod of her head.

It took Charlotte a long time to stop shaking. There was no way this was accidental. Yes, they had to cut some, but the way that one segment of her interview had been edited was obviously done to purposely make her look bad. Her mind continued to reel all evening. She sat on the couch with her father after the others had gone upstairs to bed and told him all about her problems with Brad. Other than Heidi, she hadn't confided in anyone until now. Sitting alone with her father, it all came pouring out.

"He has to be behind this, Dad," she said. "Tony's his friend. I remember when Brad first told me about the interview. He said his friend owed him a favor. I thought the favor was getting the interview. Now I know what he really meant. They made me look like a complete idiot. How am I going to face my colleagues? It's more than embarrassing. It looks like I said those things. You couldn't tell it was all done by editing out certain words until the meaning was completely changed. It really sounds like I don't know my stuff. Everyone from work was going to watch tonight. I can only imagine what they must all be thinking."

"Honey, the people who know you know better. When you go into work on Monday, you tell them what happened. It sounds like none of them like this Brad clown. They'll be on your side."

A sudden realization slammed into Charlotte. "Oh, my God. President Shepherd was watching. He'll believe I said those things. He'll fire me." She put her head in her hands. "Why, Daddy? Why did this have to happen?"

Her father rubbed her back. "I'm so sorry, Charlotte. I wish I could fix it all for you. You knew it was going to be a struggle, though, didn't you?"

"What do you mean?" she asked, sitting up to look at him.

He sighed deeply. "A lot of men don't want women in the workforce. They see it as a threat."

"Why are we a threat just because we can do the same jobs?"

He shrugged. "I guess it shows that we don't have everything over on you ladies that we thought we did. Besides, a lot of men worry that if too many women join the workforce, there won't be enough jobs to go around. Men are supposed to be the breadwinners of their families and if they can't find a job because they've been taken over by women, well..."

"You wouldn't feel threatened if a woman could do your job as well as you can, would you?"

"I might feel threatened if anyone, man or woman, came into my place of work and did my job better than me. I'd worry I might lose my job to them. But it could as easily be another man as a woman. I don't have any problem with women in the workplace. But I may be an exception to the rule."

"So, it's emasculating to a man to be equaled, or God forbid, bested by a woman. Is that it?"

"Sadly, yes. I think it is."

"So, we're not supposed to do what we're good at? Anything we find fulfilling just so men won't have to feel bad about themselves?" She could hear her voice rising in pitch. She was glad it was her dad she was talking to and not some other man who would accuse her of becoming hysterical.

"Charlotte, women are trying to change the way things have been for many a century. It's not going to happen overnight. I think it will happen. But it's going to take a lot of women like you to keep fighting to get there. You've got the brains, Charlotte. You can do anything, but you've got to expect resistance, especially from weak men like Brad."

"It's so unfair, Dad."

He sat back giving her a look she knew well.

"I know," she said. "Life isn't fair."

"When you think about it, Charlotte," he said. "Society is in a liminal phase right now and you're a big part of it."

"What do you mean?"

"Well, liminality has to do with change, moving from one thing to another. Crossing a threshold, right?"

"Right."

"Women are working hard to change some very fundamental things and have made some great inroads, but there's still a long way to go. So, you're on the cusp of that change. You're part of that liminality. Pretty groovy, huh?"

Charlotte tried to suppress a laugh that came out as a snort instead.

"Nobody says groovy anymore, Dad, but yeah. It is."

"And I still think you should go on for your doctorate. Maybe you should think whatever folklore is springing up around this liminal time for women. Maybe that could be your dissertation topic."

"Dad, my head's already reeling. I'll have to think about that another time. You know what I find ironic?"

"What's that?"

"That it's you who I can talk to about this. Not Mom. Not even Grandma. Mom is too old- fashioned and Grandma, well, sometimes I think she wants me to *be* Aunt Beatrice."

"Your grandmother had an awfully hard time losing her daughter and who could blame her. But your Aunt Beatrice was your Aunt Beatrice. You are you. You don't have to be anyone but yourself. You are more than good enough."

"Thanks, Dad."

"And I will always be in your corner."

"I know you will." She threw her arms around him. "I love you, Dad."

Chapter 53

July 1840
Birch Falls, Vermont

Jerusha progressed rapidly in her weaving lessons, giving her whole-hearted attention to everything Mrs. Wicker said and did at the loom. She knew she was making up for lost time. She had moved on to more difficult projects using multiple yarn colors and slightly more complicated patterns. She dreamed of one day creating something colorful with a very intricate design.

"I want to make something special for Mother," she told Mrs. Wicker on a hot afternoon in July. I know you have orders to fill so I won't take time away from getting them done, but I want to do it to thank her for letting me come here and learn. And I want her to see how well I am doing so she will know she was not wrong to have changed her mind. If you say I may, I will bring some yarn."

"That is a lovely idea, Jerusha. You may use my yarn. I have plenty dyed in madder root, a lovely soft orange. I know your mother loves that color. Perhaps you can make a coverlet with it shot through with indigo. It is as much my gain as yours to have you helping me, so I am happy to supply the yarn."

Jerusha watched Mrs. Wicker's expression turn wistful as she spoke. The ache it provoked in Jerusha's heart led her into what she knew might be dangerous territory, but her desire to heal old wounds proved stronger than fear. She rose from the bench at the loom to pull a chair up next to it.

"What are you doing?" Mrs. Wicker asked.

"Please sit here next to me. I wish to speak with you about something important," she said, resuming her seat at the loom, but turned towards the chair into which Mrs. Wicker lowered herself.

"You look grave, Jerusha. Is something amiss?"

"Something has been amiss for many years, but it needs to be put to rights."

Mrs. Wicker drew back, a look of suspicion crossing her face.

"Please," said Jerusha, taking the woman's hands in her own. "I think I know what drove you and Mother apart and I want you to know that I understand."

"What? How could you know?" Her expression shifted from concern to fear. She tried to pull her hands away, but Jerusha held them tightly. "Who told you?"

"I suppose you could say Nathan did."

"Nathan? Your hired man? How would he know?"

"Mr. Haskell told him—"

Mrs. Wicker gasped. "Haskell? That old fool!" This time she did manage to pull her hands away and buried her face in them.

"No, he did not tell Nathan what happened. He only said that Nathan and I shared a family secret. He refused to say what. Nathan and I talked about it, and we finally decided on the only thing it could be."

Mrs. Wicker removed her hands from her face and peered closely at Jerusha. "What do you think it is?" she asked, her words barely audible as though she was terrified of the answer.

As Jerusha related Nathan's tale, she could tell by watching Mrs. Wicker's face that she was correct.

"Dear, Lord." She breathed the words when Jerusha finished. "Does your mother know that you know?"

"So, we are right? That is what happened? Was it Lizzy who was dug up?"

"Does your mother know?" she repeated.

"No. How could I ask her that? What if I had been wrong and I needlessly put such an image into my mother's mind. I would not easily forgive myself."

"No. Of course not. She must not know. Not ever. She made us swear to keep it a secret from you." Mrs. Wicker fidgeted with her skirt, twisting it in her lap with shaking hands.

"Because I was so young?"

"Yes. She did not want you to know. She was afraid of how it would affect you."

"She has been so angry all these years. She will not even speak to you or most people in Birch Falls. Does that mean she was against it?"

"She was very much against it."

"And my father?" Jerusha leaned forward, placing her own hands over Mrs. Wicker's to still them and, she hoped, lend some comfort to the anxious woman.

"He was against it, too, at first. He went with us on the evening we did it, but it was to be certain they were all treated with respect."

"All? Were all my sisters dug up? I thought it was just Lizzy."

"We did not know which one was causing the trouble. Lizzy seemed least likely since she had only died a few months before, so she was last. Of course, it can transfer from one corpse to another, which must have been the case, I suppose."

"My father helped you do this?"

"He watched. We understood his reluctance, God bless him. It was horrific."

"What made you believe Lizzy was to blame?"

"She was different from the others. She had turned on her side. Jerusha, there was blood, fresh blood, on her mouth and in her heart. It was unnatural. Even your father could not deny it when he saw her." She brought one hand to her mouth. "It was hideous. And terrifying." Her gaze shifted so that she was staring off as if the scene were being played out there in the middle of the room.

"Her heart was cut from her?"

"Yes." A whisper.

"Then you came back to get Seth so he could breathe it in while it burned like they did with Nathan's sister? I woke up to many people in the house, but when I started down the stairs Susannah took me back to the garret. Was that why you were all there? To get Seth?"

"No. We knew he was too weak and sick to walk to the graveyard."

"So, you did not burn Lizzy's heart?"

Mrs. Wicker opened her mouth to answer, but hesitated. Returning her gaze to Jerusha, she stated, "Your mother must never know of this conversation. Please, Jerusha, you must promise me. I miss my old friend so very much. I have thought that her letting you come to weave might mean she was beginning to forgive, that perhaps there might be reason to hope for...that maybe we could..." Tears spilled down her cheeks. She tilted her head to look at the ceiling trying to hold them back. "If she knows about this, she will never–"

"I will never tell her. I want you and Mother to be friends again. But I want to know what happened. For years I have known that my family and all of Birch Falls has been keeping a secret from me. I have lost friends and been so lonely. I understand why Mother did not want me to know as I was so young. But I am not a child now. I need to know what happened."

Mrs. Wicker stared hard at Jerusha, trying to determine if she believed and trusted her. "You must understand," she said. "Your mother forbade anyone to utter a word about what happened. Not only were we not to tell you, we were not to speak of it at all lest you hear of it accidentally. That is why she did not even trust your friends, Hannah, and Betsy to be near you. She was never sure if they knew about it, but their parents did so she took no chances. She was very insistent. She still is. And we were all frightened enough not to cross her, even after all these years."

"You were frightened of my mother? All of Birch Falls was frightened of my mother?" Jerusha could scarcely imagine it.

"Yes. You see, after it happened, she was…well, not herself. She threatened to do us bodily harm if word ever reached your ears. She was in such a state that no one could doubt her word."

Jerusha released Mrs. Wicker's hands, sitting bolt upright on the bench. This was less comprehensible to her than digging up her deceased sisters. "*My* mother?" was all she could say while shaking her head.

A tear slid down Mrs. Wicker's cheek. When she spoke, it was with the rasp of one trying to talk without breaking into sobs. "I am sorry, Jerusha. I am so very sorry we drove your mother to such depths."

A fear pricked Jerusha. She was certain there was something else, something Mrs. Wicker was holding back.

"What happened when you came back to the house that night? What was it Susannah shielded me from?"

Mrs. Wicker hung her head. Almost to herself she said, "We should have found another way. It was too much for her."

"What was too much for her? Please, Mrs. Wicker, tell me."

She drew a deep breath, stealing herself before speaking. "We did burn Lizzy's heart, but we knew Seth was too ill to bring to Mr. Ward's shop so instead we brought it to him."

"I do not understand?"

"We mixed the ashes with water and tried to get him to drink it. When your mother realized what we were giving him to drink, she slapped the mug from my hand. It spilled all over the floor. He had only been able to swallow a sip or two. It was not enough. We could not save him."

Jerusha's hand gripped her stomach, which was suddenly threatening to relieve her of her dinner.

"I am sorry, Jerusha. We tried to save your brother. I am so sorry we could not. But you are well. The illness never touched you or Susannah or your parents. We were able to do that much. But your poor mother. I have tried to imagine what it must have felt like to her, to put myself in her place. I think I do understand how she must have felt, especially since she had no true comprehension of the evil that was taking place. She refused to believe it."

Lizzy loved Seth," said Jerusha when she could trust herself to talk. "She would never have done anything to harm him. And she certainly was not evil."

"Oh, child, no! Lizzy was not evil. It was not *her* doing it. Whatever that evil thing was, it was using her body as a place to rest during the day so that it could come out at night in her form and attack Seth. It would have gone on to attack you, too, if we had not stopped it. No one thought ill of Lizzy, I assure you. It was whatever was using her."

Jerusha could not help but stare gape-mouthed at Mrs. Wicker. Her head spun with the knowledge that her neighbor, this kindly woman who wove such wondrous creations, who had for so many years been her mother's dearest friend, could believe such absurdities. Then another thought struck her.

"Who else was there that night?" she asked, remembering the jumble of voices she'd heard as she'd descended the stairs.

"Chauncey Haskell, of course. My memory does not permit for everyone, but there was a goodly number."

"And everyone believed in this?"

"Some did. Others may have come out of curiosity, though I am sure the unusual condition of Lizzy's body made believers out of those who doubted."

Jerusha was silent for a while, trying to take in all she had learned. Finally, she said, "Thank you, Mrs. Wicker, for telling me what I needed to know. I promise I will never tell my mother we spoke of this. I feel unable to concentrate, though, so if you please, I will forego the weaving lesson for today."

* * *

Knowing she could not go back to the house without her mother questioning her early return, Jerusha sought out Nathan, finding him working in the field. "Where is Father?" she asked.

"Hiram Wood came by a short while ago asking for his help with something. He has gone to his farm."

"Good," said Jerusha. She did not want to explain her early reappearance to her father either. "I have just come from Mrs. Wicker."

She told him everything. By the time she finished she was weeping uncontrollably, wrapped tightly in Nathan's arms. Her entire body shook, her legs felt as though they would give out at any moment. It was an awful feeling, but at the same time, it was as if a huge weight, the weight of unknowing, had been lifted from her leaving her relieved yet temporarily untethered. When she was able, Nathan gave her a long drink of switchel from his flask.

"Better?" he asked when she finished.

Jerusha nodded. "But Mother must not see me. She will know something is wrong. I cannot tell her, and I do not wish to lie."

"Stay with me, then."

Jerusha decided pulling weeds was a good enough way to vent the unfamiliar energy that was coursing through her. She was still shaky and weak, but the more she worked, the better she felt. By the time they left the field for supper, Jerusha's body felt normal again, though her mind had not quite reached that point. They got to the house just as her father was returning.

399

She said little at supper, quickly assisted with cleaning up, and did the final milking of the evening. Pleading a mild headache, Jerusha retired early, not trusting herself to carry on as if nothing out of the ordinary had occurred. Finding that she was more exhausted than she realized, she drifted off to sleep, her last thought a hope that come morning she would be better able to hide her new knowledge from her parents.

Chapter 54

October 1973
Middlebury, Vermont

Charlotte's gut churned as she drove to work on Tuesday morning. Her grandmother, parents, and sister had all come up to see the exhibit on Saturday. Before the interview aired, she'd been so excited and proud to show her work to her family, but afterwards, she cringed just stepping into the museum. Neither Brad nor President Shepherd was there on Saturday, but she knew most of the staff had watched it. She felt their eyes on her as she conducted her family around the museum. She wished she could make herself invisible to the staff. She thought many of them were looking at her with barely veiled amusement or derision, but hoped it was only her imagination. Now that the holiday weekend was over and her family had gone home, she steeled herself for her first encounter with colleagues since the interview.

After parking her car, she sat, hands gripping the steering wheel. "Wait a minute, Charlotte," she said aloud to herself. "This isn't your fault. You gave an excellent interview. It was WVMB that screwed it up." Trying to replace fear with anger helped her to at least get out of the car and head for her office.

"Charlotte, what happened?" asked Jonathan who was exiting the building as she was going in.

"They edited my interview. I didn't say what it sounds like I said."

Jonathan pursed his lips and nodded. "I figured it was something like that. I'm really sorry that happened, Charlotte."

"Jonathan, can I ask you something?"

"Sure."

"It was only the last part that was a problem. They did edit the earlier parts, but not in a way that changed the meaning of anything. It was actually well done. But that last part about my ancestors and my future exhibit got mangled. It was more than just poorly edited. I can't shake the feeling that it was done that way on purpose. Do you think that's possible or am I being overly suspicious?" She went on to explain how words had been removed from her answers to Tony's questions in just the right way to completely change the meaning.

Jonathan grimaced. Then, with a sigh, he said, "I can't say for sure, but it does seem pretty blatant. I suppose there's the possibility that more than one editor worked on it and whoever did the last section wasn't very good, but in all honesty, that's unlikely. They're a small, local station so I'm pretty sure Tony does all the editing for his own segments."

"And he's a friend of Brad's," she stated.

"A good friend. They've been buddies for a long time."

"And Brad said that Tony owed him a favor. You know what I'm thinking, don't you?"

"I bet I do. You're probably right, but I don't know how you could prove it."

Charlotte felt her stomach drop. "Do you think he did this to get me fired? You know President Shepherd is going to freak out over that interview."

"I think, if Brad did set it up, it was probably to discredit you. You were making too good of an impression too fast. He feels threatened by you."

"That's pretty much what my dad said."

"Charlotte!" Her name was more snarled than spoken. She turned to see Brad storming down the hallway towards her. Barging between her and Jonathan he said, "Meet me in President Shepherd's office in five minutes," as he blew past them and out the door.

"I guess you're about to find out what his intention was," said Jonathan. "Good luck. I've got to get over to Curatorial."

Charlotte dropped her things in her office then headed across the staff parking lot, her stomach in knots. She stopped at the secretary's desk. "I think President Shepherd wants to see me," she said.

The secretary nodded. Not making eye contact with Charlotte, she picked up the receiver to tell President Shepherd she was there. "You can go in," she told her.

Charlotte faced the closed door wishing she could be anywhere else at this moment. She felt as though she was melting, her legs like puddles of slush more likely to sink her to the floor than walk her across it. She took a deep breath and forced herself to open the door and cross the threshold.

"What in God's name were you thinking, Charlotte?" President Shepherd bellowed before she even had the door shut behind her. Both men were standing in the middle of the office, President Shepherd with his hands on his hips, Brad with arms crossed over his chest. "Do you have any idea what a horrible light you've put this museum in? Thank God it was only a local station or we'd be the laughing stock of the museum world. And how could you say vandalism and drunkenness are just good fun and an important rite of passage? Do you know the town manager called me at home of Friday night after that aired? All of the Board of Selectmen members had already called him. And that was after I'd just gotten off the phone with a very angry chairman of our own board of directors. How do you think they felt about what you said?"

Charlotte stood with her back pressed against the door.

President Shepherd, may I, please, explain?"

"I wish to God you would."

Charlotte tried to take a deep breath, but her breathing had become so shallow it was impossible. She forced herself to stand up straight despite feeling like she was crumbling on the inside.

"They edited my interview to the point where it changed the meaning."

Something altered in President Shepherd's face, a small shift, but one that she thought meant he wanted to believe her. She saw Brad glance at him, then quickly turn to her.

"Oh, come on, Charlotte!" Brad snapped. "They always edit to keep within their time limits, but make changes to what their interviewees actually said? That would be totally irresponsible."

President Shepherd's face hardened again. Brad saw it and moved to take a seat on the corner of the president's desk, a smug look settling over his face. "I pulled some strings to get you that interview and this is how you repay me," Brad continued. "How you repay the museum that took a chance – big chance – on hiring you."

It was exactly the wrong thing for Brad to say. It pushed every one of Charlotte's buttons. She was certain now that Brad had been behind what happened. The fear Charlotte had been experiencing beat a hasty retreat in the face of the wrath that replaced it.

"I am telling the truth."

"Brad," said President Shepherd. "Tony is a friend of yours?"

"Yes."

"Be kind enough to call him and ask about the editing of that part of the interview so we can get to the bottom of this?"

"I'd be more than happy to," said Brad with a smarmy smile. "Right now."

"Please."

Brad got up from his perch on the corner of the desk and sauntered toward Charlotte. Forced to move aside for him, she glared, itching to claw the self-satisfied leer from his face.

"Charlotte," continued President Shepherd, "consider yourself suspended for the time being."

"Am I guilty until proven innocent?" she asked, unable to keep the sarcasm from her voice though inside she was kicking herself for it.

"I have our board of directors, the town manager, and the board of selectmen after me. Once Brad gets to the bottom of this, we'll decide where to go from there."

Brad reached for the doorknob. "I'll take care of it immediately," he said.

Once Brad was out of the room, Charlotte turned toward President Shepherd. She wanted to tell him that Brad was the one who set her up, that he was threatened by her competence, that even the curators could see it, that he had arranged this with Tony and, of course, he was going to come back saying it's what she really said. But how could she? President Shepherd barely believed her enough to have Brad check with Tony. If she said everything she wanted to, he would think she was making it up in a juvenile attempt to get out of trouble and put the blame on Brad.

"Charlotte? Do you want to say something?"

"No," she answered.

"Then we are done here. Get your things and go home. I hope to God you're telling the truth."

Charlotte marched back to her office, grabbed her pocketbook and lunch and headed back to the parking lot. Just as she was about to open the car door, she was stopped by a voice calling her name. She turned to see a man in a white lab coat heading towards her. It was Danny and he had Jerusha's second diary in his hand.

"Charlotte, I was just coming to see you," he said when he reached her car. "I did the best I could. It's not perfect, but I think you can make out most of it now." He handed the dairy to her.

"Thanks, Danny."

"You okay? You don't look so good."

"No. I'm, um, not feeling well. I'm going home."

"Sorry to hear that. I hope you feel better."

"Thanks. And thanks again for your help with this," she said.

Danny left and Charlotte got into her car, placing the diary on the passenger seat. She slammed the heel of her palm hard against the steering wheel. How the hell was she going to prove to President Shepherd that she was telling the truth? "That bastard!" she yelled. "What am I going to do?" Tears threatened, increasing her anger and frustration at the feeling of helplessness.

Once home, she threw her bag on the chair, placed the diary beside it, and banged her keys down on the kitchen counter then proceeded to pace the apartment floor. "Aunt Beatrice," she implored, head thrown back to stare at the ceiling, "You would never let Brad get away with this. What would you do?"

She pictured Brad having a good laugh with Tony on the phone. Damn, she hadn't ever met Tony before the interview. What did he have against her? Why would he go along with it? He must have owed Brad one hell of a favor.

Standing in the middle of the living room, hands on hips, an idea struck her. She grabbed the telephone book, flipped to the white pages, and found the phone number for WVMB in Burlington. She dialed, thinking she'd ask to speak with Tony. If she got nothing else out of this she would at least let him have it. Instead, when a woman's gruff voice answered, "Good morning, WVMB. How may I help you?" she heard herself asking, "Who is the executive producer of WVMB?"

"That would be Mark Gordon."

"May I speak with him, please?"

"One moment, please."

The phone was next answered by another female voice, presumably Mark Gordon's secretary. "Mr. Gordon isn't in right now," she told Charlotte. "May I take a message?"

"Yes. This is Charlotte Lajoie. I would like to speak with Mr. Gordon as soon as possible about a very serious matter."

"I see. Could you give me some idea what it's in regards to?"

Charlotte hesitated, not wanting to say too much, but not wanting to leave the impression of being someone who only wanted to register a complaint that he probably wouldn't want to deal with.

"I am the Assistant Director of Programs at the New England Folklife Museum. I was interviewed for your station recently. It aired last Friday evening. The editing in part of the interview was done in such a way that it changed the meaning of what I said in a very negative way. I am now in trouble with the museum president because he thinks I actually said those things when I didn't. I want to get the matter cleared up so that I don't lose my job."

"I'm very sorry you were unhappy with the outcome. I will give Mr. Gordon your message. May I have your phone number, please?"

Unhappy with the outcome. That was putting it mildly. Restraining herself from screaming, Charlotte gave her phone number, thanked the secretary, and hung up. Now all she could do was wait.

Chapter 55

October 1973
Middlebury, Vermont

It was late afternoon when Mark Gordon returned Charlotte's call. They quickly got passed the routine pleasantries, then Mark said, "I understand you are unhappy about the editing on your interview."

"Very unhappy," she said. "It was done in such a way as to make it sound like I was contradicting historical facts. Worst of all, some of my words were edited out to sound like I was promoting teenage vandalism and drunk driving. The president of the New England Folklife Museum is livid. He's been getting phone calls from museum board members and even the town manager. I'm on the brink of losing my job because of this."

"I'm terribly sorry, Miss Lajoie. It was Tony Armano who did the interview, wasn't it?"

"Yes."

"I'll speak with him and see what he has to say about it."

Charlotte let out a deep, frustrated sigh. "Mr. Gordon, I need to tell you that I have good reason to believe it was done on purpose."

"Why would you think that?"

"Because my boss is a friend of Tony's. He's the one who arranged the interview. He wants a reason to get rid of me. I'm certain he got Tony to do this."

"Miss Lajoie, that's quite an accusation. I hope you are able to back it up. Perhaps you should calm yourself. I'm sure nothing was done intentionally."

A pain shot through Charlotte's hand from gripping the receiver so tightly it was giving her a cramp. She bit her lip to curb the stream of expletives that threatened to sail into the mouthpiece, switched hands, and in as calm a tone as she could muster, she said, "Mr. Gordon, is there any way you could check the video? Before it was edited, I mean."

Silence a moment, then he said, "Actually, there is. We always keep a copy of the original, uncut version for our archives as well as the final edit."

Relief surged through Charlotte. "That's wonderful. Then all we have to do is watch the original to show that I didn't say things the way it came out on television."

"We could, but that would only prove there was poor editing, not that anything was done intentionally. Not that I approve of poor editing, but you did make a serious accusation against one of my reporters."

"All I really want to do is prove to the museum president that I'm not to blame. I just don't want to get fired."

"I'll look at the tape."

"Thank you so much. And, Mr. Gordon, would it be possible for me to watch it with you?"

"I suppose. It's too late today. Can you come to the station tomorrow morning?"

"Absolutely. What time?"

"I'll have to put you through to my secretary for that. She keeps my schedule. Hold on a moment."

"Thank you, Mr. Gordon."

The secretary scheduled them to meet at nine-thirty the next morning. Once she hung up, Charlotte felt like she could breathe again. She also felt drained. She collapsed on her bed and slept until well past lunchtime, awakening to a knock on her apartment door. It was Heidi, just getting home from work.

"I saw your car here when I pulled in," said Heidi. "Why are you home so early? You're not sick, are you? You look a little peaked."

"No. I'm not sick. Not physically, anyway."

"Oh-oh. They didn't fire you, did they?"

"Not yet. I'm on suspension. Come in and I'll tell you all about it."

After hearing the story, she agreed with Charlotte that she'd been set up by Brad. They had both wondered what the fallout might be. Now Charlotte gave her the rundown on what had transpired this morning.

"I'm glad you insisted on seeing the uncut version yourself," Heidi told her. "You may not be able to prove a setup, but you can prove that you didn't actually say those things. At least that should satisfy the president and keep you from losing your job."

"Yeah, saving my job is my number one goal, but I want to show President Shepherd what kind of person Brad really is. Otherwise, he will keep doing these things to me. I don't want to spend every day at work watching over my shoulder."

"Didn't the president say he'd call you after Brad talked to Tony? What will you do if he calls before you can get to WVMB?"

"I plan to tell him that I'm going there to watch the uncut version with the executive producer and to, please, wait until after he hears back. I'm going to ask Mark Gordon to call President Shepherd right after we watch it and tell him. Frankly, I'm surprised he hasn't called yet. It's after five."

"Probably Brad couldn't reach Tony. He is a reporter. He may be out on assignments."

"I hope so. That would at least buy me some time."

Just as she finished saying that, the phone rang. "Damn!" said Charlotte. "Oh, well. Might as well get it over with."

But it wasn't President Shepherd. It was Julie Paquette. And she was frantic.

"Julie, slow down. I can't understand you," said Charlotte who had only caught that her call had something to do with the ghostly happenings at Julie's house.

"What's going on?" asked Heidi.

"Apparently, weird stuff is happening at the Paquette's house," she said, holding her hand over the mouthpiece.

"Julie, calm down and tell me what's going on."

"It's worse than ever," said Julie, her voice shaking. "This house is definitely haunted. Stuff is flying off the shelves in the study. The floor's wet again. Andy checked the pipes again but couldn't find anything wrong. He's going to have a plumber check it out, but I know it's not the pipes. The creepiest thing is that I swear I heard a woman crying in that room. I can't stand to get anywhere near it anymore. I don't even want to be in this house. Charlotte, can you help me, please?" she begged.

"I have to go to Burlington for work tomorrow morning. I could stop by afterwards, though I'm not sure what I'll be able to do to help."

After hanging up, Charlotte turned to Heidi. "You are not going to believe this."

"What?"

"The ghost is really acting up and Julie is freaked out." She related what Julie had told her. "I don't know how she can stay in that house. I'd have moved out so fast it would make your head spin."

"Is Andy still unconvinced?"

"I don't know. She was too upset to say much about anything but what's been happening. I think she called me because she knows I won't tell her she's imagining it, but I don't know what she thinks I can do about it."

"I'm off tomorrow. I can go with you. Maybe I can connect with the ghost."

"That would be great, but I can't take you to WVMB with me."

"So, drop me off at Church Street. I'll go shopping. We can meet somewhere for lunch then go to Julie's house."

"Perfect!" Charlotte was relieved. She could only picture herself joining Julie in cowering in a corner.

"Great. I'd better get home. Aunt Iris is probably wondering what's become of me."

After Heidi left, Charlotte realized how hungry she was. She'd eaten little for breakfast because she'd been too nervous about what would happen when she got to work. Then she'd slept right through lunchtime. Now her stomach was growling. As she heated up some leftover lentil soup and threw together a salad while nibbling on a piece of French bread, she thought of what she might face tomorrow. She was as certain as she could be that she'd be proven innocent as far as the interview went and at least her job would be saved. Julie's haunted house was another story. She had no idea what to expect from that.

Chapter 56

August 1840
Birch Falls, Vermont

There was a break in Jerusha's weaving sessions with Mrs. Wicker while everyone rushed to get the hay in. Once that was over, she found herself settling into a rhythm two afternoons a week at Mrs. Wicker's loom. Jerusha not only progressed in her weaving, she also got caught up on what was happening in Birch Falls. Mrs. Wicker chatted endlessly about all the townspeople. It was all stuff Jerusha should have known, but she'd been kept so isolated that if felt more like she'd been gone for a long time and had only just returned and was catching up on all that had happened in her absence.

"You know, of course, that Lydia Mason had her baby yesterday. She must have taken my advice and put an axe under her bed as soon as her labor began. I have never been able to get Caroline to do this for all the mothers. She says there is no truth that doing so cuts the laboring mother's pain, but I know there is. I did it with all of my births and never had a problem. You will remember it, I hope, when your time comes."

Jerusha nodded. She had learned that it was better to simply agree than to try to talk Mrs. Wicker out of her superstitions. She wasn't as opposed to them as her mother had always been, though she didn't believe in any of them. It amused her to hear them and made her wonder where they had originated.

"Have you a beau?" Mrs. Wicker asked.

Jerusha felt her face flush. "There is Nathan, I suppose."

"The hired man? He seems a good sort from what I can tell. Does your mother approve?"

"She likes Nathan, but we are not courting exactly. We are..." What were they? She wasn't sure.

"You are sweet on him, though," Mrs. Wicker finished for her.

"I suppose I am." Though she stared hard at the loom, Jerusha could not hide the smile spreading across her face.

"Does he feel the same?"

"I believe so."

"Then why are you not courting?"

"I suppose in a way we are. We go for walks together after supper. We talk often. But Nathan has never asked permission to court me."

"He seems an honorable sort. He probably will before long."

Jerusha hoped she was right.

"There are several ways to determine who you will marry. At the end of October, try hanging a cabbage stump over the door. The first man to walk through the door will be the one you will marry."

"More likely than not, that would be my father."

"He does not count."

"I should hope not. But since Nathan lives with us, it is only reasonable that he would be the first man, other than my father, to enter. It hardly seems a fair test."

"Hmm...there are other ways. As I think on it, though, Nathan is quite suitable for you. It is good that your last names do not start with the same letter."

"Why is that?"

"Everyone knows if a girl marries a man whose last name begins with the same letter as hers, she will be worse off than before she married him."

Jerusha laughed. "How could that possibly matter?" Sometimes she did find it difficult to simply accept Mrs. Wicker's superstitious beliefs without comment.

"I know there are those who think these old notions are hogwash, but I learned them from my mother and she from her mother. I can tell you there is truth to them, and some are no laughing matter. Paying heed to them could save your life."

"How so?"

"Well, I never cut any of my babies' fingernails before they were a year old. Doing so earlier than a year will nearly guarantee they will die young. And just look. All of my boys have survived. None are old yet, but they have made it beyond childhood. No one can tell me there is nothing to it." Mrs. Wicker nodded resolutely. "When Susannah left for Ohio, did she take a looking glass with her?"

"Yes. She received a lovely one as a wedding gift." Jerusha wondered at this turn of the conversation.

"I hope she was very careful when packing it."

"Certainly she was. She would not have wanted it to break."

"Exactly. Breaking a looking glass while moving means that someone is going to die. You see, there are ways to prevent such tragedies, if only people would take more care."

Jerusha snapped shut her mouth. She was beginning to understand how Mrs. Wicker could believe what they had done to Lizzy would have saved Seth if he hadn't been too far gone and that it had saved the rest of them.

"It is just common sense and good practice to be aware of the things you should and should not do and learn to read the signs that come our way. For instance, I am careful never to have a total of thirteen people in the house at once especially for a meal. Even just one more or one less is fine, but if thirteen people sit down to eat together, one of them will die before the year is out. I cannot fathom why some people are careless when it is so simple to prevent."

"What would you do if you did have thirteen people and could not help it? Would one have to go hungry? Or leave?" Jerusha could not imagine turning someone away from the table for such a far-fetched idea.

Mrs. Wicker pondered for a moment. "I suppose," she said, her words coming slowly. "If it was truly unavoidable, one could take their meal elsewhere in the house. Perhaps a few of them, so that one person would not feel shunned. That might work as a solution, though I would not like to risk it."

Jerusha toyed with the idea of asking what a family of two parents and eleven children should do but did not want Mrs. Wicker to think she was baiting her. Besides, she could guess that the answer would be to have some eat elsewhere. And probably take in a boarder.

"Now, we are not always able to prevent tragedies, but there are portents that, if we are aware enough to notice them, will alert us so that we can prepare ourselves for what is to come. I remember the day Josie fell so ill. When I got to your house, I saw six crows fly over the roof. I told your mother that was a bad omen, but she did not pay me any heed at the time."

Jerusha was sure her mother hadn't needed crows to tell her something bad was going to happen, but she said nothing. Instead, she asked, "Mrs. Wicker, did you learn all of these from your mother? You know a lot of them."

"From my mother and my grandmother who learned them from their own mothers and grandmothers. This is wisdom handed down generation after generation. We are losing it, now, though. People nowadays think themselves too worldly to keep the old ways. I hate to see the old customs die out, especially those that are so useful. I do not know what this world will come to if people pay no mind to the old wisdom. There will be more tragedy. Of that, I am certain. Careful what you are doing, Jerusha. You have a snarl in the yarn. Your warp ends will become tangled if you are not watchful."

Jerusha stopped what she was doing to fix the problem. She reminded herself to focus on her weaving. She wasn't yet accomplished enough not to give it her full attention.

"While you finish that, I am going to start supper," said Mrs. Wicker, getting up to leave the room.

As Jerusha reworked her yarn, she thought about all she had just heard. She knew these were only a smattering of the superstitions held by her neighbor. Though she could understand her mother's anger, she had a better comprehension of the depth of Mrs. Wicker's beliefs. She was beginning to appreciate how the woman could so wholly accept that what was done to Lizzy was the appropriate remedy for Seth and the rest of her family. She knew that her mother had always been exasperated by Mrs. Wicker's delusional beliefs, but she wondered if she knew how she came about them and how deeply rooted they were. It was awful what had been done, but Jerusha could see that it came from a place of caring and, even, love, not to mention, fear. If only her mother could understand that, perhaps she would be able to forgive.

Chapter 57

October 1973
Burlington, Vermont

Charlotte strode to the front door of the imposing brick office building housing the WVMB station. The directory on the wall indicated that the station was located on the fifth floor. As she rode the elevator alone, she practiced keeping her spine straight, her chin held high. She presumed the executive director would not easily admit that one of his reporters was in on a plan to purposely discredit her. She would have to be resolute. If she only got vindication that her real meaning had been edited out, at least her job would be saved. That was number one. But Brad had shown himself willing to go to extremes to humiliate her and, possibly, destroy her career or, at least, her job with the New England Folklife Museum. If she wasn't able to convince Mark Gordon and President Shepherd that he was behind this, that the editing was done purposely to make her look bad, next time she might not be able to prove her innocence.

"Aunt Beatrice, help me with this, please," she whispered just as the elevator doors slid open.

To the right was a glass door with WVMB etched into the upper pane.

"I'm Charlotte Lajoie," she told the receptionist, a heavy-set, middle-aged woman with short, curly blond hair. "I have an appointment with Mark Gordon.

The receptionist nodded. "I'll let his secretary know you're here," she said in a cigarettes and whisky voice Charlotte recognized from her phone call yesterday.

The woman, whose name placard said she was Carol Armstrong, picked up her phone, pressed a button, and said, "Charlotte Lajoie is here for Mark." Then, after a second, "I'll tell her." Hanging up, she looked at Charlotte. "Have a seat. Jeannie will be out to get you in a minute."

Charlotte sat in one of the waiting room chairs, thinking that Carol Armstrong might not have been the best choice for a receptionist. She was brusque and not terribly welcoming. On the other hand, she probably made a good gatekeeper. Undoubtedly, the station had its share of viewers with complaints and one axe or another to grind. It wasn't likely they got past Carol Armstrong.

Charlotte fidgeted as the minutes passed. "Did she say how long she'd be?" Charlotte asked.

"Nope." Carol didn't even look up. No help from that quarter. Charlotte picked up a magazine and began flipping through it.

"You're that folklorist that Tony interviewed on TV the other night, aren't you?" Carol finally asked, breaking the awkward silence.

"Yes. That's why I'm here. The last part of the interview was edited in such a way that it made me sound like I said things I didn't really say." Charlotte felt as though she had to defend herself to everyone. She realized she needed to ask that the station make note of the error on air. As long as President Shepherd believed she was innocent, he would probably insist on it as it reflected on the museum, not just on her so she had high hopes for it.

"Huh. I thought it seemed odd towards the end. Especially that bit about vandalism and drunk driving."

"What I actually said was that legend tripping was harmless and all good fun as long as they *didn't* engage in vandalism and drunk driving, but the way they edited it made it sound like the exact opposite. That sort of thing happened all through the last segment of the interview."

Carol screwed up her mouth, gazing off like she was thinking intently about something. "Our reporters are pretty careful with their editing. Sure, when it's a rush job they can get a *little* sloppy, but not like that." She rolled her eyes "Maybe Tony and Brad had too much to drink by the time they got to editing that part of the interview."

Charlotte nearly fell off the chair. "Did you say Brad?"

"Yeah. That guy from the museum. He's buddies with Tony. He comes every so often. He was hanging around with Tony that evening."

"You were here?" She wondered how long the receptionist's hours were at WVMB.

"Oh, yeah. I'm here a lot even beyond work hours. The guy who owns this station is my cousin, Shirley's, father-in-law. Shirley and I are more like sisters than cousins. No one can believe that because we're so different, but you know what they say about how opposites attract. It was like that with me and Shirley. She and I grew up only a few houses apart. She's a lot more girly than me. I was always a tomboy, but we still ended up being best friends. Funny how that works out, isn't it?"

Charlotte cared little about the relationship between Carol and Shirley, but she realized she might have someone on her side. "Yeah, it is. Since you're cousins it's great that you got along so well. Tell me, do you know much about Brad? He's my boss."

"Poor you. I think he's a jackass. Sorry if you like him, but I call 'em like I see 'em." While Carol spoke, Charlotte went to stand by her desk.

"He's the same as a boss," she said. "Apparently, he's threatened by me. I think he set me up with that interview. Now that I know he was here when it was edited, I'm sure of it. He wanted to discredit me and get me fired. When he told me about the interview, he said Tony owed him a favor, but made it sound like he'd just pulled a few strings to get the interview."

"He pulled some strings all right, just not the ones you'd hoped. I'd bet you anything you're right. I used to think Tony was okay, but that was before he dated my niece. It's a long story, but let's just say he was less than a gentleman. When she wouldn't do everything he wanted, he called her some choice names and dumped her. Creep. He's been getting a reputation around Burlington lately, him and Brad."

Even though no one else was around, Charlotte leaned down and said in a conspiratorial tone, "Would you be willing to tell Mark Gordon about Brad being here when the editing was done? We are going to watch the original recording, but that would only prove poor editing, not that it was done intentionally. Mr. Gordon won't just take my word for it. I'm sure he doesn't want to believe one of his reporters would stoop so low."

Carol snorted. "You might be surprised. He knows Tony's a bit of a rogue and he doesn't like him much. He's got to stick up for the station and all, but he can't have a reporter who would do stuff like that."

With a prick of conscience Charlotte added, 'You wouldn't get in trouble for it, would you? I wouldn't want Tony to come after you or cause you to lose your job."

Carol sat back and folded her arms across her chest. "You don't need to worry about me. I told you before, I call 'em like I see 'em and everybody around here knows it. Besides, like I said, the owner is Shirley's father-in-law. He's not going to let anyone fire me. As for Tony, I'm not in the least afraid of that little turd. It'll pay him back for my niece, too."

"Oh, thank you," said Charlotte just as a trim woman in a pencil skirt and light blazer appeared in the doorway leading to a long hall.

"Miss Lajoie?" she asked.

"That's me."

"I'm Jeanne Russeau, Mr. Gordon's secretary. "I'm sorry to have kept you waiting. Please follow me."

Charlotte walked the long hallway staring at the back of Jeanne's close-cropped dark hair. At the end of the hall, they went through a door leading into Jeanne's office. Jeanne swept behind her desk, pressed a button on her phone console and said, "Mr. Gordon, Miss Lajoie is here." She barely had the receiver replaced in its cradle when another door opened and a man stepped out. Charlotte guessed he was in his late thirties. His short, neatly combed brown hair had just the barest hint of gray at the temples. He was tall, just a smidgen on the heavy side, and wore a dark business suit.

"Miss Lajoie, I'm Mark Gordon. Pleased to meet you," he said, sweeping an arm towards the open door to his office to usher her in.

"I'm pleased to meet you as well, Mr. Gordon," she said. "Thank you for agreeing to see me."

"Please, have a seat."

She lowered herself into one of the two chairs in front of his desk. He surprised her by taking the seat next to her rather than going behind the desk.

"I've pulled the tape of the uncut version," he said. "I was actually planning to watch it by myself this morning, but didn't have time. I haven't spoken to Tony yet. You and I can watch the tape first."

"I appreciate that," said Charlotte.

"First I want to apologize for putting out a final version that you found unflattering. Here at WVMB, we strive for the highest level of accuracy in all we do. If the editing is as poor as you claim, I assure you, I will contact the museum president and apologize. WVMB should not be the cause of anyone unfairly losing their position or even being reprimanded due to our error."

"I've been suspended from my job until this is sorted out so I would greatly appreciate that."

"Shall we head to the editing room?"

"Please."

When Mark began the uncut version of the recording, Charlotte realized they'd be sitting through a much longer piece than what was aired. "I have no problem with the editing that was done in this part of it," she told him. "It's fine with me if you want to skip to the last section."

"I'd like to view the whole thing. Then we'll watch the final version. I want to get a feel for what Tony was editing out. It might help me to understand why he made the choices he did."

Charlotte thought she could tell him exactly why Tony made his choices but decided to refrain until after Mark had seen both versions.

"There was an awful lot in that," he said, when it ended. "He would have had to cut quite a bit to fit the timeframe."

"I'm not upset that a lot was cut. I'm bothered by the way the last part was done."

He gave her what she thought was a condescending smile as he cued up the final version. "Did you see the aired version?" she asked.

"Actually, no. I was out of state over the long weekend. Your original interview was excellent, by the way. The exhibit looks fascinating. I'll try to get my kids down there to see it before the month ends."

"Thank you."

"Okay, let's take a look," he said, starting the final version.

They watched through the first part where Charlotte took Tony on a tour of the exhibit, then onto the interview. When Tony began asking her about her ancestors, Charlotte said, "Here. This is the part where everything I said gets changed."

Charlotte glanced back and forth between the recording and Mark's face, eventually focusing on his face alone as the section of the interview progressed.

She saw his eyes widen, his hand gripping the arm of his chair.

"Just a moment," he said, when the interview ended. He went back to the original version, rewound it to where the last section began and watched it again. Then he did the same with the final version. When he finished, he looked at Charlotte, his face ashen.

"Miss Lajoie," he said. "WVMB owes you a huge apology. I thought I was going to find some sloppy editing, but this..." He waved his hand as if words failed him.

"Do you think that it was deliberate?"

"I will have to speak with Tony first, but in all honesty, it does appear that way. I just can't fathom why he would do it."

He stood. "But we will get to the bottom of this, I assure you. Tony is out on assignment at the moment, but I expect him back before long. Would you like to wait?"

"I certainly would. Also, as I mentioned before, I suspect my boss, Brad Louden, of being a part of this. He's a friend of Tony's. He apparently, called in a favor to get Tony to do the interview with me. I believe he set me up. Carol, your receptionist, told me that Brad was here with Tony when they did the editing."

"But why would you suspect your boss? The final cut of the interview shows not only you, but, by extension, the museum itself in a bad light. Why would he do that?"

Charlotte told him all about how Brad had been treating her, what the curators believed about the way he felt about her, and everything Carol had said.

"This does put things in a bit of a different light," Mark said when she finished. "If you're right, this is a huge breach on the parts of both Tony and Brad. I can't do anything about your boss, but I certainly can about Tony."

"You can do something about my boss, though. You can tell President Shepherd."

"I'll have to be sure before I go accusing one of his employees. Hold on a minute." He picked up the wall phone and punched in an extension. "Jeanne, would you please cover the front desk and tell Carol to come to the editing room? And when Tony comes back, please ask him to come right up to editing as well."

When Carol arrived, Mark asked her what she knew about the evening Tony had edited the piece.

"I was cleaning out some files that evening. Been meaning to get to them for a while, but you know the phone's been ringing off the hook lately. So, I stayed late. I hate it when I can't find what I'm looking for especially when I've got someone on the phone waiting for an answer about something." Carol's penchant for going on and on would have amused Charlotte had she not been so eager for her to get to the point.

"Yes, so you saw Tony come in?" Mark asked.

"Yeah, I saw him. He came in with his friend, Brad Louden."

"Are you certain that's who was with him?"

"Sure am. I've met the guy before. Ran into the two of them over at Thirsty's, too." She glanced at Charlotte. "That's a bar." Then back to Mark, "They were both plastered and acting like complete idiots. Yeah, I know the guy. I'm sure it was him. Besides, Tony called him Brad."

"Did you hear them talking? Do you remember what they said?"

"Yeah, they were yakking away. It was something about finishing the edits on the museum exhibit piece. That's how I know they were working on Charlotte's interview. And I remember Brad saying he couldn't wait for it to air and that someone, I can't remember the name, was going to lose his mind when he sees it."

"President Shepherd," said Charlotte. "That's who he was talking about, I'll bet."

"Shepherd," said Charlotte. "I was thinking Farmer, but no, you're right, it was Shepherd."

"Thank you, Carol," said Mark.

Something in his voice made Charlotte glance at him. His mouth was compressed to a thin line and the muscles in his jaw were clenched so tightly that small bulges rolled like tiny pebbles beneath the surface of his skin at its hinge.

The door burst open making Charlotte whip around. Tony breezed in. His smile vanished when he saw Charlotte. Quickly, he took in Mark's furious countenance, Carol's crossed arms, and the two versions of Charlotte's interview cued up on the monitors. His swagger melted. "Oh, crap," he said so low it was barely audible.

"Would you care to explain this?" asked Mark, pointing at the monitors. "I assume you know what I'm talking about."

Tony heaved a sigh. "Yeah, well, um..." He stared daggers at Carol. "What's she got to do with this?" he asked.

"She saw you come in with Brad Louden on the night you finished the edits on Miss Lajoie's interview."

"Yeah, so?" He said, trying to sound full of bluster, but his eyes darted from one person to the next like a trapped animal looking for an escape route.

"Brad set this up," said Charlotte. "When he told me about the interview, he said you owed him a favor. Editing the interview so that it looked like I said things I didn't, things that could get me fired, was what he meant, wasn't it?"

Tony's mouth worked, but no sound came out. In the end, he just said, "Uh, yeah."

"Clear out your desk," said Mark. "You're fired."

"Aw, come on. It's not that big a deal, is it? I mean she's just some chick trying to make Brad look bad in front of his boss. She deserved it. I don't want to take the rap for that."

"You should have thought about that before you behaved in such an unprofessional manner. I now have to call the museum president and apologize. WVMB made the New England Folklife Museum look bad and we've nearly cost Miss Lajoie her job. I do not take this kind of behavior lightly."

Tony huffed, threw up his arms, then turned to leave.

"Wait," said Charlotte. They all looked at her.

"Mr. Gordon, would you, please, call President Shepherd while Tony is still here? I'm afraid he's going to call Brad and tip him off."

Tony sneered at her. Brad just got me fired. Why would I help him?"

"You got yourself fired, Tony," Mark told him. "If you owed him such a great favor, you should have found some other way to repay it. Brad used you to get what he wanted without a care in the world as to how it might affect you. Maybe you should use more discretion when choosing your friends in the future."

"Well, since I'm fired anyway, you can't force me to stay here while you make your phone call. I'll get my stuff and go." With that, he left the editing room.

"Don't worry, Miss Lajoie. Let's go back to my office. I'll make that phone call immediately. Thank you, Carol."

Once back in his office, Charlotte stood by his desk, too tense to sit, and listened while Mark spoke with President Shepherd on the phone. When he hung up, he turned to Charlotte. "President Shepherd is coming up here and bringing Brad with him. We will straighten this out, Miss Lajoie, and I'm as certain you will be keeping your position at the museum. However, President Shepherd is just going into a meeting so it will be late afternoon before they can get here. I would be more than happy to take you to lunch."

A feeling like boulders tumbling off her back buoyed Charlotte so that she could almost float to the ceiling. "That's okay," she said. "I'm meeting a friend for lunch on Church Street, but thank you for the offer. What time should I come back?”

“If you are here by four that should be plenty of time.”

“Thank you, Mr. Gordon. I’ll see you then.”

Charlotte left the building feeling much lighter than she’d entered it. Thanking Carol profusely on her way out, she practically skipped to her car. She could hardly wait to tell Heidi what had transpired. Then it was on to find out what sorts of things were happening at Julie’s house.

Chapter 58

Late October 1840
Birch Falls, Vermont

Mary spread out the coverlet on her lap. "Jerusha, this is beautiful. You have really done well. Thank you." She glanced up from the tri-colored bedding to see her daughter's face beaming with joy.

"I am so glad you like it, Mother. I know those are your favorite colors. I wanted to make something special for you to thank you for allowing me to learn weaving from Mrs. Wicker. She supplied the yarn though I had proposed using our own. She wished to be part of the gift. She said having me help her was as much a boon to her as to me."

Mary smoothed the fabric with both hands reveling in the soft warmth. Without looking up, she said, "That was kind of her. Please thank her for me."

"Of course, Mother." Mary heard the note of disappointment in Jerusha's voice and winced inwardly.

"I will go up and put this on my bed now. Thank you, darling." She kissed Jerusha on the cheek, folded the coverlet and went upstairs. Once in her room, Mary placed the coverlet on the bed then sat down. She knew Jerusha had wanted her to say that she would thank Lavinia herself. Not long after Jerusha had begun weaving, she'd been sneaking in details here and there about kind words Mrs. Wicker had said or compassionate things she had done for others. Jerusha, bless her heart, wanted to mend their broken friendship. A part of Mary wanted to mend it, too. She missed their happy times together.

"Mother," Jerusha called as she ascended the stairs. "Are we going to make the pies today?"

"Yes, dear," she answered. "I am coming."

When she returned to the kitchen, Mary found that Jerusha had begun laying out all they would need for the pumpkin and apple pies. Fall was a busy time for baking and preserving. Before the month was out, they would have enough for Thanksgiving and to last through the winter.

As they worked together, Mary noticed how proficient Jerusha had grown. She rarely had to ask how to do anything. It was not just baking. Jerusha had grown in so many ways. At seventeen, she could now care for a household on her own. Once Susannah had gone, she was the only child left and, other than Nathan, who they had taken in to help with the farm work, Mary had not wanted any others in the home. It had not been easy doing everything on their own especially since Jerusha had been so young at the time, but it had forced the girl to learn at an early age. Now she was adept at every household skill.

It had not been lost on Mary that Jerusha and Nathan had grown quite fond of each other. She had an inkling that Jerusha had applied herself to the home arts more intently of late to impress him. Mary smiled at the thought of Jerusha a few years hence as the wife of a good man such as Nathan. She had liked him since Eli hired him. He was a hard worker, honest, kind, and conscientious. As she watched them together, she saw how tender he was with Jerusha. She believed he would be good to her. How happy Mary would be if Jerusha found love with a virtuous man who would provide well for her and who knew nothing of the family's past history.

She had fretted over Jerusha's future, fearing she would never find a husband given that most of Birch Falls kept clear of them. That had been a difficulty Mary had not foreseen. If Jerusha and Nathan should marry, that problem would be solved. Mary knew Eli planned to leave the house and farm to whomever Jerusha wed. Nathan was skilled at farming. Eli thought highly of his work ethic and knowledge of husbandry and agriculture. If they were to marry, she could rest easy about Jerusha's future.

Another difficulty was the fact that Mary was getting older. Jerusha, though diligent about her work at home, had been spending more time away to help Lavinia with the weaving which left more of the work to Mary. She had begun to tire more easily than in the past but could not bring herself to curtail the time Jerusha had to indulge in the one thing she had wanted for so long and for so long had been denied. But something would have to be done about the situation. Mary had given it much thought, spoken with Eli, and received his consent.

"Jerusha, your father and I have been talking about taking on a girl to help with the housework and cooking."

"Oh?"

"Yes. We should have done so when Susannah left, but I..." Mary still had trouble speaking about that time. "Well, that is in the past. I am feeling my years these days. You are a Godsend to me, but I fear more help is needed. I have written to my sister asking if one of her girls could be spared. She has agreed, and Lucinda will arrive before Thanksgiving. She is nearly sixteen and will be a tremendous help, I am sure."

"I am glad Lucinda will come. We could use her help."

Mary was relieved to see that Jerusha was smiling. "I am happy you think so. I hoped you would not think it was because your work was not good enough."

"I know better than that, Mother. An extra pair of hands is always welcome. I have always wished Aunt Helen and Uncle John lived closer to us. I would have liked to know them all better. Now, at least I will get to know Lucinda."

Mary's heart lurched at the loneliness she saw in her daughter's expression. She was responsible for that, she knew. She had taken from her most of the people left in her life who Jerusha cared about. In trying to protect her, she had forced Jerusha into an isolated, friendless existence. Yet, Jerusha had not turned bitter or withdrawn, which was a wonder. Still, not for the first time, Mary wondered if the life she'd consigned her to had been worse than her knowing the truth. In any case, Jerusha was no longer a child, and Mary concluded, it was time Jerusha had her world back. So, once the pies were baking, Mary took a seat at the table and did the one thing she believed she would never do.

"Leave that be for now," she said, as Jerusha began cleaning up from their pie-making. "Sit with me. There is something I need to tell you."

The words were difficult to expel at first, but the more she talked, the more they simply fell out. As Mary related all that had happened, it was as if heavy weights were falling from her chest and tumbling out of her mouth. At one point, Jerusha took Mary's hand in her own, looking at her with compassion, but, to Mary's astonishment, no shock or revulsion. When she finished, she asked Jerusha, "You are not surprised by this?"

"No, Mother. I have spoken with Nathan. The same thing occurred in his family, with his own brother and sister. It is why he left. I did not know all the details, but I am glad you have told me."

Astounded, Mary sat back, staring at her daughter. She had forbidden the entirety of Birch Falls to so much as mention it in front of Jerusha, yet she came to know of it anyway from an outsider. As she took it in, the irony overwhelmed her, and she began to laugh.

"Mother?"

"I am sorry. I should not be laughing. I really do not know why I am. It is...I think it is such a relief to have this out in the open, to see that your knowing about it has not harmed you." Just as suddenly as the laughing fit had come upon her, her laughter turned to tears. "Now I am regretting so much. Oh, Jerusha, I did not ever mean to take so much from you. I only wanted to protect you."

Before Mary knew what was happening, she found herself with her seventeen-year-old daughter in her lap, hugging her. "It is alright, Mother. I know you were protecting me, and I love you for it. You did right to protect me. I was so young. I could not have withstood such an event at that age. Think of the nightmares it would have caused me." Jerusha got up, returned to her own chair, but held onto Mary's hand. "But I am old enough now to know the truth. I am grateful for Nathan. He has helped me to understand why it was done, why it was kept from me, and how to go on."

"He is a good man, Jerusha," Mary said. "Your father and I both think so. Now I believe he was sent to us by God to do what I could not."

"I believe you are right."

"Jerusha, do you forgive me?"

"Of course, Mother, but there is nothing to forgive. I only wish that you could try to forgive Mrs. Wicker."

A pang of something, guilt perhaps, shot through Mary. She was not sure how to respond so remained silent.

"You know how superstitious she is," Jerusha continued. "She tells me all the time about things she believes that I know have no true reason behind them. She was taught them by her mother who was taught by her mother. All these beliefs have come down in her family for generations. They are part of her like her blood and bones. She cannot help herself. Can you imagine what it must be like to live one's whole life with unreasonable fears, doing foolish things because of a belief that if they are not done some horrible fate will be the result? She must have believed with all her heart that she was saving us. Even when you forbade it, she risked her deep friendship with you to save us all. She was wrong, so terribly wrong, but surely you can forgive what was done out of love and fear. She is a good woman despite her faults. Anyone who would risk something so precious out of love can be none other than the truest friend."

Mary swallowed hard. She had thought Lavinia a faithless, cold-hearted person for what she had done. Now Jerusha had put it in a different light. She remembered the words Caroline had spoken to her which were not so different.

"Jerusha, I must think on this a while. And pray. Thank you, my dear. You are wise beyond your years."

* * *

Late one afternoon of the following week, Mary walked outside carrying a crock of butter. She ascended the hill between the Kendall and Wicker farms, pulling her cloak more tightly around her as the October wind scattered leaves in front of her feet. She arrived at the side door leading into the room where Lavinia kept her loom and knocked. The look on Lavinia's face when she opened the door to find Mary standing there was the same as if she was seeing her own mother's ghost.

"Mary, what brings you? Is something wrong at home?" Lavinia's words came out in a breathless rush.

"No. Nothing is wrong. I came to bring this to you." She held out the crock of butter.

Lavinia took the butter from her, staring open-mouthed from Mary to the crock, then back to Mary.

"Why? I mean, please, come in."

The door opened wider to admit her. As she stepped inside, she saw Jerusha turn from the loom.

"Mother?" Jerusha looked as astonished as Lavinia had, only much happier to see her.

Mary walked to the loom. "My, but you are becoming very accomplished," she said, taking in the

434

multi-colored strands of yarn Jerusha was weaving. "I suppose that is because you have a patient and accomplished teacher."

Mary turned back to Lavinia still standing in the doorway holding the crock of butter.

Lavinia, I came to thank you for giving Jerusha the yarn to make the lovely coverlet for me and for teaching her to weave so well."

Mary had had no idea how she would feel being in the Wicker home and speaking to Lavinia again after all these years and all that had passed between them. She found the words came more easily than she expected.

"May we leave Jerusha to her work so that we can speak alone?" she asked.

"Of course, Mary. We can go into the kitchen."

She heard the lid on the butter crock rattle and saw that Lavinia's hands were shaking.

"May I offer you a cup of tea?" asked Lavinia.

"Yes, thank you." She watched Lavinia bustle about the kitchen, keeping her back to Mary. The woman was terribly nervous. Mary wondered what must be going through her mind. She felt a sense of pity for her old friend.

When Lavinia finally set the cup of tea before Mary and took a seat across from her, Mary said, "You must be wondering why I have come."

Lavinia nodded, a wary expression shadowing her face.

Mary took a deep breath. "Jerusha knows what happened with Lizzy and Seth."

Lavinia's face turned such a mottled purple that Mary feared she was having a sudden attack of apoplexy.

"But, but...I...I–"

Mary reached across the table to grasp Lavinia's plump hand in her own. "I told her myself. Just last week. Though she had guessed at it already from something Nathan shared with her. I know you never said a thing to her about it.”

Lavinia heaved a sigh.

“It was time. She is old enough now. She has handled it well.”

“I am glad to hear it,” Lavinia said, wiping a still-shaking hand across her mouth.

“It is also time for something else,” Mary continued.

“Oh?”

“Yes. It is time I apologized to you.”

“To me?” Lavinia’s eyes widened.

“Lavinia, you know that I do not share any of the beliefs you have about certain things. I will never agree that what was done in any way saved the rest of us from becoming ill. Nor will I ever countenance that there was anything evil in my Lizzy. Not in her nor abiding in her corpse. I cannot explain why she appeared the way she apparently did when you unearthed her, but we have no knowledge of what goes on during the time between burial and when all that is left is dust and bones. But surely, no evil spirit comes to reside within a body. That is my belief, and it will not change.”

Mary had rehearsed what she wanted to say in her mind. Now that she had started, she felt like a runaway horse that no one could stop, so she was grateful that Lavinia made no attempt to interrupt her.

“However, I have come to understand that you just as heartily believe what you claimed and in so doing, you, as the dear and loving friend you have always been, undertook a most gruesome task that no sane person would relish in order to protect my family. For that, I thank you. Not for the act itself, mind you, but for where your heart was in doing it.”

“Mary, I do not know what to say.” Lavinia continued to stare at Mary as if convinced her eyes and ears were deceiving her.

"I had hoped you would say that you understand my feelings and, also, that you forgive me. I have been horribly hard on you for too long. I was determined to protect Jerusha. And I was distraught over what was done to my children, especially Lizzy."

"But Mary, I do understand. I know you do not hold with my beliefs. It is why I worry over you and yours so much. It is why I felt I had to do it because I knew you could not. Truly, in your place, I am uncertain that I could have done it. It was ghastly." She paled at the memory.

"But worse for me has been the loss of your friendship, your anger, your...hatred of me." The last was spoken barely above a whisper. Tears flowed down her cheeks. "That is what hurt the most."

"I never hated you, Lavinia," said Mary, now grasping both of the woman's hands. "I was furious. I was hurt. But I never hated. I am a Christian woman as are you. Though, I fear I have not always behaved as one throughout this ordeal."

"Mary, I am sorry I hurt you. I am so very, very sorry. That was never my intention. I have missed you so. I forgive you, though I think there is nothing to forgive. Will you forgive me?"

Mary's vision blurred as tears swam in her eyes. "Yes. I forgive you. Let us put this behind us and speak of it no more."

Lavinia smiled through her tears. Their untouched tea cups were left on the table as they stood to hug each other.

"Do you need help with anything?" Mary asked. "Preparing for Thanksgiving, perhaps?"

"I do. I have not had enough time to get to it. Phineas's cousins's girl was supposed to come, but she took ill. I shall have to write again to see how she fares. Perhaps she will be able to arrive by Thanksgiving if she has recovered.

"That will be good, but meanwhile, we could do some baking together."

“I would like that very much.”

“As would I.”

Together they returned to the weaving room.

“Jerusha,” Mary said. Her daughter stopped the shuttle and looked up at them. “I will be staying awhile to help Lavinia bake some pies. She is quite behind with them so it may take some time. Would you, please, take care of preparing supper while we work?”

“Yes! Yes!” Jerusha jumped from the bench, hugged both women, then threw on her cloak, and raced out the door for home. They watched from the window as she ran and skipped. Mary’s heart felt light at the joy she witnessed in her daughter, a joy that had long been lacking.

“She has never been so happy to abandon the loom,” Lavinia said, laughing.

“That won’t last long,” Mary assured her. “She will be back to it before you know it. Now, about those pies.”

Chapter 59

October 1973
Birch Falls, Vermont

"Can we stop at the cemetery, first?" asked Heidi after they'd finished lunch and headed towards Birch Falls. "It sounds like there's a lot of paranormal activity going on at Julie's house and I really want to try to pick up something from Mary's gravesite. I have a strong feeling about it."

"I guess so," said Charlotte. "But I have to watch my time. I don't want to be late getting back to WVMB."

"I wish I could be a fly on the wall for that," said Heidi.

"I wish you could, too. Are you sure about the cemetery? If there's activity at the house wouldn't that be where you could make some connection?"

"Normally, I'd say yes, and maybe it will be. It's just that I've had a couple of incidents at Mary's grave, and I really think she's trying to get through to me. I feel a strong pull to go there."

"Okay," said Charlotte. "We'll need to make it quick, though."

As they neared the gravestones of Charlotte's ancestors, they could see a lot of debris littering the area.

"What's all this?" asked Charlotte. A trail of beer cans led straight to Eliza's grave. Plastic vampire teeth were strewn across the ground. "Ugh! Look at this mess."

Disgusted, Charlotte began collecting the vampire teeth and beer cans. "I wish I had a bag to put these in. I can't carry them all."

"Just pile them to the side," Heidi said. "We can come back to clean up before we head home."

Charlotte started gathering the detritus, piling it up beside a tree.

"Ouch!"

Charlotte turned to find Heidi rubbing her knee. "What's wrong?" she asked.

"I just knelt down in front of Mary's grave and felt something stab my knee."

Charlotte came over to search the ground where Heidi was standing. "Was it this?" she asked, picking up a small metal tweezer-like object. "Looks like someone dropped their roach clip."

"Jeez. There must have been quite a party out here."

"Yeah, and I'm sure I know what prompted it. All those legend-tripping kids who think I practically sent them here. Damn that Brad!"

I'll try again," said Heidi, kneeling in the grass by Mary's gravestone after first rubbing her hand over the area to be sure nothing else was left behind.

Charlotte watched as Heidi knelt before the stone. After closing her eyes and taking some deep breaths, she reached out to lay her palms on the face of the gravestone. Heidi's eyes flew open the minute she touched it.

"What?" asked Charlotte.

"The stone is practically vibrating."

Charlotte set her hand on the stone, but she felt nothing other than cold, hard marble. "I don't feel anything."

"Well, I sure do."

"Okay, but what does it mean?"

"I'm not certain exactly, but she is definitely upset about something. Very upset."

"Well, look at the mess around her family's graves. Who can blame her?"

Heidi jerked her hands away from the stone and hugged them to her chest."

"Are you okay?"

"Yeah. I just couldn't keep touching it. My hands are still tingling."

"Try Eliza's stone."

Heidi scooted over to Eliza's grave, only to have her knee sink into a ditch. "What on earth?" She got up and they both inspected the ground. It appeared as though someone had been digging there.

"Are you kidding me!" Charlotte exclaimed. "Do not tell me someone tried to dig her up."

"Drunk and high," said Heidi, "I suppose they'll do anything."

She knelt again and put her hands on Eliza's stone. "Nothing. I never get anything from her stone. It's all her mom. Whatever's going on at Julie's house is probably her mom, too."

"Speaking of which, we need to get there. I've really got to watch my time."

When they pulled into the Paquette's driveway, Julie ran out to meet them.

"I've been watching for you," she said as Charlotte and Heidi got out of the car. It's freaky in there."

"What's happening?" asked Heidi.

"Stuff is falling off the shelves in the study for no reason. Every time I look in there, things have been moved around. The worst part is the feeling I get when I go anywhere near that room. It's like someone is there, watching me, but no one is. That and the crying."

"Crying?" asked Charlotte.

"Yeah. I swear I can hear someone crying in there, but when I get close, it stops. Honestly, I'd believe I was losing my mind if Andy hadn't finally seen some of this stuff."

"What did he see?" asked Heidi.

"He was working in there last night when things started falling off the shelves and no one was near them. It happened several times. And that weird puddle of water showed up again. We had a plumber come. There's nothing wrong with the pipes."

"Does he believe you now?" asked Heidi.

"He wants to believe there's a rational explanation for it and we just haven't figured it out yet. But I could tell he was kind of freaked out even though he tried not to show it."

"Is anything happening now?" asked Charlotte.

"The crying and the creepy feeling I get near that room. I refuse to step foot in it."

"Can we go in?" asked Heidi.

"Be my guest." Julie looked like she'd rather do anything other than go back in the house. Heidi took the lead and Charlotte walked beside Julie.

"Do you remember me telling you about kids legend tripping to Eliza's grave the last time we were here?" Charlotte asked.

"Yeah."

"Did you happen to see the interview with me on WVMB Friday night?"

"No. I didn't know anything about it."

"Just as well. They did an awful job of editing the end of it. They had to cut it for time, but they took out so much of what I said that it changed the meaning." Charlotte had no intention of going into the whole dust up with Brad and Tony, but she had a hunch as to why the paranormal activity had ratcheted up at Julie's house. "It came out sounding like I was saying that kids should get drunk, go to her grave, and have fun vandalizing it."

"Seriously? Why would the TV station do that?"

"It's a long story. Anyway, we just came from the cemetery. Apparently, a lot of kids took what they thought I said to heart. The place was littered with beer cans and fake vampire teeth. Heidi felt a strong vibration from Mary's gravestone."

"Mary? I thought Eliza was the vampire."

"Mary was her mother. And you might not want to call Eliza a vampire while you're in this house," Charlotte told her as they entered the kitchen.

"It's really strong in here," said Heidi. "My hands are tingling again." She held them up to show they were trembling.

They walked to the study, but Julie hung back staying just outside the room.

"Oh, yeah. I can really feel the vibes in here," said Heidi as she ambled about the room. Even Charlotte felt uncomfortable as if someone was standing right behind her, barely brushing her shoulder.

"I have a hunch," said Charlotte. "I want to try something." She drew a pair of the vampire teeth from her pocket and placed them on Andy's desk, not at all close to the edge.

"You brought them with you?" Heidi asked.

"Yup. After what I saw at the cemetery and your reaction to touching Mary's stone, something just clicked in my mind."

They all stared in disbelief as the plastic teeth slid across the desk, sailed through the air, hit the opposite wall, and fell to the floor at the foot of a bookcase. A large book dropped from the shelf directly on top of the teeth, smashing them.

"That's what I thought," said Charlotte.

"What?" asked Julie who was cowering in the doorway, near to tears.

"Mary is pissed at the way Eliza's grave is being treated. It was desecrated when her body was exhumed. I'm sure she hoped her daughter would be allowed to rest in peace after that nightmare was over with. I don't think Mary takes too kindly to the legend tripping. That's probably why she's been acting up all these years. She's trying to let people know. Now that they've gone to extremes since that interview aired, she's really furious."

"Charlotte, I think you're right," said Heidi.

"Does that mean this won't stop until there's no more legend tripping to Eliza's grave?" asked Julie. "Kids have been doing that for decades, you said. They're not going to stop."

Another book jumped from the shelf, making Julie gasp.

Charlotte had no idea if what she was about to do would have any effect. At the moment she was wishing she could lock Brad and Tony in this room overnight, preferably on Halloween. Since that wasn't an option, this was the next best thing she could think of.

She walked to the center of the room and said in a loud voice, "Mary, this is Charlotte Lajoie. I'm your great, great, great, great granddaughter through Jerusha. I'm very sorry about what happened to Eliza and about the kids that keep coming to her grave. I'm especially sorry about how rowdy they've been recently. I'm afraid that's because of me. Well, not me, exactly, but something I said that was completely misunderstood. I don't know if I can fix this or not, but I promise you I will do everything I can to make it right. We hear you and we understand. Please, just give me a chance to try to make it stop."

When she finished speaking, she looked at Heidi.

"It feels a little calmer in here," Heidi told her.

"Okay," said Charlotte who could not tell any difference. "I have to get back to WVMB. Hopefully, things should be quieter now."

"You're leaving?" asked Julie.

"I have to. I'm meeting with some people at the TV station. We've got to straighten things out about that interview."

"Oh. I hoped you'd stay a while. This is one of Andy's late nights at work. He won't be home for a few more hours. I'm still scared to be here alone."

“What if I stay?” asked Heidi. “I can’t go with Charlotte to the station anyway. Charlotte, would you mind coming back to get me afterwards?”

“I think that would be a great idea. If I can talk them into it, I’ll have the TV crew out at the cemetery anyway.”

* * *

It hadn’t been difficult to convince Mark Gordon to go along with her idea. He was practically falling all over himself to apologize to her and President Shepherd. Brad had been brought along simply so that President Shepherd could say he’d given him every opportunity to plead his cause. Faced with Tony’s admission and Carol’s information, he hadn’t a leg to stand on and he knew it and reluctantly admitted his part in the scheme. Charlotte had wanted to force him to admit to having stolen her idea for the Halloween exhibit as well but decided not to push her luck. President Shepherd had not actually fired him yet, and she was taking no chances.

Now the four of them and Joe, the cameraman, stood in the cemetery in front of the Kendall family graves. Mark had already had Joe film him in his office explaining what had happened. He’d blamed poor editing rather than stating what really occurred, but Charlotte was fine with that as long as she was publicly vindicated. At the end of his statement, he’d announced that the uncut version of her interview would be aired when he finished speaking. Afterwards he’d assured her that the segment would be shown in full immediately following his statement.

After the filming in Mark’s office, Charlotte told them that she’d been out to Eliza’s grave and found beer cans, plastic vampire teeth, the roach clip, and that the ground appeared as though someone had been trying to dig up Eliza’s grave. “That’s what the editing to my interview caused. Kids took that as license to

445

party and vandalize the gravesite of my ancestors." She glared at Brad who stood with his hands in his pockets, staring over her shoulder at the ceiling.

"I'm terribly sorry," said Mark. "We'll have it cleaned up."

"That won't stop them from continuing to desecrate it. Besides, I'm sure you wouldn't want WVMB to be responsible for kids driving drunk and getting into an accident. Someone could get hurt or killed."

"Of course, we wouldn't want that, but I'm not sure what we can do about it."

"Would you be willing to film me at the gravesite showing what was done and making a plea for it to stop?"

"We'll need to go now before the sun sets," he'd said. "Joe, pack up your equipment and let's head out.

Now Charlotte was standing in front of Mary and Eliza's gravestones. She'd taken the beer cans and vampire teeth from the neat piles she'd placed them in earlier and scattered them around in the same fashion she'd found them.

As Joe panned the camera across the mess, zooming in for a few close-ups, Charlotte said, "These are the graves of my ancestors. After seeing an incorrectly edited version of my interview on Friday, some people came out here and did this. I'm a folklorist so I understand the concept of legend tripping. I know people today think that the inscription on Eliza Kendall's gravestone means something creepy."

Here Joe moved in to get a close-up of the words *I will come for you all.*

"But what that meant to the people of her time was that she would be there to greet them and welcome them to heaven when they died. It was a statement of faith.

"Eliza is not a vampire. She was a young girl who tragically lost her life to the horrible disease of tuberculosis which was rampant in the nineteenth century. Her sisters, Rebecca and Josephine, died of it before her and her brother, Seth, died of it just months after her. Imagine the pain and grief her parents and remaining sisters endured.

"Yes, her body was exhumed months after she died because people at the time had no understanding of tuberculosis and the terror of whole families being wiped out by it got the better of them. When they couldn't cure it, some of them turned to an old folk remedy. They unearthed those who had died to see if any showed signs of being a host for an evil entity that was feeding off the living until they, too, wasted away and died. Because they didn't understand the science of decomposition, they mistook what they saw as evidence of just that. Thinking they'd found the culprit, they did to the corpse what their forebears had done back in Europe. They removed the heart and burned it, hoping that would put an end to the deaths. To them this was not some weird, ghoulish ritual, nor did they think in terms of vampires as we do. They didn't even use that word. They simply thought they were doing what had to be done to save lives.

"But can you imagine the heartache for the family members and friends? It had to have been horrendous. I can't even begin to fathom what Eliza's mother, Mary, must have gone through when this was done to her daughter's body."

Joe pointed the camera at Charlotte who stood in front of Mary's grave. Adopting the most professional pose she could muster, she looked directly into the camera.

"My ancestors do not deserve this," she said, sweeping her arms to indicate the mess of beer cans and vampire teeth. "There is even some evidence that someone has tried to dig up Eliza's grave. Her body was desecrated once already. Please, let her rest in peace. If you really must visit her grave, do so with some respect for the young girl who never got the chance to live to your age and the mother who mourned so many of her children.”

Just as Charlotte ended her speech, Mark Gordon unexpectedly stepped up beside her. Turning towards the camera, he stated, “As Executive Producer of WVMB, I want to state that the station will pay for a police detail to keep watch over this section of the cemetery. If you come here drunk, high, or with the intention of vandalism, you can expect to be arrested. This sort of disrespect for the dead will not be tolerated.”

When they were finished, Charlotte and President Shepherd thanked him for agreeing to film at the cemetery. He promised that his statement, the uncut version of the end of Charlotte’s interview, and what they’d just shot at the Kendall gravesite would air the following evening.

“And I meant what I said about the police detail. We can’t do it indefinitely, but we will cover the cost through Halloween.”

“That would be wonderful,” said Charlotte. “Legend tripping pretty much stops after Halloween anyway, at least until the next summer.”

President Shepherd handed a trash bag that they’d brought with them to Brad and told him to clean up the mess. Once he finished and Joe had packed up his equipment, they headed for their cars. After Mark and Joe pulled out of the parking lot behind the meeting house, President Shepherd stopped Charlotte before she got into her car.

“You handled yourself brilliantly throughout this whole ordeal, Charlotte,” he said.

“Thank you. Does this mean I’m off suspension?”

“Of course. I’ll see you at work bright and early tomorrow morning.”

Charlotte grinned; a huge weight lifted from her.

Brad, who was leaning against the half-open door of his Mustang, called out, "Yeah, see ya tomorrow."

President Shepherd turned to face Brad. "Oh, you won't see her tomorrow, unless it's while you're cleaning out your desk."

Brad stood up straight. "What do you mean? You're not firing me over this, are you?"

"After all the harm you've caused? What you did was thoroughly juvenile. If Charlotte didn't have the gumption and courage she does, we'd be in so much hot water with the board, they might just have seen fit to fire us all. As it is, I have to contact each of them, along with the town manager, tonight to make sure they watch tomorrow evening and hope they're satisfied with it. This was nearly a disaster for the museum, not to mention what you tried to do to a colleague. But if I really must spell it out for you, Brad, then fine. You're fired."

"You bitch!" Brad yelled at Charlotte, throwing himself into the driver's seat, slamming the door, and peeling out of the parking lot.

"President Shepherd turned back to Charlotte. "I'm so sorry."

Charlotte tilted her head. "You know what? It's okay. This was tough, but it showed me something. I can handle the Brad Louden's of the world. And I am going to be a respected folklorist and build a great career for myself."

"I believe you will," he said, smiling. "You can start by taking on the role of Acting Director of Programs. It will only be temporary until we can hire a replacement for Brad. I'm sorry I can't offer it to you permanently. As you've only just completed your degree and have just begun working in the field, I don't think the board would allow it. But working as Acting Director will give you some valuable experience. I will be sure to hire a director willing to help nurture your career rather than stifle it. The museum is fortunate to have you, Charlotte."

"Thank you, President Shepherd. I gladly accept the temporary position."

"Wonderful. We'll talk details tomorrow."

As she drove to Julie's house to pick up Heidi, Charlotte couldn't stop grinning. The relief she felt nearly brought tears to her eyes. Grandma was right, she thought. Aunt Beatrice would be proud of me. And so am I.

Epilogue

November 1980
Indiana University, Bloomington

President Shepherd had been true to his word. Charlotte was Acting Director of Programs for the better part of a year. A salary increase accompanied the title, one which he did not decrease once a new director was hired, and she went back to being Assistant Director.

To Charlotte's delight, a woman was hired for the Director's position. Sylvia Perini was a brilliant folklorist in her late forties with plenty of museum and teaching experience. She was at a generative point in her career and was sincerely happy to give Charlotte the benefit of her wisdom and guidance. Sylvia helped Charlotte get into the doctoral program at Indiana University in Bloomington, her own alma mater. Between teaching undergraduate courses and utilizing on-campus housing, Charlotte was able to afford a sabbatical despite retaining only a portion of her museum salary. She'd been able to sublet her apartment so that would be waiting for her when she got back, as well.

Charlotte had just come from a meeting with her doctoral advisor. The form of her dissertation was really beginning to take shape based on legend tripping as a rite of passage. Eliza's grave would be a focal point. The second diary had been repaired enough that with the magnifying glass and not a little eye strain, she was able to decipher most of it. Jerusha had indeed written that she'd finally found out the family secret and it was just as Charlotte had suspected. She was most gratified to read that Jerusha had had a hand in repairing the friendship between Mrs. Wicker and her mother. Now, sitting at the table in the library, she set out her books, notepads.

Before starting on the days' research, she took a moment to pull a letter from her pocketbook. She'd picked up her mail on the way to meet her advisor and been excited to see a letter from Heidi. They'd stayed in touch even after Heidi had moved out of her aunt's apartment. In fact, Charlotte had been the maid of honor at Heidi's wedding. She'd married a male nurse she'd met at the hospital, something that had put her Aunt Iris into a tailspin. "What kind of man wants to become a nurse?" her aunt had asked. "That's women's work." Charlotte and Heidi still laughed about it.

Heidi's letter was full of news. She and Ron had bought their first house almost a year ago. Now that they were all settled in, they had decided it was time to start a family. *I hope you'll be back in time to be the baby's godmother. I'm due in May,* she'd written. Charlotte had to slap a hand over her mouth so the squeal that nearly erupted from her wouldn't disturb the other library patrons.

As always, Heidi's letter asked for Charlotte's news along with an update on all her family. Since she was too excited about Heidi's revelation to focus on research anyway, she grabbed some paper from her notebook and wrote back immediately congratulating Heidi and Ron and saying that she would be honored to be the baby's godmother. Then she caught her up on her own family's news.

Her parents were fine. Her dad was looking forward to retirement in the near future and they were already planning the trips they'd take when that happened. Her brother, Russ, had recently become engaged. Tracy was excited to be graduating from Penn State with a degree in journalism, but she would miss competing on the university's gymnastics team. It had been a thrill for her to be on the same team as Ann Carr, a member of the National Team that had competed at the 1974 World Gymnastics Championships.

Her grandmother, thankfully, had finally conceded to hire a handyman who did all her yard work, shoveling, and household repairs so she could continue to live in her home. Tracy's correspondence with Keith had kept up only long enough to find out that his brother had returned home from Vietnam. More recently, her grandmother heard from Keith's grandparents that he was now teaching junior high social studies in Burlington and loving it.

She asked Heidi for any news on Julie and Andy Paquette. Heidi had stayed in touch with Julie. Paranormal activity at their home had calmed down substantially since Charlotte had made her plea at the cemetery. The police detail that had been put in place had a lot to do with curbing the legend tripping, at least for a while. Occasionally, it would start up again especially around Halloween, but there had been no incidents of vandalism. Julie and Andy had moved from the house, as Julie never could feel comfortable there, but she still wrote to Heidi now and then.

Charlotte ended her letter with her latest bit of personal news, writing that she was swearing Heidi to secrecy, at least in terms of Heidi's aunt. Charlotte had been seeing a man she'd met on campus. He was a research fellow in social science. They'd been dating for about a month. His name was Ben Adler. He was from New Hampshire and intended to return to New England when he finished his fellowship. The relationship was too new to say where it was going, but at the moment she was very much enjoying it.

She folded the letter and set it aside to mail later. Now she could focus on her research. She pulled one more item from her bag, setting the decoupaged candleholder on the table. She couldn't light the candle in the library, but it had become a talisman of sorts for her to just have it there. Notebook open, books spread out on the table, Charlotte resumed her work.

The End

9 780228 627968